Carmen Reid is the bestselling author of, most recently, *The Personal Shopper. Late Night Shopping* is the sequel, also starring Annie Valentine.

After working as a journalist in London Carmen moved to Glasgow, Scotland, where she looks after one husband, two children, various pets and writes almost all the rest of the time.

For more information on Carmen Reid and her books, visit her website at www.carmenreid.com

Also by Carmen Reid

THREE IN A BED
DID THE EARTH MOVE?
HOW WAS IT FOR YOU?
UP ALL NIGHT
THE PERSONAL SHOPPER

And for teenage readers

SECRETS AT ST JUDE'S: NEW GIRL

LATE NIGHT SHOPPING

Carmen Reid

CORGI BOOKS

TRANSWORLD PUBLISHERS
61–63 Uxbridge Road, London W5 5SA
A Random House Group Company
www.rbooks.co.uk

LATE NIGHT SHOPPING
A CORGI BOOK: 9780552154833

First publication in Great Britain
Corgi edition published 2008

Addresses for Random House Group Ltd companies outside the UK
can be found at: www.randomhouse.co.uk
The Random House Group Ltd Reg. No. 954009

The Random House Group Limited supports The Forest Stewardship
Council (FSC), the leading international forest certification organisation.
All our titles that are printed on Greenpeace approved FSC certified paper
carry the FSC logo. Our paper procurement policy can
be found at www.rbooks.co.uk/environment

Typeset in 11/14pt Palatino by
Kestrel Data, exeter, Devon.
Printed in the UK by
CPI Cox & Wyman, Reading, RG1 8EX.

2 4 6 8 10 9 7 5 3 1

LATE NIGHT SHOPPING

Chapter One

Annie at her desk:

*Tailored dress (McQueen! Yes but with a staff discount.
Anyway trousers are too weird this season:
jodhpurs? Hello!)
Genius wide-topped ankle boots
(Pucci, again staff discount)
Black hold-ups with lace top (Asda)
Sleek bronze reading glasses for ultra-private
use only (Moschino)
Extreme bikini (Hollywood Waxing Co. –
Owwwwwwwch)
Total est. cost: £780*

*'Annie, have me. Buy me. Only you can love me like I
need to be loved.'*

'Will you come to bed now? *Please?'*

Annie, still at her desk chair, eyes fixed on the computer screen shouted back, 'Yeah babes, I'm coming, I am coming this very second, promise.'

She didn't make a move. This was the third time Ed had called but she wasn't ready to go just yet. Because there was no doubt that the hours between 10 p.m. and 12 p.m. were becoming the busiest for her online eBay shop, Annie V's Trading Station.

It wasn't so surprising. What with ten-hour-a-day jobs, bum-numbingly long commutes, cooking dinner for the masses, cleaning, more cleaning and clearing up, it was only after 10 p.m. that a girl could finally pour a glass of wine, chill out, log on and get down to some serious late night shopping.

In an age of multi-taskers, Annie Valentine still made most people look like slackers. For four long days a week, she worked hard as a personal shopper, image consultant and all-round makeover maven at The Store – the über-fabulous London fashion mecca where *everyone* who wanted to know *everything* about what was so-hot-it-hurt had to shop.

Should sleeves be tight this season or loose? Tight at the bottom, loose on top? Tight on top but loose at the bottom? Where should pockets be? High? Low? Obvious? Invisible?

Annie, who was at The Store from 10 a.m. until 9 p.m. so she could pack a full working week into four days, who read every important fashion magazine, who watched the runway shows on video, who ran hourly checks on fashion websites to be utterly informed, Annie was the woman with the answer to every fashion question.

Was the new Balenciaga swing jacket for you? Or the wasp-waisted Saint Laurent? Where could you get those Miu Mius in a size 39? Should you go Missoni this season or embrace Proenza Schouler? Annie was the one who could let you know.

Not that a high fashion look was appropriate for every one of her clients, of course. But she could tell at a glance those women who needed a serious yank by their mousy locks into the twenty-first century, and those who were looking for the whisper of insider information to put them just one step ahead of the fashionista crowd. (As everyone in fashion knows, one step ahead is perfect, *two* steps ahead is as good as two steps behind.)

When Annie wasn't at The Store or manning her eBay shop front, she was bowling round London in her big, shiny black Jeep packed with hangers, hanging rails and boxes full of second-hand clothes. Either on her way to see a client in need of an urgent wardrobe revamp, or on her way back, with a bootload of things she'd weeded out from her client's cast-offs to sell on commission.

As word spread, the name and number of no-nonsense Annie was popping up in little black books and BlackBerrys all over London. Been promoted? Going back to work after a break? Husband threatening to trade you in for a younger model? Friends would whisper to each other: *'Give Annie a call.'*

She could make her clients look smarter, cleverer, three inches taller, three inches narrower, five years younger, sexy, current, informed and part of the game again. In one brisk shopping session, she could transform some-one from bewildered follower of fashion to leader of the pack. There were now a surprising number of wealthy but insecure women in the capital who couldn't add so much as a belt or an earring to their wardrobes unless Annie had approved its purchase.

Being so constantly in demand, Annie was always a woman in a hurry, never really happy unless she was doing two things at once: driving and talking on the mobile (hands-free), walking at great speed on three-inch heels while advising a client on the mobile, haggling on the mobile while eating a carefully calorie-controlled snack (in the ongoing battle to remain a size 12 . . . or else there wouldn't be a single designer item left that she'd be able to fit into). Good grief, even Donna Karan could no longer be relied on to cut clothes generously now that she'd ashtanga yoga-ed herself into a size 10.

But despite Annie's 110 per cent commitment to her many jobs, there was no forgetting the other key elements in her life. She devoted all her available non-working time to the care and attention of her two children and one still quite new live-in lover.

Her daughter, Lana, was sixteen and increasingly complicated. She had dark hair, even darker moods and some days grumped about like a firework, ready to explode with a bang and a shower of sparks at any moment. On the, fortunately rare, days when Lana's PMT coincided with her mother's, there was a threat of murder in the air.

Owen was ten and seemed shy, sweet and sunny-natured by comparison. He was musical, easy-going and very happy that the new man in his mother's life was also his music teacher at school.

Ed Leon – who Annie and her children had lived with for about a year now – had arrived on the scene with several very important assets, cunningly disguised.

A curly tangle of unruly hair concealed surprisingly warm blue eyes. The worst tweedy and baggy charity shop wardrobe Annie had ever encountered covered an unexpectedly fit and muscular body. And Ed's dingy, damp basement flat had turned out to be just one floor of the beautiful Georgian townhouse in oh-so-desirable north London that he had part-inherited.

Oh and of course, Ed was also a lovely man – funny, slightly younger, and utterly devoted to Annie . . . and he'd disguised that very well too, until she'd finally found him out.

As a woman who could never resist a project, Annie had spent considerable time renovating both Ed and the townhouse. She had sold up her own beautiful home, raised an enormous mortgage and bought a share of the house, so that they could all live there together.

The house was slightly easier to renovate than Ed, who was strangely attached to his old clothes and outraged at the price tags on the things Annie wanted him to wear. The house had offered less resistance. It hadn't complained. It hadn't blurted out things like, 'You want to spend *how* much on re-flooring my bathroom in solid walnut? But I know where I could get a nice bit of lino for buttons!' The house even seemed grateful for Annie's devotion to it. Whenever she returned, she felt it twinkle back at her and welcome her in. The glossy wooden floorboards shone, the pale walls and satiny woodwork stood to attention; the repaired windows, new bathrooms and gleaming kitchen all seemed to sparkle for her.

'Ms Annie Valentine!' called the voice from the bedroom. 'This is your last and final call for boarding!'

'Five minutes, babes!' Then, because she knew just why he was so keen to have her there beside him, she added cheekily, 'Start without me! I'll jump right in. Honest!'

Her bids had been timed to close just a few minutes apart from each other all the way up till midnight, when the shop would finally shut for the night after the sale of this evening's three prized items: a beautiful tan Mulberry handbag, thigh-high designer leather boots and a slinky floor-length mink fur coat.

Fur wasn't a thing you saw out much in London. She'd never wear it. (Well . . . maybe a beautiful wool coat trimmed with mink: a soft shawl collar, generous cuffs . . . if she was forced to.) But amongst some of the ladies she dressed, head-to-toe mink was still deeply in, despite the protesters and red paint.

But then these were ladies of the highest luxury. These were the women who could wear priceless jewels and towering glass heels and swathe themselves in fur because they went from door to door in limousines. They didn't even need to worry about door handles – their doors were opened for them, air conditioning was adjusted, tinted windows were whizzed up and down. They wore real diamond-studded sunglasses at night just to be private.

One of Annie's clients wanted to sell on this particular fur coat so she could quietly stash a little money away in a bank account. Because when your finances were so totally controlled by your husband, it was good to feel there were some emergency funds in a nameless Swiss bank account. And Annie was trusted enough to look after transactions like this because she often got surprisingly close to the women she dressed. They took her into their confidence and shared all sorts of secrets with her.

She scrolled down the list of items she'd sold online today. It was very eclectic: from high-end boots and shoes to bags and dresses, tops and high street labels.

'ANNIE!!!'

Ed was probably naked, soft and fragrant from showering, hair damp, lying on top of the duvet and waiting for her with his very welcoming body: squarish and muscular but just the right side of fleshy, not at all hard and buff. Ed was strong but soft and Annie loved to tangle up with him. Shower fresh and hungry and so, very, very into her. It made her smile just thinking of his warm body and the things they liked to do with it, but . . .

Ping! A bid was upped.

Late August was the last available chance to sell summer clothes for a decent price. Already everyone, everywhere with the slightest interest in fashion was eyeing up cashmere coats, chunky knitwear, dark leather bags, boots and big ticket items.

Looking round the spare room which she used as an office, Annie acknowledged that she still had stacks of summer things to sell from the back of her clients' wardrobes. Things that hadn't been worn for years: pristine linen Jigsaw suits, skirts with killer waistbands which had been too tight the day they were bought, let alone two babies later. Ghost dresses, thin and insubstantial, haunting the back of the cupboards for season after season. Unworn and unloved, but held on to because they cost a lot.

'You'll get over it, I promise!' Annie would insist firmly but with a smile, taking the items from her clients' uncertain hands, 'The money's gone, you aren't getting it back by keeping a reminder of it hanging in there. And anyway, it's only money! They print more of it every day.'

The clock hit twelve and the fur coat went for an astonishing £3,420. A lot of very wealthy, well-connected females knew about this virtual boutique.

And, 15 per cent of £3,420 made it worth sitting at the screen, typing up blurb, and spending entire mornings at the post office, busy as a mail order company.

'You should have your own business,' the women who visited her in her suite were constantly telling her. 'You're really good. You could be the next Miuccia Prada. Or even better: Johnnie Boden! Go for it, girl.'

Just before she closed up, Annie flicked over to the other website open on her browser: the one with all the excellent advice about setting up your own company.

She'd read many times through the helpful hints, rules and encouragement. But much as she dreamed of going into business properly, Annie wasn't quite ready yet. Maybe because, although she suspected her future was in handbags or shoes, she hadn't yet found exactly the right opportunity. But she was looking hard and she just knew that it was going to come up. Soon.

Make that very soon, she thought, glancing down at the jumble of mail tucked into her top desk drawer, where she knew there lurked a worrying brown envelope. Because she was a busy eBay trader and because she'd been self-employed for a few months last year, Annie had a 'tax situation' to sort out. She knew about it, she

14

just hadn't focused on it, and this brown envelope was almost certainly something to do with it.

It wasn't that she'd been *ignoring* the envelope, it was just that she knew she'd have to be in a certain kind of strong mood to open it. Now, with a £3,420 coat sold on eBay, she thought she could cope with whatever lay inside.

Before she could change her mind, she reached down and grabbed it. Her fingers quickly tore through the brown paper, then she smoothed out the single sheet and scanned over the words.

'Final demand', '£10,199.28' and 'within thirty days' stood out in bold.

It took a moment or two for the shock of this news to register properly.

She was going to have to raise £10,000 in thirty days? *Ten thousand pounds?!* That was about twice as much as she'd expected.

Could she earn it in thirty days? No way! Her eBay trading made £600 in a good week . . . make that an outstanding week. Maybe she could borrow it? No again. Her three credit cards were all too dangerously close to their limits for her to do that. Anyway, did HM Revenue & Customs even take Visa?

Obviously she couldn't steal it. Even if she'd known who to steal it from, Annie was cursed with very high scruples: she'd never stolen so much as a sweet from the Woolworths pick and mix.

One thing was clear: Ed wasn't to know *anything* about this. He had such an old-fashioned view of money, debts and borrowing. 'If you haven't got it, don't spend it' was one of his completely irritating sayings. Annie's attitude couldn't have been more different with her 'win some, lose some', 'got to speculate to accumulate' ideas.

But there was no way round it, raising £10,000 in thirty days was going to be a . . . she batted away the words 'nightmare' and 'impossible' as they reared up in her mind, and made herself think, 'challenge'.

It was time to power down the laptop and head for the bedroom.

As Annie approached the door, she saw the light was dim. Just the little string of flower lights over the mantelpiece was on. They cast a low, romantic light, perfect for going to bed. Perfect for looking at one another appreciatively before the touching and the stroking and the kissing began.

'Ed?' she said in a low voice as she came into the room. 'Here I am.'

He was lying on his side with his back towards her. Oh, the tease. Broad, soft white shoulders sloped down to a narrow waist, then a quite spectacularly attractive, peachy bum and muscular fuzzy legs.

'I'll just take off my clothes,' she purred at him, quickly unzipping her dress and letting it drop to the floor so that she was standing in front of the bed in underwear, hold-ups and her black ankle boots. Sensational ankle boots, she couldn't help thinking, taking another admiring little glance at them, even if they were a pointy, three-inch-high, toe-massacre to walk in.

Ed wasn't moving. Oh well, if he was in a huff with her now, she felt sure that the boots and underwear combination would help him get over it really quickly.

'Baby,' she said, kneeling on the edge of the bed.

Slowly she began to trace a finger over the outline of his shoulder and down his side.

'Babes?'

She leaned over his damp hair and looked down at his face. There was no mistaking the closed eyes and heavy breathing.

Ed had fallen asleep.

Annie unhooked her bra and tossed it over a chair, then unzipped her boots and peeled off her stockings. Finally, she loosened her long blonde bob from her trademark tight ponytail. She might as well get to sleep too. Tomorrow was Wednesday, the first of her busy, busy four days in The Store and there were some very interesting clients booked in over the next few days.

She turned off the flower lights and got into bed, pulling the covers over the two of them and moving in as close as she could to his warm naked body. Years of boarding-school dormitories had trained Ed to sleep very deeply, and he didn't even stir.

Closing her eyes and settling down into the darkness, Annie found her mind wandering almost at once towards The Handbag. The one sitting in prime position in the ground floor accessories department. The one with the four-figure price tag and the come-hither smile. The violet patent tote with subtle golden hardware that winked at and wooed her whenever she happened to pass by.

She already knew exactly how big and how scrunchily soft it was. How well it sat on her shoulder. How comfortably capacious it was inside. How tender the black suede lining felt and how many clever compartments it had. She even knew how many hours had gone into stitching it all together. It was fashionable and glamorous and current without screaming 'it' bag. It was chic and French and Yves Saint Laurent.

But she also knew that it could not be hers, because it cost far, far too much. She'd made a promise. She'd told Ed that from now on she would consult him on all purchases over £200. Anyway, she had enough handbags, and this bag cost nearly a *month* in school fees. There were so many reasons why she had to say no, absolutely not and tune that arm candy right out of her head. But tomorrow it would surely still be there, wouldn't it? On its shiny glass plinth, calling out to her.

She sighed quietly to herself. There just wasn't enough glamour in her life, she thought, not for the first time. Although she worked around all the lovely things The Store had to offer, even with the staff discount she could only afford to buy a few choice items there. She still had M&S undies, tops from Oasis, skirts from Jigsaw, and she was still a regular visitor to the Topshop rails.

Although she advised the glamorous elite on their wardrobes, Annie's life still involved commuting on foot and by bus instead of by limousine. She still had to make packed lunches and do the supermarket run. And there certainly wasn't an army of housekeepers to help her out.

But if she owned that bag with its very expensive, shiny allure, she would be *so* much more glamorous. With that wonderful bag over her shoulder, she'd feel like a film star even at the bus stop. Taking her purse out at the supermarket check-out would be an impossibly elegant event if it involved *this bag.*

But how on earth did you explain that to a man who

thought the battered old briefcase he'd had since he was thirteen was 'absolutely fine'?

No, as Annie drifted off to sleep she knew she would never be able to convince Ed that she had heard the call of the bag . . . that she really had heard it whispering, 'Annie, have *me*. Buy *me*. Only *you* can love me like I need to be loved.'

Chapter Two

Bronwen's first visit to The Store:

Blue and yellow patterned sweatshirt
(made in New Zealand)
Brown cord skirt (made in New Zealand)
American tan tights (petrol station)
Slouchy brown sandals (made in New Zealand)
Total est. cost: £95

'I just want to be comfortable. That's how I sold 27,000
toilets a quarter: people were comfortable with me.'

'You know I only ever buy MaxMara and there's no point trying to sway me,' bossy Elizabeth Maxwell told Annie sternly as she sifted through the rack of coats brought up for her to try in The Store's personal shopping suite.

The suite was a luxurious sanctuary of snowy carpet, velvet curtains and super-sized changing rooms on the second floor. It was as bright and dazzlingly lit as every other square inch of The Store, so that the gorgeousness of each item for sale could be fully appreciated.

From the sparkling beauty and accessories 'play-ground' on the ground floor, shimmering metal and glass escalators and elevators carried customers up to floors one, two and three where at each level prices expanded and exquisite creations vied with one another for attention. Rack on rack, designer concession on designer concession . . . there was almost too much: too much colour, too much brilliance, too many clothes, too many choices, too many price tags, too many zeros. It was an over-stimulation of the senses.

New, uninitiated customers often found themselves turning up at the Personal Shopping suite unannounced because they needed *help*! They needed a guide; they needed someone to make sense of the fashion jungle out there on the sales floor. Not that it looked like a jungle of course, with every collection pruned and honed and displayed to perfection. Even The Store's hangers were specially designed in shiny chrome with just the right amount of padding, just the exact angle of slope on the shoulders to hang every item to its most fabulous advantage.

'But Elizabeth, what about this one?' Annie coaxed, pulling a silvery-grey Armani cashmere from the rack and holding it out to the stocky, fifty-something barrister who was here to buy her autumn/winter essentials in a flurry of organization. 'It would go so beautifully with your hair,' Annie went on, 'and it's long too. So cosy and so this season.'

'Well . . .' Elizabeth had her hand on the fabric now. It was as smooth and supple as a puppy's ear and just as tempting.

'Slip it on, just for me,' Annie urged. She didn't exactly

like Elizabeth Maxwell. No, make that she couldn't really stand Elizabeth Maxwell. But nevertheless she was a client who came to the personal shopping suite at least four times a year and spent big, so like everyone else who paid for Annie's expert attention, she would leave with bags packed with clothes guaranteed to make her look as sensational as possible.

'Remember the silvery dress you bought in the spring?' Annie had leafed through Elizabeth's file before this session. 'Wouldn't that look amazing under this coat? And you've got to have . . .' Annie turned to the table she'd stacked with accessories: 'this!' she insisted, draping a pale violet and lilac velvet scarf around Elizabeth's neck.

'Oh yes,' Elizabeth agreed, her eyes fixed to the image of herself in the mirror. 'Yes, that is very nice. I'm going to be in Paris so much more now. Don't you think this is a very French look?'

Paris?! Elizabeth was going to be in Paris so much more now? Annie wondered again at the differences between her life and those of her clients.

'So what's happening in Paris?' Annie asked, trying not to sound too wistful.

'Oh, haven't I told you?!' Elizabeth began brightly, 'James . . .'

Ah! How could Annie have forgotten? The twins! Elizabeth's children James and Georgia were her . . . well 'pride and joy' was probably an understatement. As James and Georgia had taken their A Levels this summer and had now left school, Annie braced herself for some serious maternal boasting.

'James got four As and a starred A in music, so . . .'

Elizabeth paused for effect, eyes widening with excitement, 'he and his violin are heading for the Conservatoire in Paris. Isn't that wonderful?!'

'My goodness,' Annie agreed enthusiastically, 'brilliant. And how about Georgia? What's she moving on to?'

'Oh, Georgia got into Harvard!' Elizabeth exclaimed. 'We're just thrilled!'

Annie knew enough super-wealthy London parents to understand that the Conservatoire and Harvard were amongst the ultimate accolades. Oxford and Cambridge were now considered 'over' and 'full of the children of foreign billionaires'. These days, sending your children to university abroad proved you were cultivated, had stunningly clever offspring *and* you were rich enough for transatlantic airfares and tuition fees to be utterly irrelevant.

'And how are yours doing?' Elizabeth Maxwell added, almost as an afterthought, as she turned around to gaze again at her reflection.

'Well, Lana sits her GSCEs next summer,' Annie began, 'so fingers crossed she's going to settle down and work hard for them. Owen's doing really well, especially with his music. He plays the violin too, and the guitar.'

Perhaps because Elizabeth seemed so uninterested, Annie felt a familiar prickly worry return. Was she doing enough for her children? Was it really OK that Lana was only going to sit eight GCSEs and not ten like a lot of her classmates? And Owen . . . was he spending too much time on his music, to the detriment of everything else?

'And they're at St Vincent's, aren't they?' Elizabeth asked, perhaps wondering how a *sales assistant* could afford fees like that. But then she had no idea how hard

Annie worked. 'It's good,' Elizabeth added approvingly. 'Any thoughts about where they'll go afterwards?'

'Oh no. Not yet,' Annie told her. Thinking that if it was going to be the Conservatoire and Harvard she'd either have to marry Richard Branson or, more realistically, be running an incredibly successful business of her own.

'Very expensive business, university education,' Elizabeth added, 'some sacrifices will have to be made . . .'

Uh-oh. This was hardly music to a personal shopper's ears.

The barrister began to unwind the scarf, then unbutton the Armani.

'Let's take a look at the black MaxMara,' Annie said.

'Annie?' There was a voice behind the changing room curtain. Annie excused herself and stepped out.

Paula, one of Annie's assistants in the suite, a tall, rangy black girl, slim and elegant as a runway model, had come to let her know that the next customer was waiting. Standing next to Paula, Annie couldn't help feeling even more average-sized and chunky, not to mention more pale, than usual. One glance at Paula's feet and the reason became clear: the shoes were very, very high, in deepest pink with a purple suede trim all the way around. The curving straps, crossed artfully at the front, were held in place with tiny purple buttons at the side. They were a masterwork. A beautiful, lovingly crafted masterwork.

'Look at your shoes! Oh my God, your shoes!' Annie gave a whispered shriek. 'Those are absolutely perfect. We *have* to speak about these shoes,' she warned Paula, before heading back into the changing room.

'Time to choose!' Annie instructed Elizabeth, putting on her most friendly smile and turning to the clothes rail they'd stocked with the 'definites'. Running a hand through the chunky knitwear, slubby silks, rich colours and tweedy textures, Annie had to admit to herself how much she loved the very start of autumn, when bikinis and kaftans were pushed out of the way to make room for camel coats, conker brown boots and knitwear in dark jewel colours.

High summer and the Christmas countdown were the worst months for Annie. Even in The Store, they were the fashion pits. But March and September were the pinnacle months of a fashionable life. This was when the serious buyers came in to shop ahead.

Annie found it a little hard to sympathize with women who turned up in freezing February looking for coats, hats and gloves and found themselves gazing at chiffon wedding outfits in dismay. Did they know nothing? November is the last *possible* moment to buy something warm. After that it's sparkles, snowflakes and boxed sets only. Don't even try looking for a smart summer dress in August, when there are just bikinis and sunglasses and everything else is sagging on the sale rail.

The clothes displayed up on Elizabeth's rail were beautiful: grey flannel wide-leg trousers, creamy silk and plum blouses, wide supple leather belts, knee-length cardigans hand-knitted with complicated stitches. Layering tops in grape and salmon pink. A slightly racy brown leather skirt.

'I think you should take the coat . . .' Annie wheedled, 'it will be cold in Paris, and in Boston. It's very cold in Boston. My boyfriend Ed was at Harvard last summer and he couldn't believe how well turned out everyone was – even the students!'

Elizabeth had her fingers on the coat again.

'I love the way it's so neat and snug over the shoulders and waist, then flares out so beautifully,' Annie added gently.

She had another reason for wanting Elizabeth to buy the coat: all this talk of the cost of a university education was freaking her out. She was going to put the commission from the coat sale into a separate account and start saving for Lana and Owen right now.

'Oh well . . . as they say over there,' Elizabeth conceded, 'what the heck!'

'Bronwen! Hello my love, welcome to the suite, nice to meet you!'

After just a nanosecond in her little cupboard of an office, where Annie had gulped down the small black coffee waiting for her, thanks to Paula, spritzed herself with some sort of energizing aromatherapy spray Ed had bought her as a present and re-applied her lipstick, Annie was as fresh and ready as she could be for her next ninety-minute session.

Even the most casual of observers could tell this was Bronwen Tomlinson's first experience of Annie's shopping expertise. But in one long, careful look, Annie appraised the stunningly frumpy outfit and could tell Bronwen was a special case. An unusual client.

She looked, like Annie, about thirty-*something*. Now that Annie had passed the crucial 35, she would no longer be specific to anyone who asked about her age: 'I'm not admitting to anything! Why should I?'

It only took a few minutes of chat before Bronwen was telling Annie in a broad accent that she was the only child of a New Zealand sheep farmer.

'And I look it too,' she said cheerfully. 'Look at my legs – two bloody lumps of mutton. Look at my face!'

The face was ruddy and pink surrounded by wiry brown hair tinged ginger on top.

But the sheep farmer's daughter had been posted to London by her company after winning national saleswoman of the year, *twice*.

'If you can make it, I can sell it,' she declared. Although Annie suspected Bronwen might have a problem flogging high fashion.

As soon as Bronwen had arrived in London she'd realized that, despite her phenomenal sales figures, when it came to fitting in and looking the part, she was totally out of touch.

But someone, wishing her well, had given her Annie's name, and so, this Wednesday morning, Bronwen had brazenly marched into The Store in a 'made in New Zealand' patterned sweatshirt, a brown cord skirt and flat brown sandals.

How she had braved the withering stares that must have followed her all the way up to the second floor, Annie would never know. It proved she was made of very strong stuff.

'So what did you sell in New Zealand?' Annie asked. 'What scooped you saleswoman of the year, *twice*?'

Bronwen's answer came out loud and clear without the slightest hint of embarrassment: 'Chemical toilets. There's a huge market over there for chemical toilets. I was selling them faster than they could make them.'

Lowering her voice slightly, she added, 'With my commission, I was making more than the chairman of the company. I think that's why they had to send me to London. He didn't want me to own a bigger house than him. It's a small place, Wellington. People notice things like that over there.'

'Chemical toilets?!' Annie asked in amazement. She was intrigued to know more about this woman, because up until now Annie had always thought *she* was the best saleswoman she'd ever met. But clearly, here was someone who really could sell anything.

'Yeah . . . you're not going to go all snotty on me now, are you?' Bronwen asked with the winning, disarming smile which obviously had people reaching for their chequebooks and planning where to site their new Portaloo.

When Annie gave a hearty 'No!' Bronwen felt a wave of relief. As she'd travelled up the escalator through this slice of luxury retail heaven, looking at fragile glass mannequins draped in see-through toga dresses, knee-length wigs and lashings of intricate beads, she'd thought the woman who'd sent her to The Store must have been out of her mind.

But in front of her stood the very beautifully dressed, yes, but very real, very friendly-looking Annie. And all Bronwen could think was, *'How can I look just a little bit more like you?'*

'I'm management now,' Bronwen told her, pulling a slight face. 'I'm training and motivating the UK sales force. And I want to be just as good at that as I was at selling.'

'Why stop selling?' Annie wondered. 'Isn't it the thing

you love doing? Couldn't you make even more money selling something else? Or starting up your own business?'

'I might,' Bronwen admitted. 'But I thought I'd give the training gig a whirl. I mean, I'm management!' She seemed to find this amusing. 'Everyone takes you more seriously when you're management . . . you know, when I need to get some financial backing later on.'

'I'm very impressed,' Annie told her. 'So, any family?' she ventured, wondering if there were any mini Bronwens in mini brown cord skirts. 'Any significant other?'

'Nah,' came the casual reply, 'plenty of time for that yet, I hope.'

'So . . .' Annie took in the wiry hair and freckly face once again, 'how are we going to dress you?' she wondered out loud.

'Not going to be bloody easy, is it?' Bronwen joked. 'I like sweaters, sweatshirts, jeans that are comfy, not fancy, shoes I can walk in. I just want to be comfortable. That's how I sold 27,000 toilets a quarter: people were comfortable with me. They liked me. And look at my face, I don't suit any colours at all. Even black makes me look like a beetroot.'

Annie looked at the way Bronwen stood, slightly hunched forward, feet planted like poles in the ground, hip width apart. She really did look like a shepherd. The Store did not cater for shepherds or people who wanted to be comfortable . . . people who didn't suit any colour at all.

'I think I should measure you,' Annie suggested. 'It's a bit hard to tell what's going on underneath that sweater and skirt. You could be a size 10 or a size 18, I have no idea!

'Then, I'm going to sit you down here with a drink and I'm going to bring things up. I don't want you looking round the shop,' Annie warned, 'you'll just panic and get frightened and maybe even run out on me. No one's done that yet, but there's always a first.'

'Nah! I'll not run. I can't wait to see what you're going to come up with. I'm a disaster zone.' Bronwen was lifting up her arms so that Annie could pull the tape measure around her. 'My mum died when I was small and I only had my old man to take me shopping,' she went on. 'I didn't have any girlfriends when I was growing up. Too much of a dork.'

Although this was said cheerfully, it just broke Annie's heart. But then she knew too well that how people looked was always tied up with their complicated life stories. Bronwen's mum had died . . . she had no friends . . . she had to go shopping with the sheep farmer . . . and she thought she was a dork! That was all so tragic.

But look at her, she was so upbeat and certainly not sorry for herself. Annie wished she could sprinkle a little bit of Bronwen onto all the fragile, moaning minnies she had to pander to week in, week out.

'Well, today I'm your girlfriend,' Annie told her, 'and we're going to go shopping together and have a fantastic time. Now, you sit down – ' she pointed to the leather sofa in the vast dressing area. 'Paula will bring you drinks and magazines and even file your nails if you want her to.'

'That'd be nice!' Bronwen said in surprise.

'Just one question, babes, are there *any* colours you like?' Annie just wanted to get a clue here.

'Ermmm . . .' Bronwen had to think for a while, 'grey? Does that count as a colour?'

Annie nodded encouragingly.

'And I quite like pale green . . . any green really, so long as it isn't bright.'

Out on the shop floor, Annie did not panic. Even though there was so much to do to this woman! Looking at Bronwen in her saggy beige underwear, Annie had felt like a landscaper surveying a wild and overgrown field that she was supposed to turn into a garden overnight.

'Baby steps,' Annie reminded herself. Transformations took time. She'd have to ease Bronwen along gently, season by season.

She began to search the shop floor methodically; she had ideas and these racks had never let her down before. Out here she was going to find loads of things that a size 12–14 ruddy-faced, ruddy-haired woman who could only cope with being comfortable would want to wear.

Paula stalked past, telling her with a roll of the eyes, 'Whoaaaa, you've got your work cut out for you in there.'

'Shhhh!' Annie ticked her off, 'we'll be fine!' Her eyes slid down to Paula's shoes. 'Good fit?' Annie asked, pointing.

'Like a glove.' Paula winked and slinked on past, hips jutting and swivelling. She was wasted on the shop floor, she really was. At the very least she should be the star of her own miniseries.

Bronwen looked at herself in the mirror, hard. Annie had a name for this surprised, scrutinizing, half-astonished, half-disbelieving kind of look. She'd seen it often enough before, but she wasn't jaded. In fact, it always gave her a little burst of job satisfaction.

Yes, there was no doubt about it, Bronwen was definitely giving herself the 'I can't believe it's really me' look.

Annie had dressed her in a jumper and skirt, so she could still be comfortable and feel like herself. But this skirt was softest tweed, short and flared and flirty, by the label Annie liked to edge her novices towards.

On top was a Joseph cardigan, grey-green, mossy, cut like a military-ish jacket with a long row of buttons on each side; underneath was a pale green scoop neck top.

On a leather cord, Bronwen wore a chunky mother-of-pearl pendant of Maori design which Annie had unearthed in accessories, feeling Bronwen should have it for a touch of home.

Thick tights and flat boots made certain Bronwen was covered and comfortable. Over her shoulder was a long-handled, chunky, tasselled and casual £600 bag.

'You like?' Annie was asking, very pleased with her handiwork.

'Oh yes, me like. Me like a lot,' came Bronwen's astonished voice.

They put the jumper and top with dark grey, straight-legged jeans. They tried the skirt with a long-line slouchy grey sweater. They even put Bronwen into a simple black shirt dress with an amazing plaited leather and silver hip belt.

Everything was stunning. Everything made Bronwen younger, slimmer and prettier, and just slightly more 'management'.

Annie coaxed her into boots with a slight heel. Then mid-heeled ankle-strap shoes in wicked black patent.

'How much is all this going to cost?' Bronwen wondered a little later as she buttoned up a tweedy, but nevertheless slick, Farhi winter coat.

'Oh, a chemical toilet or two,' Annie warned her. 'Maybe even three. I have no idea how much a chemical toilet costs these days. But I'm sorry, Bronwen, if you were earning more than the chairman of the company and only buying Made in New Zealand sweaters then you're going to have to pay. I'm not letting you off! You're catching up on decades of shopping. You have to buy every single thing you love and even most of the things you just like! And by the way, you're not allowed to shop anywhere else, ever. I'm your shopping girlfriend from now on. Agreed?'

Bronwen nodded. 'You know, you may actually be a better saleswoman than me,' she said thoughtfully. 'Have you ever thought of coming to work in the chemical toilet business?'

'Paula, Paula, Paula!' Annie stopped her assistant in her tracks as soon as Bronwen and all her shopping had been helped out to The Store's courtesy car (for people who spent over £3,000 in one session and lived within a five-mile radius).

'Come. Sit,' Annie instructed, 'and let's talk about the shoes.'

Perching herself on the sofa, Paula carefully undid the

little purple buttons, eased her foot out of the vibrant cerise leather and handed the shoe over to Annie.

Paula's feet were bigger than hers – what with Paula being close to ten feet tall, this wasn't such a surprise.

'Where are they from?' Annie asked, taking a closer look. She'd only seen workmanship like this on the most expensive shoes in The Store. Shoes which came in cedarwood boxes and sold for over £500 a pair.

'Hong Kong,' Paula confided, 'I ordered them when I was there on holiday with my boyfriend. They had to be made up in my size and they arrived yesterday.'

'Which shop?' Annie wanted to know.

'It was a market stall.'

'A market stall!' Annie couldn't believe it. The maker of these shoes looked as if he'd served a twenty-year apprenticeship with a master craftsman in Italy. Look at the arch on the sole. The sweep. Check out the contrast purple piping sewn with tiny stitches even round the buttonhole. These shoes were breathtaking.

Annie studied the ornate gold lettering inscribed on the insole: Timi Woo.

'Timi Woo?' she asked. 'Is that a joke? Is that supposed to be a take on Jimmy Choo?'

'No. That's his name!' Paula insisted. 'I asked him that. He gave me his card. He said my friends could email him. He'll even make up his designs in the colours you want.'

'Really?! And . . . most importantly – ' Annie had the shoe on her foot now, pointing her toe this way and that, admiring it from every angle – 'how much did these handmade, bespoke babies cost?'

'Oh . . . I think they were about sixty quid.'

'Sixty quid! Sixty quid!' Annie couldn't believe it. 'Are you sure?'

'Yeah,' Paula replied casually, not sure what all the fuss was about.

Suddenly Annie felt overwhelmingly excited. This could be it! This could be her thing. This could be her business! If she bought Mr Timi Woo's shoes and sold them over here ... well, even at £120 they would be a bargain, a total steal. There was nothing available in Britain the quality of Mr Woo's shoes for less than £200, or £250 even. She couldn't think when she'd seen a lovelier piece of footwear that didn't come in a signed wooden box.

And the market for bespoke designer shoes was getting hotter and hotter. The Store already sold limited editions of Brian Atwoods and Rupert Sandersons at no less than £300 a pair.

'Paula, you are a genius!' she declared. 'You are a totally, brilliant, fabulous shopping genius.'

'Calm down, girl, you can order yourself a pair,' was Paula's response.

'A pair! I want hundreds of pairs!' Annie exclaimed.

'Maybe you should have a biscuit,' Paula advised.

'A biscuit? No, no, no!' Annie waved the idea away. 'Not everyone can eat biscuits all day long and still look like you. Paula, this is the best thing you've ever told me about.'

'Apart from the day that Donna . . .' Paula reminded her.

'Oh yeah.'

There was no forgetting the day that Donna Nicholson had finally left The Store. Their former floor manager, possibly the evil twin sister of Cruella de Vil.

Chapter Three

Dinah for drinks:

Mustard yellow pinafore (Barnardo's)
White, yellow and mustard floral blouse (Topshop)
Blue and white striped tights (Topshop)
Blue sequined beret (Accessorize)
Mustard Mary-Janes (Barnardo's)
Total est. cost: £65

'I'm liking your necklace.'

Five consultations later and Annie was finally packing the goodies gleaned from The Store today into white and gold carrier bags.

There was a top with a hem tear on the sleeve, which she'd bought (double discount) planning to invisibly mend it then sell it (Brand New With Tags) on her site. Then, she'd been given a generous selection of just about to go out of date miniatures by one of the Lancôme ladies, which she would either use herself or donate to her sister, Dinah.

But the best haul of the day had come from The Store's restaurant: three Tupperware boxes full of roasted artichoke salad and slices of fennel and fenugreek lasagne. Annie would offer this to whichever family members turned up at home tonight in search of dinner. She couldn't promise they'd eat it, obviously – that was the problem with The Store's restaurant leftovers, they were made for very low-fat-ladies-who-lunch.

Ed was taking Owen out to a concert this evening. She didn't know what kind of concert, except that it was at the Barbican and he'd got a special rate on the tickets. But this was a good thing, as Ed wasn't really happy unless he got a live music fix at least twice a week and Owen was always willing to tag along, whereas Annie had been dragged to several strange things (Shostakovich and Benjamin Britten, to name two) and had made it quite clear she shouldn't be his number one choice of musical date.

Lana had already phoned to say she was going to be with her new boyfriend, Andrei, this evening, *doing their homework together.* Annie had tried her hardest not to tut down the line. Probably the most irritating thing about Lana's new boyfriend was that there was nothing wrong with him – absolutely not one thing Annie could complain about. He was the perfect boyfriend and this made her twitch with annoyance because, if she was really honest, she wasn't quite ready to watch Lana fall madly in love. She wasn't ready to be relegated to the sidelines of Lana's affections . . . not just yet.

Annie turned off the row after row of ceiling lights that gave the personal shopping suite its glamorous dazzle, then, handbag and carrier bags slung over her shoulders, she walked down the escalator, already silent and still because it was after 9 p.m. and The Store was closed.

As she rounded the corner from the bottom of the escalator into Accessories on the ground floor, Annie didn't exactly mean to look, she really didn't. She'd intended to keep walking towards the front door, where she was meeting her sister in about three minutes' time, but then there was a movement which forced her to turn her head.

There, in the designer handbag corner, with its golden wooden shelving still lit from above and the new season's patent bags glowing like works of art, Sandra the sales consultant was dusting the scrunchy, slouchy, violet slice of handbag heaven which Annie couldn't seem to get out of her mind.

'Oh babes!' Annie couldn't stop herself from walking over now. 'No one's bought it today then?'

Sandra, an elegant blonde in her forties who'd spent five years in Accessories and knew everything there was to know about selling arm candy, turned to her and smiled: 'No, Annie, not yet. There was a very close call today. A woman was in here for over twenty minutes looking at it, handling it and trying it on. She said something about maybe next week when her pay cheque comes in.'

'Maybe next week!' Annie spluttered. 'It won't be here next week! Why didn't she just take it? Hasn't she heard of credit cards? Some people are just strange . . .'

'Which means it's still here.' Sandra, on tiptoe, took the bag down from its plinth and handed it to its most fervent admirer.

Ooooh, the weight, the softness, the substance, the crackle of patent leather, the gentle jangle of quality fittings. How could anyone ever think about buying a fake bag when the real thing was so very, very stunningly good? Annie herself had occasionally succumbed to the lure of the cheap, fashionable fake but it was always so woefully disappointing compared to the real thing.

And this was such a great piece! If she bought this bag, she could dress it up, dress it down. She couldn't think of an occasion that would be inappropriate for the bag. It was big, but not too big, soft but with structure . . .

Annie slipped it over her shoulder, caught a glimpse of herself in a mirrored column, then quickly took it off and handed it back to Sandra.

'I have to go,' she said sharply, more to herself than to Sandra, or indeed the handbag.

'A stunning investment piece,' Sandra, began, only for Annie to chime in with her so they said together: 'It will go with absolutely everything.'

'Definitely not tonight, my love,' Annie called, walking away from the source of temptation as quickly as she could, 'Night-night.'

She passed the Chanel counter, scooped a blob of £120 a jar face cream from the tester pot and rubbed it into her hands, then blasted herself thoroughly with the No. 19 tester bottle.

Spotting her sister on the other side of The Store's locked glass doors, she hurried over.

Outside the two hugged hello, then looked each other over approvingly for fashion pointers. Whereas Annie was labelly and slightly 'glam conservative', Dinah at the age of thirty-three was still a high street shopper, totally dedicated to fashion.

'Not just a pinafore, but a *tulip*-shaped pinafore, now that is very on-trend. Totally wouldn't work with my boobs though,' was Annie's first comment as she stroked the material of her sister's mustard-coloured dress and admired the bravery of teaming it with striped tights, a flowery blouse and a blue beret. But then Dinah did work at an art college. There were certain standards of zaniness which had to be maintained.

'Lovely material, really good quality and the exact colour of your shoes.' These things did not escape Annie's notice.

'Aha, yeah, I bought them together, matching set, at Barnardo's for twenty-five pounds.' Dinah gave a smug little smile. She just loved to subvert Annie's mantra that great quality only came at a price.

'Bargain,' Annie had to agree: 'possibly because you are the only person in the Western world who suits mustard yellow.'

'Mmmm . . . I'm liking your necklace.' Dinah was now homing in on the ornately coloured and twisted brown, black and golden whorls round Annie's neck.

'Totally plastic, Brixton market, £4. It's yours for £3,' Annie offered.

'Hand it over and I'll buy you a drink,' was Dinah's offer.

'OK. Where are we going by the way?' Annie asked, 'and is the Dry One meeting us there?'

'Oh yeah. I've made sure there's a *selection* of mineral waters available,' Dinah replied, rolling her eyes.

40

'To think, we used to really like him . . . and what very, very good times we used to have,' Annie said with mock sadness, as arm in arm, heels clicking rhythmically together, the sisters set off down the street in the direction of one of the more secluded wine bars in Kensington.

'It can't go on for much longer, surely?' Dinah asked.

'Who knows?'

They were talking about Connor, their long-term friend. Once gay, vivacious and hilarious, a highly successful TV actor with a starring role in a prime time Sunday series, he was now a far too highly successful TV actor, about to renegotiate his contract, still gay but, instead of vivacious and hilarious, stone cold sober and almost as obsessed with his health as his career.

Both Annie and Dinah were convinced if they could just force one tiny little chilled Chablis into him he'd be back to his old self. Unfortunately, in Connor's opinion, 'That's just the booze talking, you're all just as dependent on it as I used to be.' Which was just totally irritating and boring.

The sisters were already settled down with large glasses of wine when Connor arrived, looking even more tall, dark and utterly knicker-droppingly gorgeous in real life than he did on the box.

After greeting, kissing and hugging them with plenty of fuss, Connor found a barman, who obviously recognized him, hovering at his elbow offering to take his order and bring his drinks to the table.

'Perrier with plenty of ices and slices,' Connor told him with a dazzling smile. 'Anything for you, girls?'

When Annie and Dinah shook their heads, Connor

took off his slinky black raincoat and pulled up a chair.

'Service, girls,' Connor beamed at them, his newly whitened smile splitting his beautifully boned face: 'That's what we want.'

Pushing back his luxurious black hair, he stretched out his muscular arms (well, he did have a daily personal trainer) and, hands clasped behind his head, he leaned back.

'So what's the news? What's happening? How many handbags has Annie bought this week?'

Annie snorted in reply to this.

'Is Dinah still married to Bryan?' Connor asked next, teasingly because there was only one answer to this question.

Dinah gave a nod and smile.

'Is Billie still their only child? Not the slightest hint of another?'

'Yes!' Dinah insisted, 'and no!'

'Are Annie and Ed still happy?'

'Oh yeah,' Annie said, flicking up an eyebrow.

'Owen and Ed?'

'Likewise.'

'Most importantly then, is Lana still going out with Andrei and is Andrei still driving Mummy Annie up the wall?'

Gossip of a romantic nature was the kind Connor did best.

Annie nodded, groaned and took a sip of wine.

'Oh dear, oh dear, drowning our sorrows,' Connor noted snugly, 'looking for support from our faithful old poisons. You really should come to AA with me Annie, there are so many good-looking people there these days.'

'Good-looking people no longer matter to me,' she reminded him, 'unless they're wanting makeovers, babes.'

'What exactly is wrong with Andrei?' Dinah wondered.

'Oh let me see,' Annie said irritably. 'He's tall, really good-looking, very polite, speaks fluent French, helps and encourages Lana with her homework . . . erm . . . does athletics, doesn't believe in under-age drinking . . . need I go on?' she added with another groan. Dinah just looked more confused.

'Somebody's jealous,' Connor teased. 'Somebody's grumpy that their little girly-wirly has a new role model in her life taking Mummy's place.'

'Oh, I know, I know. I have to get a life,' Annie grumbled. 'I'm planning to go into business—'

'Again?' Dinah interrupted. 'I thought you were so pleased to get your job back at The Store?'

There had been a time last year when, all because of evil floor manager Donna, Annie had had to leave The Store and work for herself, just until Donna finally left – probably in a puff of smoke.

'I thought you didn't like all the stress and hassle of being self-employed,' Dinah reminded her sister.

'No . . .' and that was true, she hadn't, but, 'I'm thinking of a different kind of thing, this time. I want to sell a range, my own products, be a brand. I've got a really good idea, which I can't tell you anything about yet,' she added quelling the interested look on their faces, 'because it's just way too early, but unfortunately Ed is totally against anything like this.'

'Why?' Connor asked.

'He's risk-averse,' Annie replied, 'and that's putting it mildly.'

'No bloody wonder,' was Connor's jokey response; 'he's with you, that's enough risk for anyone to be getting on with.'

'Connor!' she treated him to an elbow in the ribs for being so unsupportive, 'I don't want to be a shop assistant for ever.'

'You're not a shop assistant!' Dinah insisted.

'You're a *personal sales consultant*,' Connor teased.

'People from all over London flock to The Store for your priceless advice,' Dinah added.

'That is sweet,' Annie told her, 'but the advice is not priceless, it costs The Store just a glorified shop assistant's salary and a bit of commission every month and I'd like to do something more. Don't you think I'd make a good businesswoman?' she asked them.

'I already thought you were,' Dinah answered. 'Don't you still do the eBay thing? And the home makeovers?'

'Yeah, but I want to import!' Annie insisted, 'I don't just want to sell little bits and pieces here and there, I want to flog things in the thousands. Have a marketing department, a PR budget, suppliers, buyers, movers and shakers.'

'Have to deal with Revenue & Customs and the VAT man,' Dinah reminded her.

'Yes, but I want a change!' Annie insisted, trying to ignore the shiver that the words Revenue & Customs sent down her spine. 'Connor, you're self-employed,' she suddenly remembered: 'can you ever get a bit of a time extension to pay your tax bill?'

'Oh no, Annie!' Dinah rushed in with immediate concern. 'How much do you owe them?'

'I've never found the tax people terribly accommodating about anything,' came Connor's reply. 'Just borrow the money on your mortgage,' he advised, 'that's what I do every year. I can't stand saving. Saving is for nerds.'

'No, Annie!' Dinah was horrified, 'your mortgage is huge!'

But Annie's mind was already whirring: borrow against her portion of the house? Maybe she could borrow enough to pay off the tax bill and a credit card or two *and* start up her own business! It would be much easier than trying to get a business loan, surely?

The barman was hovering at their table again; he picked up the Perrier bottle and topped up Connor's glass although he'd only taken a sip: 'Anything else I can get you?' he asked.

'No, no, we're fine thanks,' Dinah told him sweetly. 'So, still single then?' she asked Connor, once the barman was out of earshot. 'I don't think we're going to get any peace anywhere until you find yourself a new man.'

'Oh, I know, it's a jungle out here and I am the prey,' Connor said, so camply that Annie snorted wine out of her nose.

'Did you know that it's our tenth wedding anniversary in September?' Dinah asked, then added gloomily, 'and Bryan is planning a surprise party.'

Everyone perked up at this news. Even Annie managed to forget about her tax bill momentarily.

'A surprise party? But I think if you know that's not technically a surprise,' Annie told her sister.

'I know,' Dinah began, 'I mean, I know that if I know . . . Well, he doesn't know I know.'

'What do you know?' Annie cut in.

'I found a list of catering companies, florists and bands lying beside the telephone.'

'Oh my God!' was Annie's reaction. 'Men are so subtle! And I suppose if he was having an affair he'd just leave pants, suspenders and a condom in his trouser pockets?'

'I know, he would. There's no way Bryan could ever have an affair,' Dinah agreed, 'I'd know as soon as he was even thinking about it. He'd blush every time someone said her name, go to incredible lengths to avoid mentioning her . . . I can read him like a book.'

'So he's trying to surprise you with a tenth anniversary party. That is really sweet,' Annie had to admit.

'I know, but if I leave it up to him,' Dinah said, 'it'll be—'

'Like your wedding,' Annie finished the sentence for her.

'And that was?' Connor wanted to know.

'Tragic,' the sisters agreed.

'Marylebone Registry Office, then across six lanes of traffic to get to the Stag's Head pub for a finger buffet. We were just lucky and grateful that no actual fingers were served,' Annie summarized.

'Amen,' Connor lifted his Perrier glass, 'What did you wear?'

'Oh, a really nice dress,' Dinah told him, 'but Annie had to get it back to the film set she was working on by Monday morning, minus the wine stain. So it was a little bit stressful.'

'Ah well, we were in our twenties, nothing mattered so much back then,' Annie chipped in, 'but now we're grown-ups, we can't have Bryan putting on a crap surprise tenth. I mean TEN years. He owes you. He owes you a really decent ding-dong by now. Not to mention a *proper* engagement ring.' Annie cast her eyes down tragically, first towards her own jewel-less fingers and then over to Dinah's. 'We haven't got a decent diamond between us. Connor probably has more bling on his blooming shirt cuffs.'

'Annie!' Dinah warned, 'I'm perfectly happy with this.' She twisted at the little silver sliver on her fourth finger which had served as both her engagement and wedding ring. 'If I change rings now, I'll probably jinx us.'

'Awww,' Annie smiled at her, 'that is sweet. I can't believe it's really ten years! Well done!' and she raised her wine glass at her sister.

Connor held his glass up too. 'Good grief, I've never even made it to ten months.'

'How *is* Hector?' Annie asked. 'He's not too cut up about it, is he? I have to say, I really liked Hector,' she added.

'Yeah, so did I,' Dinah chipped in. 'Why was he given the heave-ho?'

'Couldn't handle the pressure,' Connor said and, for once, he didn't seem to be joking.

'The pressure of what?' Annie had to ask.

'Fame. He couldn't cope with my career.'

Both Annie and her sister struggled to keep straight faces at this revelation.

'But not much has changed since he started going out with you . . . has it?' Dinah asked.

'Not much has changed?!' Connor looked horrified. 'My contract's up! It's renegotiation time. Time to decide if I want to go back to *The Manor* and if I do, how much will lure me. Plus, I'm meeting a very, very important new film director from Over There, who is Over Here soon looking for a British star for his next picture. Sam Knight,' he revealed in a reverential whisper.

'Ooooh,' Annie couldn't help being impressed. 'So it wasn't just your no-dairy, no-alcohol and no-wheat diet that scared Hector away.'

'Ha-ha and for your information the Blood Type Diet is suiting my system perfectly, and Ben . . .'

'Who?' Dinah asked, trying to keep up.

'His personal trainer,' Annie sniggered.

But they weren't to hear what Ben thought of the Blood Type Diet because the barman was back asking yet again if there was anything they would like.

'No, we're fine . . . but maybe you'd like something,' Connor asked the man with a cheeky smile.

'Well, would you mind? I mean, if it's OK . . .' and he handed Connor a pen and a small piece of paper.

'No, no trouble at all.' Connor took the paper and with a flourish scribbled over it: *'Connor McCabe says "tell me all about it."'* It was his trademark catchphrase. At least once every episode, *The Manor*'s policeman had to ask somebody to 'tell me all about it'.

The barman picked up the paper with a grateful 'Thanks, thanks so much, sorry to disturb you.'

But then he looked at the signature in some confusion.

'What's the matter?' Connor asked.

'I thought you were Peter Andre,' the barman said

boldly, unaware of what an inexcusable mistake he was making.

'Peter Andre?' Connor repeated, looking completely taken aback. 'Oh! Well – I'm not!' he spluttered, and gave as gracious a smile as he could manage in the circumstances.

Annie and Dinah had to look very deliberately away from each other and think of terrible, tragic and disastrous thoughts while their lips twisted and their shoulders trembled.

Chapter Four

Ed's musical night out:

T-shirt (Woolworths)
Tweed jacket (posh gents' outfitters on Jermyn Street
– because Annie made him)
Jeans (Topman)
Desert boots (Clarks)
Leather briefcase (the mists of time)
Total est. cost: £430

'We never knowingly like to miss out if
there's food on offer.'

It was coming up to 11 p.m., and with a plate of nuked fennel lasagne by her side and another glass of wine, Annie was conducting some internet research into Paula's magical shoes.

Mr Timi Woo's website was not exactly helpful. There were some basic graphics which really did the shoes no justice at all, and lots of Chinese text, but also a promise in English to 'make any shoe you wishing of, helpful ladies of desiring'.

There was a contact email so Annie quickly typed Mr Woo a note informing him that she was interested in selling his shoes in Britain. Was he already selling shoes here? How many shoes could he make in a month? And what would he sell them to her for?

She sent the email off and turned her mind once again to extending her mortgage.

Although Ed and Annie owned the house together, Annie owned a share and had her own mortgage on that share . . . so, theoretically, Ed wouldn't even need to know about the money she'd borrowed until her tax bill was all paid off and the beautiful shoes were coming over and she was selling them at a fabulous mark-up and it was all working. Then he'd be much less resistant to the whole idea.

It wasn't that she wanted to lie to him, it was just that she knew how hard he would be to convince. He didn't like change in any form at all and he was completely nervous about taking financial risks. He'd never earned big money, he certainly didn't plan to change jobs and he'd always been very careful with the money he did have. That was just the way he was, she wasn't going to be able to change him . . . but her job was to reassure him that it was all going to be OK.

Her email flashed up with a new message. She looked at the address and was delighted to see that Mr Woo had wasted no time.

'*Greetings Annie Valentine,*' she read, '*I hope you have nice day! I very interested in doing business with your esteemed* corporation. My shoes sold in Hong Kong but made in factory of my family. Happy Feet factory. Very good workmanship shoes. I glad you like.

We can make 120 pair Timi Woo shoes this month. But if you need more next month, we can make more. Shoes only sell in Hong Kong. Very popular with high class ladies desiring much shoes. We love to sell in England with your esteemed corporation. I send order form with this message. Many styles, many colours. Each pair shoe for you $80. If you buy 100 pair shoes, $75.

Greetings, Timi Woo.'

Although Annie's heart was thudding with excitement as she read this, she couldn't act just yet as she could now hear the sound of the front door opening.

'Hi! Annie! We're back!' came the shout from the hall, so she quickly closed down the email and hurried downstairs to meet Ed and her little boy.

'Hello Owen!' She hugged her son tightly first. He felt so skinny. He was growing like a weed and his appetite didn't seem to be able to keep up with the amount of food he needed.

Owen kept his face, almost hidden under his thatch of overgrown blond-brown hair, tipped down, but he accepted the shower of kisses without protest. He liked it, really. He just didn't like to admit that he liked it. That's how it is when you're ten.

'Nice time?' she asked, directing her gaze at Ed in turn.

He looked so happy that she couldn't stop her smile from broadening when it met his. He seemed relaxed and chilled out by his evening away. He slung his jacket on the rack by the front door, then, when she'd released

Owen, he put one arm round her waist and the other round her shoulder so she was encircled, and pulled her right in.

'Hello there.' He didn't believe in half-measure kisses: *'If you're going to kiss, you might as well kiss properly.'*

Putting her arms around Ed's broad back, Annie saw the playful look in his blue eyes and felt the touch of his lips against hers. Ed was so calming, when he took hold of her he made her stand still, be still, think about no one and nothing else but him, right here and now. It was very sexy.

'Please, just no tongues,' Owen insisted, which made the adults break up a little sooner than they might otherwise have wanted to.

'Busy day?' Ed asked, now that the kissing spell was pretty much broken. 'Dressing the universe?'

'Oh yeah,' Annie told him with a smile. 'Do you boys need some food? It's late but . . .'

'Well, you know . . .' Ed began, 'we never knowingly like to miss out if there's food on offer.'

'What have you got?' Owen wondered, as he deposited his anorak on the floor and sat down on a stair to spend the fifteen minutes it seemed to require for him to unlace his trainers. By now, Ed's two fat black cats, Hoover and Dyson, had stalked into the hall and were rubbing up against every available leg and foot, desperate for some attention.

'A little bit of fennel lasagne?' Annie offered, fairly certain that this wasn't going to be met with much excitement.

'Hmm . . .' was Owen's reply.

'Fried eggs and toast?' she offered next.

'Look, there's bacon, there's cream, there's definitely a chunk of Parmesan – why don't I rustle us up a carbonara?' Ed offered. 'That'll stick to your ribs.'

Owen shot Ed a grin and nodded.

This was one of the many surprising effects that surrogate family life had had on Ed. When Annie had first met him, he'd been a sad and lonely singleton living in a damp basement – the damp basement of the house they were currently living in, to be precise. His cooking had been severely limited to putting potatoes in the microwave and opening cans of beans or, even worse, sardines.

Now, one year into his man-of-the-house role and his cooking put Annie's to shame. Yes, she could fry an egg, boil a potato, shop at M&S and heat up a ready meal just as well as the next woman. But Ed . . . Ed now *basted* things in the oven. He *crumbled* rosemary. He liked to serve stewed fruit with home-made custard. He simmered casseroles on the hob. He actually read cookbooks, hunted down hard to find ingredients and got slightly overexcited at the prospect of having a whole weekend free to cook.

It was all quite mysterious to Annie, but, just like her children, she loved most of what he served up: the braised ox tongue had been a dish too far, but otherwise she was happy for him to get on with it.

Once Owen had crammed himself full of spaghetti, Annie supervised his teeth-brushing and put him to bed before coming down to snuggle up with Ed on the sofa.

'Andrei is walking Lana home tonight, isn't he?' Annie

checked. 'You know there was a mugging the other night, two streets away.'

Ed nodded reassuringly then asked: 'So, busy on the computer tonight?

'Oh . . . you know,' she brushed the question away.

'Selling things on eBay or doing more "how to run your own business" research?' Ed didn't look quite so friendly now.

'Look,' she began, 'I'm not going to do anything stupid, OK? Can you stop worrying about this? When . . . I mean, *if* I come up with a good idea you will be the first to know, OK? I will not do anything without making sure you think it's a good idea.'

Deep down, Annie did believe this. She believed that with the Timi Woo shoes, for instance, she was just doing the groundwork, the research. When she had the shoes, when she had the customers . . . when it came to really making the move, she *would* let Ed know. By then it would all be much more clear anyway.

But Ed didn't seem ready to let the subject drop just yet.

'I'm not saying you can't have your own business, Annie,' he told her, 'I just don't think this is the time. I feel as if we're all only just settling in together. It's hardly even been a year . . . and you're working really long hours,' he reminded her. 'Four nights a week, and most Saturdays you barely see the children. I think that's enough time away from them. If you set up your own company you'd be working flat out.'

She was listening and she had to admit that some of this was true. But the whole point of having her own business was that in the long run she would be in control of her working life and her working hours, wouldn't she? She was trying to branch out so that *in the long run* there would be more money and more flexibility for her.

'It's OK,' she assured Ed, moving in close to him, 'don't worry about it and don't worry about me. Stop worrying! We do not have to talk about this right now,' and then she quickly moved on to her tried and trusted distraction technique.

She slipped her fingers under his T-shirt and began to run them over the soft, fuzzy-haired, warm skin there. Pushing a fingertip gently into his bellybutton, she asked him, 'Do you think you could stop talking now?'

Ed didn't have to be asked twice. He shut up immediately, leaned back against the sofa cushions and pulled Annie onto his chest so he could kiss her.

And then she was under the pull of the steady blue gaze. There he was, her very hot, *younger* man, absolutely focused on her, ready to do whatever it was she wanted him to do.

She moved her hips so that she could feel him getting harder right there against her, then she pushed his T-shirt up so that she could bite firmly on his nipple.

When her fingers had undone his belt, loosened his buttons and slipped inside, he said against her ear: 'We have to go upstairs. Sensitive, impressionable teenagers could walk in at any moment.'

'She'll be late,' she reminded him.

'No, no, too risky,' he said with a little gasp because she was still moving her hand (oh!) so interestingly against him.

'C'mon.' He managed to extricate himself and get up from the sofa, holding his jeans in place with one hand, taking hold of Annie's wrist with the other. 'Race you up the stairs.'

And then they were in their bedroom, with the door tightly shut and the lights off because the curtains were still open and neither of them wanted the distraction of breaking off from the urgent kissing to go over to the windows.

Annie was trying to remember when they'd last made love. Three days ago? Or four? Suddenly it seemed like a long time.

Ed let his jeans fall to the floor, but he wasn't in a hurry. The fact that he was never in a hurry was the single most sexy thing about him. He was going to take his time. He was going to make love to her in his very own sexy, but funny, but passionately intense way.

Kneeling down, he moved his head under her skirt and listened to her giggle as he tried to take her knickers off with his teeth.

Fingers winding into his curly hair, she backed slowly towards the bed, pulling him towards her.

He was starting to hum with his lips pressed right up against her clit. She lay back on the bed, stripping off her top and her bra so that his hands could stroke over her breasts as the humming continued, sending waves of warmth rushing and tingling up from the pit of her stomach.

'You make me forget about everything else,' she told him.

'No!' he broke off to joke with her, 'that's not it. Name that tune!' he insisted and put his lips against her again.

He almost always made her come first because, as he put it, 'I need to concentrate on you while I can still think straight, if I leave it till later . . . baby, it's like trying to control a volcano.'

And he was good.

Yes . . . he was very good.

She could feel the very tip of his tongue now, licking up and down with tiny, quick darts as his warm hands rubbed against the skin of her thighs.

There was no fumbling with Ed. None of that confused 'what exactly am I looking for down here?' Annie, like most women, had endured quite enough Boy Scout lovers: all that rubbing and rubbing of the kindling and still no hope of a fire.

The little darts of the tongue were getting quicker and she could feel the melting rush building and building now.

'Come in,' she urged, pulling him up by his shoulders, 'come in . . . because I am so . . . so . . . so . . . cl . . . close.'

As he pushed inside, she felt herself shudder and clench again and again around him. Oh. Yes. Yes! Nothing was better. Nothing was better than coming like this, all the way through Ed's urgent thrusts.

Eyes screwed shut, fingernails digging into his soft back, legs wound tightly around his, she clung on, feeling him pulse on through her until they were both more than finished.

'Is that a cat?!' Annie lifted her head from Ed's sweaty, post-coital arm and looked more closely at the two small glowing lights at the end of the bed.

'Down!' Ed commanded, raising himself up.

The eyes moved and with a heavy thump, four paws landed firmly on the floor.

'I don't like cats in the bed,' Annie reminded Ed, as if there was any chance he'd forgotten.

'They miss me,' he told her. 'I think they're very, very jealous of you.'

'They'd probably scratch me to death and eat me with a side helping of Whiskas if they got the chance,' Annie agreed. 'I can't believe you used to sleep with them.'

'I didn't sleep *with* them, I used to let them sleep at the foot of my bed. I'm not that strange.'

'No,' Annie slid her hands over Ed's bum, 'but you are quite nicely strange.'

And they kissed again and pressed against each other and might even have considered . . .

But then came the clinking of the key in the front door and the sound of Lana's voice and the long, long, very long goodnight.

When sixteen-year-old girls are deeply, deeply in first love with seventeen-year-old boys, goodnight is not a straightforward thing. Lana and Andrei were now wrapped around each other in the hallway kissing, kissing and kissing some more.

Her hands were wrapped round his neck, then running through his hair, his hands were stroking the small of her back, rubbing up and down her sides, while their tongues rolled over and over and over together as if this was the best thing they'd ever tasted.

Annie, lying in bed beside Ed, knew why the front door hadn't yet closed on Andrei.

'First love,' she whispered, turning to Ed. 'Do you

remember that far back? The sex is probably the worst you're going to have but the foreplay is *unforgettable* . . . I can still remember what it feels like to kiss like that.'

'Can you?' Ed leaned over her face and seemed to be offering to remind her.

'Oh yeah,' she said, but just kissed him lightly on the lips.

'I don't remember my first sex being bad,' Ed said, leaning back on the pillow and running his hands over his face.

'No, but that's because you're male,' Annie reminded him, 'and sex is never bad for men. Ever. Is it?'

'Ermmm . . .' Ed cast his mind back over a not extremely long and varied sex life and came to the conclusion that, 'No. Hardly ever. Not unless you're feeling really, really guilty.'

'Yeah . . . as in you came over to chuck her and thought you'd just have sex first,' Annie teased.

'Oh God,' Ed groaned, 'chucking people is a nightmare. I've only done it once. Since then, I've always been the chuckee. So there you go, you never, ever have to worry about me chucking you. If this is ever going to end, you'll have to do it.'

She turned onto her side and put an arm across his stomach before asking with a teasing smile: 'But it's never, ever going to end, is it?'

'No-oh,' he assured her, with something of a laugh and then rubbed her nose with his very fondly, looking deep into her eyes.

'I have to go to the bathroom,' she said abruptly, 'and remind Lana to come up for air and send that poor boy home to rest.'

'Annie?' Ed asked. 'Do you think maybe Lana should move her bedroom?'

'Huh?'

'Well, her bedroom is right above ours and right beside Owen's. It's not exactly private.'

Annie rolled onto her back and looked at the ceiling as she considered what Ed was suggesting.

'Are you thinking Lana should have a room of her own downstairs in the basement? Next to my office?'

Ed looked at her and nodded.

'A room she can take Andrei to and be undisturbed?'

Ed nodded again.

Suddenly Annie felt irritated: 'Don't you think that's just a little bit irresponsible?' she asked. 'Don't you think it's a good thing that she's kissing him in the doorway rather than rolling all over the sofa with him? Don't you think it's quite healthy that if she were to take him upstairs to her bedroom, she would have to worry about what we thought and what we heard? I think being newly sixteen with your GCSEs ahead of you is too young for undisturbed rooms on your own with your boyfriend.'

'OK,' Ed quickly agreed, 'OK, that's fine. It was just an idea. But . . . totally up to you. Just keep talking to her, though. She'll want some guidance from you.'

'Ha!' Annie laughed, 'what on earth gave you that idea?'

'She does! She's just being teenage and pretending to hate you.'

Annie really wasn't so sure about that. Sometimes when Lana was in one of her blackest moods, she could shoot her mother a look so vicious and hateful it made

Annie gasp. But then, like stormy weather, the moods would pass, leaving Annie wondering what she had done to make Lana so angry with her.

'Just for my information, Annie,' Ed began, 'how old were you when you first . . .'

'Nearly eighteen,' she broke in just a little sternly. 'What about you?'

'Er . . . twenty-two,' Ed admitted a little sheepishly, which made both of them laugh.

'It was worth the wait,' Ed added.

'I bet it was. But this does mean that you've only been having sex for ten years, which makes you a total beginner,' Annie teased.

'Better show me something new then . . .'

Chapter Five

Svetlana at The Store:

Ruched white shirt dress (Burberry Prorsum)
Black and white striped heels (Christian Louboutin)
White woven leather tote bag (Bottega Veneta)
Bright blond blow-dry (Nicky Clarke – personally)
Signature red lipstick (Chanel)
Diamonds (husbands 1 and 2)
Total est. cost: £45,000

'But isn't my one a darrrrrling?'

'Ahhhhnnah!'

Annie's favourite Russian burst thought the personal shopping suite's velvet curtains with her arms outstretched.

Svetlana Wisneski. Not that she was going to be Wisneski for much longer. The former Miss Ukraine was now in possession of a decree nisi from her third husband, the billionaire gas baron, or 'Igor Potato-face the Third', as they'd christened him in the suite.

You'd think a generous settlement, your own four-storey house in Mayfair and everything-paid-for-the-children-forever would be enough. But for Svetlana, nothing was ever, ever enough. Currently she was planning her fourth wedding to Harry Roscoff, her divorce lawyer.

'I know, I know, it even happen in *Sex and the City*. No? The hairy bald man, he called Harry too, no? But isn't my one a darrrrrrrling?'

Svetlana had taken out her digital camera to show Annie his picture when she'd first got involved with Harry. Annie had seen a small, pudgy guy in his late fifties. But then looks had never been a particular concern of Svetlana's; she was only interested in the size of a man's bank balance.

The next photo had been introduced with the words, 'But look at him in his *gowns*.'

It showed one of London's most respected divorce lawyers in a dark gown with a white barrister's wig on his head sitting on a huge, unmade bed.

'I make him wear his gowns in the bedroom,' Svetlana had confided in a low tone, 'much, much more exciting. Poor man, he has had English wife for thirty-five years. He has forgotten what penis is for! So, I remind him!' She'd let out an infectiously throaty laugh at this.

Today, Annie gave the allegedly thirty-nine-year-old specimen of Russian physical perfection a welcoming hug. Svetlana, statuesquely tall, boasted muscular, athletic curves, a hard, flat stomach and fabulous buttocks and breasts which were a little enhanced, but only with the softest, most expensive and flexible stuff.

Around her taut face, holding back the years with the help of the most expert cosmetic surgeon in London, blonde hair tumbled elegantly to her shoulders. Today's tight white dress showed off thighs strong enough to kill a man in true Russian fantasy woman style.

A blinking, winking, fat pendant of diamonds pointed directly down into her two magnificent assets. Grown men like Harry Roscoff were prepared to lose wives, homes, properties, companies, investment portfolios, even respectability in order to dive down into those assets and venture further with a woman like Svetlana.

'He is millionaire, not billionaire,' Svetlana had had to admit of Harry, 'I am now nearly as rich as him. But after Igor, I wanted a very kind man. A man who loves me, makes no trouble for me. A quiet, expensive life, that's all I want to lead now. Anyway, I am too old for a billionaire under eighty now,' she'd stated matter-of-factly, as if there were official billionaire marrying rules, 'and where is the fun in that? A defibrillator in the bedroom and then fighting and fighting with the family for money after the death. Poor, poor girls,' she'd said, with real feeling.

'No, I make good lawyer's wife, don't you think?' She'd given Annie a wink. 'And I make Harry very, very happy.'

Released from the soft and delicious-smelling warmth of Svetlana's embrace, it was the English wife of thirty-five years Annie felt sorry for now. The poor woman wouldn't have stood a chance. Not when Svetlana aimed her two missiles in Harry's direction and gave it to him with both barrels.

'Why are you here?' Annie finally had the chance to

ask. 'It's always lovely to see you, babes, but you're not on my list.'

'I know, I bring friend, she's out on the shop floor looking.' Svetlana sat down on the bright pink sofa, flashing sheerest stockings and a leg so exactly the right consistency between toned and soft that even Annie caught herself looking. That's how sexy Svetlana was.

But here was the thing: Svetlana was in fact a very good wife. Once she was hitched, she was loyal to a fault, supportive and devoted, and had seemed to genuinely love each of her husbands. But every one of them had ditched her for someone younger. Or died.

Annie hoped that Harry was going to be for good – just as soon as his very expensive divorce came through. Annie was also hoping that one day soon Svetlana might be a very good person to turn to when she needed a business investor.

'My friend Kelly-Anne is booked in with you. She needs makeunder,' Svetlana's voice dropped, maybe because she expected the friend to walk in at any moment. 'She turned forty and pfuuuuh!' this came with vigorous hand flicks in the air towards her face: 'injecting everything that move, filling up cheeks from her ass, all that thing! Botox: horrible! You can never get angry, you have to walk around like a robot.' Svetlana pulled a totally straight face and said in monotone: 'I am extremely angry with you, extremely upset, you mad, potato-faced Pol Pot.

'Mid-section facelift, much better,' she added. 'Anyway, her children, they nice boys at school with my boys, and all the kids there call her the high-class hooker. That is what she look like! I keep telling her, husband not going to leave because you now forty and have little tiny frown line and don't wear miniskirt all the time . . . but how do I know? This what happen to me.' She gave an enormous existentialist shrug.

Annie suspected that Svetlana had turned forty herself. She'd been thirty-nine for just a little bit too long now. And she definitely did things to her face . . . but it was all a question of degree and clearly this friend needed a little retuning.

'It's not nice,' Svetlana added, 'not for the school gates, ha?'

Before Annie could make any reply, the friend in question tottered into the suite, prompting Annie to give her warmest smile and welcome as she took a long, hard look at the woman.

She was carefully balanced on three-inch-high stilettos and squeezed into a black, short-sleeved wrap dress so tight it was almost a bandage.

Yes, the face on top of the cleavage looked younger than both the slightly creased breasts and the neck, but Annie could barely make the face out underneath the monstrous hair.

An enormous purplish-black beehive with a severe fringe and great long tendrils falling down round the shoulders perched on top of this poor woman's head. It was so styled and so lacquered, even the tendrils looked crunchy.

Annie checked herself: glam Addams family, yes, but it was a *look*. Maybe the woman didn't want to change. Maybe her husband adored her like this. Maybe it was just other women, like Svetlana, who were thinking: 'Hello!! Morticia!'

Annie was never too keen on women being dragged here by their friends. She lived by the psychologist's mantra that you couldn't change anyone unless they wanted to change. But anyway, she was here to suggest some new clothes. The hair was nothing to do with her.

'So! Kelly-Anne, isn't it?' Annie ushered her in and made her sit down on the sofa next to Svetlana. 'Tell me what I can do for you today. What kind of things are you looking for?'

'Well . . .' Kelly-Anne looked a little unsure of herself, 'I've never done this before. I have such a good idea of the kind of things I want, usually.'

'Pschuuuuut,' Svetlana tutted unhelpfully beside her. 'You need Annnah.'

'That's great,' Annie smiled at Kelly-Anne, hoping to cancel out Svetlana's comment. 'Some new things for the autumn . . . a coat? A bag? I have amazing new day dresses, just in . . . or maybe you want to look at something more casual.'

'Maybe a haircut too,' Svetlana put in.

'No, no!' Kelly-Anne said, looking anxious, 'you don't do hair here?'

'Yes, we do now have a new hair salon in the basement,' Annie told her.

'Kelly-Anne, you need haircut,' Svetlana told her firmly, 'this hair looked good when you were fifteen. Now you need something more modern.'

Kelly-Anne looked faintly terrified now.

'Well, anyway,' Annie gave Svetlana a look which was intended to make her shut up about the hair, 'let's talk about clothes.'

*　　*　　*

The trying-on session wasn't a great success. Everything tight and black Kelly-Anne wanted. Everything colourful, elegant and stylish, Svetlana and Annie wanted, but Kelly-Anne resisted.

It was shaping up to be one of Annie's very rare personal shopping deadlocks, when suddenly Connor breezed into the suite unannounced.

'Whatcha think Annie?' he asked, holding out his arms and wanting her immediate appraisal of his new, all-important outfit, 'I've been shopping with Dale downstairs in the big boys' department. This is what we came up with for the Sam Knight lunch. You like it?' Suddenly he noticed the other women in the room.

'Svetlana!' he exclaimed, and rushed over to take her hand and kiss it showily.

Annie gave him the glare, which was supposed to mean: *I'm busy, make an appointment, like everyone else.*

But Connor read it as disapproval. 'No? Not the blazer?' he asked her, 'I thought the blazer was a bit much as well. But it's Ralph Lauren, baby and I'm loving the cashmere T-shirt underneath.'

He posed in front of the full-length angled mirror, knowing full well he looked like sex on a stick and even Annie was going to have to admit it.

Kelly-Anne was looking at him with the wide-eyed look of surprised recognition. Annie hoped this was a good thing. Maybe if Kelly-Anne knew she dressed the famous Connor McCabe, she might be just a teensy bit more open to some honest advice.

'Hello there!' Connor schmoozed at Kelly-Anne. 'And I'm not Peter Andre, if that's what you're thinking.'

'I know!' she squeaked. 'You're Connor McCabe,

from *The Manor*! I love that programme. I think you're great!'

Kelly-Anne, who was currently wearing slim grey flannel trousers with a cream off-the-shoulder jumper (an outfit she'd just told Annie and Svetlana she'd never be seen dead in) stared at him quite transfixed.

'You're looking very foxy in that,' Connor told her generously. 'You're even giving me the horn.'

Kelly-Anne was well enough up on Connor's love life to know why that was funny.

'But the hair!' Svetlana complained to him, 'the hair should be silky. Moving, no? Connor, tell this woman.'

'Come to Connor and sit,' he instructed, pulling up a chair and placing it in front of the mirror.

Kelly-Anne obeyed without a word. She sat in the chair and faced the mirror as Connor, enjoying every moment of the attention, sank his hands deep into the dark tresses and started to shake them about.

'Stiff as a board,' was Connor's verdict. 'That's not sexy, baby, we want to be stroked with silk, not have our eyes taken out with bits of twig. Go shorter,' he urged, 'look at your lovely neck – ' he ran a finger along its length. 'Show it off!'

'Eeeek!'

Clearly, the thought of short hair was making Kelly-Anne squeak with fear.

'Eeee . . . yeowch . . .' she added. Maybe something was actually hurting.

'Ooops I seem to have got a little tangled in here,' Connor explained, as his hands remained buried in Kelly-Anne's hair. 'Annie, her hair's caught on my blazer button!'

Annie bent down and tried to investigate. Caught on a blazer button? Connor had four buttons on each arm. Big, shiny gold buttons, sticking pompously proud of the material. Kelly-Anne's hair was tugged and tangled, snarled and snaggled right across all eight buttons.

It would take Annie hours to sort this out. She began to try and unwind the muddle.

'Oh for goodness sake!' Connor was starting to fidget, 'it can't be that bad, there must be a way of just fishing it out from under the buttons.'

More long minutes went by as Annie fiddled away at the mess of snarled hair and hard, unyielding brass.

'Yeeeeouwch,' was the only sound Kelly-Anne made every now and again.

'No, it's not going to work, babes, we'll have to either cut off some hair or cut off the buttons,' came Annie's verdict.

'Well, we can sew the buttons on again, can't we?' Connor was trying to sound calm and pleasant, when he was in fact deeply regretting ever having stepped into this room and interfering with this crazy woman with the hair.

'Where do I get scissors?' Svetlana asked in her deep, dark voice.

Annie knew the suite only had tiny nail scissors for snipping stray threads and cuticles and a great big pair of dressmaking shears for cutting off whole trouser hems . . . and on occasion, rescuing women trapped in dresses. Once she'd had to free a leg bound so tightly by a pair of skinny jeans it had started to swell. Yes, if

Annie ever hosted a TV series, it would be called: 'When Clothes Can Kill'.

She directed Svetlana to the drawer, sure that plenty of progress could be made snipping off the brass buttons with the nail scissors. A little hair might be sacrificed, and if it wasn't working out they could always go down to the salon. Although Annie wasn't sure she wanted to lead Kelly-Anne all the way through The Store with a TV star stuck to her head.

Kelly-Anne seemed to be suffering. She'd gone very quiet, her shoulders were shaking a little and her breathing was shallow.

'You're going to be fine,' Annie assured her, 'this is just a little hiccup, it will all be over really soon.'

'I haven't cut my hair since I was seventeen,' Kelly-Anne whimpered, 'I don't want to cut my hair. Donnie loves my hair. I love my hair. I don't even want any scissors around . . . I don't want to see any scissors . . .' The anxiety in her voice was obvious; clearly some sort of hairdressing phobia was kicking off.

'It's OK, don't worry,' Annie soothed, 'we're just going to snip Connor's buttons off and the problem will be solved. Honestly, you'll probably lose a strand or two at the most. Do you want me to do it? Or we could get one of the hairdressers up . . .'

Because Annie was kneeling down at Kelly-Anne's side, patting her hands and trying to reassure her, she saw Svetlana return, but did not see what she had in her hands.

'Arms up,' Svetlana instructed Connor.

'Are you sure?' Connor asked. Then, before Annie could say a word, two sounds came all at once.

A dramatic: 'Aaaargh!' from Kelly-Anne as her hair was yanked up high with Connor's arms and then a very firm, very final, metallic 'clunk'.

'There!' Svetlana said, brandishing the dressmaking shears.

'Phew!' Connor freed his arms as an astonishingly large clump of purple-black hair slid to the ground.

Kelly-Anne's bloodcurdling scream brought every member of staff currently on floor two rushing to the scene.

Annie bustled everyone out of the suite just as fast as they'd come in. 'We're fine thanks, just a little anxious moment. Don't worry, don't worry we'll be fine! Paula,' she instructed her assistant, 'a glass of champagne, love, just as quickly as you possibly can and get Marco from the salon up – right now! I don't care if he's blow-drying Madonna's fringe, he needs to come here now.'

She dispatched Connor and Svetlana as well with a brisk: 'I think I can manage this better without your help, thank you!'

'I phone you Annah!' Svetlana promised.

Yes, well, maybe Svetlana wasn't going to be the dream business partner Annie had hoped. What else was she capable of when armed with a pair of shears?

But back to the poor trembling, gibbering, weeping woman in the far corner of the room, who had not even been able to open her eyes since she'd first seen the scissors and the clump of hair hit the ground.

'Kelly-Anne,' Annie began, kneeling down again beside the woman's chair, 'you are going to be fine. Honestly, please, please, please trust me here. I've worked with hundreds of women who haven't wanted to change a thing about their appearance and when it had to happen, it was OK. They coped.' Annie put her arm round Kelly-Anne's shoulder and squeezed comfortingly.

'I've had clients who've gone bald with chemotherapy and one of my ladies has gone from double-D to double mastectomy. Now that is a big change, babes. Your beautiful hair will grow back, Kelly-Anne. No doubt about it.'

Paula came into the suite with an elegant glass of champagne balanced on a small silver tray.

As soon as Kelly-Anne saw it, she waved it away, but Annie took the glass, handed it to her and insisted kindly: 'Go on . . . I think you deserve it and absolutely no one is looking.'

By the time hairdresser Marco arrived, Kelly-Anne had drunk the whole glass down, wiped her eyes, blown her nose and although she wasn't exactly cheerful, she had at least stopped weeping and shuddering.

Marco, having heard some of the details of the disaster from Paula, came armed with a second glass of champagne. Then with all the charm of a 27-year-old straight guy who loves all women, he flattered, wheedled and cajoled Kelly-Anne to come down to the salon.

'I can't do anything up here,' he insisted, taking her hair tenderly in his hands and stroking it, 'I need to wash it, deep condition it, handle it, really get the feel for it before I *reshape* it for you.'

As Kelly-Anne reached for her second glass of complimentary champagne, Marco told her, 'I'm going to need some of that too. Apparently I'm the first person who's been allowed to reshape this in twenty years or something.' Then with disarming sincerity, he added: 'does that mean you last cut your hair when you were *seven*?!'

As Kelly-Anne finally smiled, Annie could hear the trill of her mobile sounding out from her office.

'I'll be right back,' she told them before heading over to answer it.

'Annie!'

Straight away she recognized the voice of her mother, Fern, sounding slightly stressed.

'Sorry to call you at work, love,' Fern apologized.

'No, no no,' Annie insisted, 'you're fine. You couldn't make my day any worse, believe me.'

'Oh yes Annie,' came Fern's reply, 'I think I probably can.'

'What is it?' said Annie suddenly worried. 'You're OK, aren't you?'

'I'm fine, absolutely fine . . . but it's Aunty Hilda.'

'She hasn't died, has she?'

'No, dear. And you're not allowed to say "what a shame",' came the snippy response.

Aunty Hilda was an eighty-something widow aunt of Fern's and therefore Annie's great-aunt. Hilda was opinionated, pompous, generally difficult and increasingly deaf, but as they were her only family, they had to care about her. Also, the poor old dear had just had a hip operation and seemed to be taking a long time to recuperate, so she had been living with Fern for several weeks now.

Fern was worried because Aunty Hilda didn't seem to be recovering as quickly as she'd expected.

'I'm going on a little holiday,' Annie's mother told her.

'It's been booked for months and now I don't know if Hilda's going to be well enough to move back into her own home in time.'

'Black run skiing in the Alps again?' Annie joked. 'Or no, let me guess, Saga bus booze cruise over the Channel to France?'

'Saga booze cruise!' Fern exclaimed. 'It's a fascinating tour of the Bordeaux wine region.'

'Mmm . . . good choice, bound to be many, many single septuagenarians on that holiday. GSOH and OCB.'

'Good sense of humour and – OCB?' Fern was baffled.

'Own colostomy bag.'

'Annie!' Fern ticked her off. But as Annie's mother had been single for such a very long time now, dating jokes were not just permissible, they were an expected part of their conversation.

'So you want me to put Aunty H up for a week? Is that what I'm picking up?'

'Oh would you?!' Fern gushed, as if the idea had just occurred to her. 'It's not a whole week dear, it's about five days. She's getting quite mobile and she can manage the best part of the day on her own, so between you and Ed . . . and now that you have that nice big house. Dinah just hasn't got any space at all and I'll bring Hilda down myself, obviously.'

'Which week are we talking about anyway?' Annie asked, waving a cheery goodbye to Kelly-Anne as Marco ushered her off to the salon.

And here was Paula, showing in Annie's next client for the afternoon. This woman had very short hair, Annie noted, at least nothing could go horribly wrong on that front.

'September the 18th,' Fern told her, 'from Thursday until Tuesday. I'm back on Tuesday.'

'You know, I think Ed and the children are off . . . there's some special Centenary Founder's Day long weekend,' Annie told her. 'One hundred years since the old boy who set up the place popped his clogs or something. I've only just got them back into school and then they're coming out again,' she added with exasperation. 'Well, we've no plans. We'll all be delighted to look after Hilda for you, Mum.'

'I know, she's not the easiest,' Fern admitted.

'It's no problem, Mum,' Annie assured her, 'you'll need the break. I have to go, darlin'. Love you.'

Clicking off the phone, she hurried out to meet her new client, passing the rack of clothes Kelly-Anne hadn't bought and would never, ever buy. Annie doubted whether the poor woman would ever set a stiletto inside The Store again. She might even try and sue them. Maybe Annie should be filing an accident report for The Store's insurance policy right now . . .

She tried to overlook the lost commission and put all thoughts of owning The Bag Downstairs to the back of her mind.

'Hi, I'm Elsa,' her next client began. 'I know it's a bit boring, but I'm looking for some new suits.'

The most surprising thing happened halfway through Elsa's session. The bank executive was in one of the criminally chic grey dresses Annie had brought down for her, examining herself very closely in the mirror, when in breezed Kelly-Anne.

Well, not that it was immediately obvious.

The great towering, lacquered beehive construction was gone. Completely away! Instead, a short, silky-soft dark bob framed a sweetheart face, highlighting the most delicate of features.

Kelly-Anne didn't even make a big deal out of her first haircut in twenty years, she just waved over at Annie and said, 'Please, don't let me disturb you, I've just come down to get the clothes.'

Before Annie could even ask *which clothes?* Kelly-Anne went over to the rack that Paula had put to the side but not yet had time to set back out on the shop floor, and scooped up the lot. Then she left, thanking Annie profusely and promising she would be back soon.

Marco must have slipped her a Valium. This was the only conclusion Annie could come to. No doubt about it.

Chapter Six

Owen's comfort clothes:

Green camouflage combats (Army Surplus Shop)
Orange and white T-shirt (Quicksilver)
Khaki sandals (Geox)
Total est. cost: £70

'No, not raspberry, I think we have to go with . . . Aunty
Dinah's homemade plum.'

'I'm thinking thick white bread toast with butter and honey,' Ed was telling Owen as they walked along the pavement together.

'Yup, toast,' Owen agreed, 'but not honey. How about peanut butter with jam?'

'Mmmm,' Ed had to concede, 'I like your style. Peanut butter with raspberry jam?'

'No . . . not raspberry, I think we have to go with . . .' Owen considered carefully for a minute then threw down the decider, 'Aunty Dinah's homemade plum.'

'Plum! Yes!' Ed nodded, full of enthusiasm. 'We have

a winner. Do we have white bread and peanut butter in the house? Or do we have to stop at the shop?'

Monday to Friday, Ed, who was head of the music department at Lana and Owen's school, walked home with Owen. Lana, being older, would rather have had hot needles stuck into her eyeballs than be seen walking home with a *teacher*, obviously. But Owen wasn't quite so fussy.

Anyway, Ed and Owen would usually talk a little bit about how their day had gone, but as both had hearty appetites, which the twenty-minute walk home always seemed to sharpen, the main focus of the journey was on planning their afternoon snack.

'We're not going to have time to eat supper before the recital this evening, so we're going to need a lot of jam and peanut butter,' Ed warned.

'Is Mum coming to see me play?' Owen wondered.

'I hope so, she said she would,' came Ed's reply. He knew that the school's junior string quartet wasn't Annie's idea of a thrilling night out, but Owen was playing violin and had been practising so hard that Ed had made her promise she would come and watch him as his reward.

As they turned into Hawthorne Street, Ed ran his eye approvingly over the front gardens still bursting with green and bloom. Well, OK, the garden of number eight was in need of a little attention, particularly in the way of hedge trimming, but there would hopefully be time for that at the weekend.

However, the house looked amazing. A narrow, four-storey Georgian townhouse, it was quaint, ever so slightly wonky and just utterly charming. The window frames, recently repainted, gleamed bright white. The door was a shiny light blue. Two large blue pots at the front door brimmed with the pink and blue flowers Ed had planted in the summer.

Annie, although a genius at house renovating and redecorating, turned out to have something of a kiss-of-death effect on everything she touched in the garden.

'Leave everything inside to me,' she'd insisted, 'but you'll have to go out there and get dirty, babes.'

As Ed pushed the key into the brass-rimmed keyhole of the solid wooden front door, he thought of his mum. Coming in though the front door still made Ed think of his mother because she'd lived in this house for twenty-seven years, until she'd died just two years ago.

For several years, Ed had lived in a flat in the basement, and on his mother's death he and his sister should have had to sell up the family home and move on. But then Annie had bustled into his life, Annie with her big plans and snap decisions.

She'd moved in, she'd redecorated, then she'd sold her place and bought enough of a share in the house for him to be able to afford to own the rest.

He must be just about the only teacher in London living in a townhouse in north London's lovely Highgate. That was for sure. He would always be grateful that Annie had enabled him to stay here.

The mortice lock had already been opened, so Ed knew that Lana must be home. He pushed in the Yale key and opened the door.

There were two schoolbags in the lobby. The brightly patterned number he recognized as Lana's, the dark rucksack he suspected might be Andrei's.

'Hi, Lana!' Ed called into the stairwell, 'just to let you know we're back!'

'So you can put your clothes back on,' Owen muttered in a low aside.

Ed tutted him.

There was silence. Lana's room was on the attic floor two flights of stairs up from the lobby, but she should still have been able to hear them.

'Everything OK?' he called up.

When there was still no response, Ed told Owen to go and put the toast on in the kitchen and he'd be down in a minute.

Once he was on the first floor, he told himself that he was just being silly and anxious and maybe even too nosy. He was not going to go up to the attic room and knock on Lana's door. Whatever she was doing up there, she was fine and it was her business . . . and certainly not his.

So he swung a left into the sunny bedroom he shared with Annie. If Ed were to be ruthlessly honest, he'd admit that Annie had made this room just a bit girlie. There was white and pink paper with a bold pattern on the wall, a white and crystal chandelier and an ornate white mirror above the fireplace.

A whole wall was taken up with the bank of white wardrobes she'd insisted they would need. And it turned out she was right. She had enough things to fill them almost single-handedly.

Planning to hang up his jacket, change his shirt for a T-shirt, then go down to join Owen, Ed had just pulled the shirt over his head and was heading over to drop it into the laundry basket, when he saw them.

Lana and Andrei were lying almost completely naked underneath the leather-upholstered bed: Annie's Christmas present to him, bought for some small fortune on who knows what credit card. Something he didn't like to think about.

'OK,' he said firmly. 'Game over.'

This was met with little gasps of horror from under the bed.

'I don't want to know,' Ed added, 'I really don't. But you have a room of your own upstairs, Lana. I'm going to go down to the kitchen now and maybe you two should . . . tidy up, then come and join us there.'

Ed and Owen ate peanut butter and plum jam toast steadily, working methodically through the loaf. Owen, now happily changed into his favourite combat trousers and fluorescent orange and white T-shirt (in case he wanted to disguise himself as a traffic cone lost in a wood) ate with much more enthusiasm than Ed, because Ed knew he was about to have to have a really awkward conversation with Lana.

Finally the romantic duo appeared at the foot of the stairs, where Andrei pulled his rucksack onto his back in the lobby and scarpered out of the front door. Clearly he didn't want to hang about to see what Ed, who was also his teacher, thought of the situation.

'Goodbye, Andrei,' Ed called after him, then couldn't resist adding, 'hope we'll be seeing *more* of you.'

Ed, who'd been at a boys' boarding school from the age of seven till eighteen, had no recollection of ever being caught doing something like this. But, as he'd taught in co-ed boarding schools all over Britain for the first seven years of his career, he'd certainly come across a few teenagers in slightly comical states of undress.

'Owen, would you mind going out to the trampoline for a few minutes? Just don't bounce too hard because . . .'

Owen, cramming the remains of his third sandwich into his mouth, nodded with understanding and headed out of the room as Lana came in slowly and slouchily.

Even Ed could appreciate that Lana was very pretty in a sort of pale and gothy kind of way. Her long hair was dyed a shade or two darker than the original colour, her pretty freckles had been blanked out with foundation and she was wearing a black top, black leggings, bare feet and dark-green nail polish on all twenty nails.

'Are you going to tell my mum?' was Lana's first question as she sidled into the room, slinking along the wall.

'Come in and sit down,' Ed tried to reassure her. 'Do you want some tea? Some toast?'

'Yeah, please,' she agreed.

As Ed boiled the kettle, put bread in the toaster and fetched mugs, Lana chewed nervously at the skin around her nails.

'We were just . . .' she began.

'It's OK,' Ed told her, 'I don't need to know – I really don't.' Although he might actually quite have enjoyed listening to whatever excuse Lana had been about to give him . . .

'Andrei had a wasp in his trouser leg and he had to take them off and then the wasp went up my skirt . . . I was just coming out of the shower when . . . we were playing strip poker, I don't know why . . . but my contact lens rolled under the bed.'

'Ed, do you think I'm old enough to have sex?'

Lana didn't even look round at him, just continued with the skin-chewing as soon as the words were out. For a moment or two only the sound of the kettle coming to the boil could be heard in the room.

Maybe because the silence was too intense for her, Lana quickly blurted out, 'It's not a big deal, I just wanted another opinion. I mean, I know what I think. I know what Andrei thinks. I know what my friends think. I just was kind of interested to know what you think.'

This was the really difficult thing, because all the time, Lana made things sound so cool and flippant and as if she didn't care. But all sorts of feelings and major emotional issues were just beneath the surface and Ed was sure that he and Annie could mess it all up at any time. Just with one single wrong word.

He felt as if he was walking around the most precious, fragile china shop in the world whenever he spoke to Lana about anything. She was confident and assured in so many ways, but still such a baby in others.

Coming back to the table with two mugs of tea, he set one in front of her, then went to get her plate of toast.

'Peanut butter and jam?' he asked her.

'You're avoiding my question,' she hissed at him.

'I'm not avoiding your question at all,' he told her gently, 'I'm giving myself time. I want you to have something to eat and drink and then I'm going to sit down beside you and talk about it properly.'

She looked up at him to see if he was being straight, and when she didn't see any hint of a smile or a joke about him, she said, 'Thanks.'

'But it doesn't matter what I think,' he told her when

he'd settled himself down in the wooden kitchen chair beside hers. 'It only matters what you think.'

When she didn't reply, he added, 'If you're having sex, Lana, be very careful and respectful. Of your body and your feelings. If you're not having sex, don't feel you have to rush into it. There's a big difference between snogging someone and sleeping with them. Big difference.'

Lana's head was down over her toast, which she was carefully smearing with peanut butter.

'Is there any way,' Ed wanted to know, 'that I can get you to talk to your mum about this?'

Lana gave a snort, 'I think we all know my mum's POV: *Pull up the drawbridge, take aim and fire. No men anywhere near my daughter. Ever.*

'Well . . .' Ed had to laugh a little at this, 'you're her daughter. She finds everything about you growing up just a bit scary. She doesn't want to lose you. That's her number one worry, she's only really happy when we're all together in this house and . . .'

'She has a mobile clamped to her head making some kind of deal,' Lana interrupted.

'Hey, that's not very fair—'

But now he'd blown it, and Lana just got up and walked out of the room.

Chapter Seven

Nicole Wilson on a service call:

Pinstriped black trouser suit – too tight and
too short (Next)
Pink wrap top (M&S)
Black pumps (M&S)
Tan knee-highs (M&S)
Black and pink saucy underwear (Agent Provocateur)
Total est. cost: £270

'We could lend you £125,000 against the
current value of your property.'

'Bryan, hello! Yes, it's me, Annie. Hi! I'm really sorry to call you at work, but I wanted this to be private, you know . . . away from Dinah,' she added in a stage whisper. 'I was just thinking . . . isn't the big one-zero coming up for you two? You know, your tenth wedding anniversary?'

Annie pretended to sound as surprised as she possibly could when her brother-in-law confided that he was planning a celebration and he didn't want Dinah to know anything about it.

'That is such a great idea! How romantic! You know what?' she added, trying to sound completely spontaneous, 'I have this friend and he's just brilliant at this kind of thing. He works as an events manager but I'm sure he'd love to help you out, Bryan. Because I know how busy you are and planning a party like that . . . that's a really big job to take on . . .'

She hoped she was making the point strongly but subtly enough. There was no way Bryan could be left alone in charge of this party. His wedding had been cheap and depressing and anyway, he was an architect now, a very minimal, hyper-pernickety architect. If he was in charge, they'd be eating off white plates in a white room, all trying to share a tiny slice of a minimal white cake. No, what Bryan needed was a gay man. A professional party planner. What Bryan needed was one of Annie's newest friends: Hector.

Yes, unfortunately Hector had been Connor's boyfriend for a brief spell, and it had ended badly and sadly because Connor, *allegedly*, spent too much time obsessing about his waistline and career trajectory. But Annie didn't see why she and Hector couldn't still be friends. Especially when Hector would be just brilliant at organizing Bryan and Dinah's tenth wedding anniversary party.

'Look, why don't you just let me call Hector and get him to hook up with you? No, no!' she assured Bryan, when he made extremely dubious-sounding noises, 'it won't cost much. Honestly, he'll charge mates' rates and he'll save you loads of money on all sorts of things because of his party contacts. Honestly, trust me.'

Her mobile was beeping with a call waiting, so Annie said goodbye to Bryan, promised Hector would be in touch and that Bryan was going to love him, then switched over to take the other call.

'Mssss Valentine?' came the voice at the other end of the line.

'Yes?'

'This is Nicole Wilson from Simpson mortgage brokers, you wanted to talk to us about releasing some equity on your property.'

'Borrowing more money?' Annie wanted to make sure they were talking about the same thing.

'Freeing some of the capital tied up in your share of Hawthorne Street,' was Nicole's take. Obviously 'borrowing' was a bad word these days.

'Yes, we're thinking about putting in a second bathroom,' Annie began. A second bathroom would be nice, no doubt about it . . . but Annie was fibbing because she thought Nicole would prefer to hear this than talk about tax bills and vague plans to import Chinese shoes from Mr Timi Woo.

'So what sort of figure are we looking to release?' Nicole asked briskly.

'What's my limit?' Annie wondered. She wasn't going to go there, obviously, but it wouldn't really hurt to know, would it?

'Well . . .' Tapping noises came down the line as Nicole asked the computer. 'We could lend you £125,000 against the current value of your property. Obviously that would bring up your monthly payments by . . .' the tappity-tap sound came again.

£125,000!! Annie had thought she might borrow £20,000 or so just to pay off the Revenue & Customs and get started with the shoes, but with so much available and at such a low cost really . . . well, what was the interest on £30,000 going to be per month?

Nicole tappity-tapped then told her.

Done. Annie agreed to it there and then. Well, she did pause for a moment to think of Ed and how she'd promised to discuss this with him – but then Nicole had reminded her that for this week only there was a special interest rate available: 'Only another two days left on this equity release offer . . . you don't want to let this one go if you're serious about borrowing more. You're not going to get another deal like this anywhere.'

Now, if Annie could just hold on for a few minutes while Nicole went through the terms and conditions and blah, blah, blah with her on the phone . . . yes, there would also be some forms to fill out, but Nicole would send those on to her straightaway.

When the call was over, Annie checked her watch and saw that there were still eight minutes to go before her next client arrived at 7.30 p.m. She was supposed to have rearranged this appointment, but she had no recollection why. Anyway, she'd been too busy to get round to it. And if she couldn't remember why she was supposed to have rearranged it, it surely couldn't have been so important, could it? She told herself this to make the vague feeling of unease go away.

Eight minutes meant there was time to do the one thing that she really *needed* to do, now that she was going to be the head of her own luxury goods empire, now that all this cash was about to land in her private back account. She'd be able to pay off all her credit cards, take the family on holiday, and . . .

Rushing down the escalators, taking two steps at a time, she made it to the ground floor.

Cutting through the vividly perfumed air, she made straight for Accessories to claim her bag.

The Bag?! She could see straightaway that the bag was not on its plinth. Somebody else had bought it! Oh no!

Hurrying to the concession counter, she spotted Sandra deep in conversation with a woman, and there was The Bag on the counter top between them.

Annie knew quite enough about shopping psychology to know that the last thing to do was rush up and say, 'Hands off, that's mine.' Nothing made any shopper want anything more than a rival.

Instead, as she strained to hear what Sandra and the woman were saying to each other, she picked up a beautiful brown Mulberry bag, supple as a well-worn saddle, and began to fondle it. She slung it over her shoulder and walked this way and that in front of the mirror.

'Hmmm . . .' the customer was telling Sandra, 'I just can't quite decide. I mean, it is beautiful, but it's *so* expensive.'

'It's a very limited edition. Only twenty of these bags will be sold in London in total.' Sandra was ignoring Annie and leaning in for a serious sales pitch. 'This is the opposite of a fashionable "it bag". This is completely exclusive. There's a letter inside, hand-signed by the designer. Not Saint Laurent himself,' she added quickly, 'he's retired now. But by the bag's creator.'

'For that kind of money,' the customer joked, 'I'd expect the creator to invite me to their house for dinner.'

'But look at the workmanship,' Sandra went on, 'the lining is quilted suede, all the zipped compartments inside are satin lined with a solid brass zip. This bag will last a lifetime. Probably two. You'll be able to hand it down.'

Annie wasn't getting anywhere with the Mulberry: she ditched it and picked up Chloé's new season tote. Now this was a lovely bag, jade blue and creamily soft. It jangled and slouched up against you. Snuggled, even.

She walked just a little more obviously past Sandra and the customer.

'Lovely bag,' she called across to Sandra, 'I might come down to get this in my next break. Can you hold it for me?'

'Yes Annie, I can hold it for you.' Sandra's voice was a touch weary. She knew exactly what Annie was up to.

Ooooh, but the customer had turned. The customer was looking.

Annie glanced at her watch. She had to go! She was going to have to leave it in the lap of the gods. Taking one last, long look at her bag, she set the Chloé back on the shelf and sped back upstairs.

Irena was from Romania, but she'd moved to London for a decent job. She was in her late twenties, much younger than Annie's usual client, but she had made this appointment asking specifically for Annie Valentine.

She wasn't going to be hard for Annie to dress because she was so pretty, with a figure that Annie understood perfectly because it was curvaceous with a nipped in waist, just like hers.

Slipping in and out of Irena's changing room with dresses, skirts, jackets and belts, Annie was impressed with the extravagance of Irena's deep burgundy underwear.

Finally, Irena, who had come for 'just two great outfits,' seemed to be settling on a dress, a skirt and a blouse, then a fantastic swing jacket with wide sleeves which went with all three.

'Thank you,' she gushed at Annie, 'you are very good at your job. I hear so much about you. I have been wanting to meet you for a long time.'

Annie couldn't help feeling there was something a little strange about the way Irena shook her hand and looked so deeply into her face.

'Have you been in London long?' she asked.

'Just a few months now,' Irena told her, 'but I visit one time before, about four years ago.

'You are not married? No?' Irena asked her, out of the blue.

Annie, whose heavy platinum wedding ring was still one of her most treasured possessions, stored safely in her jewellery box at home, shook her head.

'I used to be,' she said simply.

'Ah,' Irena said with her head to the side and a look filled with too much sympathy for Annie to feel comfortable.

'But . . .' Annie went on quickly, 'luckily for me, I've met someone new.'

'Not easy,' Irena intoned, 'not easy to meet nice new man. I'm still trying.

'And you have children?' she wanted to know.

'Yes,' Annie told her, unwrapping a pair of spike-heeled, wide-topped ankle boots which would be perfect with Irena's new pencil skirt, undo all the Miss Moneypenny connotations, 'two children, Lana who is sixteen and Owen who's ten.'

And now the feeling of unease was there again. There was something at the back of Annie's mind, something she was supposed to be doing. Maybe it was to do with her eBay site? Maybe there was something she had meant to buy? Or meant to sell?

By 8.45 p.m. Irena was still in the suite, still trying things on, still looking at her reflection this way and that, still asking lots of irritatingly personal questions: 'Where are you living?', 'What is Lana interested in?', 'Does she look like you?'

Annie was beginning to twitch. This was the seventh person she'd dressed today and it was a little hard to stay enthusiastic.

Meanwhile, Irena was scrutinizing her back view and making the tutting, sighing sounds that Annie knew were the self-critical musings of almost every woman on the planet.

She wanted to shout: *'Oh for God's sake, you're beautiful with a gorgeous ass. Get over yourself. Are you buying or are you not buying?'*

'The tills are going to close down in about five minutes, babes,' was what she did say, as nicely as she possibly could, 'so it's time to make some decisions. Or if you like, I can hold some of these things until tomorrow,' she added, although every one of her natural sales instincts went against this policy. People who put things on hold could never be trusted to come back and buy them.

'Five minutes!? OK, I choose.' Irena stripped off the outfit she was wearing, stood for a moment in the impressive underwear and ankle boots and then quickly tried on one of the dresses for a third time.

When Annie had finally bundled Irena and her purchases out of the suite, she rushed around tidying up, powering down the computer, packing up her bags and her booty for the day.

When all her chores were done, Annie at last clickety-clicked down the escalators in her heels.

'Sandra!' she called out from the bottom step. 'What's the news then? Is it still there?'

On the plinth there was now a maroon bag she'd never seen before, so with a heavy heart she turned towards the saleswoman for an explanation.

'She *bought* it?'

Sandra bent down under her counter top and emerged holding The Bag in her hands.

'No . . . she put it on hold,' Sandra said with a slightly wicked smile.

'Oh no, then I can't . . .'

'Oh yes you can, I'm not in tomorrow. So even if she comes back, and I'm not convinced that she will, we'll just make sure Pippa is hugely apologetic but never got the message!'

'I like it,' Annie cackled, then she slapped her credit card down on the counter top and picked up the bag.

'Hello baby, how are you doing? Come on, come to Mama.'

'You're a little bit cracked,' Sandra told her, tapping her head.

'I'm tired,' Annie confided, rolling her shoulders back to try and ease some of the tension out of them, 'I'm really tired,' but with a smile, she added, 'This will perk me up, though.'

'Staff discount? You do have some left for this month, do you?' Sandra checked.

'Oh yeah,' Annie assured her, 'I've been saving it.'

'Do you want me to wrap it for you?'

'Well . . . you know what?'

As Annie typed in her credit card PIN, she remembered a little too vividly her recent promise to Ed that 'big' purchases were to be checked with him. This was so that he could try and talk her out of it. There was no other reason. He'd told her he was worried about her spending and was going to try and help her 'manage' it.

There was no doubt that he would never, ever allow her to buy this bag. He wouldn't even begin to understand why she would want to spend so much money on a new handbag, especially when she already had 'so many'. Ha! Ed had carried the same leather briefcase around for *seventeen years*!! What would he know of the need to buy a new handbag every season? Absolutely nothing!

'I'm going to start using it, right now,' Annie told Sandra. If she just put all her things into it and carried it about blatantly, he was far less likely to notice. Wasn't he? One bag pretty much looked the same to him as the next. She could just say it came from the bag stockpile at the back of her wardrobe. How would he ever know?

Opening the satisfying brass clasp and then zip, she sniffed at the delicious new suede and carefully unloaded her purse, keys and mobile phone into The Bag.

Slipping her old bag into her big canvas tote, she slung the tote and her laptop bag onto her shoulders, but carried the new handbag carefully in the crook of her arm. It was close to nine thirty when she finally hurried out of the building.

Only on the tube platform, waiting for the delayed Northern Line train, did she see a poster with a violin on it and realize, with tears springing to the back of her eyes that she was supposed to have left work early so she could get to school and watch Owen playing in the junior string quartet.

Chapter Eight

Lana at home:

Blue vest top PJs (Topshop)
Blue sheepskin boots (Ugg)
Frazzled blue and red dressing gown
(Her dad's)
Total est. cost: £95

'Is that new?!'

Rushing in through the door of her house, Annie dumped everything but the new bag in the hallway (it wasn't ready to be thrown on the ground in a heap just yet) and ran up two flights of stairs.

'Owen!' she called out, 'I am so sorry!' She hurried into his bedroom, already dark with the lights turned out, and crouched down at his bedside.

Owen's eyes were shut, but he opened them drowsily at the sound of her voice.

'Hi!' she whispered and ran a hand through his messy hair, 'I am so, so sorry I couldn't come. I needed someone to cover for me and they couldn't, so I didn't get out of work until after 9 p.m.'

'Don't worry,' Owen told her, sleepily but cheerfully, 'it went really well and Ed says there's going to be lots more performances.'

Annie leaned over and kissed his cheek. 'Will you play it for me on Sunday, when I'm home and we can catch up?'

'Yeah.'

'Night-night.' She ran a hand through his hair again: she could never resist it, soft and tumbly, on the longish side, boy hair.

Then she crossed the landing and knocked on the door of Lana's room.

Lana was sprawled across her bed with her laptop open. Annie doubted that she was writing an essay or doing homework research on the web. She was probably busy emailing Andrei and all the other people she would see again in only a few hours' time.

Annie settled herself down on a chair, ready to have a little bit of a chat with her daughter, but Lana seemed grouchy and uncommunicative.

'Was your day OK?' Annie ventured.

'Fine,' Lana insisted, although the crossed arms and screwed-up mouth suggested something different.

'Is everything going OK?' Annie asked.

'Fine,' Lana told her again.

'How's Andrei?'

'Fine! Mum? Can I come down and see you in a minute? I'm just finishing something off up here.'

Annie, feeling offended, stood up, picked up her handbag and headed out of the room.

But then Lana, spotting the bag, had to ask, 'Is that new?!'

'Shhhh!' Annie put her finger up to her lips and smiled conspiratorially.

Lana got up to take a closer look, her eyes widening in surprise. *That's my girl*, Annie couldn't help thinking proudly.

'Is that really a YSL?' Lana asked, although she'd already clocked the label.

'Shhhh!' Annie repeated.

'You are in so much trouble! It's gorgeous, can I just hold it?'

'No! No!' Annie warded her off. ' Don't even think about it! You are never, ever borrowing this bag. Get off! Now I have to go down and say hello to Ed.'

'You better leave that here then, he'll kill you.'

'He won't even notice.'

'He's not stupid, you know.'

'Yeah, but he's a little bit blind to the finer things in life.'

'Hello baby!' Annie greeted her man enthusiastically. He was in the sitting room on the sofa with his back to her. So she came in behind him, slid her arms over him and was planning to tumble right over the sofa to land beside him.

But he gripped her arms tightly and pulled them away from his chest as if he wanted her off.

'I know, Ed, I know. I'm so sorry about the violin thing. I've already been up and apologized to Owen.'

'Violin thing?' Ed repeated with some heat in his voice. '*Violin thing*? Annie, the junior string quartet was giving its first concert. We've been practising really hard, *two hundred* people turned up to watch. Owen was totally brilliant and you missed all of it! Even worse, I don't think you even begin to get it.'

Annie was surprised to see Ed so annoyed. She came round and sat carefully down on the sofa beside him.

'Owen is doing really well, thanks so much to you,' Annie told him, with complete sincerity and gratitude. 'I would have come. I really wanted to come. I just . . . didn't get cover in time.'

Ed still looked really angry, and she wasn't used to it. Yet. He sometimes got a bit grumpy, but this could usually be solved with sex or food. The two were close contenders in his life.

'So how's your day been then?' he asked her now. 'Any big news? Any big decisions? Anything I should know about?' He sounded unusually snappy.

'No.' She was a little bewildered, 'No, just an absolutely usual day. I just couldn't get anyone to cover my last appointment, so I had to stay on.'

'So absolutely nothing to tell me?' he asked again.

'No . . . don't think so . . .' she looked at him carefully. He was behaving strangely. Was he really not going to get over this concert thing at all? He couldn't possibly know about the bag. He couldn't.

'So why did I get a courtesy call from Nicole Wilson informing me that my house ownership partner was about to draw down £30,000 worth of equity on our property?' Ed asked her in as steady a voice as he could muster.

Annie's mouth opened and momentarily stayed open.

Courtesy call? *Courtesy call?!* Why had Nicole not told

her anything about this? Nicole had gone through the incredibly long and detailed terms and conditions and so on . . . was it possible that Annie might have just tuned it out a tiny bit? But phoning Ed? There was no way Nicole had mentioned phoning Ed. Surely Annie would have heard that?

'Just one week ago – ' Ed turned to face her. He was threatening to really kick off now – 'you agreed that big purchases would be discussed. With me. Hello! Your partner. The new man in your life. Your other half. The person looking after your children four nights a week and most of the rest of the time as far as I can see. The person having in-depth, life-changing discussions with your teenage daughter because you never seem to be around for her. And when you are, all you want to talk about is nail polish.'

Well, that was it. Now he had gone too far. Annie could feel her breath rising up in her lungs, she seemed to be blowing air in and out too quickly. She flashed furious eyes at him. 'You know, Ed, I wish you wouldn't tell me how to run my life! Or how to run my family. It's just not any of your business!'

'Yes, it is!' he shouted straight back. 'And I want it to be. You live with me now, you can't have everything your own way, not all the time. Anyway, this is our house, you can't make a major money decision like that without at least letting me know! That's just insulting.'

'I don't want your help,' she heard herself shouting back, 'I don't want your advice and I don't want you to interfere!'

'Well, that's just great, Annie,' came Ed's response. 'Maybe you don't want me here at all? Maybe you'd just like to live on your own again, would you? See how you'd like that!'

'Fine!' She snatched up her handbag, but Ed immediately caught hold of it, pulled it closer so he could examine it then exclaimed, 'Oh my God! You promised! You said you would check with me before buying anything over two hundred pounds. I know perfectly well this cost much more than that.' He took a deep breath and stung her by adding, 'I really can't trust you.'

'Shut up!' Annie shouted, just as furious as him now, furious at feeling so humiliated and caught out.

'It's my money and it's my life. And these are *my kids*,' she added, deeply upset by his criticism.

In a blind stumble of tears, she snatched the bag away and stalked out of the front door, slamming it hard for effect.

Outside, it was surprisingly chilly and dark. But then she'd left without her jacket, which was her second mistake. Her first mistake was leaving the house at all. Now that she was outside, she would have plenty of time to reflect on the fact that it was always a mistake to storm out of your home in a huff. Because eventually you had to go back in with your tail between your legs.

This was her first big row with Ed. She and Roddy, her first husband, had had countless raging rows, walkouts and arguments and looking back, she'd thought it was something to do with being younger. She'd begun to believe that she and Ed weren't going to do big rows and heated disagreements. So she was surprised at this outburst. She hated shouting. It never got you anywhere anyway, just raised your blood pressure. Made you more likely to die of a heart attack before you were fifty.

Now that she was out here on the street, she thought she would walk to the nearest pub; there was quite a nice place on the high street, where she could calm down. Maybe she'd phone Connor and he could come and join her for a beer. Or mineral water. God, when was he going to stop with the AA thing?

She walked on briskly, intending to fish her mobile out of her pocket, not paying any attention at all to the tall man jogging towards her on her side of the pavement when all of a sudden he stuck out his hand, right in front of her face. Before Annie could even grasp what was happening, she felt a terrible pain smack hard into her forehead and she was falling helplessly backwards.

Chapter Nine

City banker Manzoor Khan:

Custom-made dark grey suit (Oswald Boteng)
Blue shirt with white collar and cuffs (Thomas Pink)
Blue tie (Gieves & Hawkes)
Custom-made black brogues (James Taylor & Son)
Black overcoat (Gieves & Hawkes)
Black briefcase (Mulberry)
Total est. cost: £4,600

'Over £1,000? My word!'

'Mrs Valentine? Is that you?'

Annie opened her eyes very slowly. It was dark but she could make out in the glimmer of the orange street light that a man was bending over her.

She felt the most terrible throbbing and aching in her head. All over her forehead, down into her eyes and nose.

'Are you OK?' the man was asking, although it was pretty obvious that she was not. 'I'm Manzoor Khan from number ten,' he added.

Ah, Annie was able to register the flashy City banker from next door. He must have been coming home late from work.

But what the hell had happened to her? It had taken her some time to work out from the angle of the street light that she was lying on the ground. She put a hand up to her aching head and felt it very gingerly. The skin was grazed, burning and weirdly spongy.

'Do you think you can get up?' Manzoor asked.

Annie lifted her head and, with Manzoor's arm under her shoulders, managed to wobble up to her feet, feeling sick to her stomach.

'Did you fall?' he asked her.

'No . . . someone was running towards me and I think he must have hit me in the . . .' Annie began and that was when she realized what had happened. She'd been hit *deliberately*! She'd been *mugged*! Oh. No! NO! Despite her raging head, she looked down, scanned right across the pavement, but there was absolutely no sign of it . . .

'Someone's taken my bag!' she wailed. 'Someone's stolen my new handbag!'

'Oh dear,' Manzoor sympathized, 'that's very bad luck, but it might turn up. Muggers often take out the contents and throw the bag away round the corner, I could go and have a look around if you like. But I need to get you home first.'

'Throw the bag away?' Annie repeated in a dazed horror. 'Throw it away! That bag cost over a thousand pounds even with a staff discount.'

She was still too shocked even to feel upset yet.

'Over a thousand pounds? My word!' Even Mr

106

Six-Figure-Salary sounded a little taken aback at this information.

With Annie leaning heavily on his shoulder because she felt so sick and dizzy, they walked the thirty metres or so to her front door.

Once Manzoor had rung the bell, Annie could hear Ed walking down the corridor then calling out to the closed door: 'And I suppose you've forgotten your keys, have you? Forgotten to put them into your totally overpriced handbag!'

But when he had opened the door and spent several shocked seconds taking in Annie and her battered head, his expression changed instantly from stormy to seriously concerned.

'Oh my God! Annie!'

The verdict of the two paramedics who turned up with the ambulance was that Annie should have a very quiet night at home and go to see her GP in the morning.

They put a cooling compress on her ballooning fore-head, shone a torch into her eyes, decided that she wasn't concussed and warned her that going to hospital would mean spending the night in the waiting room instead of in the comfort of her own bed.

One of the two police officers who called at the house to take Annie's statement told her cheerily, 'That is going to swell right up, you're going to look like something from *Dr Who.*'

'He took my bag,' Annie wailed, 'and I only bought it today. It's Yves Saint Laurent!'

The woman police officer did at least look a bit sym-pathetic.

'My mobile with all my numbers!' Annie's losses were beginning to stack up, 'my wallet, my credit cards, my house keys!'

'You'll have to change your locks and cancel your cards,' one of the officers advised. 'You never know, he might try some of the doors in the street.'

Throughout the comings and goings of the evening, Ed made tea, held her hand, plumped the pillows up under her head, and looked distraught because he blamed himself for the whole thing. When she was finally in bed, propped up on pillows and loaded with painkillers, he pulled up a chair and sat beside her, holding her hand.

'I hope you're not here for the big make-up talk,' she told him with a little smile, 'because I need to sleep.'

'I know,' he told her, squeezing her hand. 'You could have been really badly hurt. You have been badly hurt . . . but it could have been . . .'

'Shhhh!' she told him off, 'I'm going to be fine. Don't go "if"ing and "but"ing about it,' but with a sigh, she admitted, 'I am going to look a fright in the morning.'

'Yeah, like . . .'

'Something out of *Dr Who*,' Annie finished his sentence, 'thanks. But what exactly?'

'I don't know, you'll have to ask Owen tomorrow. He slept through the whole thing.'

'Good.'

Ed pushed his unbuttoned shirtsleeves up and ran his fingers through tangled ringlets that looked even wilder than usual. 'I'm sorry we were arguing,' he said, casting his eyes down to the floor.

'I'm really sorry,' she told him quietly. 'I hate shouting and being shouted at.'

'I'm sorry,' he repeated, leaning over to run a finger gently down her arm. 'Let's not do that again.'

She looked over at him, then catching his eye, she smiled cheekily and said: 'So does that mean I can borrow the £30,000 then?'

Ed did not smile back and the hand on hers moved away.

'OK, we'll talk about this later,' she assured him; she was not in any state for another disagreement right now.

'Yes,' he agreed, 'it's just . . .' the hair shuffling was starting up again, so Annie knew he was agitated, 'I'm just thinking of you. I mean, your own business . . . can I just remind you: you hate the admin and the tax things and all paperwork in general. Annie, you love clothes and you love dressing people and you're great at it. Play to your strengths! Plus,' Ed's hands moved back to hers and he interlaced their fingers, 'we want to spend more time with you, not less!'

Annie felt the warm fingers squeeze tightly against hers. She understood, she really did. But she wanted to move on with Ed on her side, not holding her back.

'I don't want to talk about this now,' she told him, because that was the simplest thing, 'I have to go to sleep.'

When Annie woke the next morning, she looked at the ceiling in confusion for a few minutes before she remembered why her head felt just exactly as if it had been hit by a brick. The police officers had in fact found the brick and taken it away for analysis.

Because Ed was already awake and out of bed, she couldn't ask his opinion on how she looked, so she staggered over to the mirror at her dressing table. The face that looked back at her almost made her cry out with fright.

The skin on her forehead was pulled so tightly over the hard swelling underneath that it looked shiny. Even worse, it was deep dark purple and angry looking. The dressing seemed to have shrunk in comparison to the swelling the size of a large grapefruit that was now protruding from her head.

'Oh my God!' she was saying as Ed, wrapped in a towel, came into the room.

'Have you seen this?' she turned to face him, still not able to keep the astonishment out of her voice.

'Yes, I've seen it, you poor old thing.' He came over to her and put an arm carefully round her shoulder.

'It's all superficial,' he assured her. 'They said it would go down really quickly. So please get back into bed and rest.'

Annie turned her head slowly to look in the mirror again. 'So no plastic surgery on the NHS then?' she added, pretending to sound sad. 'Look, the swelling has made my frown lines disappear!'

'Oh well, there's an unexpected bonus,' Ed said just to join in with the joke for a moment, but then he couldn't help reminding her: 'You've been so lucky. He could have smashed your nose or taken out one of your eyes. He could have killed you if he'd hit you any harder. Annie . . .'

'Ed, stop it,' she reminded him and patted the arm around her shoulders. 'You're such a softie. I can't believe I've never been mugged before. You're not a real Londoner until you've been mugged. The only thing I'm really upset about is the bag.'

'The bag, the bag,' he said, then let out a breath. She wasn't sure if it was a sigh of sympathy or exasperation.

'I can't go to work looking like this, can I?' She sounded almost annoyed.

'No,' he insisted, 'don't even think about it.'

'But I never don't go to work!' she reminded him, 'I don't think I've had a day off sick since . . .' she strained to remember, but couldn't. Streaming colds, blazing temperatures, twisted ankles, sore backs – all these conditions had been dragged into work with her before. But even Annie had to accept that today she would have to take it easy. Plus, who would want to take wardrobe advice from someone out of *Dr Who*?

'I think Owen and Lana are on their way down,' Ed said at the sound of hurried footsteps on the stairs. 'Do you think I should go out first and warn them: "your Mum's been abducted by aliens, but don't worry, we're getting her back slowly"? Do you want me to take the day off school,' he added, 'so I can look after you?'

'No, no!' she insisted, 'I'm going to be absolutely fine.'

'Oh Mum!' Owen said when he'd burst into the room and taken a shocked look at his mother, 'you look just like a human Dalek Sec.'

'That's it!' Ed had to agree.

By 9.58 a.m. Annie was bored rigid.

She'd had breakfast in bed. She'd tried to get back to sleep, she'd attempted reading a magazine, then the book on Ed's bedside table. But it was all boring her to death.

She just wanted to be well and back at work and out of this bedroom and doing something!

'For goodness sake, just take a day off will you?' Dinah

insisted over the phone once she'd listened with horror to the full details of Annie's handbag saga.

'How's Bryan's secret party coming along?' Annie wanted to know.

'Definitely happening,' Dinah confided. 'I keep seeing the strangest notes and there are bizarre messages on the answering service. It is out of my hands. I'm just going to make sure that no matter where I am on that day, or what I'm doing, I am buffed, bronzed, gorgeous and wearing a beautiful dress. I mean, surprise parties, what a terrible idea!'

'Especially for women,' Annie had to agree. 'Men can turn up at anything looking like whatever, but for us it's so very different.'

'Agreed. Annie? Why can I hear tapping?' Dinah asked. 'Are you on your computer?'

'Oh, just having a little check on sales,' Annie admitted. 'I can't ignore eBay, not even for a day.'

What she didn't tell Dinah was that she had just emailed Mr Timi Woo with a substantial first order and she'd decided to cross all her fingers and take out the mortgage extension. It was going to work out. It really was. She believed in herself, even if no one else did.

'Annie, please go to bed,' Dinah pleaded. 'You should be resting.'

'I am in bed, but it's just so boring,' Annie told her. 'Ed and the kids have three days off school coming up,' she remembered. 'We never went away all summer and now I'd really like a long weekend somewhere. When's your next holiday?'

'Don't know,' Dinah replied; 'no plans in the pipeline.'

'We should do something together,' Annie said,

'especially as I'm probably not going back to work before then. I'll just be here, boring my face off.'

'I'll have a think about it,' Dinah promised her.

Once they'd said their goodbyes, Annie continued to fiddle about on the computer. What could she do? A little bit of online shopping? Nothing major – just some toiletries maybe? There were always good discount deals at her favourite online chemists. She knew that her bottles of shower gel and body lotion were about to run out, and she would hardly be able to go out to the shops looking like this.

With a few clicks of the mouse, Annie was logged on to one of her favourite cosmetic sites. Now she was looking at the offer of the week: an amazing deal on Sisley products. Sisley creams were very, very expensive. One hundred pounds a pot and upwards. They were also very, very good. Hollywood beauties apparently coated themselves head to toe in the really expensive anti-wrinkle face creams.

This really was a great offer: two tubes of face cream for the price of one, plus a pot of facial sun protector thrown in for free . . . direct from the manufacturer in Italy.

Annie made a snap decision to go for it. Fortunately, there was a credit card she kept in her desk which the mugger hadn't been able to steal from her.

Direct from Italy . . . that set her off on a fresh train of thought. She loved Italy. Home of the delicious leather shoe, birthplace of the beautiful handbag.

She had once spent four months in Tuscany working on a film set, back in her previous life as a wardrobe mistress. Although it had been some time since she'd used it, Annie considered her Italian surprisingly good.

Out in Tuscany, some of the local set designers had taken her under their wing and made sure she'd had a daily dose of language learning. Annie had been taught all sorts of unusual and colourful expressions and made to repeat them over and over again until she was fluent.

She was confident that it would all come flooding back once she was over there again.

She'd been thinking about looking into an Italian summer holiday next year. Maybe with Dinah's little family in tow, maybe even Connor. They could all rent a big villa with a pool together.

So, why not do a little research now that she had the chance?

Soon, she was busy trawling through Italian villa rental websites. Tuscany, which she'd had in mind, seemed to be terrifyingly expensive: you couldn't rent a garden shed in midsummer without spending £2,000, so she started to look through some of the houses on offer in other regions.

Le Marche looked much more promising. Even better, it was near the coast. So there would be swimming and maybe even surfing, which might suit Owen and Lana more than touring round vineyards, olive groves and medieval churches.

She had a feeling that Ed would be big on medieval churches, though.

Clicking through the available accommodation, she glanced at a villa, another villa, an apartment, a beach-side apartment, a villa with a pool . . . now that looked lovely. She opened up the photo of a big, whitewashed farmhouse with a red clay tiled roof. There was a wrought-iron balcony on the first floor which looked out towards the ocean, only a thirty-minute drive away. The house was described as 'within reach of Ancona and surrounding towns'.

Annie was supposed to be looking at dates for next summer. But she couldn't help noticing the flashing red 'late availability' sign.

The house was unbooked for the weekend that Ed and the children would be off and it was going for a song. The whole house and its lovely swimming pool. It was a steal. Really.

What a lovely, relaxing break they could all have, enjoying the late Italian summer sunshine. Her head injury could mend in peace and quiet. Ed could take a proper break away from school and evenings spent marking essays and all the out-of-hours music. He would be much less grouchy if he had a proper holiday. Maybe she'd be able to persuade Dinah, Bryan and Billie to come along and even Connor. He could tan up and drop a few pounds before his lunch with Sam Knight.

And if they divided the villa and the car hire between them, it would practically be cheaper than staying at home. And anyway, she was about to get £30,000 from the mortgage company, so surely she could treat everyone to a little break, especially after what she'd been through? She and Ed had never been away with the children. It would do them all so much good.

Annie pinged the owner an email straightaway, asking him to reserve the house.

Now, she just had to sort out some flights . . . then hire a car big enough for everyone . . . and make sure Dinah and Connor could come . . . and then obviously, there was the little matter of convincing Ed.

Chapter Ten

Persuasive Annie

Blue, yellow and white fixed wrap dress (Whistles sale)
Yellow heels (LK Bennett sale)
Cloud of perfume (Chanel's Coco)
Total est. cost: £130

'Maybe your dad liked surprises!'

Just one day before the start of the Founder's Centenary school holiday, almost everything was going very, very smoothly for Annie.

Connor had agreed to the Italian trip immediately, totally delighted at the prospect of turning himself into a bronzed screen idol by swimming in a sunshine-flooded pool for five days.

Dinah had needed some persuading, especially as she was going to have to take Billie out of primary school, but as soon as she'd come round to the idea, she'd grown enthusiastic and had promised to try and persuade Bryan to come with them.

Although she had marvelled at the bargain price, Dinah still had to ask Annie in today's phone call, 'What about the money you owe the taxman? You have sorted that out, haven't you?'

'Yeah, yeah,' Annie had breezed.

'You didn't borrow it, did you?'

'I've found some great things to sell so it's all going to be all right,' Annie had told her, not wanting to lie, but not wanting to worry her.

'Is Ed pleased about the holiday?' was Dinah's next awkward question.

'Totally!' Annie had insisted. This, unfortunately, was not true . . . well not yet, because she still hadn't found just the right moment to tell him about the holiday, even though the flight was departing from Stansted in less than twenty-four hours.

But Ed was due to come home for lunch today, so because she was still off work, she was planning to make a bacon and avocado salad with care and attention and warm garlic bread in the oven, in the hope of softening him up for the big news.

Just as Ed stepped into the house at lunchtime, Annie's mobile rang and she found herself trying to have a conversation with a woman from the mortgage company, about which account to deposit her £30,000 into. Something she definitely didn't want to remind Ed about. He still didn't know that she'd decided to go ahead with the loan because once again the ideal moment for the conversation about it just hadn't really presented itself. Well, not ideally.

'My personal account? Hmmm yes, that would be

great,' she said, trying to turn away from him and speak as quietly as possible. 'Do I have the number? Ermm . . . let me just go upstairs . . . if you could just hold on for a moment.' Annie took her chance to get somewhere private as quickly as she could.

When she came back into the kitchen, she found Ed had already served himself and was eating quickly, telling her that he had to get back to school sooner than he'd expected.

'Was that your bank?' was his next question.

'Yeah . . . some cheque I paid in, they were just wanting to check . . . the cheque . . .' she trailed off, hoping he wouldn't ask any more.

After he'd swallowed several mouthfuls of garlic bread, Ed suddenly struck up a new and worrying conversation. 'My dad was always doing things that my Mum would only find out about later.'

'Oh?' was all Annie said to this, although she tried to look as sympathetic as she could.

'I don't mean really big, bad things, like he had a mistress and she only found out about it later,' Ed continued, 'but still, significant things, like he would sell the car and buy a new one without even mentioning it to her.'

'Really?' Annie had to act surprised now, although she was starting to feel agitated. If Ed knew about the holiday, why didn't he just say so? Why beat about the bush like this?

'Yeah,' Ed went on, 'I remember Mum hunting all round the house for the car key and then Dad piping up with, "oh, I traded the old banger in, there's a new one parked outside."'

Looking up at Annie, Ed added, with worrying seriousness: 'I don't want us to be like that. OK? Mum found it hurtful. She wanted to be involved with decisions like that, and she should have been.'

As both of Ed's parents had died before Annie had met him, she couldn't know if this story was true or if he was making it up for a reason.

'Maybe your dad liked surprises!' she said defensively, 'Maybe he was just trying to make life more interesting.'

But there was no getting out of it. This time tomorrow, they were booked on a flight from Stansted to Ancona, and she was going to have to tell him.

'Ed, I'm sorry,' she began, ' but I've organized a surprise. I'm sorry, I didn't know that you didn't like surprises . . . but . . .'

The doorbell rang.

Annie jumped up and insisted that she would get it, relieved that the difficult conversation was going to be put off for just a few more minutes. But when she opened the front door her mind was not exactly set at rest by the scene outside.

Most of the entire width of narrow Hawthorne Street was taken up with a mighty articulated lorry. On her doorstep stood a man in a boiler suit bearing a clipboard.

'This is for you to sign, love, eight boxes of Chinese import via Dover.'

Oh. Good. Grief. The shoes! The Timi Woo shoes! While Annie couldn't help thinking that it was fantastic that they'd arrived, and so soon, this was exactly the wrong moment. Where was she supposed to put a hundred pairs of shoes while Ed was in the kitchen fuming about couples keeping secrets? In fact, she reminded herself, there were two hundred pairs of shoes, because she and Mr Woo had come to a very good deal: two hundred pairs for $15,000. A hundred were arriving this month and another hundred were following in October. Starting a business with $15,000 worth of stock was just nothing, she had reassured herself. People borrowed much, much bigger amounts with far less chance of success. The shoes were genius. She just knew it.

The driver on the doorstep was waving the clipboard at her now. 'You've got to sign here, love. Obviously there's import duty to pay, so Revenue & Customs will be on to you.'

'Annie? Is everything OK?' Ed called from the kitchen.

'Yes, yes!' she yelled back, but really this wasn't OK at all.

'You can't bring them in just yet,' she told the driver in a low voice. 'You'll have to give me fifteen minutes.'

Ed would have headed back to school by then and she could save the shoe/mortgage extension/holiday in Italy discussion for this evening. Couldn't she?

Annie, with her Stilton-coloured, swollen forehead, was looking a bit ropy to the driver and that was before she'd seen the size of the boxes he was about to try and fit through her front door. But still, he wasn't in the mood to be sympathetic.

'Fifteen minutes will be extra,' he told her firmly.

'How much?' she asked.

'Thirty quid. Cash.'

She had to agree. So he turned and went back to his

cab, then switched on the engine and just sat there. Oh that was subtle, that really was.

Annie shut the front door and hurried back into the kitchen.

'What was that about?' Ed wanted to know as he mopped bread around his plate, making sure every last little bit of salad dressing was scooped up.

'Mail order,' Annie said as brightly as she could. 'I bought some new sheets for us. Total . . .'

'Bargain?' Ed finished the sentence for her and decided not to make any comment at all about her spending: 'So was that the surprise?' he asked.

'Yes!' she said cheerfully. She would tell him all about everything else . . . tonight. They'd sit down, they'd relax, it would all be much easier then.

Once he was in the hallway, Ed called out, 'Why is the delivery lorry still here?'

'I dunno,' Annie replied casually, 'maybe he's checking his map or something . . . taking a break?'

Ed shrugged his shoulders and set off through the front door, cord jacket on, battered leather briefcase in hand, tartan scarf flying.

As soon as Annie could be confident Ed was safely round the corner, she went back out to the lorry driver.

'OK.' She tried to sound much more cheery than she felt once she'd taken a look at the four enormous cartons in the back of the truck, 'I'm going to need your help. Because the room these are going into is at the top of a flight of stairs.'

With a great sigh, the driver informed her that that too was 'going to be extra'.

*   *   *

121

That evening, supper was early in Annie's household because everyone, apart from her, had plans to go out.

Owen, Lana and Ed were all in very good spirits, because there was no school ahead for five whole days. Already they were buzzing with plans because not one of them knew yet that Annie had already made other arrangements.

Annie was finding it hard to sit still. She kept hopping up and down from the table to get a glass, to find the pepper – anything to put off this conversation. But the plane was leaving at 11.45 a.m. tomorrow morning. Unless she said something very, very soon, only Dinah, Bryan, Billie and Connor would be on it.

Maybe she should just go without them? The thought flashed across her mind. She could leave them a note . . . but then, that wasn't really the point, was it?

The phone began to ring and Ed was up and answering it before she could stop him. He returned to the kitchen with the phone in his hands, and passed it to Annie. 'It's Dinah, she sounds very excited. She wants to talk about tomorrow. Have you invited her over or something?'

Annie took the phone and fled out to the corridor to speak to Dinah in privacy.

Once the conversation was over, she came back into the kitchen, took a deep, steadying breath and blurted out her secret. 'I'm really sorry, Ed and Owen, I'm really, really sorry but you can't go out tonight. Neither can you, Lana.'

'What!?' Lana cried.

'No, because . . .' Annie put a smile on her face, made a big effort to announce this like the huge treat, the amazing surprise she'd really thought it would be.

122

'You've got to pack. Because tomorrow . . . we're all going to Italy for five days! Da-nah – surprise!'

'What?!' This time it wasn't just Lana who looked completely outraged. Ed seemed to be growing flushed and furious too. Only Owen's face broke into a smile. 'Cool,' he told his mum.

Annie rushed to explain, 'I got us all really cheap flights and this big villa with a pool, but it's a total late deal special and Connor and Dinah are coming with us, so they're going to split the cost . . .'

But Ed didn't stay to listen to any more, he just stood up and left the room.

'I wanted to be with Andrei!' Lana shouted, 'we've already planned to do all kinds of things together. You never let anyone choose to do anything, you're just such a control freak!' then she turned and flounced out of the room after Ed.

Now Annie felt hurt and just a little angry, 'Good grief!' she cried, 'if I left it up to you lot, we'd never do anything good at all. We'd just be stuck inside the house, snogging Andrei or counting our pennies.' Heading out into the hall to make sure no one missed a word, she added loudly, 'You can't take it with you, you know! What's money for if it can't be enjoyed? If it can't buy you a nice life? With nice things?!'

Neither Lana nor Ed made any reply and Annie ticked herself off for shouting again. She wasn't going to shout. She didn't want to turn into one of those ranting mothers. She would be calm and see how the evening panned out. Maybe Lana and Ed wouldn't come . . . maybe she would go with Owen and the others. Would that be so bad?

When she came back into the kitchen, Owen was still sitting at the table. He shot her a grin.

'Cool,' he said again. 'Can we dig for Roman remains, Mum?'

Annie nodded, feeling quite dazed.

'And Mum . . . is there any pudding?'

Ed was sitting on their double bed moodily playing the guitar when Annie decided she felt brave enough to go in. Playing the guitar moodily was Ed's way of having a big huff, she'd discovered over the course of their time together.

'I'm not coming,' he said as soon as he saw her.

'I thought you might say that,' she said, sitting down on the bed beside him.

'We had an agreement! Big ticket items have to be discussed. That was our agreement and you've not done it yet. Not even once. You've just gone ahead and bought major thing after major thing without even mentioning it.'

'But you'd just have said no every time!' Annie exclaimed in frustration.

Ed gave a sigh of exasperation and looked away from her again. 'Right, do you need me to explain what a discussion is, then?'

'I'm used to having my own way,' she told him.

'Oh, great argument.'

'I don't want to go without you,' she said and moved closer to him on the bed. She dared to lower her head gently onto his shoulder, wheedling, 'My head's still sore. I need you to look after me.' Maybe appealing to his sympathy would be a wise move. 'I thought a little holiday would be really, really good for us all. We didn't get away all summer . . . we've been so busy doing up the house . . .'

When she felt Ed's arm move from his guitar to slide around her waist, she knew she was doing something right.

'Where is this villa?' he asked.

'Oh it looks gorgeous,' she began, 'it's in the country-side, but not far from the sea. About two hours' drive from the airport. I've hired a big car . . . very cheap. Total . . .'

'Bargain,' Ed couldn't help smiling. 'Which airport?'

'Ancona,' she told him, lying down across the bed and rubbing the small of his back, determined to win him over by all means at her disposal.

'Ancona?' Ed sounded surprised.

'Do you know it?' Annie asked.

'Erm, yes! You might remember me telling you about my Italian . . .'

'Girlfriend!' Annie broke in, remembering almost every word Ed had told her about this woman. No one can help wanting to know every little crease and crinkle of The One who came before them.

'Yeah, she's from Ancona.'

'Oh! Right. I didn't know that. Is that bad?' she wondered.

'No. It's nice . . . and I suppose you had no idea either that Ancona and the towns round about are the shoe and handbag capital of Italy?' Ed lay back on the bed beside her, seeming almost quite willing to make up with her now.

'That's where almost all of Italy's leather goods are

made,' he added. 'Am I really supposed to believe that you didn't have the slightest idea about that either?'

'I didn't!' she said, truthfully, 'I honestly didn't know anything about that!' Now she was struggling to keep the excitement out of her voice. *The shoe and handbag capital of Italy?!*

'So, will you come with us, babes?'

'Yes . . . OK,' he agreed. 'I give in once again . . .'

'That's what I like about you,' Annie told him, kissing his cheek.

'Yeah, you've twisted my arm,' Ed said, 'but now you have to go upstairs and work on Lana. She will not be so easy to persuade.'

'Maybe if I tell her about the shoes and handbags . . .'

'Yeah, good luck with that.'

Chapter Eleven

Fern's going away outfit:

Pink and blue print summer dress (Monsoon)
Beige sandals, extra wide (Van Dal)
White clip-on earrings (Vintage eighties, back of
jewellery box)
Practical white handbag (John Lewis)
Total est. cost: £160

'Oh no!'

By nine the next morning, the entire household was in a state of pandemonium. Now it was Owen's turn to sulk because Annie and Ed had agreed that he couldn't take his violin to Italy.

'There's a pool!' Annie was shouting at him in exasperation. 'It's going to be sunny! You'll be outside, swimming and having a lovely time.'

'You know we should be grateful that he's so keen to practise,' Ed reminded her. 'Some of the other kids . . .'

'Stay out of this,' Annie warned him.

Meanwhile Lana, who had finally been persuaded with the promise of a new handbag, shoes and boots – Annie had secretly been impressed with her daughter's uncompromising negotiating tactics – was weeping down her mobile. 'I'm going away! I won't be able to see you! No, not until Monday night at the earliest . . . I know, it's just terrible.'

Annie's large suitcase was packed, but now she was bossily interfering with Ed's packing.

'Don't you own anything ironed?' she snapped, 'or anything that's white and not grey? Where are those nice shirts I bought you at the start of the summer?'

Everyone was acutely aware that the taxi would arrive in about twenty minutes. Still, it was something of a shock when the doorbell rang.

'Oh God! It's early!' Annie cried. 'Come on! Bring your bags down. I've got the passports and the tickets.'

As Ed, Owen and Lana bumped and banged bags down the wooden stairs towards the hallway, Annie opened the door for the taxi driver.

To her astonishment, there on the top step looking fresh and smelling fragrant, in a brand new flowery dress, was Fern, Annie's mother.

'Good morning, dearie! How are you doing?' Fern asked raising her arms for a hug and a kiss. She stopped in her tracks, 'Oh my God, your head! You said you'd had a bit of an accident but I had no idea . . . oh darling, I'm sorry, I've not phoned you for days, I've been rushed off my feet.'

'Mum!' Annie exclaimed as she was pulled towards a soft, carefully made-up cheek and enveloped in a cloud of Givenchy.

'Hilda's in the car, dear,' Fern went on. 'We left really early to miss the worst of the traffic. But I thought I'd get Ed to help me with the wheelchair, it's a bit of a struggle getting it out by myself.'

'Hilda?' Annie asked, wondering why on earth her mother could have thought to bring hideous old Aunty Hilda with her for a visit so early on a Thursday morning.

Just then Lana came to the front door and looked round from behind her mother, suitcase in one hand, mobile phone in the other.

'Hi, Gran!' she exclaimed cheerfully. 'What are you doing here?' Turning to her mother, she added, 'Dinah's just phoned, Bryan can't come to Italy with us, he's not going to be able to get away from work. Hey, why don't you come, Gran?'

Just as Fern was beginning to grasp the meaning of Lana's words, Annie was coming to the vaguest recollection of a hurried conversation with her mum, something about Fern going away and Hilda needing care and Annie volunteering and . . . could she seriously have agreed to look after Aunty Hilda *this* weekend? Founder's weekend?

Annie looked over at her great-aunt again. The old bat was so infuriatingly opinionated that it wasn't possible to bite into a sandwich without her letting you know what she thought about your bite, your bread and your choice of sandwich filling. Someone else would have to have her.

'But I'm leaving for France in three hours!' Fern exclaimed with horror. 'You can't be going away! You're the ones who are supposed to be looking after Aunty.'

'But I'd completely forgotten!' Annie tried to defend herself. 'I got mugged and whacked on the head and since then, I've not thought about it at all. You should have reminded me!'

'Oh my God!' Fern's voice was growing more and more high-pitched. 'Why didn't I phone you yesterday to check? I meant to. I even tried, but the line was engaged and then I was busy packing . . .'

'What's the matter, Annie?' Ed called down the stairs.

'Oh! Hello Fern,' he greeted Annie's mother in astonishment. 'You've picked the wrong moment for a surprise visit.'

He jogged down the stairs and was brought up to speed astonishingly quickly by both extremely agitated women.

'And Bryan's not coming,' Lana announced to them all once again.

Although Ed's first reaction to the Italian long weekend had been fury and a flat refusal to accompany them, in the hours since then he'd decided it was too late to complain about the money, because it was already spent, so he might as well look forward to the trip. Now, the idea of swimming in the pool, basking in the sun, eating some fantastic Italian food and drinking a little too much Chianti was all highly appealing.

The fact that an elderly aunty he'd only met once before was about to jeopardize it all was not exactly great news.

'Where else could she go?' Ed asked, trying not to make it sound too brutal.

'I don't have any time to find anyone else!' Fern exclaimed, her cheeks growing pink with stress. 'I'm supposed to be catching my bus in three hours.'

'Where does she live?'

'In a nice little village not far from Bishop's Stortford.'

Ed's face seemed to light up. 'Isn't Bishop's Stortford right beside Stansted?' he asked.

Annie saw Ed's look and, all at once, caught the meaning of his question. 'Oh no. No, no you don't,' she warned.

'Is she fit to travel?' Ed directed this question at Fern.

'Who?'

'Aunty H.'

'Hilda? Well, she has her wheelchair, she can walk a little more these days, she's coming along . . . Oh no!' Fern added, also catching Ed's meaning, 'You can't take her to Italy!'

'Why don't I go over there and have a little chat with her? She must be wondering what on earth's going on up here,' Ed said and before anyone could stop him, he bounded down the steps towards Fern's sleek green Jag, parked right in front of the house.

Annie could see Aunty Hilda sitting primly in the front seat, looking just as disapproving as ever. Oh, she was going to love this, wasn't she? She was never going to let Annie forget about this mix-up.

Fern, Annie and Lana waited anxiously on the threshold of the house as Ed crouched down at the car door, which he'd partly opened in order to chat to the old battleaxe.

'He's really a very nice man,' Fern couldn't help commenting, 'I don't know what he's doing with you,' she added huffily. Annie knew then how much she'd annoyed her mother; this wasn't the sort of comment she'd usually make.

'He clearly has a way with older women,' Annie snapped back.

'Does Ed seriously think Aunty Hilda should come to Italy with us?' Lana was asking in a tone of disbelief. 'That old bat?'

'Lana!' her mother warned her.

But Owen was now behind them, sitting on the stairs lacing up his trainers and declaring, 'WHAT? Aunty Hilda!'

'I see you're bringing them up to respect their elders,' Fern snipped.

'Oh yes,' Annie shot back. 'It's *so* important.'

It was with no small amount of horror that Annie watched Ed stand up and head towards the boot of the car.

'He's getting out the wheelchair,' she said faintly. 'He's persuaded her to come with us.'

'Well, thank goodness for that – even though it's absolute madness,' was Fern's reaction. 'At least if she dies when you're in charge, it won't be my fault.'

'Dies?' Annie spluttered. 'Look at her! She's going to outlive all of us. Owen included.'

As Ed carefully unloaded Aunty Hilda from the passenger's seat and into the wheelchair, the long-awaited taxi arrived.

Fortunately Annie had specified 'a big car' and a super-sized people-carrier was now pulling up in front of the house.

'Hello everybody!' Aunty Hilda called up from her wheelchair to the little crowd on the doorstep. 'Well this is quite a surprise, but Frank and I used to go to Italy every summer and I've always wanted to go back . . . just not on my own.'

And even Annie, who suspected this was because

132

Aunty Hilda couldn't possibly have any friends, suddenly felt just a tiny bit sorry for the old dear.

Look at her, sitting in her wheelchair smartly dressed in a summer frock with a pink and white necklace, pink lipstick and sensible white shoes. Annie could always find sympathy in her heart for a woman who accessorized. Aunty Hilda's hair was a bit skew-whiff though, as if she'd done it before putting on her glasses.

In a flurry, the house was made ready and locked up while bags, luggage, children, wheelchair and Aunty were loaded into the people carrier. The plan was to stop off at Aunty Hilda's house as quickly as possible to pick up her passport and a few essentials.

'She *can* go to the bathroom herself, can't she?' Annie whispered into her mother's ear frantically as they said frantic goodbyes.

'Yes. But no stairs and she might need a hand getting out of the bath,' Fern informed her, adding nervously, 'I can't believe I'm letting you do this. Are you sure you're going to manage?'

'Of course, it's only for a few days and anyway, Connor's coming, he loves old ladies and Dinah's going to be there.'

Fern seemed to relax slightly when she was reminded of this. Dinah could be trusted not to do anything too crazy, whereas Annie . . . well, sometimes Fern wondered what was coming next with Annie.

With a final wave and a cry of 'Have a lovely time!' the taxi containing Annie, her family and their latest addition pulled off and disappeared round the corner.

Chapter Twelve

Holiday Connor:

Loud Hawaiian-style short-sleeved shirt
(Paul Smith)
White jeans (Armani)
Sandals (last holiday – Morocco)
Foot wax and pedicure (The Men's Room)
Total est. cost: £230

'No bread, no pizza and no pasta. No wheat.'

'Hallelujah! This must be the place!' Connor enthused as he brought the mighty people carrier beast to a standstill outside a rather dingy-looking rustic-style restaurant bearing the sign 'Taverna' and a flickering light above the door.

Everyone was hot and exhausted, crammed into the car. Owen, on Annie's lap in the back, had puked six times between the airport, the villa and the restaurant. To comfort him, Annie had had to give up driving on the twisty roads. She'd had to hold him across her lap as he groaned into a plastic bag for the grindingly long journeys.

A quick tour of inspection of their holiday home had found it pleasant enough but it was in such a remote spot that the village shops were a twenty-minute walk away and of course, on a Thursday evening, all shut.

'A restaurant? *Ristorante*?' Annie had begged the villa owner, adding theatrically and with a really very pretty accent, 'Sono mormorare di fame, dove manghi pronto,' which was supposed to mean, 'We are dying of hunger and need to eat straight away' but actually meant something like, 'I have been to murmur of hunger, he needs mangoes straight away', much to the villa owner's bemusement.

Nevertheless, he got the idea and gave them directions to a restaurant he assured them was not too far away.

A twenty-minute journey had followed, which had passed fairly quietly apart from Owen's nauseated groaning, Billie's incessant 'Are we nearly there yet? You said we were nearly there!' and Aunty Hilda's stream of disapproving complaints.

'Goodness me! Self-catering! Frank and I would never have done something like that,' she'd warbled from the back seat. 'When you arrive after a long journey, you want it all laid on for you. You want dinner to be served in a nice restaurant with no cooking and no washing up afterwards. I suppose it's too expensive for you though is it, Annie? A nice hotel?'

Annie had curled her fingers up into her hand and told herself that punching old women who were currently wheelchair-bound was pretty indefensible. Probably even more so in Italy, where grannies were sacred.

She looked out of the window and tried to make out something of the view, despite the fact that it was dark out there and she had an exhausted, limp figure on her lap who probably wouldn't be able to eat one mouthful and would still have to face the journey back home again.

Dinah was pale, Ed was quiet, only Connor in the driving seat was jollying everyone along. Hallelujah for Connor! Annie couldn't help thinking, not for the first time in her life.

Parked up in front of the Taverna, everyone piled out of the car. The place looked deserted. Fortunately, two waiters seemed to spring to life when the party entered though the creaky wooden door.

It was after 8 p.m., surely not too late for dinner in Italy? No, no, too early, Annie assured everyone. In her crazed Italian, she instructed the waiters that this was 'Many, many big family of London, much mangoes and very big wine.'

Nevertheless, they ushered everyone to the large table in the centre and hurried to bring menus, bread, olives and little earthenware jugs of water and wine.

Several platefuls of antipasti were also brought out without much delay, and once everyone had started digging into slices of salami and strips of red pepper a feeling of relief and relaxation spread over them.

Owen was thoroughly washed down in the bathroom and after he'd had a glass of water and a small piece of bread, began to perk up considerably.

The devoted waiters, chatting to the children, charming the grown-ups, flirting shamelessly with Annie, went through the menu at length, discussing their recommendations in full in both Italian, which Annie went to great lengths to translate, and broken English.

A large selection of home-made pizzas and pastas was ordered to follow the antipasti, and when the fabulous pizzas were brought out they were on crusts so crispy and fine that even little Billie wolfed down the anchovy and caper toppings without blinking.

The problem wasn't with the toddler at the table. It was with Connor. He was trying to explain to one of the waiters that he couldn't drink any alcohol and he wasn't going to eat anything with wheat.

'No bread?' the waiter was trying to establish.

'No bread,' Connor confirmed, 'no pizza and no pasta. No wheat.'

'No pasta!' The waiter sounded utterly appalled. 'Perche no?! Che problema con pasta?!'

Then began a long, impassioned speech which seemed to be about how this was the best pasta in Le Marche, no one had ever said no to the pasta, it was his mother's own recipe, the most tender, delicious, light and flexible pasta once again, in the whole of Le Marche, if not all of Italy. It was an insult to his mother's memory not to enjoy the pasta, without doubt the best pasta in all of Le Marche. That was clear.

When one of the waiters held a plateful right up in front of Connor's face, twirling the moist quills round in the oily green sauce, then offering up the forkful to him with a look of pleading, he had no choice but to give in.

Everyone watched as he opened his mouth and the waiter fed him the forkful. He began to chew slowly and started to smile, then, sensing his audience's anticipation, went into full-blown raptures of delight.

'Oh! Mama mia! Fantastico!' he enthused, 'That is so good, brilliant. Bella! Bella! Delicious! I must have all of that!'

Everyone around the table began to laugh, even Lana, who seemed finally to be getting into the holiday spirit.

'How's Andrei?' Ed, who was sitting next to her, turned to ask quietly. 'Is he holding up without you?'

'He's doing OK,' she smiled at him. 'You can actually speak Italian, can't you?' she had to ask, suspecting this was why all Annie's attempts to do so were sending him into silent hysterics.

'Un po,' he confided in her.

'Why don't you tell Mum?' Lana wondered.

'What and miss out on all the fun?' Ed confided. 'Do you know what she's just told that waiter?'

'I think she wanted a fresh jug of water.'

'Yup, but she told him to bring her some rushed broccoli.'

Lana spluttered her drink.

'Oh, I love your mum,' he added, but Lana had worked that out a long time ago.

Meanwhile, across the table, the waiter was asking Annie, 'So you come to Ancona for handbag and shoes, no?'

'Si. Of course!' Annie told him and, remembering how much the Italians she had known had loved to show off what 'insiders' they were, she asked him, 'Where is the best place to go? I need to know the very best place. Very best shoes and bags but at the very, very best price. *Best price,*' she thought she'd repeated in Italian, but the waiter wondered why she was talking about 'precious millet'.

'Yes, I go talk to my brother, we come back and tell you all best places.' He treated her to a showy wink, then asked, 'Shop? Or factory?'

'Factory?'

There was no mistaking the gleam in Annie's eyes as she asked, 'You can go to the factories?'

'Si, si,' came the emphatic response, 'big tourismo in the factories.'

Dinah caught the gist of this conversation and turned to Annie to confirm what she thought she'd heard. 'We can buy things direct from the factories?' When Annie nodded happily, Dinah had to agree. 'That's got to be worth a visit!'

The waiter returned with a list of all the best shops and factory stores in and around Ancona. Lana wanted to take a look through the names and even Aunty Hilda seemed to fire up with enthusiasm.

'Frank bought me a beautiful navy crocodile handbag when we visited the lakes, oh back in the sixties. Navy crocodile, so hard to find, goes with everything. I still use it. Not like you girls – ' she directed a sharp look at Annie and Dinah – 'a different bag for every outfit. And they're not cheap, I know that.'

'So I think it's going to be just you and me exploring the territory around the villa tomorrow then,' Ed informed Owen, 'unless Connor, of course . . .'

'No, no, I'm with the bag ladies,' Connor told him without hesitation.

*   *   *

When Annie had booked the three-bedroomed villa, she'd thought Bryan, Dinah and Billie would all share the biggest bedroom and she and Ed would be in the other double. Then, she'd planned for Connor and Owen to have the room with the single beds and Lana, the foldaway sofa bed in the sitting room.

Now that Aunty Hilda was with them and obviously needed a large ground floor bedroom to herself, everything had been thrown into disarray.

Annie went through every possible combination in her mind, but the best she could come up with was Lana, Dinah and Billie in the family room, Aunty Hilda in the other double, Owen and Connor still sharing the singles . . . which left Annie and Ed on the sofa bed.

'No! Have our room,' Connor had offered. 'I can slum it on the sofa bed and we could make Owen something comfy on the floor with the sofa cushions.'

But Annie thought there was going to be quite enough chaos in the villa without creating a boy's dorm right in the middle of the sitting room.

Lying uncomfortably beside Ed on the sofa bed's thin and narrow mattress that night, she regretted her generosity to Connor and Owen.

'This wasn't really quite how I pictured it,' Ed turned his head to whisper into her ear.

'No, me neither,' she told him.

They lay side by side, trying to get used to their new night-time surroundings.

'What *is* that noise?' she asked. They both listened to the low rumbling that rose and fell, louder for a few moments, then quieter again, then louder once more.

'Tractor in the distance? Revving up its engine?' Ed suggested, but not with any great certainty.

'No, I don't think – Oh my God, it's Aunty Hilda's snoring!' Annie realized.

Splayed across the comfortable double bed in the garden bedroom with doors out to the terrace, where Annie should have been cuddled up with Ed right now, the octogenarian snorer was deeply, deeply away in the Land of Nod.

'Well, that's the sign of a good evening!' Ed said with amusement. 'Did you see how much wine she put away?'

'Yeah . . . and how much pasta,' Annie added. 'I don't think Mum's been feeding her properly. Mum's probably been on a diet to look hot for her Saga booze cruise.'

The sagginess at the centre of the sofa bed had rolled Ed and Annie in very close together. Because it was warm in the sitting room, even with the windows wide open to let in a breeze, they'd gone to bed with very little on, so their nearly naked bodies were brushing against each other.

'Italy is a very sexy country,' Annie said, feeling her way around Ed with her fingertips.

'Yes . . . I had noticed that,' he replied, sliding the slim strap of her camisole slowly down her shoulder. With his lips against her earlobe, he added, 'What was all that about handbag factories? I was at the table too, you know.'

She ran her fingernail around his bellybutton and lower into the tangle of hair below, then her lips found his damp, minty mouth and she kissed him luxuriously.

'Shhhh . . .' she insisted halfway through the kiss, 'let's not talk about that right now.'

'Oh,' he said, lightly stroking her nipple into a little point, 'now you want to get friendly . . . now that I'm questioning your divine right to shop no matter where, no matter when.'

'Stop talking,' she insisted, moving her mouth down to the soft and sensitive side of his neck.

'You're not allowed to spend over two hundred pounds without consulting me,' he reminded her, then bent his head so that brushing his hair against her breasts, he could lick deftly with the very edge of his tongue against the nipple point. 'We had a deal,' he reminded her. 'Would I spend over two hundred pounds without asking? Even of my own money?'

'Ed!' she argued, although he was kissing her stomach now, he was moving lower and in a moment she wouldn't be able to say anything at all. 'You've never spent over two hundred pounds on anything, ever. Apart from that one time I made you go shopping for clothes you actually look good in. And didn't that turn out to be a fantastic investment? You got me!'

Ed came back up the bed, squeaking the springs with every move. She pulled him on top of her so she could feel his hard warmth leaning into her.

His face above hers, he told her with a smile, 'I think, technically speaking, you're an asset. Not an investment. You're an asset that needs constant maintenance.'

He moved onto his side, so he could touch between her legs in search of exactly the right place . . . and he didn't miss. She could rely on him never to miss.

'I think, technically speaking . . .' she whispered with

142

her lips against his ear, 'you've got a boner,' and she moved her fingers onto it. 'I might have to go down there and do a full inspection.'

Annie had just begun to move down underneath the sheet into Ed's furry warmth when she felt his hands pulling her to a stop.

'Owen?' Annie heard Ed ask in surprise, 'is anything the matter?'

'Just going to the bathroom,' came the sleepy-sounding reply.

Ed and Annie lay perfectly still on the sofa bed, their hands still in place, their fingers applying just the right amount of pressure and almost imperceptible touch to keep them both throbbing with pleasure, desperate to move and on the very brink of coming, while Owen meandered to the bathroom, did a startlingly audible wee, then stumbled out and back to bed again.

Once he was safely in his room, the lovemaking that followed was hot and hurried but almost completely silent. With Ed moving deep inside her, his guitar-playing fingers strumming against her clit, Annie came as quietly as she could, swallowing down the sounds.

'I love you,' she heard herself whispering into the pillow and then again, 'I love you. I love you.'

It sounded strange, because she didn't say it often. Usually she said 'me too' after Ed had said it.

'Yes,' came Ed's whisper, as he moved against her, hurrying now that he knew she'd come, 'Yes . . . yes . . . yes . . .' he rocked, 'YES!'

Lying side by side in the sofa bed's hollow, just as Annie thought they were finally going to go to sleep, Ed broke

143

the comfortable silence with the unwelcome but not entirely unexpected question. 'You're not really serious about setting up your own business are you, Annie?'

There was only one reply she wanted to make to this right now: 'Babes, it's been a very, very long day. Can we talk about this tomorrow?'

Chapter Thirteen

Holiday Dinah:

White, lime and beige tunic dress (Topshop)
Flat yellow sandals (Barnardo's)
White sunglasses (Brick Lane market)
Large lime shopper bag (Topshop)
Total est. cost: £75

'Well, if you like it Billie, we'll take it.'

The next morning, Ed got up early and walked down to the village where he found a bakery, a greengrocer's and a tiny general store.

Both Owen and a bright-eyed Connor were awake when he got back, so they helped him set out the table on the terrace with crusty white bread and jam, coffee blacker than the night, apricot juice, fresh pears, figs and a tub of goat's yoghurt.

When the girls surfaced an hour later, still in their pyjamas or nighties, they were much more cranky, Dinah and Annie both suffering from the many jugfuls of wine consumed at the Taverna, Lana, Billie and Aunty Hilda still grouchy with sleep.

As Annie poured herself a coffee, Connor emerged from the pool and his first swim of the day and she had to stop mid-cup to admire the glorious chiselled torso.

'God, you're looking fantastic, Connor,' she called over to him. 'I'd have you.'

His six-pack was straight off the cover of a Calvin Klein boxers box.

'Do you think you could show Ed a few of your stomach crunches?' Annie asked cheekily, shooting a grin at Ed.

Connor, dabbing at himself with a towel, told her off gently. 'Annie Valentine! You've got a very good man there: handy about the house, an early riser, layer of breakfast tables, maker of fantastic coffee . . . but he still squeaks your sofa bed. So, if you ever change your mind, you make sure you let me know so that I can move in on him straight away!'

This brought a shocked cackle from Aunty Hilda, and even a little smile.

'Hands off!' Lana warned Connor.

Then Owen added, 'He's ours.'

All this blatant affection made Ed blush right up to his ears.

'OK, OK, that's enough sucking up to Ed, just because he went to the village and got breakfast,' Annie said, shooting Ed a wink. 'Much more importantly, how are we dividing up for the morning? I thought I might drive into the next town with my little list of places to visit – ' she couldn't repress her smile. 'I know Lana and Dinah want to come with me . . .'

'Yup, put me down for the ladies-only shopping trip,' Connor said, pulling up a chair at the table and reaching for the yoghurt.

'We're staying here, aren't we, Ed?' Owen asked, his mouth crammed with bread and jam. 'I'm not going in that car again, ever, and anyway, I want to go exploring.'

He waved his hand expansively at the countryside surrounding the villa. There were fields and hills, fruit orchards, small twisting dust roads, so many places to wander. He couldn't wait. He still couldn't believe he'd managed to sneak his penknife through Customs by hiding it in his shoe and he was planning to put it to good use.

At this moment Lana's sparkly pink mobile, on the table right beside her glass of juice, beeped and a smile flashed across her face.

'Ooooh!' Connor teased, 'Lanie's got a textie from her boyfie.'

'I know I said I would come into town with you,' Aunty Hilda began from her corner of the table, 'but after last night, I think I'll have a quiet day. I never usually eat so late at night, it just doesn't agree with me. I can wheel myself from my room to the poolside and back again, so no one needs to worry about me.'

'Are you sure?' Annie had to ask, trying not to sound too relieved. 'We have to look after you, Mum would never forgive us if you weren't looked after properly.'

'Your mother is a bit of a fusser,' came Aunty Hilda's verdict, 'and that's all I'm saying.'

Annie let it go. She even congratulated herself for letting it go.

'We'll keep an eye on you,' Ed told Aunty Hilda with a

smile, 'in between very exciting expeditions, obviously,' he assured Owen, whose face had fallen.

'So what about you, Billie?' Ed asked, turning to Dinah's five-year-old daughter. 'Would you like to come out exploring with me and Owen?'

Billie, in an angelic pink and white nightie, was spooning down yoghurt and chopped fruit like there was no tomorrow. She broke off to look up at Ed, then over to her mummy, as if weighing up the choices carefully.

'We're going round the shops,' Dinah told her, 'it might be quite long in the car and a little bit boring for you.'

But this didn't deter Billie in the slightest. Fixing her gaze firmly on Mummy, she said, 'I'll come with you.'

By 4 p.m., the long and meandering shopping trawl had not brought Annie a great deal of joy.

In all the little shops and boutiques the party had been into, the clothes and accessories for sale had been so . . . well . . . just so Italian: fussy little pointy pumps in mock croc, sweaters that were cashmere, yes, but with pastel-coloured stripes, or cartoon faces, or appliquéd ice-cream cones for God's sake. Who in their right mind wanted to go around in a pale blue cashmere jumper with a pink and white ice-cream cone on the front? Even if it was only fifty euros. If someone were to pay Annie 50 euros she still wouldn't wear it.

Both Lana and Dinah had been luckier. With Annie's money and rapturous approval, Lana had bought navy patent pumps with dainty heels and brogue detailing in suede at the front.

'Oh they are so sweet!' Lana had declared.

'To wear with ankle socks?' Annie had asked and

when Lana had nodded in reply, Annie had agreed: 'Very cute.'

Dinah had bought a pair of cream-coloured cashmere gloves and a little evening bag made of plaited gold leather. Annie had spotted the bag and had it brought out for them all to look at, but as she had (at the last count) thirty-seven evening bags and a calendar not exactly chock-a-block with glamorous evening events, she thought she'd better just let the bag pass and declared quite happily to Dinah, 'No, no, you go ahead. It's all yours.'

'I like it, Mummy,' Billie had chipped in solemnly, taking the handbag out of her mother's hands and examining it carefully.

'Well, if you like it Billie, we'll take it,' was Dinah's verdict.

For a five-year-old, Billie was already in possession of precocious dressing and mixing and matching talents. Annie had an eye on Billie as a future business partner, no doubt about it. Take Billie's Italian shopping outfit, picked out all by herself, without a word of advice from Dinah (not that Billie took much of Dinah's advice anyway). She was wearing a pink, green and blue flowery skirt, teamed with a pink and blue striped T-shirt which exactly matched her cornflower blue eyes and blush-pink cheeks.

Pink flip-flops and handbag completed the look, as well as the killer accessory: pink heart-shaped sunglasses.

You could get away with a lot when you were five though, Annie would be the first to admit. After thirty-five, it got a lot harder to look fabulous every day. That was when all the girls who'd looked effortlessly good throughout their teens and twenties went to pieces and all the natural-born groomers began to stand out from the crowd.

Ageing always hit the boho girls hardest, Annie knew. She'd seen quite enough of them turning with confusion to her in the personal shopping suite. 'But I used to wear any old thing and look great. Now I look like I got dressed in the dark!'

Give Sienna Miller just a few more years and she'd join Helena Bonham Carter in looking like a bag lady. After thirty-five, a girl's gotta groom. Something the Italians seemed to understand instinctively Annie couldn't help thinking as they entered another bijou boutique and spotted the glamorous, coiffed to perfection mamma behind the counter. The arms of her spectacles exactly matched the caramel gold of her highlights, Annie noticed admiringly. Now that was good grooming.

'I am *so* bored,' Connor whispered to Annie as the boutique owner talked them leisurely through her inevitable collection of scarves, brooches, dangly gold earrings and pastel-coloured sweaters. 'Any moment now, she's going to go over to the wooden drawers and bring out her silky sock collection. I'm sorry,' he pouted, 'I am just not gay enough for silky socks and you know it.'

'Signora?' Annie put on her most charming smile, 'We want to go to the factories. Los fabbricos? Handbags and shoes? Borsettas e calzoleria. Dove?'

'Ah!' the woman smiled with understanding and nodded vigorously, setting her earrings a-jangle. 'El distrito fabricante? Mario!' she said to them and fished under the counter into a drawer.

She brought out a little business card and handed it to

Annie. Then she went to the shop door and seemed to be giving directions.

'There's a driver? To the factory?' Annie asked, getting the gist of the instructions although they were delivered in rapid-fire Italian.

'Si, si! Mario,' the woman insisted.

Annie didn't need to be told twice. She gathered her party together and herded them out of the boutique and briskly down the pavement following the woman's directions. Around the corner was a broad and sunny cobbled street. A street lined with shady plane trees and café terraces spilling out onto the pavements, dotted with bright sun umbrellas. A skinny waiter in a white shirt and black waistcoat buzzed between the marble-topped tables. Over the exhaust fumes from the odd Vespa moped puttering through floated a tantalizing smell of coffee, lemon peel and Italian cologne.

Connor came to a standstill and drank in the scene.

'You know what?' he announced, 'I'm not coming to the factory to look at any more pink cashmere jumpers and silky socks. I'm staying right here. I'm going to find myself a little table over there, line up a row of espressos, then enjoy the sun and the view. I'm here to relax!' he insisted, 'and get a light bronzing. Not a tan, that would be too ageing, just a little colour. Anyone want to join me?'

'Yeah,' Lana, whose face had been set to bored rigid for some time now, answered with conviction, 'I do!'

'Aha, you've spotted the talent buzzing by on the Vespas, have you?' Connor asked her with a nudge.

'No! I'm just tired,' Lana insisted, 'we've been shopping for the whole day. I can't take any more.'

'We spent nearly an hour having lunch!' Annie argued. 'C'mon, you can't wimp out on me now. I bet there's a lovely café up at the factory.'

But Connor and Lana were already sidling towards a table and it didn't look as if there would be any stopping them now.

'Dinah!' Annie warned, just in case her sister, who was looking gorgeous, if a little wilted in a vibrant white and yellow summer dress, thought she was going to get out of the factories tour.

'I want to go to the factory with Aunty Annie!' Billie insisted.

'That's my girl,' Annie told her. 'OK, OK, you two can stay here.' She looked at Connor sharply. 'But behave. You have got your phone on you, haven't you, Lana?'

Lana nodded.

'OK, we'll be back for you by six. Right, c'mon Billie, let's go and find Mr Mario.'

Through a side street, up a flight of winding stairs above a bakery, they finally tracked Mario down to a tiny, chaotic taxi office, which somehow managed to function without a telephone, radio or any other visible means of communication.

Mario turned out to be a small, neatly dressed and charming man in his sixties. Maybe he was the uncle of the woman in the boutique who'd given them his card. Once they said hello and were all greeted in turn, including Billie, they explained to him where they wanted to go.

'Ah si, si, va bene,' Mario enthused, taking a little black peaked cap down from a shelf, slipping on a dusty grey jacket and then directing them out of his office, back down the stairs and out into a rear courtyard.

There he showed them his shiny silver Seat saloon, opened the doors for them and helped them into the back seat.

When he was buckled into the driver's seat, he turned to them and asked, 'La zona industrial?' with a smile.

'Molti, molti borscttas e calzoleria,' Annie checked.

He smiled and nodded, and she added, 'Forty euros?' which was the price scribbled across the back of the card.

'Si,' he assured her and then gabbled something which she understood to mean that he would wait for them and bring them back.

'Forty euros?' she repeated.

'Si, tutto,' he assured her with a wave of his hand.

They swept out of the courtyard and then slowly, with a very restrained amount of horn-honking for an Italian taxi driver, headed out of the town.

Billie, leaning back in her seat, seatbelt fastened tightly around her, pushed her sunglasses up into her hair and declared, 'This is cool.'

Back at the café, Connor and Lana had settled into chairs close beside each other, which gave them a ringside view of the road and the interesting passing scene.

'Person who spots the Vespa rider in the tightest T-shirt wins a prize,' Connor had suggested.

'Are you ever not looking?' Lana had to ask.

'Got to keep looking,' Connor told her, pulling his shades off and putting them down on the table so he could take her in properly, 'otherwise the good ones get away. I'd have thought your mother would have taught you that by now.'

The skinny waiter was soon at the table, pen at the ready, offering to take their drinks order.

'Hello there,' Connor gushed, 'so what does one drink on a beautiful, bella, bella, afternoon in this part of the world?'

The waiter seemed to understand and fired back something that sounded deliciously fruity.

'No alcohol?' Connor wanted to check.

'Not vay alcohol, no, rinfrescante,' the waiter assured him.

'Refreshing?' Connor repeated, 'yes! We want long, cold, refreshing drinks. Perfetto.'

'Si, si, pronto!' The waiter executed a theatrical turn on the heel of his shiny shoe and disappeared back into the café.

When he returned he was bearing a tray loaded with one small bowl of freshly roasted almonds, one small bowl of black and green olives and for Lana, an icy, freshly pressed lemonade garnished with slices of lemon, straws and a sprig of mint.

Then Connor was handed a tall tea-coloured drink, jangling with ice cubes and decorated this time with mint, straws and fresh slices of peach.

'Oh God, look at that beauty!' Connor declared. 'Is that not just what the doctor ordered?'

When Connor put his lips to the straws, he sucked up a good long mouthful. He could taste iced tea and sweet peachy syrup cut with the sharpness of lime juice. There was definitely something else though, something a little dusky and not entirely innocent.

He rolled the taste around his mouth and wondered for a moment what to do.

It had been months since he'd had a proper drink. He could spit this mouthful out and send the drink back ... that was his first thought.

But how very long the past few months had been. How very, very long.

Connor swallowed the delicious mouthful: 'Oh Mama! That was good!' he told Lana, smacking his lips.

He could feel it travelling warmly down to his stomach. Yup, he was going to hoover this drink swiftly down and line up the next. Hang the consequences.

Chapter Fourteen

Holiday Ed:

Blue Aertex polo shirt (Boden sale c. 1996)
Combat shorts with extensive pockets (Gap sale c. 1999)
Black plimsolls (school lost property auction)
Total est. cost: £15

'Sonos Inglese'

'Ed, how old do you think these trees are?' Owen asked through a mouthful of the apple he was munching.

They'd spent an hour or so walking around the hillsides surrounding the villa and had now stopped for a picnic lunch. Although the grass was short here and slightly singed, they'd thrown themselves down on it and were busily working their way through cheese, bread and the handful of ripe apples and pears they'd picked as they roamed around.

Ed leaned on his elbow and took a look at the gnarled olive trees Owen was gazing up at.

'I don't know . . . apparently they can live for over three hundred years,' Ed replied, ever the schoolteacher. He added, 'Olive oil is one of Italy's most important products. People used to get paid in it.'

'In olive oil?' Owen asked, incredulously. 'But then how did they buy things in shops?'

'Swapped oil for them, I suppose. There was a time in the past when people didn't use to buy that much. They grew almost all the things they needed to eat, they kept animals, fished, made their own clothes and shoes . . . there was a time when you hardly ever went shopping at all.'

'It's a good thing Mum wasn't alive then,' Owen joked. 'She wouldn't have known what to do with herself.'

Ed just smiled at this and began to spread another piece of bread thickly with the creamy yellow cheese he'd brought along.

'So, if you don't like shopping much, what do you like to do with your mum?' Ed wondered, because it was something that worried him a little. He didn't think Annie spent enough time with her children, and when she was with them, he wasn't sure if she was quite on their wavelength, or in the moment with them.

'Ermmm . . . well . . .' Owen was considering the question carefully, 'she's not really into the violin . . .'

'No.'

'I used to like it when she read out my books to me,' Owen brightened up, remembering this, 'because she used to do lots of silly voices.'

'You used to like it?' Ed repeated.

'Yeah, she doesn't do it any more. She never has the

time,' Owen said lightly and tossed his apple core in a high arc behind his head.

'Well, that's a shame. I'll have to help her find some more time, so that she can read to you again.'

'OK.' Owen smiled, ever chirpy. That was the cheering thing about Owen. Hardly anything got him down. He was altogether a much happier little soul than when Ed had first got to know him. When Ed had become his form teacher two years ago, Owen had been so excruciatingly shy that he had rarely spoken to anyone outside his immediate family and had spent the entire school day in silence.

He was really coming along now and Ed couldn't help feeling a little proud of his part in this. He rested back on his elbows.

Then, just below them, further down the hill, Ed thought he could hear something . . . voices?

'Can you hear someone talking?' Owen asked, getting to his feet and looking out into the distance with his hand shading his eyes from the bright glare of the sun.

There were definitely light, chattering women's voices heading up the hill in their direction.

'Are we going to be in trouble?' Owen worried. 'Are we trespassing?'

'No,' Ed reassured him, 'we're fine. We're not going to be in trouble for having a picnic. Different story if we were picking their olives, or trapping rabbits or something.'

The voices were drawing closer and then up over the ridge of the hill towards them came a dark-haired woman, hand in hand with a girl about the same age and size as Owen, with two ponytails and long, thin legs, made to look even more so by the baggy white shorts she was wearing.

'Buon giorno!' Ed called out and got to his feet as the pair approached.

'Buon giorno!' the woman called back with a broad smile which showed her straight white teeth.

She pushed her hair out of her face so she could take a better look at these strangers. Owen saw that she was carrying a big basket full of pears. She and the girl must have been picking from the trees he and Ed had visited earlier in the day.

'Sonos Inglese,' Ed warned her, before she went off in quick-fire Italian.

'Ah, Inglesi!' She gave him a sunny smile. 'La villa?' she pointed in the direction of the house they'd rented.

'Si,' Ed replied.

She turned to the little girl and let off a barrage of rapid Italian, with the result that the girl turned shyly to Owen and stumbled over the words: "Ow you do? I Maria. This my mamma.'

Not to be outdone, Owen's response was, 'Buon giorno. Owen.'

'You like?' the woman asked them both and held out her basket to them.

'We've picked some already, I hope that's OK,' Ed confessed.

'Si, si,' the woman assured them, 'Nocciuola?' she asked next. 'You like nocciuola?'

Ed nodded enthusiastically, then turned to explain to Owen, 'I think she's going to show us where to pick nuts.'

'Yes, come,' the woman said with a smile.

*　　*　　*

Halfway down his third long peachy-tea drink, it began to dawn on Connor that he was well and truly tipsy.

He didn't blame himself: hadn't he tried to explain to the waiter at the start that he wanted a non-alcoholic drink? And he didn't blame the waiter, because the waiter had probably tried to explain to him . . . so there really was no reason to get upset.

And he couldn't imagine getting upset anyway. He felt far too good. He felt like a big, warm, lazy lion, sitting in the sun, watching the world go by.

'This is very nice,' Connor told Lana, putting his hands behind his head and stretching out his arms, 'so very, very nice.'

'Aha,' she told him. 'You do know you're drinking cocktails don't you, Connor?'

'Yeshhh,' he confirmed, 'but how did you know?'

'Hmmm . . . let me see,' she smiled, 'maybe it was when you started telling me you were "deshperate to get a shhcooter."'

On the table between them, her phone began to bleep. Tipsy or not, Connor made a lunge for it and got there first.

'Give it back!' Lana cried. 'That's personal.'

'Oh good! I should hope so too,' Connor told her and clicked on the message box: 'Going out tonight to see elephants. Chat later A kiss kiss,' he read out.

'OK, no need to guess who A kiss kiss is. But elephants? Please explain?'

'Oh, it's some people from school, they've formed this band . . .' Lana wasn't looking too happy now.

160

'Aha, so A is going out tonight . . .' Connor deduced, 'with all your school friends . . . with other girls, no doubt . . . and he's going to be having lots of fun without you?' Connor elaborated.

'Oh shut up!' Lana snapped.

'OK! No need to be so tetchy, baby-cheeks. Now look . . .' Connor leaned in to confide his words of dating wisdom to his favourite moody teenage girl, 'don't text him. D'you hear me? Not another word, OK? Not till Monday morning at the earliest. Nothing will drive him more wild and crazy about you than the thought of you *not* thinking about him every minute of the day. I promise you! This is how men are. So simple to understand.'

Before he could hear what Lana had to say about this, a tall, blondish surf dude kind of guy in an oversized T-shirt slouched up from the pavement and pulled up a chair at the table next to theirs.

'You English?' he asked with a heavy Italian accent.

'Yes,' Connor told him with his lazy lion grin.

'Cool,' was the guy's response. He turned his chair to face them, leaned forward and seemed to be ready for a nice long chat.

Although to Connor's dismay, this surfer dude was pretty obviously more interested in Lana than in him.

'Oh my God, I have died and gone to heaven!'

There was no containing Annie's enthusiasm when she hit the first of the factory outlet shops. This was it! This was unbelievable bargain central. She decided immediately that what she had to do was dig deeply into the borrowed money sitting in her bank account, buy a load of stuff here and somehow get it back to London to flog at a handsome mark-up to her eBay buyers.

'I am officially dead! No doubt about it,' she told Billie and Dinah as she tried not to skip with excitement around the shelves. 'Do you know what these are?!' She pointed to the rows and rows of leather moccasins in every colour lined up along one of the walls. 'These are Tod's driving shoes! Actual, genuine Tods. I'd recognize them anywhere, and in London they cost nearly three hundred pounds a pair. Here they are – a hundred euros?' Annie stared hard at the price tag, to convince herself that she was not in fact hallucinating.

Dinah picked up a shoe and scrutinized it carefully. 'It's nice,' she agreed, 'really nice leather. But Annie, they're seconds,' she reminded her over-enthusiastic sister, 'and you don't wear flats. You never, ever have done and you never, ever will.'

'I know!' Annie agreed, unfazed. 'But the faults are tiny and I know loads of people who wear flatties. Loads who will snap up a pair of these beauties for . . . let's say, a hundred and fifty pounds?'

Annie seemed to speed up, she began to flit about the shop spotting something even better than the last, desperately trying to hide her astonishment at the amazingly good prices from the shop owner.

The woman in charge managed to explain in a jumble of English and Italian that if Annie had her own business she could buy as much as she liked, but if she was a private client, there was a limit.

Never had Annie wanted to have her own business more.

'Then I could come over here all the time!' she told

Dinah. 'Stock up with all this brilliant stuff and import it straight back to London.'

After ordering the maximum twenty pairs of Tods allowed for a private client and arranging for them to be shipped directly to her London address, Annie led them out of the first shop and straight into the second, then on to the third and fourth.

Each one they went to had its own special supply of goods and unique treasures. Annie racked up carrier bag after carrier bag of goodies and Dinah gave up trying to restrain her. Instead, she chose carefully for herself and her little family.

In honour of the tenth wedding anniversary, she bought Bryan a supple, luxurious, leather single buckled messenger bag. 'He's going to love this! Isn't Daddy going to love this bag?' she asked Billie, who fiddled with the fat brass buckle approvingly.

Billie snagged herself a pink cashmere wrap cardigan. Rose pink.

'Baby's first cashmere,' Dinah couldn't help smiling.

'No,' Annie disagreed, 'I think if you cast your mind back to when she was born, I gave her a cashmere cardigan, hat, gloves and matching bootees.' There was just the slightest hint of huffiness to this.

'Oh yes! How could I forget?' Dinah said quickly and bit her tongue as she wondered again how on earth Annie had imagined that a new mum would have time to hand-wash cashmere baby bits? The lovely pink things had been worn twice then languished in the hand-wash bag until tragically, they were totally outgrown.

For herself, Dinah had already bought a soft leather purse, a bright red tote bag and several of the velvet quilted headbands which Annie thought were hideously Italian Sloane but Dinah, being Dinah, having the eclectic, quirky fashion girl look that Topshop stylists would kill for, was obviously going to get away with.

Mario's car boot was filling up too quickly, Billie was looking dangerously pale and sleepy and although Dinah probably didn't want to say 'Let's not go into the last place', Annie knew she was thinking it.

'C'mon, I'll be really quick, honest,' Annie wheedled. 'I could even give Billie a carry if you like.'

She couldn't bear the thought of missing out on another treasure trove. Yes, she'd already spent about £2,000 on the Tods, some belts and some bags but she was so confident she'd be able to sell all these lovely things on with her eBay site in about ten minutes flat, that she wasn't even slightly nervous.

Well . . . yes, she was maybe slightly nervous of explaining this to Ed. Annie had still not had the big business talk with him; she still hadn't told him that she had gone ahead and borrowed the money . . . and she wasn't sure when or how she was going to be able to raise it. At the moment, she was forging ahead in the hope that it would all go really well, really quickly, and she could break good news to him a bit further down the line, without worrying him. He worried far too much about her anyway.

As soon as Annie pushed open the door of the last factory outlet shop, she could see that this was a very special shop.

Beneath her feet was the gleam of polished limestone flooring and at first glance she could tell that the lighting in here was bright and flattering, nothing like the glaring strip lights of all the other stores they'd visited. Already Annie's eyes had lighted on the handbags. Shiny bags and matt bags; jewel greens, purples and reds; traditional tans and blacks; quilted bags and slouchy bags; the dainty, the chunky and everything in between; buckled bags, tasselled bags, bags trimmed with bronze, bags trimmed with chrome . . . every kind of bag anyone could ever want was here on these dark, wooden custom-built shelves.

But before Annie could rush over and begin a detailed inspection, she was greeted warmly by a man and woman who were standing, as if waiting for them, at the front counter.

'Buona sera, signoras,' the man spoke first.

'Sera?' Dinah looked at Annie,

Annie flashed a glance at her wristwatch and saw with astonishment that it was 6.30 p.m. already.

'No wonder Billie's flagging,' Dinah said.

'I'll be quick, honestly. I'll shop like the wind,' Annie assured her.

Then, turning her attention to the couple behind the counter, Annie smiled brightly and told them: 'Buona sera, I'm Annie Valentine, from London.' Then: *This is the most beautiful shop I've been into today, with the loveliest things,* was what Annie hoped she told them.

In fact, what came out was closer to 'This is a beautiful négligé, with good principles.'

The couple at the counter looked momentarily confused, but recovered and the man asked her, as if to confirm the important points, 'You from London? Shopping here? Today? We are speaking English.'

'Yes!' Annie assured him. 'Multo, multo shopping.'

'Signor Berlusponti-Milliau.' He smiled at her and offered his hand for her to shake. Annie took the hand and gathered herself together enough to focus on him properly.

He had a handsome, tanned face. He was in his early forties maybe, with brown hair held back by the tortoise-shell sunglasses perched casually on top of his head. His open-necked shirt was of creamy linen, beautifully pressed, and revealed a smooth brown chest. He exuded the subtle but delicious, Italian smell of sun oil and beach air, orange peel and basil.

For a split second, Annie was stopped in her tracks and had a strange *déjà vu* kind of feeling. She knew exactly what it was. She'd been married for six years, been partnered up since the age of 20. She knew that this was the flash of something in between disappointment and panic that you had when you met someone attractive and fascinating, who you could possibly have started something very interesting with, if only you weren't already . . .

She let go of his hand a little too abruptly and told him, 'I'm never going to remember your name, I'll call you Mr Bellissimo.'

Mr Bellissimo gave a hearty laugh at this, as did the woman by his side, an equally attractive, immaculately groomed and beautifully dressed Italian, Annie assumed must be his wife.

Mr Bellissimo introduced himself to Dinah and Billie and shook their hands as well. The couple then made the obligatory fuss over Billie, which all Italians seemed programmed to do at the sight of small children.

'You live in London?' he turned his attention to Annie again. 'You work in London?'

Peeking beyond the front counter to the bags arrayed behind him, Annie could barely concentrate enough to answer him.

'Yes, I work at The Store, it's a beautiful shop, full of clothes, shoes, bags. You must have heard of it, if you sell such lovely bags. *Such simultaneous sacking,*' she added in Italian.

'No, no, I not exporter yet.' There was a little gleam of humour to his eye as he said this. 'I have things here from three wonderful factories who make and I very interested in selling in London.'

He stepped out from behind the counter and Annie was surprised to see he was over six feet tall; she'd assumed he was on a slight platform.

'Here,' he began, walking towards the nearest set of shelves and waving his arm at the bags, 'here you find things the factory make for me . . . and some handbag made for famous designer, but not perfetto, you understand.'

Yes, she understood perfectly: the designer seconds. The bargain hunter's zeal broke out in Annie: 'Show me those things first!' she instructed him.

'You go and look,' Mr Bellissimo challenged her with a smile, 'see if you find them.'

He walked back to the counter and from underneath, brought out a cool green bottle and set out one, two then three delicate glasses. 'Pro-secco' he declared, 'because I come from Venice.'

'You're from Venice?' Dinah had to ask, because it seemed slightly unreal that someone should actually come from Venice.

'Si, the home of all beautiful. Tutto belli,' he added, the way Italians did, because they didn't trust English to sound lovely enough. And they were right, it didn't.

'Patrizia, una pasticcino por la bambina,' he instructed the woman, who disappeared through a side door.

A moment or two later she re-emerged holding a plate with the most incredible fruit tart on top. Peaches, little blueberries and redcurrants all shimmered under a glaze of the palest pink.

Mr B took the plate and leaned down, smiling indulgently at Billie. 'You like?' he asked.

'Am I *apposed* to eat this?' Billie asked her mummy, because the tart did look almost too perfect to be edible. When Dinah gave her the nod of approval, Billie carefully took the plate, said 'grazie' politely and fell on the cake with an audible 'Ummm!'

'Forgive me, this is Patrizia.' Mr Bellissimo introduced the woman properly and Annie shook her hand, taking in the long, dark, curly hair, strong Italian nose and eyebrows, wide mouth defined with a sweep of pale brown lipstick and her stunning dress.

It was a chiffony creation, but in muted creams, browns and oranges, with ruffled sleeves which ended well above the wrist to show off slim arms and long olive brown hands.

Best of all Annie liked the woman's necklaces: ropes and ropes of chunky glass beads, which glowed orangey brown and gold, just like her eyes. Because Mr B had given her no clue, Annie quickly scanned Patrizia's hands for wedding or engagement rings. There was a stunning hunk of smoky topaz on one of her fourth fingers, but nothing else.

'I love your necklace,' Annie told her.

'Oh thank you,' Patrizia replied, then in much more fluent English than Mr B's, she added, 'it is from a special shop I know. If you like, I tell you where to find it.'

'Thank you!'

'But first you must look here, see what you like—' Patrizia waved a slender arm around the shop.

Annie did not need to be asked twice. With a slim glass of fizz in her hand she began to tour slowly around.

Everything she set eyes on was wonderful. She picked up the handbags and examined them carefully: the leather was soft and supple, the workmanship was as good as any she'd seen and the designs and colours were just perfect.

'Many bags made with one thread.' Mr B was at her side again: 'just like Hermès. If the thread break,' he made a chopping motion with his hand, 'start again.'

He picked a random bag from the shelf and told her with emphasis, 'Made in Italy. Everything . . . Patrizia!' he called over and they shot out a volley of Italian.

'He want me to tell you,' Patrizia began, 'EU rule mean bag made in China, but handles sewn on in Italy can say "Made in Italy" on bag, you understand?'

Mr B pulled a face, raised his hands to the sky and shrugged to express his disgust at this state of affairs.

'Terrible!' he told Annie.

'I didn't realize,' she assured him, suitably horrified, then with her own unique grasp of Italian added, *this is a malignant truffle!*'

Here on Mr B's shelves, there was nothing, not one bag, that was too fussy, or just slightly off like so many of the things she'd seen today. Here everything was simple, elegant and right on the money.

The big questions running through Annie's mind were: how much can I buy? And how can I get it back to London?

And then she saw it . . . she saw *her* bag. Up there, on a shelf all of its own, basking in the respect it deserved, was her violet blue YSL tote bag.

'Oh my God!' she exclaimed at the bag, 'how did you get here?'

'Aha!' Mr B followed her gaze, 'you know this bag?'

'Of course!' Annie told him. 'I owned this bag, I bought it, but the first time I took it out, someone stole it from me . . .' She pointed to her forehead which was still slightly bruised.

'Terrible!' Mr B sympathized, 'they do this to you for the bag?'

'Yes, with a brick,' Annie confirmed, 'but how do you have one of these in here?' she asked, astonished. 'They are very, very rare.'

'Patrizia, per favore . . .' Mr B asked again, because obviously it was complicated to explain.

According to Patrizia there was a top quality factory near Ancona which made some bags for YSL. Mr B and several other outlet stores were allowed to sell off the items rejected by quality control. These bags did not have the YSL logos or letters of authentication, but they were less than half the price of the authentic items.

'You are joking!' was Annie's response as she removed the bag from its shelf and began to inspect it. Apart from the missing logo, she could not see the slightest difference between this bag and the one she had so briefly owned.

Mentally, she was tussling between buying this bag and keeping it for herself, or buying it and re-selling it on her eBay website to make some serious pocket money.

'Well, I'm having this!' she told Mr B.

'Annie!' Dinah warned. 'Can I just remind you what else you've bought today?'

'I was hoping you wouldn't,' Annie told her, 'but I'm selling *almost* all of it on.'

'You have a business?' Mr B asked with some surprise. 'Then we do trade discount,' he said and headed off to his counter where he brought out an official-looking invoice pad.

'Well . . . I'm not a proper business just yet,' Annie had to confess, 'not officially. I have a shop on eBay, I sell second-hand clothes, bags, shoes and discount things I've bought from the shop I work in.'

Mr B repeated 'eBay??' in a way that made it clear he didn't approve. 'Many, many bad bags on eBay,' he warned, shaking his head, 'fake! Not good quality,' and he leaned over to rub his finger and thumb against the strap of the caramel-coloured handbag closest to him to make his point.

'I know,' Annie agreed, 'but my eBay shop has a good reputation. 'Annie V's Trading Station'. My customers come back again and again because I sell good things. Maybe we can find my shop on your computer?' she offered, hoping that this would dispel any fears that Mr B might have that she was some kind of rogue trader.

Despite Dinah's eye-rolling and the fact that Billie had found a comfortable armchair and looked dangerously close to drifting off to sleep, Mr B directed Annie into the back office to search for British eBay on the internet.

It didn't take them long to locate 'Annie V's Trading Station' and once Mr B had scrolled down the range of things for sale, he at once understood that he was dealing with a saleswoman who understood fashion and quality.

'This is good, very good,' he told her, draping a very nice cashmere sweater over his shoulders against the slight evening chill.

Without taking his eyes from the screen, he rolled the end of one of the sleeves into the other, so they fell in a loose knot against his chest, as Annie watched in admiration. He'd probably been doing this since he was a teenager, so it was effortless, natural and so stylish.

'Nice sweater,' she complimented him and reached out to stroke the cashmere on his shoulder.

'You like?' he asked, shooting her a little sideways smile.

'*Oh . . . I like, I definitely like,*' Annie thought.

'Why you not in business for yourself?' Mr B asked. 'Your shop is wonderful, why you still work for The Store?'

'Good question,' she agreed. 'Why are you not selling your wonderful bags on the internet?'

He gave his raised hand shrug again. 'I think we must talk,' he said, swivelling his desk chair round to face her, 'I am looking for agent in London. Someone who work with me and sell my bags in London. Maybe you,' he pointed at her with the index fingers of both hands, 'maybe you, Mizz Annie, the person to do this with me?'

Annie could not believe her ears, could feel her smile stretching across from one side of her face to the other.

The charming Mr Bellissimo, with his Aladdin's cave of beautiful bags, was throwing out an opportunity like this to her . . . And they'd only just met!

But it was funny, there were some people with whom you just clicked. Even though she and Mr B could not understand everything they tried to say to each other, she nevertheless believed that they understood each other perfectly and she could feel a fuzzy, happy surge of warmth spreading through her. She didn't think it was just the wine.

'Annie, we have to go!' Dinah called to her from the front of the shop.

'We must talk,' Annie agreed with Mr B, 'but I have to go back to the villa now, my sister and her little girl are really tired.'

'Yes,' he nodded sympathetically, 'But you come back here tomorrow – ' this was more of a statement than a question – 'in the afternoon? Then we talk about our business?'

'Yes!' she agreed happily. 'Fantastico! But I'm buying the Saint Laurent bag right now, just in case someone else takes it.'

When Annie, Dinah, Billie and all their purchases were finally loaded into Mario's silver saloon well after seven o'clock, Dinah asked suddenly, as if she'd just thought of them, 'What about Connor and Lana?'

'Oh yes!' Annie was ashamed to realize she hadn't thought of them once – and hadn't she said she would pick them up from the café at 6 p.m.?

'I'll try their mobiles, see if I can get a signal,' she told Dinah and then, to reassure herself more than her sister, she added, 'but you know, he's a big boy and a very sober one, so I'm sure he can look after himself and Lana. They've probably taken a taxi home by now.'

Annie tried her daughter's mobile but was put through to voicemail, so then she dialled Connor's number and heard the line ringing.

Finally, the phone was answered but when all she heard down the other end was a cheerful but very slurred: 'Hello . . . hello who ish thish? Oooops!' followed by a clatter and the line going dead, she suddenly wasn't quite so confident about Connor being Mr Responsible.

She looked over at Dinah and said with concern, 'That was Connor and he sounded completely smashed.'

'No way! He's so sanctimonious about drinking at the moment. There's no way. Have another go.'

The line rang again, but this time went through to voicemail.

'Connor, phone me!' was Annie's urgent message. 'Do you and Lana need a lift back to the villa? We're heading back to the car right now.'

When they reached their hire car back in the car park, the place was almost completely deserted. There were just a few motorbikes and Vespas parked in a corner by the kids who had come into the town centre for the evening.

Dinah, now weighed down by a sleeping Billie, decided to wait in the car once all the carrier bags and packages had been transferred into the boot by Mario. He was paid his forty euros by Annie, and of course he got a generous tip on top.

'I'll have to go out and have a look around for them,'

Annie warned Dinah, 'I can't get them on their phones and Ed says they're not back at the villa.'

Ed, on the end of his mobile, had sounded exasperated. He hadn't been able to understand why the shopping party wasn't back yet, let alone why half of it seemed to be missing. 'What do you mean you're just going to go and look for Connor and Dinah?' he'd asked in surprise. 'Have you lost them? They're not gloves, you know! People don't usually cruise about town mislaying their daughter and their best friend! I need you back here,' he'd hissed, 'your aunty and I have completely run out of things to say about the weather.'

Annie hurried past several sedate cafés and restaurants where, for a Friday evening, it looked quiet. Only a few people were about, eating antipasti, or chilling out with espressos or glasses of wine.

But it didn't take her too long to find the raucous bar down a side street, where Connor was busy leading a group sing-along, while Lana was entertained at a table occupied by three very attentive Italian teen boys.

Annie marched straight up to Connor, took him by the arm and told him kindly but firmly that it was time to go home. She'd had plenty of experience dealing with Connor drunk. It was the strangely sober Connor she'd found tricky to handle.

Despite Connor's protests at the break-up of such a fun party, Annie and Lana took an arm each and led him outside into the fresh air.

'Hallelujah,' he declared once he was out of the bar, 'I am well and truly off the wagon. Think of all the drinking time I've been missing! I must have been out of my mind! I'd forgotten just how much fun it is to be trollied . . . wellied . . . plastered, stocious . . .' here, he looked dramatically up at the starry night sky, before calling out: 'and gloriously blootered!'

As they led him along the pavement, Connor continued, 'Hector says that everyone from Scotland knows fifty different words to describe how drunk they are. I have to phone him right now and tell him how clever they are!'

Connor fumbled his mobile out of his trouser pocket and promptly dropped it onto the pavement.

'Maybe tomorrow, babes,' Annie suggested, stooping to retrieve the phone for him.

'It's all a question of moderation!' Connor shouted out into the quiet side street. 'It's not all or nothing. It's a question of moderation!' With that, he tripped on a cobblestone corner, and if Annie and Lana hadn't had a firm grip on him, he'd have gone flying, right onto his pretty face.

Chapter Fifteen

Holiday Hilda:

Fuchsia pink kaftan (the 70s . . . the original 70s,
rather than another 70s revival)
White sandals (Van Dal)
Fuchsia pink lipstick (Estée Lauder)
Prescription sunglasses (Boots)
Daily Mail *(airport)*
Wheelchair (NHS)
Total est. cost: £70

'I've seen that Jane Asher . . .'

It was approaching 9 p.m. when the people carrier finally rumbled up the dirt road towards the villa, which was ablaze with light. Annie wondered if Ed was pacing from room to room in annoyance.

They were late. Very, very late . . . much later than she had expected they would be and then there was the matter of the mountain of purchases in the back of the car. Annie was bracing herself for a heated debate with

Ed because, once again, she had gone and spent well over two hundred pounds without discussing it with him.

There he was, coming out of the house, bounding over to the car, hair bouncing . . . a surprisingly big smile across his face.

'There you are!' he exclaimed, 'I was beginning to think I'd never see you again. Come on, come in.' He kissed Annie hello on the mouth. Clearly, he was so pleased, or maybe relieved, to see them again, he'd forgotten to be angry.

'Don't be shy,' he told her, 'however many thousands of pounds' worth of things you have in there, just bring them in. Bring them all in, hide them under our bed – if you can fit them under there – and tell me about it in the morning.'

This made Dinah laugh. 'You've no idea, Ed,' she said.

'Oh God,' Ed groaned, causing Annie to splutter, 'Dinah! Don't exaggerate!'

'Come on, I'll carry the stuff in for you. I won't moan, honestly,' Ed insisted and although he gave something of a double-take when he saw the mound of bags and packages in the back of the car, he just pinched Annie affectionately on the bum when she leaned in to pick up as many things as she could carry at once.

'I like you on holiday,' Annie told him from behind her armful of bags. 'Obviously we should go on holiday much more often.

'Oh yes,' Ed answered, 'I'm like a tomato. I improve in the sun. I'm definitely much more tasty in the sun.'

'And more red,' she couldn't help noting.

Once all the bags were unloaded and Owen had been greeted, Ed led them all out to the terrace where the table had been set with salads, bread, and lots of little dishes: olives, salami, sardines . . .

'Goodness me!' Aunty Hilda, already settled at the table, declared at first sight of them. 'And what time do you call this? Gallivanting about the countryside . . . you got lost, did you?'

'No, no, we're fine, thanks,' Annie told her, eyeing up the food and realizing how long it was since she'd eaten anything. 'Have you had a nice day?' she asked her great-aunt.

'Well . . . I suppose so,' came the grudging reply. 'I've not been able to get much out of your boy, though. He's a bit silent still, isn't he?'

When Owen began to turn red at this, and Annie threatened to turn nuclear, Connor, who'd sobered just slightly on the car ride, stepped in with, 'If it's a good gossip you're after, I'm your man', and cheerfully pulled up the chair next to the old dragon.

'Oh!' Aunty Hilda looked almost animated for a moment: 'I've seen that Jane Asher on your programme. She's lovely, isn't she?'

'No, no!' Connor dived straight in with the scurrilous gossip, 'Jane? No. She's a total nightmare, you wouldn't believe it. Fresh cream cakes in all the dressing rooms or she flounces straight off the set . . .'

Midway through the meal, Annie found herself looking around the table with pleasure. Owen and Lana were laughing over some joke together, and Aunty Hilda and Connor were still deep in conversation – he'd always had a thing for much, much older ladies. They were his core telly fan base, after all. With bread smeared in tomatoes and olive oil, Dinah was lovingly feeding Billie, who'd rallied following her nap in the car back to the villa.

It was noisy with chatter. The pool lights were winking in the water. It was still warm and tiny moths were flitting about the terrace. Finally Annie felt glad that she'd dragged them all out here. Despite the expense, despite the hassle, despite the travel sickness and not to mention the hangover Connor was going to have in the morning, for an evening like this, it was worth it.

And then she saw a forkful of food coming towards her.

'Try,' Ed, sitting beside her, commanded.

A grilled prawn, carefully peeled by him and smudged with a little garlicky sauce, was hovering at her lips.

She turned and let him put it into her mouth.

'Good?' he asked as she chewed and nodded.

She put her hand on his leg and squeezed gently. 'I think you're lovely,' she told him with a garlic blast.

'Oh good,' he said, 'we'll try and do something about that . . . when everyone else has gone to bed.'

'Are you glad we came out here?' she had to ask.

'Yeah.'

'It was a good idea then?'

'Your ideas are always good,' he told her with a teasing smile. 'Don't listen to anything I say from now on.'

'Oh really, I'll remind you of that . . .'

'When you're unpacking your shopping?' he interrupted.

'Exactly!'

Aunty Hilda was the first to head off for bed, complaining about eating so late and the hideous things that were bound to happen to her digestive system as a result.

Dinah took Billie off soon afterwards and Ed insisted that he and Lana would clear up, giving Annie the chance to spend some time with Owen.

'Get into your pyjamas, Owen and your mum will read to you for a bit,' Ed encouraged him and before Annie could even think about saying she didn't have time, he added quickly in her direction, 'Don't worry, it's an Alex Rider book. You're going to love it.'

Half an hour later, when Owen's story time was over and Annie had heard all about his day, kissed him thoroughly and turned out his light, she went back out into the terrace and found just Ed and a bottle of wine.

'Where's Lana?' she asked.

'I think she had some urgent texts to attend to.'

'Connor?'

'Locked in the bathroom . . . said he may be some time.'

'Ah.'

'You've driven the poor man to drink,' Ed couldn't help adding.

'Me? I wasn't even there!' Annie came over to stand behind Ed and ran her hands fondly over his shoulders.

'How about a walk?' he asked, taking hold of her arms: 'A little stroll, just you and I into the fig trees at the bottom of the road?'

'Sounds nice,' she agreed, 'sounds a little bit more fun than the sofa bed.'

'Definitely.'

As they walked hand in hand along the gravelly path

which led from the villa to one of the little country roads, Annie had to talk about Mr B, his incredible handbags and his interest in finding someone to sell them in London.

Ed listened, leading her by the hand from the road and into a field where dry grass swished against their ankles as they walked.

'Do you know where we're going?' Annie asked.

'Oh yes,' he assured her, 'I saw this place earlier today with Owen and I wanted to come back with you.'

It was dark. Now that they were well away from the bright windows of the villa, they were relying on just the light of the pale half-moon in the sky to find their way through the velvety darkness.

'You should have brought a torch,' Annie told him.

'A torch? Where's the romance in that?' he laughed.

There was a fig tree just ahead of them with branches bent low, close to the ground, and thick green leaves almost still in the windless air.

'Doesn't it smell nice?' Ed asked, leaning up against one of the thick branches and pulling Annie in close beside him.

Annie breathed in the dark green, spicy-sweet smell of the leaves and the small unripe figs hanging between them.

'Mmmm . . .' she had to agree.

'I'm a bit worried about you,' Ed said, landing a kiss on her forehead.

'Why?'

'You sound like you have a big crush on this Mr B,' he told her. He didn't sound as if he was teasing, 'and we've been here before,' he added. 'Mr Flash in a big flash car,

182

promising he'll keep you in handbags and posh knickers for ever more . . . and look how badly that ended.'

'Ed!' Annie exclaimed with as much horror and disbelief as she could muster, because way deep down where she could hardly admit it, she wondered if she did have the tiniest crush on Mr B. 'Are you jealous? Are you really jealous?'

'Of course I'm jealous,' he confessed. When he'd first fallen for Annie, she'd been dating and then had even moved in with a rich dentist, causing Ed the kind of jealous agonies which, at the time, he'd thought might be terminal.

Annie slid her hands into the back pockets of Ed's trousers and pulled him right up against her. 'Good,' she said, 'stay jealous, babes. It makes you much more interesting.'

Just as he moved in to kiss her, she pulled back her head and had to ask, 'What's this Owen was telling me about you hanging out with some incredibly attractive Italian woman all day?'

'Oh!' Ed spluttered, 'that's a total exaggeration. We ran into someone, literally, she said hello . . . she had her daughter with her . . .'

'Fabulously attractive though? Yes or no?'

'She wasn't bad . . . she was OK . . .' Ed answered in some confusion. 'I didn't really notice.'

'You didn't really notice?'

Their kissing was growing much more heated. Fingers were on buttons, fumbling to undo them and feeling urgently for skin.

'I'm going to see Mr B again tomorrow,' Annie confided, 'and you should be fine with that.'

'OK . . . OK,' Ed agreed, feeling Annie's cool hand slip into the open front of his trousers. 'How much did you spend?' he asked suddenly, feeling her tongue slide down to his nipple.

'I can't tell you,' was all the reply she gave.

'C'mon,' he murmured, feeling her lick down his chest and then against his stomach, knowing she was going to go lower. 'Two or three? Or more?'

She took him in her mouth, so when he repeated the question, it was in a very low voice, with his head pulled back, trying to find support against the branch of the tree.

'Just over three, but don't worry,' Annie broke off to tell him – but quickly carried on, deciding this was probably the best remedy.

'OK, OK,' Ed sounded a little surprised, but then murmured, 'I can live with that.' He ran his fingers through her hair. 'Another three hundred on your credit cards . . . we can sort it. We'll get there. We'll get there,' he repeated. 'Oh! I like that!'

Three hundred? Now it was Annie's turn to be surprised. Three hundred pounds? No, no, she had just spent over three thousand . . . using the money borrowed against the house.

She had wanted to tell him then, she had wanted to have the conversation and clear the air, really she had. But obviously this wasn't the moment.

'And jus' where have you two been?' Connor, on the terrace with another bottle of wine, called out when he spotted them walking in from the garden.

'Fruit picking,' Annie called out to him.

'Fruit picking? A likely story . . . Squeezing his plums and chewing his banana maybe.'

'Connor!' Annie had reached the terrace by now and seeing how pale and sweaty her friend looked, she reached over for the remains of the wine.

'You have to go to bed now,' she instructed him. 'Your liver can't take any more. You've been pure for four months, you'll have to break yourself in gently. I know, babes, because it's just like after childbirth when the first glass of champagne makes you high!'

Connor drained the glass he had in his hand and then tried to stand up. But he wobbled dangerously and had to sit down again.

'Oh babes,' Annie sympathized, 'you are going to feel so bad in the morning. I don't know if I can let you share a room with Owen tonight, he might get drunk just breathing in the fumes you're giving off.'

'Shud *up*,' Connor said, holding out a hand for Annie to pull him to his feet.

'C'mon,' Ed joined in and together, each with an arm of Connor's over their shoulders, they led him first to the bathroom, where he insisted he'd be fine and shut the door on them, and then helped him to his bed.

'Just take off my shoes,' he groaned, sinking down onto the mattress, 'I'll just sleep in these.'

'Can't I at least take off your trousers?' Annie had to ask. 'Make my day?'

'I thought Ed had already done that?' Connor wasn't too drunk to tease. 'OK, you can admire my trunks. I think you bought them for me anyway. In medium!'

'It goes by waist size, gorgeous,' Annie retorted, briskly

hoicking down his cargoes, 'otherwise you'd obviously be extra, extra large.'

Connor was already curling up on his side, eyes shut, falling either asleep or into a coma. Annie was going to put a big plastic bowl at his bedside just in case. She was feeling deeply guilty about him now. She shouldn't have left him in the café with Lana for so long. Temptation must have come breezing by and although Connor was a big boy, he still hadn't learned to stop before he fell over. Maybe he was an alcoholic. Maybe he should abstain. Maybe she had not exactly been very supportive of his attempts to address the problem.

But he was so much fun just a little bit drunk. It was hard to give that side of Connor up. Even Hector had agreed with that.

'I only love him when he's at least one glass down,' Hector had told her. 'That's not a very healthy basis for a relationship, is it?'

'You know, I can think of worse,' Annie had replied.

Chapter Sixteen

Italian Annie:

Vibrant orange and pink chiffon dress (Boutique Nina)
Pale camel fake snake heels (Boutique Lorenzo)
Bouffant hair (by Patrizia)
Total est. cost: £110

'When in Rome . . .'

The next morning, straight after breakfast, Annie got into the people carrier and drove herself back to Mr Bellissimo's shop.

No one else had volunteered to come with her. Not that she'd minded: she was sure it was more professional to go and talk business with Mr B on her own. Besides, Ed and Dinah wanted a quiet day by the pool, maybe with a touch of exploring round the villa, even a little light food shopping in the afternoon, and Billie and Owen were happy to stay with them. Connor and Lana were still in bed, which wasn't so surprising, whereas Aunty Hilda, the creature of habit, had woken at 7 a.m. and wheeled herself into the kitchen for a cup of tea.

'Lipton's . . . it's just terrible stuff. You can't get it in Britain, but you can't get anything else abroad, of course. It's just one of those strange, strange things,' she kept telling everyone who hung around long enough to listen.

'Are you really going back to Mr B?' Dinah had wanted to know.

'Yes! He wants someone to sell his bags in London and I think I—'

'Are you sure?' Dinah had asked, 'You don't think he was just saying—'

'Shhh!' Annie had interrupted her because Ed was coming back out to the terrace.

'So you're off to speak to your new handbag guru,' Ed had smiled at Annie, 'and we're stuck here just sunbathing, swimming in the pool and all that terrible stuff.'

'If you're going to sunbathe, you've got to have my posh sun cream,' Annie had insisted and went off to rifle through her suitcase to find it.

'Sisley,' she'd showed Dinah proudly as she'd rubbed some lovingly over Ed's forehead, nose and cheekbones.

'Nice!' Dinah had said. 'Am I worth it though? Isn't this stuff about eighty pounds a pot?'

Ed had spluttered with horror and moved Annie's fingers from his face. 'I'm definitely not worth it!'

'It's OK,' Annie had assured them, 'I got it online, fabulous deal. It's fantastic. For tanning without wrinkling.'

'Oh good, because I was so worried about that.' Ed snaked an arm around her waist. 'I think you should stay here,' he'd wheedled, 'I've still not seen you in your swimsuit and that's the only reason I agreed to come to Italy, to see you in your new swimsuit. How have you managed to come on holiday and fill up your time with appointments and meetings and things to do?'

She'd looked at him with some sympathy. 'Ed, I *am* in the shoe and handbag manufacturing capital of the world,' she explained.

'Annie, if I took you for a minibreak to Outer Mongolia, you'd spend the whole time negotiating the best price on saddle-bags because they are just *so this season.*'

Annie had to concede that maybe he had a point.

'I don't really like . . . well . . . lounging,' Annie had to confess. 'If I had to lie by the pool for more than an hour or so, I'd probably get a bit bored.'

'Aha!' was Ed's response. 'Now we're getting to the truth of it – we're not interesting enough for you. You're running away.'

'Just for a few hours,' Annie had promised them. 'And Ed, don't worry, I'm going to sell all this stuff, for so much money that you're not going to regret anything!'

'No, regrette rien!' he'd joked, 'that's my motto.'

'I don't think it's Connor's though,' Dinah had to add at the sound of loud retching coming from the direction of the open bathroom window situated just a little too close to the terrace for comfort.

Having parked on the edge of the town, Annie meandered in on foot through the quieter, dustier streets and drank in all the sights on the way.

A pair of heavy wooden doors was pulled open by a wiry man in a straw hat, who began to drag a wooden crate of lemons out onto the doorstep. The grocer was setting up shop. Annie looked at the doors with their ragged and flaking sun-bleached blue paint. If she'd seen them in London, she'd just be itching to pick up sandpaper and paintbrushes and re-do them. But here in the dazzling morning sun, it looked just right. Ancient, faded blue, set off perfectly by the acid lemon yellow heaped beneath it.

As she approached the town centre, Annie walked towards a café and spotted a supremely elegant woman seated at an outside table reading the paper. Her huge tortoiseshell sunglasses, already on against the glare of the sun, glinted darkly just like her chunky brown and black necklace.

There was a tiny white coffee cup in front of her and there she was, dressed to the nines, happy to be alive.

This was the essence of what Annie tried to inspire in her clients: dress to express yourself! Dress to make yourself feel good! Who cares what anyone else thinks? If you want to wear the green shoes with the yellow skirt, go for it!

Dressing well was the one genuinely creative and artistic thing most people were allowed to do all day. It wasn't about fashion and it wasn't about how much things cost . . . but then maybe she'd been in danger of forgetting that too.

To her surprise, the woman in the sunglasses looked up, seemed to study her briefly and then called out, 'Annie? Is it you? Buon giorno.'

Only when the glasses were removed did Annie recognize the woman behind them. It was Patrizia, from Mr B's glamorous factory shop. Annie had decided yesterday that Patrizia wasn't Mr B's wife, but looking at the glamorous lady now she still wasn't sure if there was anything between them or not. How could they resist one another?

'Allora,' Patrizia patted to the chair beside her, 'come, you sit and have a little coffee with me. Beautiful morning, no?'

Annie was delighted to be asked. She pulled up the spindly little metal chair and sat down, not opposite Patrizia but beside her, so they could both, from behind their glamorous shades, look out onto the street, watch the comings and goings and take little glances at each other now and then.

The coffee brought by the waiter was so strong, it was like drinking hot whisky. It tore down Annie's throat, burning a hole, shot through her blood and made straight for her heart, which began to pound. No wonder they only served it by the thimbleful. It should come with a health warning.

'So?' Patrizia leaned back in her seat, pushing her long, wavy hair away from the nape of her neck and releasing a lovely blast of the complicated citrus perfume everyone here seemed to wear their own version of. 'You came to town for the mercato?'

'Yes, maybe I'll have a look around.'

'Delicious, delicious things,' Patrizia enthused. 'Wonderful food from all around the region. The prosciuttio and olivas!'

'I was going to look for your necklace shop,' Annie confided, since she was trusting Ed to look after the food side of things during the trip, although, just to be nice to him, she might go to the market and buy him something special to cook with. 'Where did you buy this wonderful piece?' Annie asked, pointing at the fat beads Patrizia had wound several times around her neck. 'Is the shop in town?'

'Ah!' Patrizia looked genuinely pleased at the compliment, 'I take you! Yes!' she insisted when Annie raised her hands to protest. 'No! No problem. I show you some of my favourite boutiques on the way. Today, you shop like an Italian lady.'

Patrizia insisted on paying for the coffees, then they fell in step along the delicate stone pavements, complimenting each other on their shoes.

'It is very English to love shoes,' Patrizia said. 'Mr Berlusponti-Milliau say this because English women too fat to get excited about clothes, only shoes.'

'Oh no!' Annie reacted in outrage on behalf of every English woman, 'it's because English men love our shoes and . . . English women have beautiful feet,' Annie declared. No, it wasn't necessarily true but it was the best excuse for the shoe thing that she could come up with on the spot. How long have you worked for Mr Bellissimo?' she asked next.

'Mr Berlusponti-Milliau?'

'Yes, but I can't pronounce that.'

'So you flatter him and call him Mr Very Beautiful.'

'Well, I don't think he minds!'

'No, no, and I am sure he not mind. He has, how you say? Ego . . . gigantico!' She spread her arms wide to demonstrate, 'Oh,' she interrupted herself, 'but first you must come and see the shoes in here.'

Annie, who had a hundred pairs of Timi Woo shoe perfection neatly boxed up at home in London, was not exactly bowled over by the shoes on offer. They were quite elegant and very reasonably priced, but they bore no comparison to the genius shoes she had discovered. However, Patrizia was an insistent shopping companion. She wanted to know Annie's size, she instructed the sales assistant to bring out a selection of shoes to try and before Annie knew it, she was at the till paying for a pair of creamy fake snake-print slingbacks.

A quick jaunt along the cobbled pavement later and they were in a boutique which Patrizia insisted had the very best dresses at the very best price.

'I buy *everything* here,' Patrizia informed her and indeed, the woman in the shop greeted Patrizia like her very best customer.

'You like? You like this?' Patrizia kept asking, holding out dress after dress from the rack. Somehow it would have been almost insulting to both Patrizia and the owner to say no. Anyway, the dresses were beautiful and most of them were less than a hundred euros, which seemed astonishing for such intricately patterned silk.

Before she was able to say much more about it, Annie was in the changing room admiring herself in a floaty, chiffonish creation, all reds and oranges and vibrant pink. When she ventured to suggest that it might be just a little over the top for day wear, Patrizia clapped her hands and insisted: 'No! You are not thinking like Italian woman yet.'

Then, seized with the sort of enthusiasm Annie usually had for her clients, Patrizia asked permission to loosen Annie's hair from its tight ponytail. Before she knew it, Patrizia had snapped open her small leather bag, brought out a comb (in what else but coordinating tortoiseshell) and within a few quick moments, she had bouffed Annie's just below the shoulder blonde bob up to about four times its normal size.

'Now, put on the new shoes, then we go to my special shop to buy necklace. Then, you truly stunning Italian-style woman . . . this the kind Mr B-M do business with.'

Truly Italian-style tarty woman, was Annie's thought as she tried to smooth down the bouffant hair surreptitiously. But when in Rome and all that . . .

In a tiny shop, slightly bigger than a booth, a dark-haired, darkly tanned man with a winking gold front tooth sold necklaces with price tags only half as much as Annie had expected. In imitation amber, topaz, or multi-coloured Murano glass, they were all jaw-droppingly beautiful, every single one of them.

Annie took her time looking carefully through them. She wanted to buy everything, but having to narrow the selection down, she decided that she liked the chunky glass pendants best. Fashioned from amazing whirls of colour, each was like an oversized jewel strung along strands of shiny glass beads. Every colour combination was as intricate as a miniature constellation, absolutely unique and beautiful.

'So tell me more about Mr B,' Annie said as she and Patrizia tried to make a choice from all the amazing things on sale: 'is he a good businessman?'

'Yes, I think so,' Patrizia told her. 'I've only been working with him for four months. He has good connections and he has just opened the shop. But now he does not have enough customers. This is why he so interested in you. You are the way to customers. He has the very nice things to sell. You are the one with customers.

'I think he was impressed with your eBay shop,' she added. 'He has spoken of something like this. But I don't think he want to be posting handbags by himself every day. Anyway, post here, not so good.'

'Yeah, well, we have that problem too,' Annie confided picking up a small pendant of many shades of blue swirled with gold dust. This was for Lana, no doubt about it. One of the blues spiralling in the mix was exactly the colour of Lana's vibrant eyes. And her daddy's, Annie remembered with just the tiniest of shivers.

'But do you think he will be a good business partner?' Annie asked Patrizia a little anxiously. She'd only just met the man, but felt she was going to have to make a decision. If she was to take this chance, she had to decide as soon as possible, before someone much more impressive than her walked into his shop and took the bull by the horns. 'Is he honest?' Annie asked.

'Everything I see of the business, fine,' Patrizia said firmly, 'Buona. But you should know,' her voice lowered, 'he has a lot of girlfriends. He big lady man.'

This made Annie laugh, although she understood that it meant Mr B was big into ladies, not – judging by his shoe comment – into big ladies.

Patrizia held up an emerald green pendant decorated with rich brown and yellow whorls, then lighter green inside. It was strung on a multi-strand of tiny brown and gold pearls, and when she held it against her neck, her brown eyes glittered gold.

'Oh, you have to have that. Have to,' Annie commented, 'that is just perfetto for you. So Mr B is a ladies' man . . .'

'Si, but I think this is not a bad thing for his business, no?'

'And between you and Mr B . . . ?' Annie thought it might be rude to spell it out exactly, but she was curious to know if there was anything at all going on between the two of them.

'What?' Patrizia didn't seem to catch Annie's meaning at first but then . . .'Oh!' she smiled, 'you mean a romance between him and me? Oh no, no, no,' she laughed as if this was a completely ridiculous idea, 'I have fiancé,' she said and to prove the point she raised her right hand and held out the chunky smokey-coloured topaz ring on her fourth finger.

'That is lovely,' Annie told her, but felt some confusion. *Topaz?* For an engagement ring?

'Much more beautiful than diamond, no?' Patrizia asked. 'This is the ring I choose.'

'Oh yes,' Annie agreed, but really she was lying. When it came to engagement rings, she'd have to love someone very, *very* much to let them get away with anything less than a truly stonking diamond.

'But he try, of course, ' Patrizia added, fastening on the green necklace and looking at herself in the mirror with concentration, 'he lean over and say "something on your face Patrizia, let me move it away", this sort of thing. But for me is nothing,' she added, 'I wave *him* away,' she batted her hand vigorously to demonstrate, 'like mosca.'

Annie got the idea.

*   *   *

In the flamboyant pink and orange dress and new Italian heels, with the still scarily bouffant hair, Annie got out of the mighty people-carrier as elegantly as she could and headed towards Mr B's factory shop.

Mr Bellisimo was in for a surprise, she thought as she caught a glimpse of herself in the car window.

'Signorina Valentina!' he gushed as soon as she had pushed open the glass door. There he was, just as tall and smooth and handsome as he'd been yesterday, sunglasses still perched on his head. Today he wore a flattering pink shirt but still sported the cashmere sweater over his shoulders.

And yes, he was calling her Miss. Yesterday, just as she was leaving the shop, he'd caught hold of her hands, inspected them for rings and said, in a tone of astonishment, 'You are not married?'

She'd begun her explanation, about how she used to have a husband and now she had a partner, but he'd merely waved his hand and shaken his head at her.

'You Signorina Valentina to me,' he'd told her. 'Come in, come in,' he now ushered her into his shop, 'I open the pro-secco and we sit down and we talk beeeesinezzz.'

'I have the car,' she began, a little startled by the two kisses he was bestowing on each of her cheeks and not sure she wanted a numbing glass of fizz. She wanted to be totally sober for this meeting, thinking as clearly as she possibly could.

But, 'Si, si, si, vene,' Mr B was insisting, already bringing out his tray and his glasses and his chilled green bottle.

Chapter Seventeen

Dinah poolside:

White micro shorts (old Levis, cut down)
Yellow and white bikini top (Primark)
Flip-flops (Brick Lane market)
'Sisley' suncream (Annie)
Vintage white sunglasses (Oxfam)
Total est. cost: £35

'Allergic reaction?!'

'But will she actually be able to make contact with the water?' Ed asked Dinah as Billie prepared for the pool in a swimsuit with inbuilt floats, bright yellow inflatable armbands and an inflatable ring. The little girl looked like a mini Michelin man and was almost as white, with a layer of factor 300 all over her. 'Isn't she just going to float on top like a little hovercraft?' Ed continued.

'Better safe than sorry,' was Dinah's response to this. 'If I'm going to lie down on this lounger and leave you and Owen in charge, I need to know she'll be totally safe.'

Ed understood that Dinah had anxieties about her one and only precious child, so he didn't say anything else, just pulled his battered fisherman's hat further down over his eyes and nose against the fierce glare of the sun and sat watching the two children play together in the pool for a long time, until a glance at his watch told him that it was 3.30 p.m.

The siesta was nearly over and it was time to be thinking about dinner . . . and where the hell was Annie? Ed was now well and truly wound up about this. If he'd had his phone within reach, he'd have tried giving her a call to find out. She'd promised she would spend just a couple of hours in town, and would then pay a quick visit to her brand new best friend 'Mr B'.

Ed had not expected to come to Italy to be Annie's full-time babysitter and chef while she tore around every available retail outlet in the area. She was always so frustratingly unavailable. Not to mention annoying. And she took him for granted. There was absolutely no doubt about that.

'I think I'm going to walk down to the village,' he announced, getting up from his deckchair, deciding action was better than sitting about mentally whingeing about Annie. 'Who wants to come with me?'

Neither Aunty Hilda, dozing lightly in the shade of the terrace, nor Dinah lying flat out in the sun showed much sign of interest. Connor and Lana had gone off for a short walk together, so Ed's only chance of company was from Owen and Billie.

Owen swam over to the side of the pool, pulling Billie

in her rubber ring and rubber wings and polystyrene weighted swimming suit along behind him like a little dingy.

'Shall we go for a walk, Billie?' Owen asked his cousin, who was bobbing in the water beside him.

'Yes!' she answered. Clearly a full hour of splashing about in the pool had finally been enough.

'What do you think, Dinah?' Ed called over. 'Can Billie come to the shops with us?'

Dinah came over. She had to dry Billie thoroughly, apply another basting of factor 300 grease, put her into a dress, matching sunhat, socks and shoes and then finally, making Billie promise she would be 'very, very good and do everything Ed says', she agreed that her daughter could go with them.

'You will watch her on the roads, won't you?' Dinah added anxiously, to which Ed answered 'Of course', and Billie crossed her arms and gave a great long withering sigh before adding, 'Just chill, Mummy.'

They were almost a full ten minutes or so down the road. The gnarled olive trees ahead shimmered in the full force of the afternoon's heat. Dust swirled up from their steps, stones rattling along loosely, the grass at the side the colour and texture of straw after the long hot summer.

Owen and Billie walked ahead of Ed, holding hands, which must have been a bit sticky, Ed couldn't help thinking, but clearly they were enjoying each other's company. And that's when the awkward thing happened.

Billie turned to Ed and said, 'Oh dear, there's something I've forgotten.'

'Oh? What's that?' he wondered.

'I've forgotten to go for a wee.'

'Oh!'

Well, that was a bit tricky, to say the least.

Ed ran through the possible solutions in his head. Obviously there weren't any handy public toilets out here, or any obvious private ones for that matter. It was a full ten-minute walk back to the villa . . . but would she be able to last that long? Holding a child over the grass for a wee was the kind of manoeuvre that teacher training encouraged you to steer clear of with children you didn't know extremely well. Make that all children you hadn't actually fathered.

'Do you want to go behind that tree?' he ventured. 'You could just crouch down and do a little wee and Owen and I will wait on the other side?'

She looked at him with her head to one side and she might have agreed had Owen not delivered the killer blow at that moment. 'What about snakes? Aren't there snakes in Italy?'

'Yikes!!' Billie exclaimed and shook her head vigorously. So peeing behind the tree was a no-no.

'Well, we'll have to walk back to the house then. Do you think you can manage to hold on?' Ed asked kindly.

Billie nodded.

'Why don't I take her back?' Owen offered. 'It's just straight up the hill . . . we'll be fine . . . honest.'

Ed considered Owen's pleading look. He obviously really wanted this little chance to be independent and responsible.

He paused . . . he never took risks with children. He was far, far more careful with other people's children than he would ever be with his own. But on the other hand, Owen was nearly eleven. All he was asking was to take his very sensible five-year-old cousin up a hill to the villa. When Ed was eleven, he used to spend entire days on his own roaming about on a bicycle. In five minute's time, Owen would only be five minutes away from Dinah. He'd be almost within earshot of an adult for the whole walk.

'We'll be fine, I promise,' Owen repeated, seeing Ed dithering.

Surely Ed was just mollycoddling if he didn't let Owen do this? Owen would be fine. He always did exactly as he was told.

'Please?' Billie joined in with the pleading.

'OK, but you have to walk very quickly and get back to the house as soon as you can and stay there with Dinah. Billie can't be hanging around. She needs to go fast. OK?'

A grin split Owen's face. 'Yes, sir!' he said and gave a salute. Then turning on his heel, he issued a commanding 'C'mon Billie!' And the two of them began walking at speed back towards the villa. They would be there in no time.

Ed watched for the full three minutes it took them to reach the bend in the road, then he turned in the direction of the village again and carried on at a brisk pace, his mind gradually letting go of Owen and Billie and filling up instead with thoughts of what he was going to buy and how he was planning to cook it.

There was no way Ed could have guessed that just around the corner, as soon as they were out of sight, Owen and Billie were going to run into Maria, carrying a large empty basket in her arms because she was off to pick pears.

'Ciao!' she greeted them.

'Ciao!' Owen replied.

'Ciao, bambina,' Maria cooed at Billie enthusiastically. 'You like pear?' she added.

Billie nodded, then turned to Owen and said, 'Is this the girl you went pear-picking with?'

'Yeah,' Owen replied. 'She knows where to get nuts and blackberries as well.'

Billie gave a grin of excitement. 'Can we go with her?' she asked.

'But don't you need the toilet?' Owen reminded her.

Billie shook her head, crossed her arms and stuck out her bottom lip just slightly. Owen knew Billie well enough to understand that this was a Bad Sign.

'I want to go pear-picking,' Billie said with great determination.

'Are you sure you don't need the toilet?' Owen made a last attempt to dissuade her. 'Ed said we had to go straight to the house.'

'Toletta?' Maria asked, understanding the gist of the problem. 'Come with me' – and she held out her hand to Billie.

While the girls went into a field and headed for a tree, Owen made the calculation that so long as they were at the villa before Ed got back, no one would be in the slightest bit worried about them, so they had at least an hour, they would definitely be fine for a little bit of tree climbing and fruit-picking with Maria. He turned off the road and began to follow them slowly into the field.

Maria was much more matter-of-fact than Ed. She

203

took Billie behind the tree, helped her out of her pants and showed her how to squat down, lifting her dress and making sure her sandals were well clear.

The pants, a touch damp, were hung up on a low branch to dry and the children walked on down the hill towards the cluster of pear and nut trees.

'Are there snakes?' Billie wanted to know as she waded through grass, which to her was waist high.

'Yes,' Maria told her. 'Little tiny snakes.' When she saw Billie's horrified expression, she quickly added: 'They very, very frightened of people. They hide.'

It was close to five o'clock when Ed arrived at the villa laden down with two bagfuls of shopping. Tomatoes, more tomatoes, bread, melons, cold ham, cheeses, wine . . . he'd loaded himself up with slightly more than had been comfortable to carry. It would have been much easier if he could have taken the car, or been able to reach Annie on her mobile and asked her to pick him up. Instead, he'd had to struggle up the steep hill. Although the sky was beginning to darken, it was still close to 30 degrees in the sun.

Connor and Lana were sitting at the kitchen table drinking iced juice when he came in.

'Aha! Thirsty walk?'

He put the food on the table in the kitchen and was just starting to unpack when Dinah came in.

They all turned to stare at her.

'What's the matter?' she asked in response to the shocked looks.

'What's happened to you?' Connor said. 'Been in the sun too long?'

Her face, chest, stomach, upper arms and shoulders were covered in an angry red rash.

'What?' Dinah quickly took off her sunglasses for a look. This produced a peal of laughter from Connor and Lana because with the glasses off, the white of the skin all around her eyes made her look even more unusual.

'Oh my God!' she exclaimed, 'what's happened?'

Connor stood up and came over to take a closer look at the pimples.

'Allergic reaction', was his verdict. 'Nasty. Those things take ages to clear up. When I was filming in—'

'Allergic reaction?!' Dinah cut him off. 'To Sisley?'

'Erm . . . I think you'll find that's totally dodgy Sisley that my mum got cheap on the internet,' Lana piped up. 'You should have seen my face when she got me supposedly Lancôme Juicy Tubes. I looked like the elephant man for weeks.'

'Oh no, you're joking.' The full horror of this – the fact that she might still be covered in a scaly rash for the surprise party – was only just beginning to dawn on Dinah when Ed, busy stacking wine bottles in the tiny fridge, casually asked, 'So I take it Owen and Billie made it back OK then?'

'Owen and Billie?' Dinah repeated, her mind completely clearing of pimples, all her attention now focused on Ed.

'Yeah – ' Ed was still stacking – 'not long after we set off, Billie needed the toilet, so they came back here . . .' he turned towards Dinah now, with just the slightest prickle of anxiety.

'Owen and Billie?' There was clear agitation in Dinah's

voice now. 'Back here? Just after you set off? No. *No!!* They're not here, we've not seen them, they're not here!' And then she let off the most ear-piercing scream, so that Ed dropped both the wine bottles he was holding, and they exploded against the tiled kitchen floor sending wine and shards of glass flying everywhere.

'Whoa!' was Connor's reaction as he swung his feet clear of the mess. 'Hold onto your hats, everyone. We'll go and look round the garden and we'll probably find them out there having a giggle at us.'

'Owen is the most boring kid in the universe,' Lana offered; 'believe me, nothing exciting ever happens to him. *Now* please can I have my phone back, Connor? Pleeeeease?'

None of this was having any sort of calming effect on Dinah. In her flip-flops and bikini, she was already tearing out of the kitchen shouting, 'Billie! Billie!' at the top of her voice.

'Harrods! *This* is the where I want to sell my bags!' Mr B was holding forth. 'This is the ultimo. The pinnaculo of success.'

At the back of the shop, he was flicking excitedly through a ring-binder of drawings and photographs of handbags.

'Look at these beautiful things from the two best factories in Italy, all for very, very best price for you, Signorina Valentina.'

Annie didn't really want to break it to him that Harrods was not exactly the cutting edge. It was a bit stuffy, packed with expensive but unadventurous luxury goods and the tubby, middle-aged tourists who'd come to pay their respects at the Diana and Dodi shrine. But now that she'd sunk a third, or could it even be a fourth, glass of fizzy wine, she didn't really have the head for a debate, so was just agreeing with him.

'Harrods, yes! And The Store and maybe Harvey Nichols . . . although everyone wants to have things exclusive,' she reminded him. 'Exclusivo? Their shop only, that's the thing.'

'Esclusivo!' Mr B pounced on the word. 'My bags very, very esclusivo. And such a wonderful price for such fantastico quality. No?' He kissed the fingertips of his left hand extravagantly.

Annie decided that it really was time for her to get up gracefully from the sofa, where she seemed to be sliding ever closer and closer towards this charming man and his fragrant embrace.

Then she noticed that her back was already making contact with his right side, his right arm was casually slung across the top of the sofa and he *appeared* to be stroking her hair ever so gently with his right hand.

'*It must be late*,' Annie hoped she'd conveyed, but she'd just told a surprised Mr B that she had to be reprinted.

She lurched forward and attempted to stand up but wobbled on her heel and fell back down onto the sofa again, now even closer to him.

'Whoops!' she said out loud, then, taking a glance at the clock hanging from a nearby wall, she saw to her horror that it was almost 5 p.m. The extensive tour of Mr B's stock and catalogues had obviously taken much longer than she'd thought.

'I have to go!' she exclaimed. 'It's nearly five o'clock! I said I'd be back for lunch.'

'Ha!' Mr B nodded. 'Five o'clock is late for lunch, even in Italy.'

'Why have there not been any customers?' she wondered. 'I see what you mean about not much passing trade . . .'

Well that's what she'd meant to say. Mr B was looking at her in confusion. 'Tassing Parade?' he asked. 'What is this?'

Once she'd made herself understood, he boomed, 'Oh, the shop is shut. Saturday afternoon in Italy. Chiuso. Closed. Fermé.'

'Saturday afternoon!' Annie was incredulous. 'A half-day on Saturday? Mr B, that is where you are going wrong.'

The squashy sofa seemed to have flung them very close together once again. And now Mr B's warm finger was under her chin, drawing her face closer to his.

'I like you,' he said, leaning in still closer.

He had very nice lips, it occurred to her, dark pink, full for a man, with a defined cupid's bow at the top. Despite the numbing blanket of booze, Annie knew she should not be contemplating Mr B's lips in close-up like this. She dived down for her handbag and came back up with her mobile phone in her hand, which she held between them like a protective shield.

'I thought I heard it beep,' she said and looked closely at the screen, which read, 'fourteen missed calls'.

'Oh good grief, I have to go,' she insisted and stood up, wobbling dangerously.

'You leave your car here,' Mr B, who was now up on his feet too, said firmly. 'I drive you back to the villa and tomorrow when you get car . . . we make our deal.'

'Careful!' Owen was instructing Billie. 'Careful! Don't let go of my hand too soon.'

He and Maria were up on the higher branches trying to lower Billie out of the pear tree the three of them had climbed for a very successful picking session.

This was the third tree the trio had scaled, because, as any budding fruit picker could see, the best stuff was always at the top.

Billie had turned out to be extremely brave and skilful at climbing up, but just about entirely useless at coming back down again. Maria, on the other hand, could leap between the branches like a monkey.

Owen had a tight hold of his cousin's hand, which was just as well as she'd lost her footing and he was now urging her to let herself drop to the ground. She was only a foot or so up in the air.

'Just jump!' Owen told Billie. 'Let go. You'll be fine.' The ache in his arm meant he couldn't hold onto her much longer.

'Let go!' he ordered sharply now because the pain was becoming quite unbearable.

But still Billie hung on, her other hand gripping Owen's wrist tightly. 'No!' she wailed. 'Too high!'

'OW! Let *go*!' Owen shouted, beginning to feel his grip on the tree branch loosen a little. 'You'll be fine, you'll land on the grass.'

Billie was clinging even tighter.

Owen closed his eyes and just concentrated on his left arm which was clinging to the tree branch and now hurting as much as his right.

'Let go, let go, let go!' he said calmly, 'or I'm going to fall on top of you.'

At last, her grip on his arm relaxed and Owen opened his eyes to see that Maria, understanding the problem, had hurried down the other side and run to get hold of Billie from underneath so that she was spared even the small drop to the grass.

He let himself slide down the fat branch he was holding and then climbed down to join the two girls.

'We'll have to go,' he said casually. Neither he nor Maria had a watch and a quick glance at the sun (tribesmen could tell the time incredibly accurately by the sun) told him only that it was still very hot.

Maria held out the smaller of the two fruit baskets to him. It was full of warm, ripe pears and some squashed-looking blackberries, a mushroom or two and a few other edible leaves Maria had insisted they add to their haul.

'Um . . . so how do we get back to the house from here?' Owen asked, trying to sound casual. He didn't want her to think he was like, lost, or anything deeply uncool like that.

And if he was lost . . . he'd be able to find his way again. Another glance at the sun . . . did it set in the west? Or was it the east? But anyway, their villa was up a hill, so that meant north didn't it? But then, they had walked quite far with her, from one field to another, so that he had lost track of which hill the villa was on.

Maria turned and looked thoughtfully around her before giving them the simple directions she had worked out for them.

'. . . and then,' she concluded, 'after the field, you see

the road and walk up. But in the field, by the tree, attention. Very profondo.'

Which meant absolutely nothing to Owen. But he repeated the route they were to take carefully: 'Top of this hill, turn left into the field. Cross field, join the road.'

'Si!'

She leaned forwards as if she was going to give him a kiss, but Owen quickly leaned back, making it clear that he didn't want anything like that to happen.

Instead, Maria turned and gave Billie a hug and a kiss on her cheek.

'Ciao,' she said.

'Bye-bye,' Billie told her.

'You do understand the way?' Maria just wanted to check.

'Yeah, no problem.'

So with the basket of fruit and other pickings in one hand and Billie holding on cheerfully to the other, Owen set off.

He hoped they would make it back before Ed, so as not to worry anyone, but he had the slightest of misgivings that they might have stayed with Maria much longer than he'd intended.

He looked at the plants growing in the grass as they walked. How did she know so much about them? How could she just pick things so confidently and announce 'For salad' when every leaf she'd chosen had looked exactly like the next? She'd be able to live in the wild. She'd even told him that she could trap rabbits. He'd always wanted to be able to do that. Even though he wasn't exactly sure about killing them, let alone eating them.

'Look! There's a butterfly! Bright blue!' Billie called out and let go of Owen's hand.

They were in the big field on the left now. The one Maria had said just needed to be crossed before they were back on the road to the villa.

There was a large, gnarled olive tree right in the middle of the field. Both the butterfly and Billie seemed to be heading straight towards it.

What was it Maria had said about the tree? Pay attention, it's very profound? Maybe he was supposed to study the tree closely for some reason.

Something to do with living out in the wild.

'I'm going to catch it!' Billie called out and began to run a little faster towards the butterfly.

Maybe because they were on a slope, heading down, Owen felt himself speed up. Felt himself start to run too, after the butterfly and after Billie.

Then all of a sudden, with just the tiniest flick of her hair, she was gone.

'Billie?' Owen shouted after her in surprise.

She must have fallen down. She must've fallen into the long grass. Yes . . . yes! That was surely a much more logical explanation than the other one pounding in the back of his head: *alien abduction*. Well, he was an avid *Doctor Who* fan. He was sprinting now. Sprinting to the spot where he'd seen that last curious flick of hair before she vanished.

But just as he got there, the ground beneath his feet dropped away and, flailing frantically with his arms, Owen felt himself falling.

Chapter Eighteen

The seductive Mr B:

Pale blue chambray shirt, ironed to within an inch of its life (Ralph Lauren sale)
Red cashmere sweater tied over shoulders (sample sale)
Dark blue jeans (Armani sale)
Brown belt, brown ankle boots (discounted at his cousin's shop)
Sunglasses in hair (Armani sale)
Generous application of aftershave (Acqua di Parma)
Total est. cost: £150

'How do you like my vroooooom?'

Mr B drove a bright red Maserati, which made Annie smile because it brought Ed's words to mind: 'Mr Flash in a big flash car promising to keep you in handbags and posh knickers for ever.'

Annie stepped as carefully as she could through the door being held gallantly open for her and then sank gratefully down into the leather passenger's seat. Mr B settled in comfortably beside her. When he fired the engine up, he revved on the accelerator and there was a throaty vroooom of power.

He turned his head, met her eyes and raised his eyebrows questioningly, which she suspected meant, *'How do you like my vroooooom?'*

'Very nice,' she said.

She had already decided how he was going to drive – just a little too fast with too much braking at corners and junctions. But as they set off through the business park, she realized she was going to have to re-evaluate. Mr B drove at a steady speed, carefully, almost professionally.

He flipped on a CD and something smooth and smoky snaked into the car. Ah yes, he was definitely a big seducer. But seducers got such a bad press, she thought. They did always know how to look after you. Well, at least at the beginning, even if they let you down at the end. But it was nice to enjoy just a little taste of the beginning. And she was a grown-up, she could do that without hurting anyone.

'Who is at the villa with you?'

Annie listed her children (Mr B giving the appropriate cries of disbelief when she gave their ages), then her sister and niece, then gave Connor a properly swanky introduction, explaining that he was famous in Britain. Finally, suspecting that this would put an end to all the Mr B's seductive attentions, Annie told him, 'And Ed, my boyfriend.'

'Boyfriend?' Mr B asked.

'Ragazzo,' Annie clarified, relieved that the Italian word had come back to her.

'Un *ragazzo*?' Mr B asked with a slow smile. 'Signorina

214

Valentina!' he made a tutting noise but didn't stop smiling. An urgent trilling took his attention away from her and he pulled a tiny mobile from his trouser pocket.

As she heard him jabbering at high speed, Annie took out her phone and tried dialling Ed's number again. But she just got through to his voicemail.

'I'm on my way back,' she told him, 'I'll be there by about half-past five . . . and I'm bringing Mr B . . .' she wasn't sure what more to say about this, so she just finished with 'see you', and clicked off.

Annie listened to Mr B's animated mobile conversation and it was safe to say that she couldn't make out a single word. Well, OK, he seemed to repeat the word 'commercio' a lot and she had a feeling that this was beeeeziness. She wondered if Mr B was blowing out the date he had surely lined up for this Saturday night.

The car turned from the main road and began to twist along the narrower country road towards the villa. Darkness was falling quickly and already the sky was an inky blue with just a strip of gold low down on the horizon. As they rounded a corner, the headlights Mr B had just switched on swept over a field.

Annie's attention was immediately caught by a tall, thin woman in white shorts and a bikini top running across the field. The woman seemed to be shouting and waving her arms, and even at this distance Annie could see she was very upset. A moment later Annie registered who she was looking at. She lurched forward and shrieked at Mr B, 'Stop the car! Stop! That's my sister!'

Quickly he applied the brakes and the car came to a standstill.

Annie flung open the door and hurried towards the

field, calling out to Dinah. Mr B got out as well but stood by the car, trying to work out what on earth was going on.

'Dinah!' Annie called, 'Dinah, it's me! What's wrong?'

Now that Annie was in the field and her eyes had adjusted to the dim evening light, she could see that Connor was there as well. He was about 200 metres or so behind Dinah, carrying a long stick, which he was using to swish at the grass.

'We've lost the children!' Dinah screamed back at her.

'What?' Annie screamed back, unable to take in what this meant.

'Billie and Owen! We can't find them!' came Dinah's terrified reply, her hands falling helplessly to her sides.

As Annie ran towards her sister, her mind briefly registered that Dinah was the colour of an overripe strawberry before filing it away as unimportant information.

OK . . . Annie was trying to think as clearly as she could.

'Where are Lana and Ed?' she asked, but before Dinah could reply, Annie went on: 'what were Billie and Owen doing?' She still didn't feel as if she'd taken this news in. She was too buffered by surprise and pro-secco even to feel properly frightened yet.

'Lana's looking all around the garden and staying near the house, in case they come back, Ed's doing the field behind the house. Annie,' Dinah couldn't help asking hopelessly, 'where are they?'

'What were they doing? Were they playing?' Annie asked. She was almost beside Dinah now, hadn't noticed Mr B striding through the field behind her.

'Ed let them walk back. A ten-minute walk. He last saw them at four o'clock,' Dinah was shaking, her voice flying up and down, totally uncontrollable.

Annie put both arms round Dinah and held her tightly, 'We'll find them,' she said, as steadily as she could.

'Owen!' Connor boomed out into the field.

'The children are lost?' Mr B was catching on.

Then Connor called Dinah over, and both Annie and Mr B followed. There wasn't much time for formal introductions, because when they reached Connor, they could see he was holding out a small pair of pink pants.

'Annie? Are these Billie's?' he asked hopefully, as if this could be a good sign.

Dinah started to scream and wail.

'Dinah, hang on in there,' Connor told her, calmly.

'We'll find them, babes,' Annie tried to reassure her, holding her tightly across the shoulders, but a very anxious feeling was taking hold of her heart now.

'Didn't Ed say Billie needed the toilet?' Connor reminded them. 'Well, maybe that's why pants were hanging on this branch. To dry off . . .' He pointed to the tree from which he'd unhooked the knickers.

Dinah's shallow breathing seemed to calm just slightly as she hoped that this explanation could be the right one.

'Maybe Billie did a wee and then they went off to play,' Connor continued. 'I'm sure they're fine, just a bit disorientated.'

'They've been here,' Annie said and squeezed Dinah. 'We're looking in the right place. We just need to spread out and make lots of noise. I'm going to go down there.

Maybe I can climb that big tree and get a view from the top.'

'I'll go this way, Connor can go over there . . . Ed's phoned the police,' Dinah told her. 'They're going to be here soon.'

Annie began to march purposefully down the side of the hill in the direction of the big tree. When she was halfway down, she stopped, took a deep, deep breath, put her hands up to her mouth and roared 'O-WEN!' at the top of her powerful voice.

She listened, straining her ears, hearing only crickets, the rumble of a car passing miles away, and the breeze stirring the grass all around her. But there, so very, very faintly she could hardly even be sure of it, was something else, a ghost of a cry . . . She began to run towards it. She thought she had heard just the slightest trace of her son shouting back, 'Muuuuuum!'

'*Over here!*' Annie bellowed at the top of her voice again, this time hoping to attract Dinah, Connor and Mr B as well.

'*Over here!*' she shrieked again.

Now, as best she could in her fake snake Italian heels, Annie was racing, stumbling and tripping towards the bottom of the hill.

'*O-wen!*' she paused to yell at the top of her voice again, desperate to hear something back, so she could reassure herself that it really was him.

'Muuuuum!'

There it was, coming back at her, clearer than before. She wasn't imagining it! It *was* him.

'Thank God! Thank God! Owen . . . Owen,' she heard herself saying under her breath as she hurried on.

'Mum! Watch out!' Owen called. His voice was close now, close enough for her to be able to see him surely, but she couldn't. She slowed down and looked carefully all around her, then up into the branches of the tree, but there was no sign of him.

'Owen?' she shouted, frightened again. 'Where are you?'

'In a deep hole,' came his reply.

Slowly she began to walk forward in the direction of the voice.

'Have you got Billie?' Annie asked and realized she was close to tears. The thought of Owen not having Billie was just too scary to even think about.

Before Owen could reply, Annie was parting the tall, dry grass to reveal a gaping black hole in the ground. Crouching down, she leaned over and called, 'Owen?'

About nine or ten feet below she could just about make out her son sitting with his legs spread out in front of him. With a leap of fright, she saw Billie's dress and legs down at the bottom of the hole too . . . Billie's head was on Owen's lap.

'Oh God!' Annie exclaimed, 'Is Billie hurt?'

'No, she just fell asleep,' Owen called up. He sounded incredibly matter-of-fact, considering. 'But I've hurt my ankle, otherwise I'd have tried to climb out.'

Annie leaned in as close as she could to take a look at her lovely boy. They smiled at each other in happy relief.

'Hello, Mum!' Owen said warmly, 'I've been waiting for you. You're always late, but I knew you'd show up eventually.'

'Have you any idea how frightened we've all been?'

'I was pretty frightened at the thought of spending the night in here,' Owen admitted, 'especially with Billie. She screams a lot. I was glad when she fell asleep.'

'It's a shame she didn't keep screaming, we'd have found you a lot sooner.'

Owen was holding something in his hand. Casually, he bit into it.

'Are you eating?' Annie asked with amazement.

'Yeah.'

'What?'

'Some pears . . . we went pear-picking with a friend of mine. We met her on the road and she took us all around . . .'

'Owen, I don't think you should tell Auntie Dinah that . . . not just yet,' Annie advised. 'Shall we just stick with Billie needed a wee, so she went behind the tree and then you fell in this hole.'

Owen nodded in agreement.

'What is this?' Annie asked. 'Why is it here?'

'I think it's an old well,' Owen called up. 'It's a bit soggy at the bottom and the sides are made of brick.'

'Oh Owen!' was all Annie could say as she tried not to think about how unlucky the two children could have been.

Annie wished there was some way of capturing Dinah's happiness as she galloped down the hill towards them, once she'd heard Annie's shouts that she'd found the children.

'Billie, Billie sweetheart!' Dinah kept saying from the top of the old well, 'are you OK?'

But Billie, who'd spent a long, hot afternoon climbing trees, walking through fields and then playing an interminable game of paper, scissors, stone down in the well with Owen, could not be woken.

It was Connor and Mr B whose minds quickly turned to the practicalities of getting the children out.

'So shall I go down and lift them up to you?' Connor volunteered.

'But how we get you out?' asked Mr B, who was now, sleeves rolled up, as deeply involved in this family drama as everyone else.

'No idea,' was Connor's helpful response.

'Just go down!' Dinah, who couldn't even think about relaxing until Billie was in her arms, urged Connor. 'We'll worry about you later.'

'OK . . . deep breaths, Dinah,' he added because Dinah's fright had been so severe that she was now trembling with happiness and relief.

Using the muscles he'd honed so hard in the gym, Connor lowered himself over the edge of the well and, scrambling for toe- and hand-grips, began to climb down.

'Stay out of the way!' Annie warned Owen.

But the well wall wasn't quite as simple as the plastic and rubber artificial climbing wall in the state-of-the-art fitness studio Connor attended. Just as he reached the halfway point, something didn't quite go according to plan. Maybe the wall jutted out roughly there, maybe there was a rogue loose stone or he couldn't find a toe hold. Whatever the reason, there was a loud 'Ow', followed by a thud and a cry of, 'Bloody hell, I've skinned my nose!'

Annie and Dinah found it hard to care, 'Oh dear . . . well, just bring up the children,' Annie encouraged him.

Sleeping Billie was lifted out first. Connor raised her up as high as he could, then Mr B and Dinah leaned in to get hold of her. Next came the carrier bag full of fruit, which Owen didn't want to leave behind, and finally Owen, whose ankle was clearly swollen and causing him some pain.

Mr B had to get involved in Connor's undignified scramble to the top of the well, which resulted in both of them getting very dirty.

'Don't they have well covers in Italy?' Annie asked irritably as soon as Owen was safely out. 'Don't they think holes like that should be covered up instead of just sitting there waiting for people to fall into them?'

'We were warned,' Owen, who'd had a lot of thinking time in the well, told her. 'I think the Italian for deep might be profondo.'

Owen hopped on one leg, supported by Annie and Connor, whose face was now bleeding freely. Billie stayed fast asleep in Dinah's arms and Dinah would not be persuaded to let go of her, even when it was obvious she was struggling with the weight as they walked up the hill.

Just as they approached Mr B's car, intending to cram into it for the brief ride up to the villa, they were met with the bright headlights of a shiny police car in one direction and the beam of a lone torch in the other.

'*Ed!*' Annie shouted out, as the police car illuminated the figure carrying the torch. 'We're all here. We've got them.'

Somehow in the excitement of finding the children and the complication of fishing them out of the well, Annie had unforgivably forgotten to at least try and phone Ed and Lana, who'd had forty minutes longer to worry than anyone else.

Annie could see Ed's face in the car headlights. A grin was splitting across it and he began to run towards them. He shot Annie a smile, but his eyes were fixed on Owen. As he bounded up to them, he reached out, flung his arms round Owen and lifted him into the air.

'Watch his ankle,' Annie warned.

'Owen!' Ed said over Owen's giggles, 'you . . . you total . . . you *idiot!*' but like everyone else, he was grinning with relief.

Spotting Dinah and Billie, Ed asked, 'Is Billie OK?' Dinah nodded curtly in response, and Ed suspected he had some major apologizing ahead of him.

Meanwhile a black leather jacketed, capped and armed Italian police officer was climbing out of the police car.

'Would you talk to them?' Annie asked Mr B, who nodded and strode forward, happy to be the group translator.

'Who's that?' Ed asked, now that he was beside Annie, now that he had slung a comforting arm around her waist.

'Mr B from the handbag factory – the one I was telling you about.'

'Oh . . .' There was something of a pause before Ed said, 'Let's get back to the house, we need to tell Lana and Aunty Hilda.'

Aunty Hilda! Annie hadn't thought about her since she'd left the house that morning. She didn't think she'd even mentioned her to Mr B.

It wasn't quite the evening Annie had planned. Once the wine debris from earlier had been swept and mopped from the kitchen floor, everyone congregated round the table on the terrace for whatever could be cobbled together from Ed's afternoon shopping trip.

They were hardly the 'glamorous and gorgeous people from London' that Annie had thought would wow Mr B. They looked just like an ordinary, exhausted and slightly grubby family. And somehow Mr B had ended up in the chair next to Aunty Hilda.

'What was that?!' Annie kept overhearing Aunty Hilda ask him in her deep and penetrating voice.

'You know, she leaves the children with that man of hers all the time. He's not the father, of course, and Owen . . . well . . . a difficult child . . .'

Now Annie had to make a superhuman effort to tune out the old battleaxe.

The two policemen stayed for coffee because they had to file a report anyway. Mr B drank coffee too and ate a plateful of the food on offer. He ignored his mobile, which burst into life every so often. That had to be his irate date, Annie suspected.

Lana, sitting opposite Annie, had looked touchingly pleased when Owen finally made it back to the villa that evening.

'Did I even have *you* worried?' Owen had wanted to know.

'Just this much,' Lana had told him, holding her

thumb and finger just a tiny bit apart, but her smile had been genuine.

'How's Andrei?' Annie leaned in to ask her daughter. 'Have you had a chance to speak to him with all this going on?'

'No . . . I've not got through to him yet, I'll try again later.' A flicker of concern passed across her face.

'Don't worry,' Annie reassured her, 'he's probably trying to keep busy so he doesn't miss you too much.'

Connor would possibly have liked to make some punchy response to this, but he was too preoccupied with the policemen and their leather jackets and truncheons. Not to mentions handcuffs.

Undeterred by everything that had happened to him this afternoon, Owen stuffed bread and tomato into his mouth. His ankle, carefully bandaged by Ed, who'd promised to call a doctor if it looked worse tomorrow, was up on a chair and whenever his mouth was empty, he launched into a new and increasingly lurid description of his time in the well.

There had now been a 'medium-sized' snake down there at the bottom of the well, along with a 'pure white' scorpion and a 'vicious-looking' one-eyed lizard.

Connor, when he could tear his gaze from the policemen, felt it was his duty to provide topical jokes. 'Well, well, well, Owen,' he began to everyone's groans. 'Let's hope you *fall* into a *deep, deep* sleep tonight.'

Dinah had put Billie to bed and stayed there with her for a very long time. So when she finally came out to the terrace, the policemen and Mr B were saying their goodbyes.

Maybe just as well, as Annie could see from Dinah's

stormy expression that the words 'post-mortem' was definitely in the air.

After being lavishly kissed, four or maybe even five times on the cheeks by Mr B, who had told her to 'meet me in café for late beeeziness breakfast', Annie made Dinah sit next to her and poured her a large glass of wine. She urged her to drink it down and then poured her another one.

'You've had a horrible fright. Forget about sweet milky tea and get some of this down you,' she insisted. She was also hoping that the row Dinah looked as if she was ready to have with someone might be tempered a little by a glass or three of wine.

Aunty Hilda declared that she had to get to bed, Annie told Owen and Lana to go inside, wash and think about bed, so only Connor, Annie and Dinah were left at the table when Ed returned from showing the Italians out.

'You're seeing him tomorrow?' were Ed's first words to Annie and she could hear the edge to his voice.

'I have to go and get the car,' she explained. 'I had just a bit too much wine at his shop and that's why he drove me back. So we're going to meet in town, then he'll drive me up to get the car.'

'So what's going on with this guy? Is he offering you some work or something?'

Annie ignored the obvious snort that this provoked from Dinah. 'I'm going to sell his bags in London, through eBay or maybe though a couple of shops. He's got some great stuff – at brilliant prices,' she added quickly, aware that she was making it sound very easy.

'Right,' was all Ed said. He pulled up a chair and reached over for the wine bottle.

Sensing the awkward silence, what with Ed glaring at her and Dinah glaring at Ed, Annie took a mouthful of wine, then asked her sister, 'So . . . you got really sunburnt then?'

'Annie Valentine!' Dinah spluttered. 'Your pseudo-Sisley did this to me! Whatever is in that jar, I'm allergic to it. Totally allergic.'

Dinah had actually forgotten about her vibrant red rash. Now, thanks to Annie, she had another reason to be angry.

'Nasty allergy,' Connor agreed. 'I'll give you my dermatologist's number when we get back to London.'

'Oh just shut up!' was Dinah's not entirely grateful response. Then turning to Ed, all the terror of the last few hours rushing out, she began to rant, 'I just can't believe you sent them back to the villa on their own! How could you have been so selfish and so stupid and so completely irresponsible? Anything could have happened to them! Anything!'

Ed had already decided that he wasn't going to do any explaining, or justifying, he was just going to apologize. Dinah was far too upset. Anything else he said would just make it worse.

'I am so sorry,' he told her softly, 'I am so, so sorry. If there was any way I could go back in time and re-make that decision I would. I am so sorry to have put you through that.'

'You're a teacher!' Dinah was clearly going to have to get this off her chest, whether the others liked it or not. 'You know the dangers. Billie could have broken her neck falling down that well.'

'I thought Owen—' Ed began.

'Leave Owen out of this,' Annie snapped. No one was going to blame Owen for what had happened.

'Owen! Owen?' Dinah blurted out. 'Owen is a total space cadet who couldn't be left in charge of a glass of milk because he'd probably knock it over.'

'Dinah!' Annie turned angrily to her sister. 'Just because you're the most over-protective, over-anxious mother in the entire universe!'

'Please don't,' Ed said gently. 'You've both had a terrible time, please don't take it out on each other.'

'Just stay out of it,' Dinah ordered, 'you know nothing. Don't ever make decisions about other people's children again, OK? Never, ever. You've got enough to worry about trying to stop Annie from shopping you right out of house and home.'

'What's that supposed to mean?' Ed asked, the calm note missing from his voice now.

'Uh-oh,' Connor muttered from his end of the table.

'Dinah,' Annie warned, making a mental note never to give Dinah more than one glass of wine ever again. They were sisters, they'd had plenty of disagreements in the past, but it was a long time since they'd had an out and out open row.

'She's not told you, has she?' Dinah was unstoppable.

'Dinah!' Annie warned again.

'She's not told you she's sunk at least three thousand pounds in the factory shops and she's probably going to spend much, much more at schmoozy Mr B's outlet shop.' Then came her killer blow: 'Oh and by the way, she owes the taxman ten thousand pounds . . . but knowing Annie, she hasn't told you that either, has she? But don't worry, she's just going to add it all to her mortgage.'

A stunned silence followed.

'Oh boy,' Connor decided it was time to weigh in. 'C'mon, Dinah, I think you and I should take a little walk around the garden.' He moved round to escort Dinah from her chair.

As they walked down the steps into the garden he couldn't resist adding, 'Don't think there's going to be any squeaking from the sofa bed tonight.'

Chapter Nineteen

Aunty Hilda in town:

Herbaceous border summer skirt (Vintage M&S)
Matching summer blouse (Vintage M&S)
White, square-heeled slingback sandals (Scholl)
White handbag (Sorrento c.1975)
Wheelchair (NHS)
Slightly too much perfume (Chanel No. 5)
Total est. cost: £160

'You're more like her nanny than her man.'

Ed was trying not to listen too closely to Aunty
Hilda. He'd agreed to take her into town by taxi
because she'd woken up in a sour mood and spent
the hour after breakfast complaining to anyone who
would listen that she'd been in Italy for nearly three
days and had done nothing worth doing, and seen
nothing worth seeing and what she really wanted to
do was go home.

Ed, satisfied that Owen's ankle was improving and

that everyone else just wanted to be left in peace by the pool, had offered Aunty Hilda the trip.

'C'mon, we'll order a taxi, then we'll buy some English papers and have a coffee out in the main square,' he'd told her.

It was for his benefit too. He wanted to get out of the villa where the atmosphere was horribly strained because Dinah was still avoiding him and, as just about everyone knew, he'd had a big row with Annie last night.

The row was still unresolved, because they didn't seem to be able to reach any kind of agreement. Annie was determined to 'go into business', although as far as Ed could see all she was doing was getting further and further into debt by buying things she was supposedly going to sell. Ed had argued till he was blue in the face that it was far too much of a risk. It was far too much of a time commitment. He just wanted them to do their jobs, pay the mortgage and be happy.

Then Annie had argued back that having her own business was what she was desperate to do and Ed was just holding her back because he was over-anxious and never dared to take a chance.

'What about the tax money you owe?' Ed had fumed. 'Why couldn't you even tell me about that?'

'Because I knew you'd use it against me! You'd just say I can't be trusted to do the business admin and I can. I want to learn!' she'd insisted.

'I told you not to borrow against the house,' he'd stormed.

In the morning, when the row had kicked off again after their broken night's sleep, he'd asked her heatedly, 'Why can't you just be content with what you have?'

'I can do better,' she'd snapped, and to him, that had sounded like a warning.

'Fine,' he'd shot back, 'go ahead! Flounce off with your new handbag friend and see how well that goes, why don't you?'

'Oh don't be so stupid!' Annie had fired back, but soon afterwards she'd left the house in a taxi of her own, dressed to the nines in a red summer frock and her ridiculous new Italian shoes, to meet Mr B and make 'final arrangements' about consignments of handbags.

'And I suppose I'm babysitting everyone again?' had been Ed's parting shot to her. 'Thank you so much, Annie.'

'Dinah and Connor have said they'll do that,' she'd shouted back. 'You can do what you like! You can go home for all I care.'

In the taxi it became obvious that Ed had one person on his side, but unfortunately it was Aunty Hilda.

She had nothing good to say about Annie and was full of advice for Ed.

'You make life too easy for her,' she insisted, 'you cook all the meals, you do all the shopping, you look after her children. You're more like her nanny than her man. Frank would never in a million years have stood for that kind of nonsense. I knew my place.

'You should teach her a lesson,' she warbled on, 'believe me. I was married for forty-eight years. I should know. She'll respect you much more if you stand up to her . . . You should just fly home with me today and leave her to get on with it.'

Bouncing about in the back seat as she fired her views

back at him, Ed wondered how much more of this he could take. Should he argue tactfully back? Or just let her carry on until she'd got it out of her system?

'What is this nonsense that she's on about? Selling handbags from that man? You want to watch that situation. He couldn't keep his eyes off her,' Hilda added.

That little detail hadn't passed Ed by either.

'Yes, you need to watch out,' Aunty Hilda told him ominously, 'you'll be left with her children while she goes off gallivanting with the wealthy Italian.'

No, it was no use, Ed was going to have to stand up for Annie now.

'Hilda, Annie is interested in doing business with this man.' He was trying to be as restrained as he possibly could. 'She goes in at the deep end sometimes, but she has our best interests at heart and I trust her absolutely,' he added: '110 per cent. I don't think it's very kind of you to make these suggestions.'

'Well then!' Aunty Hilda folded her arms across her chest and turned her head away to look out of the window.

Ed looked outside too, with a little more concentration than before. It was another beautiful day. Bright sun, clear sky, the small town on the horizon ahead of them with its church steeple soaring high into the blue air.

Having once spent a whole summer in a small Italian town, Ed was already imagining the clang of the bell, the cooing of pigeons and the clip and clatter of shoes on the cobblestones of the central courtyard.

He and Hilda would drink coffee together, they'd read

through the papers side by side and this silly rant would be forgotten. Surely?

Maybe Annie could even finish up with Mr B and join them there. Prove to him that Aunty H had got it all totally wrong.

'This is not difficult,' Annie was telling Mr B as they strolled along a little street towards the town centre. 'You just give me some of your lovely bags and then I sell them!'

She felt much better now that she was in town, away from her fractious family, away from having to justify every single one of her decisions to Ed all the time.

She didn't know how to get around this. She was doing what she wanted to do – why did Ed have to be against that? Why did her following a dream have to cause him such a headache? Why couldn't he just let her work this out on her own? If only Dinah hadn't blurted everything out, that's what she would have been able to do.

Dinah would of course be contritely sorry today, but that was no bloody use.

'And then,' she looked up at Sandro – that was Mr B's first name and he was insisting she call him by it – with what she hoped was a very persuasive and charming smile, 'I send you money and you send me more things.'

'Ha, ha, ha,' Sandro cracked a little smile. They'd had a coffee together and now he was giving her a quick tour of the town before he drove her back to collect her car.

Annie was having to concentrate harder than she would have liked to on her fake snake shoes. She'd strapped them on this morning at the sound of the taxi outside the villa, completely forgetting that they'd been subjected to severe abuse in the hunt for Owen and Billie yesterday. Running down the hill towards Owen seemed to have done them a serious injury and now they were even more fragile and unstable than before.

'Annie, I cannot *give* you my things,' Sandro was telling her mournfully.

What?!

Had she been completely wasting her time with him? What did he mean he couldn't give her his things?

He looked relaxed enough, strolling along in his white linen trousers and light shirt, jangling his keys in his left hand and carrying one of those big Italian wallets with handles in his right. The kind of thing middle-aged British wives were always buying their husbands on holiday, but to no avail: *'Carry a bag? Are you out of your mind?'*

'I cannot *give* you my things,' he repeated. 'You will have to *buy* them, at discount of course, and I give you very good discount on the price, but then you sell them. When you selling many bags, then you can have and pay me after the sale.'

'Money first, from me?' Annie clarified in Italian.

Well, what else could she have expected? He couldn't know if she was genuine or not. She might be about to take a great consignment of bags from him and never be seen again.

'Fifty per cent discount on your shop price,' was what she said, instinctively.

'Fifty! Cinquanta! No, no,' Sandro shook his head, 'thirty! Trenta is generoso, the most I can do.'

Annie's heel struck an uneven paving stone and she

felt it wobble dangerously beneath her foot. She caught hold of Mr B's arm for support.

'OK?' he asked, placing his hand over hers, assuring her it was to stay there.

Annie, walking gingerly forward on the injured shoe, nevertheless told him confidently, 'Quaranta-cinque, forty-five per cent.'

Sandro gave another little laugh and squeezed her hand. 'Signorina Valentina! You sell my bags very well in London, I know this!' he added.

Before he could say anything else, Annie removed her hand and told him in a tone of complete finality, 'Forty per cent. Quaranta. I can't do it for less,' She shook her head with genuine sincerity.

Sandro's brow furrowed slightly, Annie turned her eyes to the dangerously uneven pavement. She didn't want to fall on her face just at this moment. Just when she was trying to impress him with her hard-headed business skills and her no-nonsense negotiating.

She kept her gaze down and saw a drain cover with dangerously wide gaps, so she skipped in what she imagined was a dainty and gazelle-like way over the drain and landed.

But as she hit the ground, the heel of her fake snake snapped clean off, rolled straight into the drain with a splash and pitched her over sideways, straight into an (up until now) invisible waiter who had been swooping gracefully towards an Italian couple waiting for their morning caffe latte.

The coffees and the metal tray took flight through the air for quite an astonishing distance before arcing, tipping, then smashing to the pavement. The tray

236

wobbled with long, harsh metallic rings before it finally came to a standstill.

'Forgive me, forgive me . . .' Annie gushed, 'I am so sorry and so clumsy', she imagined she was saying, although what in fact came out was, 'Losers, losers . . . I am a very poor whirlpool.'

Without great fuss, Sandro felt in his man-bag for his wallet, drew out a note, passed it to the waiter and with a series of charming words and smiles told the couple that today their coffees were on him. Well, technically, the coffees were all over the pavement, the waiter's shoes and the bottom of the tablecloth . . . but . . . nevertheless.

After the apologies, Annie and her new business partner tried to keep on walking with some dignity, Annie wondering how long she could tiptoe on her heelless right foot before terminal cramp set in.

'Forty per cent is fair,' she began again, once a reasonable distance had been set between them and the drain cover, the invisible waiter and the somersaulting coffees.

Sandro stopped walking. He turned to Annie and she was delighted to see he had a broad smile on his face and was spreading his arms wide as if he expected a hug.

Oh God. Maybe forty per cent was too low? Maybe she'd caved in? Maybe she should have stuck with fifty no matter what?

'Annnnie!' he gushed. 'You win! Minimum purchase fifty bags,' he added quickly.

'Deal.'

Annie could see that any moment now, the arms

were going to close in on her . . . and thought that would probably be quite nice. She wouldn't mind an affectionate little seal-the-deal hug with Sandro.

She let him and his cloud of citrus cologne move in.

'Isn't that Annie over there?' Aunty Hilda asked, her head moving sharply to the side. Ed behind her, pushing her wheelchair along the pavement, looked up.

'Where?' he asked.

'Down there at the bottom of the street, on the other side of the road,' Aunty Hilda insisted. 'I can only see her back, but isn't that the dress she was wearing when she left this morning?'

Ed followed Hilda's blatantly pointing finger.

It was Annie! He could see that immediately. That was her dress. That was her loose 'Italian' hair, rather than her usual ponytail, but most of all, he recognized her by her unmistakably luscious behind.

Ed began to push the wheelchair again to bring them closer to her.

'Just look at that!' Hilda exclaimed as Annie's waist was encircled by Mr B's arms and his head bent towards hers for what was obviously a kiss.

Sandro was kissing her full on the mouth! This was surprising . . . this wasn't just beeeziness. Well, maybe it was in Italy. Maybe this was how you sealed a beeeziness deal in Italy.

But now that Annie could feel just a hint of Sandro's tongue brushing against her lip, she had to take action. She jerked her head back.

'Is something wrong?' he asked.

She moved her hand quickly up to her eye. She wasn't desperate to hurt Mr forty per cent discount's feelings just yet. Not at this fragile stage in negotiations.

'There's something in my eye,' she said, leaning back and away from his face, although he was still holding her tightly around the waist. In fact his hands were definitely sliding down to the top of her bum.

She smudged at the corner of her eye with her finger-tip.

'Oh, I look,' Sandro said, bending closely down over her face, scanning her eye with careful attention.

He was looking right at her, very, very intently, and Annie found herself staring at the sculpted furrow above his top lip. Another kiss wouldn't be so bad. Just one more, proper kiss. After all the rowing she'd been through, another little fragrant, coffee-flavoured kiss would be really very nice.

No.

No.

She shouldn't. No matter how soft and responsive his lips looked.

She pulled her face a little further back, but his hand was on the back of her head now, holding her in place.

'Tranquillo,' he murmured and looked in her eye with concern. His lips were only a centimetre or two from hers and Patrizia's words of warning were ringing in Annie's ears: *'He big lady man . . . he lean over and say, "something on your face, Patrizia, let me move it away".'*

'Just look at that!' Aunty Hilda repeated loudly. 'Absolutely shameless!'

Ed was standing transfixed. He could see the back of Annie's head and he could see Annie's arse. Mr B had a hand on each.

He was holding Annie far too tightly for this to be anything businesslike. They were clearly having a very long snog.

Ed couldn't think of anything to say or anything to do. For several long moments, he couldn't think of anything at all. Then a memory sprang into his mind, of Owen playing a mournful melody on the violin. Suddenly with a snap, the D-string had broken, curling into a spiral and flopping over the edge of the violin, where it had dangled uselessly. They had burst into laughter.

But now . . . now he could feel strings of his own snap, snap, snapping inside him, curling up and dangling and there wasn't the slightest thing funny about it.

Briskly, he wheeled the chair around and began to head very quickly in the opposite direction.

'I want to go home today,' Aunty Hilda announced, 'and I need somebody to help me.'

She sounded smug and almost quite cheerful about this horrible turn of events. Without turning to look at him, she announced, 'I think you, Ed, should be that person.'

Chapter Twenty

Annie felt considerably happier as she pulled up at the villa later that day. She'd let Sandro down gently, telling him that he was wonderful, charming, very tempting and so forth, and that if it didn't work out with her *ragazzo* he would be the first to know.

Then they'd gone to his shop where she'd picked out the fifty bags from his catalogue for her first delivery, to be sent to her just as soon as her cheque had cleared.

Now, with Sandro's bags and Timi Woo's shoes, she was ready! This was the start, this was the launch pad, this was the beginning of Annie Valentine, sales-woman, career woman, businesswoman, entrepreneur and fashion retailer!

All the way home, she'd planned how to make it up to Ed, how to win him over to her side. She could understand his concerns, she really could. But she was going to reassure him, make sure he didn't worry so much. He had to give her this chance to prove herself. He just had to. Then, when she and Ed had made up, she thought they could all celebrate (well . . . just as soon as she and Dinah, then Dinah and Ed were all friends again, obviously). She would take everyone back to the Taverna and buy them all a wonderful evening meal.

And tomorrow was going to be a proper holiday without one single mention of bags or shoes or shops. They would do whatever Ed wanted to do. Go to the coast . . . or even spend hours admiring the stained-glass windows in some dusty old cathedral, if necessary.

By the evening they would all be refreshed and ready to fly back to London, where she would make a start on her Timi Woo sales campaign.

'What do you mean they've gone?'

What on earth was Lana, in the kitchen drinking coffee while her thumb darted over the keys of her mobile phone, telling her? Ed and Aunty Hilda had gone? They had left? They had packed their bags and headed for the airport in a taxi?

'They've gone to the airport?' Annie didn't believe she could have heard this right. 'That's a two-hour drive.'

'I know . . . Hilda said she was paying. Said she couldn't stand it any longer.' Lana gave a shrug.

'What?! I thought she was having quite a nice time. Has something happened?'

'Mum!' Lana folded up her phone and turned her full attention to the slightly crazed bouffant-haired woman in the, quite frankly, tarty dress, 'I think you know what's happened. You've fallen out with Ed and Dinah. Maybe Hilda couldn't take the aggro.'

'The aggro?' Annie was astonished. 'But I was going to make it up with everyone. I was coming back here to celebrate.'

Lana looked at her in some disbelief. 'Ed and Hilda went to town to have a cup of coffee and get some newspapers and when they came back, he was really, really angry. Furious. I don't think he's quite in the mood for celebrating just yet.'

'I have to speak to him.'

Unbuckling the disastrous fake snakes with one hand, Annie rummaged in her handbag with her other.

She called Ed's mobile number, but infuriatingly, her call went straight through to voicemail.

'Don't leave Italy!' her message began. 'This is crazy. Come back, Ed, please. We need to talk this through.'

'What did Ed say?' Annie asked her daughter, slowing down, deciding it was only sensible to ask one question at a time.

'I don't know . . . that Hilda was desperate to get home today and that he was going to go with her. Then they packed their bags and left. I thought he'd have spoken to you about this. I thought you'd know about it. I didn't know you were so busy with Mr Perfume Pants to even speak to Ed.'

'Ed hasn't phoned me!' Annie insisted. 'He hasn't told

me!' and then she snapped, 'Perfume Pants? What's that all about?'

'That Italian guy stinks! He must put on his aftershave with a ladle.'

'Oh right, how very observant and kind of you! Do I make cruel, personal remarks about your friends?'

'Yes!' Lana didn't hesitate to tell her. 'All the time. You even make them *to* my friends.'

'I do not!' Annie retorted, checking her mobile's list of calls received.

'You told Greta her green skirt made her arse look big!'

There was no sign that Ed had made any attempt to contact her. Nothing at all.

'I just answered her question truthfully and then I advised on camouflaging . . . and darker colours,' Annie said in her defence. Why hadn't Ed phoned her? She couldn't really believe this was happening. He had left the villa, and he was about to leave the country without her. Without even telling her.

Out on the terrace, Dinah and Connor were sitting on the sunloungers while Billie and Owen splashed in the pool.

'Well, that was obviously quite a row,' were Connor's words of greeting. 'He's stormed off back to London. Look on the bright side, though, the old battleaxe is out of the picture. At least he's done us that favour, your man.'

Connor had a big padded plaster over his skinned nose, cobbled together out of Elastoplast and cotton wool.

Dinah looked equally unusual, in a long-sleeved white T-shirt and jogging bottoms, her red face hidden behind dark glasses and a baseball cap. Her only visible bits of skin looked as if they had been coated in Billie's sticky white suncream.

'Did he say much about it?' Annie wanted to know.

'Erm . . . no,' Connor told her, 'he looked so angry that no one really wanted to quiz him. He even chewed Owen up about something and you've got to admit, that's not usually his style.'

'Oh great.' Annie sat down heavily on the deckchair beside them.

'Hi, Mum!' Owen shouted over, obviously not too upset.

'Annie?' Dinah ventured, 'I shouldn't have . . . I mean . . . it wasn't really . . .'

'Any of your business?' Annie snapped. 'No, it bloody wasn't. You're lucky we're very closely related or I would never, ever speak to you again.'

'Sorry,' Dinah offered.

'Well . . . you were freaked out,' Annie managed, 'it was Ed's fault and let's face it, it *was* Ed's fault. And then he finds out about everything I've been doing without telling him . . . and well . . .' she shrugged her shoulders, 'here we are. It'll blow over,' she said, trying to convince herself as much as the others.

'Why's he so uptight about you running your own business?' Connor had to ask. 'Anyone can see you're going to be fantastic! I couldn't believe it when you went back to The Store, I thought you were going great guns on your own last year. This is what you should be doing,' he assured her.

Despite her deep disappointment that Ed was not here and just didn't see it that way, Annie mustered up her warmest smile for Connor. 'Thanks,' she told him, 'you're my best friend and I love you, even when you're sober.'

'Oh God! Don't talk about sober, in fact' – he flicked a look at his watch – 'It's nearly lunchtime, not too early to open a cold white, I don't think.'

'I will if you will,' Annie answered.

'Leave me out of it,' Dinah told him, 'I'm staying off the booze till we get home.'

'Too right,' Annie agreed, 'there's no knowing what you'll come out with next . . . and bring Lana out, will you?' Annie shouted after Connor, 'she needs to put her phone down. I'm starting to panic about the bill.'

'Have you tried to phone Ed?' Dinah asked. 'Would it help if I phoned him?'

'Yes and I don't think so, but nice of you to offer.'

'Is it you he's really angry with . . . or is it me?' Dinah asked next.

'Oh don't worry, I'm sure it's me . . . but . . . I can't give this all up for him.'

'Could you delay it?' Dinah wondered.

Annie thought of the one hundred boxed pairs of shoes waiting for her in London and the four-figure cheque she'd just written out for Mr B. 'No,' she said, 'not really. He's got to trust me. He's got to let me go ahead and cock it all up really badly if I have to.'

'He doesn't want to lose the house,' Dinah reminded her gently. 'That's his family home.'

'Yeah!' Annie broke in, 'which he wouldn't have been able to keep anyway if it wasn't for me. He and his sister would have sold it last year. I'm the one who owns one third of that house, if I want to borrow against my share, that's up to me!'

'Maybe that's not how he sees it.'

'No,' Annie had to admit, 'but I don't want to lose the house either! He can't really think I would, can he? I'm only borrowing a bit and I know this will work.'

Annie sat back with a sigh and stared out across the fields. 'The problem is, babes,' she said, in a lower voice, 'I don't remember having a situation like this with Roddy.'

'Of course you did!' Dinah insisted, determined that Annie shouldn't bathe her husband in a saintly glow. 'You used to have the most monumental rows.'

'Rows, yes. Any number of rows, terrible rows,' Annie agreed, 'but I don't remember him ever saying I couldn't do something I really wanted to do. He believed everyone should do the things they wanted to do. He always used to say, *"compromise and die!"* He did!'

'Well . . .' Dinah looked at her sister dubiously, 'that's easy to say. Not exactly so easy to do. What if Bryan wanted to live in the countryside and I wanted to stay in London?'

'It is easy,' Annie insisted. 'You have to let the other person have a go. You can't just clip their wings. You'd have to move to the country with him for a few years on the promise that then, if you still couldn't stand it, you'd both move back. The compromise would be to move to the suburbs and then you'd both be miserable. See? Compromise and die!

'If Ed keeps saying no,' Annie added, 'I'm just going to resent him, and then I'd have to leave him.'

'Annie!' Dinah sounded shocked now. 'You are not going to leave Ed over this. Ed is a great guy and he's the right person for you.'

'How can you say that when he doesn't want me to do the one thing I want to do most?' Annie asked her with exasperation.

Dinah just gave her a raised eyebrow look, which Annie took to mean: Ed knows better than you.

'Oh shut up!' Annie said and stormed back into the villa.

In the sitting room, the sofa bed had been neatly made and folded away. The jumble of clothes which had been exploding from Ed's open suitcase when she'd gone out this morning had now gone and only her own open suitcase with her clothes neatly stacked inside was left on the floor.

Annie sat down on the armchair opposite the sofa and stared at it glumly. She cast her eyes about the room looking for anything that Ed might have left behind for her. A note? A scribble of explanation?

Her eyes fell on the villa's telephone – a heavy, old-fashioned cream-coloured one with a dial – resting solidly and silently on the side table beside her chair.

Next to it was a slim pad of paper and a navy and gold ballpoint pen.

Annie bent over to take a closer look at the pad of paper and there, although the page was blank, she could see the imprint of a name and a number which had been left when someone had written on the sheet above.

She snatched the pad up and looked at it closely. Apart from a capital G and some fours, she couldn't read it. But she'd read Owen enough mystery stories to know that what she needed was a pencil.

She searched the room as quickly as she could and finally found a stub of pencil in one of her suitcase pockets, tucked in there for emergency airport lounge games of hangman. With care, she gently shaded over the markings until clearly legible was the name 'Giovanna' in Ed's scribbly handwriting followed by a telephone number.

Giovanna? Giovanna?

Annie was absolutely certain that Giovanna was the name of Ed's Italian ex-girlfriend.

She leaned back in the sofa and stared at the piece of paper. Ed had gone in a taxi with his luggage, an elderly aunt and the telephone number of his ex-girlfriend in his pocket. Whatever problems she and Ed were having, they were definitely not going to be helped by the reappearance of a Giovanna in his life, that much Annie did know.

She scrunched up the paper and threw it hard against the wall. Punching Ed's number into her mobile again, she told his voicemail: 'You really better phone me, Ed. Before someone else makes our problems even worse.'

Chapter Twenty-one

Lana in a gloom:

Black knitted tunic (mother's wardrobe)
Black leggings (Asda)
Black baseball boots (Converse)
Black mood (homemade)
Total est. cost: £45

'We should never have gone!'

As the taxi from the train station pulled up outside their home at close to 9 p.m. on Monday evening, Annie craned her head out of the window to get a better look. The house was ominously dark. Only the porch light was on, and she knew that was on a timer.

There had still not been one word from Ed. She'd tried his mobile regularly, leaving various messages ranging from sulky, contrite and pleading, to just plain angry. But not a single call had been returned. Finally, just before they took off from Ancona airport, she'd texted:

'U r a jrk,' which she regretted almost as soon as she'd pressed send.

She'd tried to make the last day and a half of the holiday as enjoyable as she could for everyone, especially the three children. There had been dinner out, late night swimming, more sunshine and even an excursion to some very decrepit Roman ruins for Owen's sake.

But on Sunday night, when Owen had nestled up against Annie and asked her if Ed had left because he'd fallen in the well with Billie, Annie could just about have cried.

'No,' she'd told her son emphatically, squeezing her arm tightly around him, 'Don't think that. You didn't do exactly the right thing, but we all make mistakes, babes,' she'd reassured him. 'It turned out all right and no one's even thinking about it any more. No, Ed's had a fight with me. But when we get home, I'll sort it out with him and everything will be OK again.'

'But Ed shouted at me before he went,' Owen confided. 'It wasn't very nice. He told me not to be so rough with Billie in the pool, but we were just play fighting and she was laughing.'

'Don't worry, please,' Annie had soothed him. 'I'm sure we'll sort everything out.'

But in her heart she was furious that Ed had upset not just her, but her son as well. And Lana too, Annie was sure, although Lana was too guarded to say anything yet.

At Stansted, Annie had waved goodbye to an exhausted Billie, pimply Dinah, plus Connor and his plastered nose because they were taking a cab home together. All Annie's extra shopping luggage meant that she and her children needed a taxi to themselves.

'Chin up,' Connor had instructed, 'I'm sure you and that nice man will work it out. You have to,' he'd added, 'we'd all miss his cooking too much.'

But when Annie and her children hauled their luggage in through the front door, it was obvious that no one else was home.

'Where's he gone?' Owen asked, not needing to name Ed because they were all thinking exactly the same thing.

'Oh, he must be out doing something, I'm sure he'll be back soon to see us,' Annie told them, but she had really expected him to be there to meet them.

'Maybe he'll make us supper,' Owen said hopefully.

'Where are the cats, though? They were supposed to be dropped off this morning. He must have taken the cats.' Lana pointed out, because Hoover and Dyson, the big, black, fluffy furballs, usually stalked out into the corridor purring whenever anyone came in through the front door.

'He's taken the cats!' Lana repeated, now sounding upset.

'I don't believe this,' Annie said, more to herself than to the children.

She turned and shut the front door behind them then, dumping all her things down in the hall, hurried upstairs to the bedroom she shared with Ed. Surely there would be something up there? Some note, or explanation, or clue . . . or *something*?

'Take your things to your rooms,' she told the children, over her shoulder, 'I'll try and find out what's going on.'

It was very tidy in the main bedroom. It was almost exactly as Annie remembered leaving it. But then, looking carefully around, she saw the very significant difference.

Ed's second, larger suitcase was missing from its place on top of the wardrobe. With a heavy heart, she opened the wardrobe doors and saw that not all, but a large portion, of his clothes were gone.

'No,' she heard herself say under her breath.

Scanning the room desperately for any further clue, Annie's eye fell on her bedside table.

There it was, the dreaded note. Folded neatly in half.

Annie approached the table with a tight feeling in her chest, her mind whirring frantically. What if Ed had decided he'd had enough of them? What if Aunty Hilda had poisoned him against the three of them for ever? What if he'd phoned up Giovanna and met her in Italy and decided she was the one for him and he'd packed up his clothes and his cats and was moving back to be with her?

Her hands were shaking with panic by the time she had the note in her fingers, making it difficult to open . . . difficult to read the words inside. But the words didn't solve any part of this puzzle for her, they simply read, 'I've gone to Hannah's.'

That was it, as if he'd just popped out and would be back any moment now.

'I've gone to Hannah's' she read again. And again. And once again. He'd gone to stay with his sister? How did that help anything? What use was that? What exactly was his point here?

Feeling a flash of anger at his refusal to talk to her, see her or deal with her on any level, she scrunched up the note and hurled it at the window. Right, that was it. She'd put on her coat, get the car keys and whizz round to Hannah's, right now. She'd had quite enough of this sulky silence. Ed was going to talk to her. Nothing would be solved until they had a decent conversation. And she wasn't going to put it off for one moment longer . . .

Muuuum!' Owen called from the hall.

'Yes?'

'I'm hungry.'

Right, she would go round to Hannah's just as soon as she'd made something for the three of them to eat.

Annie poked about in the fridge and the freezer. Ed had obviously spent some time in the house: there was fresh milk in there, along with eggs and a loaf of bread.

She put oven chips in to cook and brought out the frying pan for the eggs. This was Ed's frying pan, carbonated steel or something . . . it had to be wiped down with olive oil on a kitchen towel and never washed. Usually she stayed well clear of it, but today she banged it down on the hob, determined to cause it some damage if she could.

'Get Lana to come down, will you?' she ordered Owen when the food was ready and she'd put the pan in the sink and covered it with soapy water.

'Isn't Ed coming?' Owen asked.

'No, not right now,' Annie answered without turning to her son. She didn't want him to ask any further questions.

'Right,' Owen said, then turned and went out of the room to get his sister.

When Lana came into the kitchen, Annie could see at once that something else was wrong and it wasn't just because Lana had changed into head to toe black.

'Have a seat, babes,' Annie said gently, 'you must be hungry.'

'I'm not,' Lana replied, her voice strained.

'Please,' Annie urged, 'have a little bit.'

About three chips and a small corner of egg had gone down before Lana blurted out at her mum, 'Andrei isn't answering any of my calls or messages.'

'We're having the same problem then,' came Annie's gloomy response.

'And Greta says,' Lana went on, 'Greta says she saw him snogging Daisy at the party on Saturday night.' Big breaking sobs followed this revelation.

Something of an astonished smile crossed Owen's face at this news, for he'd lived through Lana mourning a boyfriend for weeks before and he'd found it very entertaining. But the smile quickly disappeared at the sight of Annie's warning frown.

'Oh, sweetheart,' Annie said with as much sympathy and concern as she could muster, 'is Greta sure?'

When Lana nodded at this and carried on sobbing miserably, Annie could only say, 'Oh Lana, baby, that's terrible. I am so sorry.'

'We should never have gone!' Lana wailed. 'If we hadn't gone to Italy none of this would have happened!'

Annie put her arm round her daughter. A long evening of tears and snotty tissues was in store. They would have to break into the duty-free chocolate, no doubt about that. Annie would have to dust down her talk about unfaithful boyfriends: why they're no good and should never be taken back.

And any showdown with Ed at his sister's house would have to wait until she finished work tomorrow.

Chapter Twenty-two

Dannii's daywear:

Tightest jeans (Juicy Couture)
Frilly floral chiffon top (DvF)
Silver heels (Gucci)
Silver bag (Gucci)
Platinum and diamond watch (Gucci)
Total est. cost £7,000

'Outplay her. Outflank her every move.'

The next morning in The Store, Svetlana's verdict on Ed fleeing to his sister's house without a word of explanation was simple: 'Nothing, nothing, nothing! Ahnnah, you don't want *nothing* to do with this man! What more can I say? I have had two, three husbands who not treat me the way I want to be treated. And I stay and I try and I do this and that and sexy underwear and lovely dresses and everything they ever want . . . and what do I get?'

She turned and fixed Annie with an expectant look in

her glittering green eyes. 'I get cheating on and divorce court and fighting over every penny they owe me! So, no, no, no!' She shook her finger with its long magenta fingernail in the air emphatically.

'I learn my lesson. At the first sign of trouble, get out! Find someone crrrrazy about you,' she added with an extravagant roll of 'r's.

Annie thought she had, though, that was the point.

'Like my Harrrrrry!' Svetlana went on, 'Yes . . . I know, he not as rich as Igor of course.' Well, only a handful of people in Europe were, so no shame there really. 'But Igor never gave me any money anyway, so vot the point?'

Annie couldn't help feeling a large house in Mayfair counted for something, at least . . . but Svetlana was now asking, 'Am I too old for zis?'

The statuesque Russian turned to offer Annie a three-quarters view of herself in the red tropical print swimsuit, matching sarong and red platform heels. She looked fabulous. Breathtaking. Like a sumptuous Miss World, ready to stride across the platform and announce her intention to work with children.

Of course, this may have had something to do with the fact that Svetlana had once been Miss Ukraine. Although Svetlana had not told the judges she wanted to work with children. Instead she'd informed them with a dazzling smile that she 'Vant to marry very rich man', which according to Svetlana was the only reason they awarded the Miss World crown to Miss Thailand. ('*She vas midget! You not believe!*')

'The swimsuit looks stunning,' Annie insisted. 'What do you mean, are you too old for it?'

'No, the purse!' Svetlana raised her leg at a graceful

angle – fifteen years of ballet lessons hadn't been wasted on her – to show off the tiny, quilted Chanel ankle bag.

'I love it,' Annie told her: 'very glam Caribbean.' Because where else would Svetlana be spending the winter holidays?

'Vill I get my credit card in it?'

There was no question of Svetlana ever carrying cash.

'I miss when you worked from home Ahnnah,' Svetlana said mournfully, 'then we had more time, more privacy to talk, to work out all the looks. When are you going back? When you leave here and vork for yourself again? You need to make more money with your business, huh?' she asked in just the sort of cheery, jaunty way of a woman who's never had to worry for one moment about meeting the mortgage payments.

'Well, I have some new ideas,' Annie told her, but she didn't feel like giving Svetlana the whole business pitch today.

Today, her heart wasn't really in it. Today, she felt oddly flat and unenergetic. About as drab as the boring old black dress she'd put on for work this morning with only a necklace to accessorize it. No sparkly earrings, no fascinating belt, nothing worn in a different way to add interest. No, this morning Annie had woken up alone, flung on the dress and the necklace without a great deal of thought and got on with the business of starting the day.

'You need a good man to take care of you,' Svetlana told her sympathetically, 'you are a wonderful woman going to waste. You are looking tired, you are looking vorried. You need someone to take veight from your shoulders, not add to it.'

'Ha!' Annie managed, but she didn't want to meet Svetlana's eyes all of a sudden, because she thought if she saw too much warmth and sympathy there, she might be tempted to feel really sorry for herself.

'Come on!' Annie encouraged, as if to her client, but really to herself, 'we have this whole rail to get through before eleven o'clock.'

And with that her hands went to the next outfit: a shimmering, radiantly multi-coloured, long and lean Missoni evening dress. The kind of thing Svetlana would probably slap on over her bikini – whereas Annie would kill to have this very dress to wear at Bryan and Dinah's party.

Annie hadn't been able to resist making a quick call to Hector to find out how the 'secret' party preparations were going.

'He's not really very open to new ideas,' Hector confided, 'but we're getting there. I definitely couldn't persuade him to have doves, though. Doves were a total no-no.'

'Doves?' Annie repeated. The Hector she thought she knew was an only slightly camp, posh Scot. The kind of guy who wore tartan trousers – seriously – as daywear. She'd thought she could count on him to make Bryan and Dinah's party classy.

'Yeah, I was going to release ten pink doves at the end of the ceremony. One for each year they've been together.'

'Oh! That's quite a sweet idea,' Annie had to agree, 'but I don't think Dinah likes birds, they make her nervous.'

'That's what Bryan said.'

'Did you say "ceremony"?' Annie asked, thinking she really should know more about this. She'd thought it was supposed to be a party, not a ceremony of any kind.

'Yeah . . .'

'What kind of ceremony? How can it be a secret party if there's going to be a ceremony? Won't Dinah have to say something? Or know what to say?' Annie was starting to worry on her sister's behalf.

'Well, Bryan's going to do some home-made vows . . . and hopefully she'll be able to think of some to say back.'

'Hopefully?!' Annie spluttered. This was all getting very elaborate – very complicated. She thought it was really her duty to at least prepare Dinah slightly.

'I've been speaking to Hector,' she informed Dinah on the phone five minutes later. 'There's going to be a bit of a ceremony and some very low key, sort of, home-made . . . er . . . vows.'

'VOWS?!' Dinah leapt straight into panic mode. 'Dear God! Vows? I have to put a stop to this immediately! You know how bad I was at the registrar's.'

And Annie did. Dinah had cried and giggled intermittently throughout the short service.

'I'm not doing vows, that's so embarrassing. Cringeworthy! No way is this Bryan's idea. This is all Hector's fault. I'm calling this whole thing off!'

'But it's a secret!' Annie reminded her, only too aware that if Bryan found out Annie knew everything about the party from Hector and had passed the information on to Dinah, who had then called off the party, it would all be Annie's fault. And Bryan and Annie's relationship was . . . well . . . not exactly relaxed, more like openly polite, but covertly hostile. It had been like this for years, ever since Annie and Bryan had decided they both loved Dinah but didn't really like each other.

'I'm still covered in those bloody spots!' Dinah wailed. 'I don't think they're going to go away in time. The party's on Saturday!'

'Could you wear a veil?' Annie suggested, trying to keep the giggle out of her voice.

'Oh ha bloody ha.'

'I see you again in five weeks,' Svetlana reminded Annie, leaning down to kiss her on both cheeks before she sailed out of the changing room, leaving Annie and her assistant to bag and box up her purchases and send them down to the waiting car, 'and if you need to speak to me before then, you call,' came the instruction, 'I am always here to give advice. Harrrry says I give very good advice. He says I could have been vonderful lawyer.'

'Thanks darlin', have a lovely holiday,' Annie called after her.

'And what's up?' Paula, Annie's assistant, wanted to know as soon as Svetlana was out of earshot.

'Oh nothing much,' Annie tried to shrug her off.

But Paula, in all six foot two of her black gorgeousness, was not going to be put off so easily. She ran bright orange talons though her long beaded braids and urged, 'Yes there is. You look rubbish, and Svetlana's offering you advice. What's up? You have to tell me . . .'

'So you can tell everyone else in the whole shop,' Annie said, but with a smile.

'Yeah! 'Zactly.'

'OK, well, if you have to know, Ed has gone off in a huff. He's packed his suitcase and gone to his sister's.'

'Oh no!' Paula gasped, suitably shocked. 'Why?'

'Let's just say there are a few things we can't agree about,' Annie replied, 'and he's having a sulk. There's no other word for it. But I've decided: fine, if he wants to sulk, I'm going to let him. I've not had a sulker before,' she confided. 'My husband was a shouter, he always wanted to get it out there, off his chest, into the open.'

'But he was an actor,' Paula reminded her.

'True, he liked the drama of a really good row. I've tried phoning Ed, babes,' Annie couldn't help telling her, 'I've left loads of messages for him, but, nothing. So I'm not sure what I'm supposed to do now.'

'Here's the girl who can help you!' Paula cracked a wide smile as Annie's next client bustled into the suite on deadly heels.

'Dannii!!' Annie tried to sound as enthusiastic as she possibly could, 'Dannii, Dannii, here to bring joy and juicy gossip into our lives.'

'Help you do what, girl?' came the cheerful reply.

Dannii with her long bleached blonde tresses, tightest jeans, highest heels, fussiest top, bling watch, serious jewellery and bag, complete with ridiculous Yorkie dog with pink bow in its hair, was a force of nature.

No, that wasn't right. There was nothing natural about Dannii at all from her hair colour to her skin tone, to her lip and bust size. She was a force of un-nature.

'Man trouble,' Paula said, pointing at Annie.

'Oh no, girl.' Dannii put her hand up in a stop sign and said, 'We don't want to go there. Been there, done that, never want to go there again. So what's the story?'

She set her bag with her dog down on the floor and turned her head slightly to the side, just like the dog, to listen.

'Oh let's not go into all that,' Annie insisted, 'it's not that interesting.'

'Has he got someone else on the go?' Dannii couldn't resist asking. 'There's only one way to deal with that, my love. Outplay her. Outflank her every move. Outclass her . . . and grab the game for yourself.'

It wasn't at all obvious that the love in 24-year-old Dannii's life was a Premier League footballer. How else would she have four or five thousand pounds to drop every time she popped in for a consultation with Annie?

'Darlin',' Dannii went on before Annie could stop her, 'you can't go sulking about in a black dress. If you want him back, you've got to doll up and knock him dead.'

'Why is everyone going on about this dress?' Annie said. 'This is a very nice dress. It unbuttons low, it's a great fit round the waist, it's flirty! This is a lovely dress.'

Dannii looked at her doubtfully. 'Men don't like black,' she said finally, 'unless we're talking underwear. You need to brighten up and tighten up!'

Annie, who was usually the one dispensing wardrobe advice much more tactfully than this, wasn't sure how to react.

'OK, well, I will bear that in mind, babes. Let's talk about you now, what are you in for today?' she asked. 'Special occasion? Some new things for the new winter wardrobe?'

'Both,' Dannii told her happily, 'but first there's something I have to show you!'

'Down you go, Gucci,' she told her dog in a baby voice as she set her lavish, gold-trimmed bag on the floor and rummaged around inside.

'Gucci?' Annie had to ask.

'Yeah! Gucci-coo my little poochy, isn't she sweet? She's my baby, aren't you darling?' She bent down and made kissing noises while the dog licked her right on the lips.

Annie and Paula exchanged an uneasy look. Annie quite liked dogs but that was definitely taking it too far.

'She won't wee on the carpet, will she?' Annie wondered.

'No, she'll stay in her baggy, won't you, Gucci?'

From the other side of the handbag, Dannii brought out a copy of *Heat* magazine.

Dannii's relationship with the weekly glossies hadn't begun well. Because she was young and pretty with a famous boyfriend and far too much cash to lash on herself, the magazines had had it in for her from day one.

'Trashy Dannii', 'Dannii misses again', 'Dannii spent five grand on this outfit, but she still looks cheap' – all that sort of headline horror had been landed on her lovely little head.

On several occasions, Annie had been the one on hand with the tissue box to help mop the devastated tears. She was the one Dannii had turned to for advice on how to achieve more restrained and elegant dressing.

But Dannii wasn't exactly easy to rein in. No matter how many beautiful, simply cut items Annie urged

Dannii towards, she would wear them out on the town with all the wrong kinds of accessories: open-toed high heels, visible knickers, a bottle of vodka and three drunken football players.

Nevertheless, Dannii was standing in front of her flicking though *Heat* with a triumphant look on her face.

'Here!' she said finally. 'Take a look at this!'

She handed the magazine to Annie, open at a double-page spread on footballers' girlfriends. The women had been divided up into columns headed 'scores' and 'misses', and then right in the centre there was Dannii. She was labelled a 'hat-trick', 'because we love Dannii's dress, bag and shoes!' the magazine trilled.

Annie had selected every one of those items and had suggested putting them together. Despite her mood of general gloom, she couldn't resist a smile of pleasure . . . and if Dannii was now a style-setter, then Annie had a brilliant idea.

'This is fantastic!' Annie enthused, 'Look at you! That Cavelli dress is stunning on you. What a brilliant picture, blimey you'll be on the cover of *Vogue* next!'

Dannii beamed.

'Before we go out and look at some new things, I have to tell you about Timi Woo shoes. Have you heard of them?' Annie's voice lowered a little, because she was being totally disloyal to The Store here, something she never liked to do. 'They're just amazing! Brilliant quality, gorgeous colours and you can only get them on the internet. Insider's secret. C'mon, I'll get Paula to show you hers.'

*   *   *

If Dannii and her boundless enthusiasm had managed to revive Annie's mood slightly, it was about to be killed off again by Paige, who walked into the suite just as soon as Dannii wiggled out, along with her £4,000 worth of evening dresses, tight jeans and sparkly tops, not to mention her little hairy Gucci-Coo.

Paige had been here twice before, although Annie wasn't quite sure why because no matter what Annie suggested, Paige just chose the things she would have bought on her own anyway. And these things were always neutral. They were beige or taupe or light grey. They were sand, or greige or putty. There was no dragging Paige away from neutral. Even her hair and skin were beige.

Maybe it was because she worked for an accountancy company where no one was allowed to stand out, maybe it was because she was single, childless and more than a touch neurotic, or maybe it was just because her name was Paige and she liked to wear beige.

When Annie had taken her down to the cosmetics counter, in the hope of persuading her to try out some slightly more enlivening colours, Paige had picked out the beige eye shadow, the taupe cheek colour and the nude lipstick. In other words, she'd looked almost exactly the same when she left the counter as when she arrived.

Whenever Annie brought her an outfit to try on, she would ask, 'Doesn't it come in something just a little bit more neutral?'

Until Annie wanted to shriek, 'NO!! It doesn't! That's the point!'

On previous visits, Annie had tried to fight against

the beige tide by bringing up rails of carefully selected, mouth-wateringly tempting colours: a blouse in grape silk, a teal blue cashmere cardigan, a bottle-green shirt dress, a heathery pink jacket . . . for them all to be rejected in favour of 'something that will go with everything'. This was the phrase which drove Annie mad. Why did *something* have to go with *everything*? No one ever wore their somethings with everything! The terror of having a lone something left in the back of the cupboard which went with *nothing* explained why some people only ever bought black or navy, or in Paige's case greige. And they missed out! They missed out on grass greens and sky blues, inky purples, juicy watermelon, sharp lemon, comforting coffee, earthy greens, rich russets, pillarbox red, the energy burst of orange . . .

So today, Annie in her black dress and black patent shoes was going to introduce Paige to colour, but only one tiny step at a time.

As soon as Paige was safely inside a swish grey trouser suit, Annie brought her a chunky bracelet – cheap for The Store, just plastic stones strung together with elastic – and slipped it onto her wrist. Crucially, the bracelet was olive green.

'Hmmm . . .' Paige didn't seem to object, she was concentrating on the suit, which once some necessary alterations had been done, was going to be a total winner.

Next, Annie handed her a sleek, lizard print clutch bag in grey and . . . olive green.

Paige held the bag, as intended, in the hand with the olive green bracelet. Oh that was so nice! Annie was now desperate to run out onto the shop floor and get a thin green-fringed velvet scarf to slip under Paige's jacket so that it peeked through with its hint of softness just at the collar and below the buttons. But she stayed still . . . careful not to undo all the progress they were making.

When Paige put her narrow frame into a stone grey day dress, Annie risked a red, white and smoky grey necklace made of multiple bead strands twisted artfully together. Then, holding her breath, she removed the narrow black belt the dress came with and threaded a slim scarlet one through the belt loops in its place.

'Hmmm . . .' Paige considered herself in the mirror.

'You know you could consider a red lipstick with this,' Annie encouraged, 'but you've got to break yourself in slowly with red lipstick if you don't usually wear it. Start with red lip gloss, then gradually add just a trace of lipstick with the gloss, smudge it round with your finger, get used to the bold new red lips on your face . . .'

Next, a beige chunky-knit cardigan was paired with green-blue leather gloves, and an outfit of unrelenting mushroom, even if it was Armani mushroom, was draped with the softest spun cashmere wrap . . . in dusky pink.

'I need to go through my wardrobe,' Paige told her, 'pack away all the summer things, get the winter clothes out.'

'Mmm,' Annie agreed, 'me too. I love doing that! Folding away all the bikinis and summer dresses, getting out the woollies and the scarves and gloves. Planning all my new outfits! Thinking about the lovely new things I *need* to buy!'

She was going to do that tonight, she decided. If there was no sign of Ed, no word from Ed, she was going to leave him to it. Instead, she would soothe herself with a long, deep delve into all the darkest corners of her ward-robe.

'I love this bag,' Paige declared, holding out the green lizard print clutch, 'it's so elegant and different.'

Annie wanted to do a little victory dance: Paige likes something that isn't beige!! Instead she said, 'I have a lovely little velvet scarf, gold and olive – would you like to try it on with the suit?' If Paige liked the scarf, maybe they could even consider green shoes . . . Don't rush it, Annie reminded herself.

'I thought things weren't supposed to match, you know . . . *accessories*,' Paige said the word as if it was for-eign to her.

'I know,' Annie replied, 'they *weren't* supposed to match. Nothing was supposed to be too matchy-matchy, but now we've come full circle. Now everything's supposed to match. What goes around comes around. Personally,' Annie went on, 'I like two matching items, it looks so nicely pulled together, but I think the third needs to be a bit different: a pattern incorporating the colour of the other two but mixing it with something else, you know, something a little offbeat.'

'It's so complicated!' Paige declared.

'No,' Annie insisted. 'Just buy what you like, take baby steps. I love the bag with the bracelet, that's not hard. Try that out. If you want to add the scarf, great; if not, forget it.'

'Scarves scare me,' Paige confided.

'I know, I know,' Annie had heard this before, 'I have clients who can do heart surgery but they're frightened of knotting a scarf.'

'I'm worried I'm going to look . . .' Paige began.

'*Matronly?*' Annie whispered the word and Paige nodded in fear. 'Trust me,' Annie said, 'we won't even tie the thing, we'll just place it under your jacket, do up the buttons and let it get on with its job quietly. There will be no knotting, no tying and certainly no hint of a . . . *brooch.*'

Annie could hear the trill of her mobile from her office. Secure in the knowledge that Paige was happy and definitely about to buy quite a few things, she asked if it would be OK to take the call.

As she picked up the phone, she checked the screen. The number was unfamiliar and it certainly wasn't one of Ed's .

'Ahnnie!!! How are you?'

Annie was delighted to hear the booming tones of Mr B coming to her all the way from Italy.

'Your bags are with the courier,' he told her. 'Did you speak with Harrods?'

The completely true answer to this was, to be precise, 'No'. But because Annie was sure that she would speak to Harrods and that Harrods would at least want to see her, she didn't think it was so far-fetched to answer, 'Yes! They're going to see me next week.'

'Fantastico!'

Chapter Twenty-three

Nic's new look:

Black, lime and cream tunic (Dorothy Perkins maternity)
Black pencil skirt with elasticated tummy gusset
(Formes maternity)
Black boots (Hobbs)
Lime bag (Hobbs)
Total est. cost: £380

'I can't believe I'm going to go through the whole turning
into a hippopotamus thing again.'

As Annie smoothed down Owen's hair and kissed him goodnight, he quietly asked the question he'd been meaning to ask all evening.

'Mum, is Ed coming back?'

'Oh babes, I hope so,' Annie told him. 'Would you like him to come back?'

Although the bedroom was dark, Annie could see that Owen was nodding.

'So, what's happened?' Owen asked next.

'We've had an argument . . . that's all, really.'

'Well can't you just make up? I have arguments with Lana all the time.'

'I know, but we're grown-ups . . . we're much more . . .'

'Stubborn?' Owen offered when Annie struggled for a word.

'Maybe,' she agreed with a little laugh. 'Did you see Ed in school today?' was her next question.

'I saw him and he waved at me and smiled, but we didn't have a lesson with him, so I never got to talk to him. I walked home with Lana, like you told me. I like that you're going to come home early now that Ed isn't here.'

'Oh, well . . .'

Arranging several days of temporary cover so that she could leave work at 6.30 and come home to look after her children hadn't exactly been easy and she didn't know how long she could keep it up. A week at the most. Then there was the lost commission to consider. Surely she and Ed would have made up by the end of the week? This couldn't go on for much longer, could it?

'Don't worry about us, OK?' she told Owen. 'Sleep tight and I'm sure it's all going to look different in the morning.'

'G'night,' Owen yawned and gave her a sweet little kiss on the cheek.

Closing the door on Owen's room, Annie considered knocking on Lana's but then decided she would leave it for a bit. Their suppertime conversation hadn't exactly gone brilliantly. Annie hadn't meant to bring up Andrei or ask anything upsetting at all. But somehow she'd asked about school and Lana had mentioned Greta and before either of them could stop themselves they were talking about Andrei and whether or not it was true about Daisy, and Annie soon heard herself declaring, 'If it is true, don't even bother making up with him. I definitely don't want to see him again, even if you do. He's not welcome here. Anyone who hurts your feelings totally hurts mine.'

Which resulted, as she could have predicted, in Lana shouting, 'I don't want to talk to you about this!' storming out and heading for her room, declaring that she had 'tons of homework' to do.

'I'm sorry, Lana,' Annie called to her daughter on the other side of the closed door.

For a moment she heard the frantic keyboard-bashing stop, but then it started up again, so Annie decided it would be best to try again later. Right now, she would stick with her plan to go downstairs to the main bedroom, where she would fling open the doors of her wardrobes, haul everything out and get busy in there.

Half an hour later, great armfuls of clothes were heaped all over the double bed, a huge tangle of colours and fabrics, styles and labels, impulse buys and 'investments', cheap thrills and expensive flings. There were a lot of dresses, because Annie hated suits, was 'so over' jeans and didn't seem to suit any of this year's trouser styles. Anyway, dresses were her thing right now. They could be smart. They could be casual. They could be warm as well as cool. And buying a dress meant you didn't have to worry about choosing a skirt and three different tops to go with it.

So she began to look through the dress mountain critically. Anything with bell-shaped angel sleeves was going straight to eBay. She'd decided after three – no . . . five – dresses that it was a loser look on anyone over fifteen. Plus the sleeves dangled, they got into the washing-up bowl, they scooped up ketchup from the corner of your plate; even more alarmingly they got singed on the gas when you removed the pasta from the hob.

Much, much better was the balloon sleeve, preferably three-quarter length with a narrow cuff holding the fabric in check. Now that was elegant, especially if the top of the sleeve was tight and it ballooned from just above the elbow. Yes, all of those dresses were staying. Along with the Michael Kors shirt dress and the Chloé shirt dress . . . but no, no, the zebra print D&G, that was off. It was so tight and so short. What was she thinking?

She held the dress up and remembered exactly what she'd been thinking. She'd bought this at a whopping great discount to wear at home . . . just for Ed.

She tossed it quickly into the 'sell' pile.

The bedroom phone burst into life. It was an old-fashioned one, black with a dial. It had been Ed's mother's, one of the many, many things already in the house that Annie had had to make room for during the renovation of the place. There was no telling what the number was. She let it ring three, four times – then snatched it up, breathing in tightly.

'Hello, it's Annie.'

'Annie! It's me,' she heard her mother's voice at the other end of the line. 'I've just been speaking to Aunty Hilda,' Fern continued. 'What's going on?'

'Oh . . . hello, Mum,' Annie began, sitting down on the edge of the bed, 'did you have a good holiday? I didn't know you were back yet.'

'Just got in. Lovely,' but she didn't want to be side-tracked. 'What is all this? Hilda says she came back early with Ed because you're carrying on with some Italian . . .'

'What!' Annie broke in. 'Talk about getting the wrong end of the stick! She's an old lunatic that woman, she really is.'

'No,' Fern insisted. 'She says she and Ed saw you with this man and that's why he came home with her on Sunday.'

'WHAT!' Annie exclaimed. 'Oh, this is just stupid. The man sells *handbags*. I'm going to buy some *handbags* from him to sell on. Ed knows all about it. Ed's in a total huff about it . . .' Annie added. 'It has nothing to do with me *"carrying on"* with anyone.'

'Well Annie, she seems to think that she definitely saw you and this other man, *together,*' Fern emphasized the word.

'Vicious old bats like Hilda see what they want to see,' Annie snapped.

'There's no need to be rude. Have you and Ed sorted all this out then?'

The easy thing to do would be to tell her mother yes. She didn't want Fern's interference right now, she didn't want Fern's opinion or advice. All of a sudden, Annie understood exactly how Lana must be feeling.

'We're having a bit of a row . . .' Annie began carefully. 'I'm sure it's going to blow over. I'm sure we're going to sort it out . . . but at the moment, he's gone to his sister's—'

'Oh Annie!' Fern was horrified. 'For goodness sake! What is this all about?'

So then Annie had to tell her about the Italian bags and the Chinese shoes and the taxman's £10,000 bill and the mortgage extension . . . and her plans to turn it all around.

'I just don't know,' was Fern's verdict when she'd listened to it all. 'If Ed doesn't think it's such a good idea—'

'But what does Ed know?' Annie burst in. 'He's a schoolteacher. What he knows about fashion or selling things I could fit on the back of a stamp in very big letters.'

'Yes, but he's your partner,' Fern insisted, 'you have to work these things out together.'

'Oh and you'd know all about that, of course,' Annie blurted out. Fern had ditched Annie's feckless, reckless and generally unreliable father so early on that Annie had only the vaguest memories of him.

'There's no need for that,' Fern told her briskly.

'Mum, you're a very strong, very independent person,' Annie reminded her, 'you brought us up all by yourself, you worked so hard and sent us to a great school. I can't believe you're telling me to shelve my ambitions because of what Ed thinks!'

'Annie,' Fern began quietly, 'I never found anyone else. Maybe I would have done things differently if I had. Maybe the way I did things wasn't the best, how do I know? All I can tell you is that Ed makes you happy. I know that. I can see that. You need to think very, very carefully before you throw that away.'

'I'm not throwing it away,' Annie insisted.

'Good,' Fern said, not wanting to add any more. She knew exactly what happened when you poked into the hornet's nest of other people's disagreements. You got stung.

'Who'd have thought . . .' Fern began, on a fresh track, 'that I'd be going to Dinah's tenth wedding anniversary party while you and your big sister carry on in your forties like a pair of teenagers?'

'I am not in my forties!' Annie retorted.

'Won't be long,' Fern reminded her.

'Yes it will! Anyway, what's up with Nic?'

'Haven't you heard? She's pregnant.'

'No! That's not carrying on like a teenager! Well, I suppose it is where you grew up.'

'Annie!' Fern sniffed.

'Nic's pregnant! Well, that's nice. She and Rick make a great couple.'

'She's forty-one,' Fern said, 'I can't believe she wants to go through all that again – babies, broken nights, toddler tantrums.'

'I know,' Annie agreed, but she felt a pang at the thought of it. She'd absolutely howled when Owen had left nursery school because the days of toddlers and beakers and chubby little faces overcome with delight to see '*Mummy!*' were so finally over.

'I'll see you next Saturday then. We're meeting at the Parkes Hotel for dinner, which sounds nice,' Fern added.

'I think it's a bit more than dinner,' Annie warned her. 'We're being told it's a family dinner, but that's just to keep Dinah in the dark. It's a big party.'

'Oh how nice. But . . . organized by Bryan?' Fern asked a little doubtfully.

'Don't worry, secret helpers are involved.'

'Do you know more than you're letting on?'

'Mum, even Dinah knows more than she's letting on.'

'You take care . . .' Fern added. 'You can always phone me.'

'Hilda is OK though?' Annie thought she'd better ask.

'Yes, she's at home, walking with a stick. You managed not to do her any harm in Italy, thank God. One of those home helps pops in every day to check on her.'

'Ah well, that's coming to us all,' Annie added.

'Oh aren't you full of cheer!'

One forty-minute conversation with her big sister Nic later and Annie was still miles away from completing the cupboard clearout.

'I'm huge!' Nic had complained. 'I'm fourteen weeks pregnant and I'm the size of a bus. I can't believe I'm going to go through the whole turning into a hippopotamus thing again!'

'Babes! It's brilliant!' Annie had scolded her. 'And everyone does fantastic maternity clothes now, so spend the money! You'll wear all that stuff for at least a year. No one I've ever met has stopped wearing their maternity clothes until at least five months after the birth.'

Once the phone call was over, Annie looked at the untidy heaps she'd made on the bed and the bedroom floor and realized she'd bitten off far more than she wanted to chew tonight.

She lifted up the telephone receiver again to check if any messages had been left while she was speaking to Nic. Nothing. In her handbag, her mobile was reporting the same news. Nothing. Not a voicemail, not a text, not a beep. He hadn't tried to phone, and that was that.

For a long minute, Annie toyed with the idea of phoning him but then decided she had tried enough yesterday. He knew where she was. He knew she wanted to talk to him. It was up to Ed to make the next move now.

She would have to start putting these clothes back. Leave the organizing of the Annie Valentine autumn/winter collection to another quiet evening . . . well, looked like there were going to be a few of those coming up.

It was when she approached the empty rail with the first armful of clothes to hang back up again that Annie caught sight of the Box. It was down there, at the bottom of the wardrobe, partially hidden by two handbags and a box of shoes.

But tonight there was no ignoring it. It wasn't that she didn't know it was in there; she did know, somewhere at the back of her mind. It was just some time now since she'd thought about it or looked at anything inside it.

Once she'd hung up the clothes she was carrying, she bent down, lifted away the handbags and the shoes and then gently took hold of the box and pulled it forwards. It was large, the size of three shoeboxes together side by side, but it wasn't heavy.

Once it had been slid out onto the floor, Annie wasn't sure what to do with it. She didn't know if she wanted to lift the lid or not. It had been a while. She could picture almost every item inside quite exactly . . . but there was always, every time she looked, something unexpected that still managed to take her by surprise and bring her to her knees.

And then the box was open: she'd grabbed the lid and moved it away quickly, before she could think about it too long.

With a little gasp of pain, she caught sight of her wedding photo, staring up at her. She took it in her hands and brought it up close to study it. Look how pretty she was then! And how deliriously happy. Her hair was all piled up with ivy leaves and tiny snow roses pushed between the tresses. And that wonderful gold dress. So beautiful, so elegant . . . and to think she'd bought it second-hand from a theatre costume sale, then just made some alterations herself . . . then had to make a few more because she was three months pregnant with Owen.

Just look at that lovely man she was cuddled up against. They were cheek to cheek, laughing and flushed with happiness. They'd broken off kissing for this photo . . . she could remember that.

He was so handsome! With his quiff of dark hair, deep-blue eyes and movie star jawline. Looking at this lovely photo, she thought how lucky they were not to have been able to see into the future. How would they have been able to smile at the camera like this, so broadly and proudly and with such wild optimism, if somehow they'd known that in just six years' time Roddy would be dead?

It was a blessing to have loved him for every day she'd had him without the slightest shadow, the slightest hint of how quickly it was all to come to an end. That was what she told herself, because four years on, she had made some kind of peace.

She had finally come through the rage, the furious injustice, the helpless and hopeless denial and all the other tormenting emotions which had stalked her after that terrible day.

Annie set the photo aside and now saw the blue and gold box with their wedding rings inside. Annie had only put hers in here, alongside his, a year ago when she'd moved in with Ed, because finally it had felt as if it was time to move on, to no longer be a widow in mourning.

And now she was burrowing amongst watches with well-worn straps and a half-emptied bottle of aftershave and photos and photos and more photos. She caught a glimpse of Roddy with baby Lana on his knee and had to avert her eyes quickly.

It was down here . . . now she had her hands on the thing she suddenly desperately wanted. The slightly scratchy Shetland wool jumper. The one with wool unravelling at the cuffs and suede elbow patches, the one with a neckline pulled wide with over-use. The one magical item which when she had it pulled over her face and breathed in and felt its scratch across her face, was the only thing which could just for a fleeting second or two bring a big strong bear hug from Roddy right back.

Annie pulled the arms of the jumper around her shoulders and covered her face with the chest. Here in this warm and private woolly place, she let go of the hard, tight feeling which had been building at the back of her throat all evening and let herself cry.

Losing Roddy had been absorbed. It had become part of who she was. Some days it made her feel stronger than anyone else because the worst had already happened. Some days it made her feel helplessly weak because she knew that the worst did happen. And could happen again. That was her now: flapping about between invincible bravery and total terror.

'Mum?'

It wasn't until Annie felt the hand on her shoulder

that she realized someone else was in the room with her. She'd been sobbing so hard into the jumper that she hadn't been able to hear anyone approaching.

'Oh . . . hello,' Annie managed, reluctant to take the jumper away from her face because she suspected she'd covered it in snot and tears and anyway, she always hated her children to see her like this.

'Mum, are you OK?' Lana asked gently, although it was obvious that Annie really was not. Seeing the open box, the wedding photo and her mother kneeling on the floor weeping into an old jumper, Lana's next whispered question was, 'Are you crying about Daddy?'

Although at first this made Annie cry even harder, pressing the wool tightly against her eyes, she finally managed to say, 'No babes, I'm crying about Ed.'

Lana crouched down and comfortingly began to rub her mother's back, but she knew better than to say anything else immediately.

'I mean, I miss your daddy,' Annie spluttered out, still with the jumper over her face. 'He'd love to have seen how well you and Owen are doing and how pretty you are . . . we all miss Daddy – ' Annie stretched out an arm and pulled her daughter in close – 'but I'm really upset about Ed.' She struggled to contain the fresh sobs desperate to break out at the mention of his name.

'You're going to be OK aren't you . . . you two?' Lana asked.

'I hope so,' Annie said, swallowing down her tears and finally pulling the wet jumper away from her face. 'Bet I look a fright,' she told Lana as she used the jumper to wipe under her eyes and her nose.

'You're fine,' Lana replied and squeezed her mum's shoulders.

'Well . . .' Annie smiled weakly at her daughter, 'that's the easy bit over. I thought it would last a bit longer than this, but there we go.'

'What d'you mean?'

'Me and Ed,' Annie went on, 'the nice easy bit at the start when everything is totally lovey-dovey and happy. That bit is over, I think.'

Lana passed her a tissue and Annie blew her nose before telling her daughter, 'Oh baby, relationships are really, really hard work. That's why so many people don't have a very good one.

'I was with your daddy for fourteen years,' Annie reminded her. 'You learn a lot about how love works in fourteen years . . . but Ed, he has no idea. He's being a big baby sulking at his sister's instead of coming home and talking to me. What on earth does he think he's going to change with his sulk? Does he think I'm going to rush over there and say, "Darling you were totally right, have it all your own way, run back into my arms"? We have to work this out, hammer it out, together. I should have told him what I was doing,' she admitted more to herself than to her daughter, 'I just didn't want to have the big showdown until I knew a bit better what I was going to do . . . I knew it was coming. I just tried to stall.' Annie reached for another tissue.

'Mum, why don't you just go round to Hannah's and talk to him?' Lana asked, 'I don't mind being here on my own for a bit, just go and see him.'

'I will, babes,' Annie said finally, 'but not tonight. It's too late and I'm too tired . . . and I'm just too upset.'

Annie gave her face another hearty wipe and then had to ask Lana, with all the kindness Lana had just shown her, 'How are you? Are you having a horrible time?'

'I spoke to Andrei tonight,' Lana said calmly, 'he's really sorry and wants me to forget about what happened. He says it was nothing . . . a mistake . . .'

Annie clenched her teeth shut to make sure that no murmur of disapproval should escape.

'So, I'm just thinking about that. I need to be sure. I need to be able to trust him,' Lana added.

She sounded so grown up, Annie thought all of a sudden, and with a fierce pang of pride.

'Yeah,' she agreed, 'take your time. No one's rushing you into anything.'

Lana looked up at her. 'Did Ed tell you about the time he found me and Andrei under there?' She pointed underneath the bed in front of them.

'Under there?!' Annie asked. 'No! What were you doing under there?'

'Well . . .' Lana's were eyes cast down again and she stumbled slightly over the words, 'I think . . . I mean . . . we were thinking about . . . sex . . . I think.'

'Oh!' was Annie's first reaction, but she quickly tempered her astonishment. 'Oh, right. And Ed found you?'

'Yeah,' Lana admitted a little sheepishly.

Ed hadn't told her a word. Annie wasn't sure whether to feel annoyed or impressed that he'd kept Lana's secret.

'I think he knew nothing major was going on . . . so maybe he didn't want to make a big deal of it,' came Lana's explanation.

'So you haven't . . . ?' Annie began and Lana shook her head shyly.

'I'm glad,' Annie told her. 'If you'd slept with him, you'd be feeling even more confused.'

'Yeah, I know,' Lana admitted, but then maybe because she wasn't quite ready for a big long talk about all that just yet, she got to her feet and asked, 'Do you want a hand putting all this stuff back in the cupboard or shall I go and make us some tea?'

'I would let you help me, but I'm too worried you'll just try and nab a few plum items for yourself.' Annie tried her best to sound cheerful again.

'Nah!' Lana insisted. 'We've got different taste these days.'

That was definitely true. Annie had decided, not long ago, to give up trying to understand her daughter and her daughter's friends' taste in clothes. It was all so frumpy and retro: slouchy pointy boots, weird baby doll jackets, batwing sleeves and carpet-bags. What was it with those cheap and nasty carpet-bags? Lana was always slouching off to school with a carpet-bag, a flat cap, ankle boots and black cape, looking like a Victorian orphan on her way to the poorhouse. It was too complicated.

As soon as Lana had gone out of the room to boil the kettle, Annie picked up her phone and without thinking about it too much, called Ed's number.

Once again, she was put through to voicemail. 'Ed,' she said calmly, 'please phone me, or come and see me. I would come and see you, but I don't want to leave the children at night. We need to talk. I'm sorry I've upset you . . .' After a momentary pause, she added, 'I miss you.'

Chapter Twenty-four

Tom Dickinson in the office:

Black merino polo sweater (John Smedley)
Black light wool trousers (Boss)
Black knee-length socks (Paul Smith)
Black lace-ups (Patrick Cox)
Fig-flavoured cologne (Diptyque)
Total est. cost: £560

'So what's the label?'

'Yes, hello? . . . yes I'm Annie Valentine.'

When the man on the other end of the line told her he was phoning from Harrods, Annie's heart skipped several beats: 'Oh hello! Thanks for calling me back!' she said excitedly.

Tom Dickinson apologized for not getting back sooner. It was approaching 7 p.m. and Annie had spent most of the afternoon hovering over her mobile waiting anxiously for his call. He wanted to know more about the bags she was selling.

In a voice which sounded so much more confident and professional than she was feeling, Annie began, 'Oh they're wonderful. Beautiful bags, entirely made in Italy from the three small factories commissioned every year to make bags for Tods and Yves Saint Laurent. They really are stunning quality at a stunning price. Obviously, I was hoping you'd like to take a look at some samples and see if you're interested.'

'So what's the label?' Tom Dickinson asked.

The label? Blimey, she hadn't given that a moment's thought. With just a brief pause, she found herself replying, 'Bellissimo Bags'.

'The reason I'm interested,' he went on, 'is that we're thinking about expanding our range of own-label bags. We're speaking to some suppliers but we haven't found quite the right thing at the right price yet. Would you be interested in working with us in this capacity?' he asked.

'Absolutely!' Annie told him, sure that Sandro with his Harrods obsession wasn't going to object to this.

'And how many bags can you supply?'

'How many do you want?' Annie countered.

'Well, initial orders might be in the 50–100 range.'

'Right, well I will speak to the factories and come back to you with figures at our meeting.'

There was going to be a meeting – wasn't there? She hadn't jumped the gun here?

'Erm . . .' Tom Dickinson paused, then said, 'Let me just check with my accessories merchandising manager. I'd want her in on a meeting.'

When he came back on the line, he asked if 10 a.m. on Friday would suit.

'Perfect!' Annie said, managing to rein in a shriek. She would have to take a few hours off work but otherwise it was totally perfect!

As Annie hurried in her heels down Hawthorne Street towards her home she found it had to keep the crazed grin from her face.

Supplying handbags to Harrods? Working with them on their own-label range? Could there have been a more dizzying start to her career in retail?! Whatever she'd thought about Harrods being a little bit staid and touristy and not cutting edge . . . she took it all back.

As she came in through the front door, things were not entirely as she'd expected. She'd expected the lobby to be a chaos of coats, schoolbags and shoes, just the sound of the TV coming from the sitting room, because that's where Owen and Lana would be, ready to greet her with, 'Hi Mum, what's for supper?'

Instead, the hallway was tidy. Everything had been put away. The kitchen lights were on, the warm and welcoming smell of sizzling garlic and onion was wafting through the hall and Annie could hear the sound of chatter.

Then she saw the raincoat and scarf hanging on the rack of coat hooks and her hope that Ed had come home was confirmed.

'Ed!' she shouted warmly from the hall, 'Hello! Hello guys!'

She hung up her own coat, dumped her bags and walked quickly towards the kitchen door.

Lana and Owen were at the kitchen table, Owen with his violin books spread out in front of him, Lana with a kitchen knife busy chopping her way through a pile of vegetables.

And there at the stove, in his butch blue and white striped apron, shirtsleeves rolled, stirring busily, was Ed.

'Hello,' she said to him, softly and with some surprise in her voice, 'are you making us supper?'

'Yes, I thought you'd all be hungry . . .' He carried on stirring, so Annie wasn't sure whether he wanted her to go up to him and kiss him hello or not.

But she did it anyway. She folded her arms around his waist and aimed to kiss him on the lips, but he turned just slightly, so her kiss landed at the side of his mouth. Oh! she thought to herself. If he was coming back, there were clearly still terms and conditions to be discussed.

'Nice to see you, babes,' she told him. 'We've missed you,' she risked.

'Yeah and your cooking,' Owen chipped in.

'We've eaten a lot of egg and chips in your absence,' Lana added.

'Only twice!' Annie insisted. 'I went to M&S on the way home, I was going to give you lasagne.'

'From a packet?' Owen asked as if this was the most horrible suggestion he'd ever heard. Lana also pulled a face at her.

'Is there anything I can do to help you?' she asked Ed, looking away from her ungrateful children. Her arms still ached after hauling the groceries home on the tube.

'No, I don't think so. The table's set, just open the wine.' He gestured to the bottle on the counter top, still wrapped in tissue, which he must have brought along with him.

*　　*　　*

The meal went smoothly enough. Lana and Owen did most of the talking. Owen and Ed were trying to decide which piece Owen should play at Dinah's party, because Bryan had phoned and asked him if he'd like to perform.

'Why don't you accompany me on the guitar?' Owen asked. 'That will sound much better than if I just play on my own. Plus I won't feel such a complete twinkie standing up there on my own.'

'Well . . .' Ed hesitated.

'Go on,' Owen wheedled.

'You've got to admit, Owen's violin sounds a lot better if you're drowning it out with some decent guitar,' was Lana's contribution.

'Lana!' Annie ticked her off.

'OK, OK,' Ed finally conceded, 'but we'll have to practise it together at least once before the off. Otherwise it might go horribly wrong.'

Once the main course was over, Ed had to confess that he didn't have anything for pudding, so Annie's M&S trip turned out to have been worth it after all. She microwaved chocolate sponge pudding, served it with cream and didn't hear a single complaint about it coming from a packet.

Every time she met Ed's eyes during the meal she gave him a smile. He smiled back too, but only small, tight, fleeting smiles as if he definitely couldn't relax into this yet.

'So . . . you two have probably got a bit of homework to do,' Annie suggested, when the pudding bowls had been scraped, or in Owen's case licked, completely clean. 'Maybe upstairs?' came her unmistakable hint.

And then she and Ed were on their own and at first there was a moment's silence before both of them began to speak at once.

'I'm . . .'

'I didn't . . .'

They stopped and smiled at each other. Annie didn't think Ed's smile was quite so tense now, so she began again, 'I'm really sorry. I'm really, really sorry – ' she put her hand on his forearm and rubbed it soothingly: 'I can't believe you were so angry with me that you endured Aunty Hilda on your own for the entire journey back to London. My God! If I'd known you were so angry I wouldn't have gone anywhere that Sunday morning. I'd have stayed with you.'

'Would you?' Ed asked.

'Yes,' Annie told him, 'you're much more important than any of this!' But she regretted the words as soon as she'd said them. Because wasn't he now going to insist she gave it all up for him?

'We're going to find a way of working this out, together,' she told him, 'we're going to make sure we are *both* very happy.'

Ed's arm moved out from under her hand and, leaning back in his chair, he crossed his arms. She didn't need to be an expert in body language to know that this wasn't a good sign.

'I have no idea what's going on,' he said.

'Yes you do,' she said, not quite so friendly herself any more, 'and maybe if you hadn't stormed off in a huff to your sister's you'd know more.'

'I would have moved to the spare room, but the spare room is full of shoes,' he exclaimed, 'not that I've ever been told anything about them!'

Ah.

'It's like living with a total fantasist,' Ed continued angrily, 'I don't know what's going to happen next. Maybe I'll go to the cash machine tomorrow and find there's no money in my account, it's all been used to buy belts. That's what's missing, isn't it? You've got a roomful of shoes, your Italian boyfriend is supplying the bags, all you need is the belts.'

Annie felt a terrible need to explode with laughter but she managed to keep it together. This was ridiculous.

'I've not touched a penny of your money,' she retorted. 'I would never do that.'

'What exactly is going on with you and that Maserati driving tosser?' Ed spat out.

'Oh, that's very mature!'

'Well, what are you doing with him?'

'This isn't hard, Ed: we're doing *business* together! He's going to sell me some bags!' Annie stormed. 'Why, what else did you think was going on? Just because someone bothers to iron their shirts . . .' her critical look didn't go unnoticed, 'doesn't mean I have to run away with them. In fact, how dare you suggest that—'

'I saw the two of you together,' Ed said, and although his voice was lower now, it was absolutely furious. 'I *saw* you. Do you understand?'

'No, I do not!' Annie was angry but she was also struggling to follow this. What was he getting at?

'I saw you!' Ed repeated. 'Do you need me to paint a

picture? Your arms around him, his hand on your arse, your face sucking the life out of his.'

Oh dear God.

Annie instinctively knew that saying '*I had something in my eye, he was trying to get it out,*' was not really going to work. She would have a job convincing herself with that line, let alone Ed.

'Jesus, Ed!' she began, her voice rising, 'I think you saw what you wanted to see there. That is not what happened. The guy's Italian and a bit flirty, we'd just agreed a deal and he moved in on me. Yes, I was caught a bit off guard, but there was nothing . . . absolutely nothing to it. No tongues, no *face-sucking –* ' suddenly she wanted to laugh again. This was just so childish. 'I can't believe you stormed all the way back to London over that . . .'

For a moment, Ed's face seemed to relax. Maybe he was going to laugh too. Maybe this was all going to be over in a moment.

'How completely immature,' she added and knew at once she'd pushed him too far.

'Oh for God's sake!' he snapped. 'If anyone's being immature, it's you. Shoes? Bags? Belts? A ten thousand pound tax bill? Are you out of your mind?'

And then Annie was listening to Ed offloading all his anxieties yet again: what a terrible risk this all was, and at the wrong time . . . putting their home and family life in jeopardy.

'Please, Ed,' Annie tried to reassure him, 'I wouldn't do anything to hurt us. I wouldn't risk our home. I'm good with money!' she insisted. 'I might overlook the odd bit of paperwork, but I'm great at selling! And I believe in this. I really do believe it will work . . .' She hated the pleading tone in her voice.

Even more, she hated the way he was making her feel as if she needed his permission. It just fired up her independence and her pride and made her want to charge off in her own direction without him.

Finally, they stopped talking and just stared at each other in exasperation because neither of them wanted to budge but they both knew there was no way they could split up over this.

Then Ed asked if it would be at all possible for her to put her idea on hold . . . just for a month or two. Just until she'd made a business plan, taken some samples round a few stores, made some proper connections.

Annie understood that this was a big shift. He was offering her the chance to go ahead but in a way he could be more comfortable with. She also understood that she should definitely agree. Agreeing would be a major breakthrough. Agreeing would probably solve everything, at least for the time being. Agreeing would definitely get Ed back into the house . . . tonight.

But she couldn't. The shoes couldn't be sent back to Hong Kong. The Italian bags were already on their way; in fact, they were supposed to have arrived this morning, before she left for work. And the meeting with Harrods was in the diary for Friday.

But there was Ed looking at her so intently, offering to back down, just needing her to meet him halfway.

'I could try and put things on hold,' she said and when she saw the relieved smile breaking out across his face, she added, 'That's probably not a bad idea.'

'Annie!' he reached out to put his arm over her

shoulder, 'that's great! Please, I'd be so grateful and I don't think you'd regret doing this . . . planning it out a bit.'

She put her arm around his shoulder and pulled him in.

It was very nice to have him again, to be holding him tight like this, his hair brushing against her face, and she didn't care for a moment that it smelled of fried onions rather than lime cologne. It was so nice to have him back that she felt obliged to say, just to reassure him, 'I haven't ordered any bags from Italy yet. I'm sure that could wait.'

His lips were on hers and they were up on their feet so they could pull each other close together.

'I've missed you,' he was murmuring into her ear, 'I've really, really missed you. I thought you were going to leave me for Mr Maserati.'

'Will you stop it?' She squeezed her hands into his back pockets. 'Don't ever do that again.'

'What, spy on you while you snog Italians?'

'No! Don't ever go off to your sister's and not return any of my phone calls or I will be really, really angry with you.'

'Yes . . .' his hands were running busily down her back, around her sides, over her buttocks, 'I think I'd quite like that.'

'Boarding-school boy,' she whispered in his ear. 'I always suspected you'd like to be spanked.'

The clear tone of the doorbell rang out, causing them both to look in the direction of the hall.

'Who's that?' Ed asked. 'Are you expecting someone?'

'No. D'you want me to go?'

'No, I'll get it.'

As Ed set off down the hall, a terrible thought occurred to Annie . . .

'Hello,' the man at the door began, 'I've got a delivery for Ms Annie Valentine.'

'Right,' she heard Ed reply. And it was too late. There was nothing she could do about it now.

'Is she here? She'll need to sign, it's a consignment from Italy.'

'Ms Valentine,' Ed's voice sounded flat, 'you'll need to sign for your Italian bags.'

When she reached the hall, Ed had already taken his coat and scarf down from the hook and was putting them on.

'Don't go, Ed,' she said, looking at him with her most pleading expression.

'Don't lie then,' he snapped. Then, brushing past the delivery man on the doorstep, he headed out into the night. When Annie put her hands out for the clipboard, she saw that they were shaking.

When it was time to turn out Owen's light, Annie lay down on top of his duvet and snuggled against him for a few minutes.

This was usually their quiet chat time when they had a little talk about how the day had gone and shared a joke or two. Annie liked to make him kiss her on the cheek a few times, insisting, 'You've got to keep practising your kissing!'

'For my teenage years,' Owen would joke.

Tonight, neither of them said anything until finally Owen asked, 'Is Ed still going to come to my birthday party?'

'Of course,' Annie told him. 'I might be having an argument with Ed, but that doesn't mean that you have to.'

'I like Ed. He's funny,' came next.

And Annie suddenly had to sniff away tears.

'He was going to give me a really cool birthday present. We'd already talked about it.'

Annie ran her fingers through Owen's hair. 'What was the present?' she had to ask.

'The Celestron Firstscope 114 EQ,' came Owen's reply.

She had no idea what this was . . . or what it meant. Well, it meant one thing anyway, it meant that Ed knew Owen and knew just exactly what to get him (whereas she'd been thinking bike . . . he needs a bigger one . . . even though he hadn't ridden his small bike once in the past year).

'You don't have a clue what that is, do you?' he asked.

'Of course I know what that is!' she said with as much indignation as she could muster. 'The Celestron First-scope 114 EQ. It's exactly what I was going to get you, so I'll tell Ed not to bother, shall I?'

'Mum!'

'Night-night sweetheart,' she told him, landing a kiss on his lips.

'Bet you're off to go and look that up on the internet, aren't you?'

'Do you think I should wax it right off or not?'

'I don't know . . . I don't care. What should I wear for the meeting?'

'Why are you asking me what you should wear?' Dinah's voice on the other end of the line sounded astonished. 'Can I just remind you what you do for a living?'

'Yeah, but I'm nervous, babes. I'm nervous. This is serious. This is walking into Harrods and trying to persuade them that I can supply them with expensive handbags.'

'You'll be fine,' Dinah said, with touching conviction. 'You'll be great!' she added. 'But c'mon, landing strip or take it right off?'

Party preparation was going into overdrive. Dinah was in danger of giving away that she knew all about Bryan's surprise party by over-prepping.

Somehow, touchingly, Dinah had got to the age of thirty-five without getting anywhere closer to extreme waxing than the standard bikini line. No beautician had yet instructed Dinah to 'put your leg around my back'. But she was considering the all-off as a 'surprise' for Bryan.

'Ten years of marriage,' she'd told Annie, 'there are a few new things we have to try, really.'

'You owe it to yourself,' Annie agreed: 'take it all off. Who wants a little Hitler moustache left down there anyway? Just don't be surprised if the beautician asks you to *turn over.*'

'NO!! I don't need to know that! I really don't!'

'Sometimes, you can be too prepared,' Annie had to admit.

'It is 11.30 p.m. and I'm taking it you are still on your own . . .' Dinah began to broach the difficult subject of Ed with her sister once again.

'He was here earlier,' Annie told her, 'but my Italian collection arrived and that sent him out of the door again.'

'Ah . . . I think you should go round there.'

'To his sister's?'

'Yes.'

'No,' Annie said, 'not tonight.'

'You haven't done anything,' Dinah wondered, 'I mean, you haven't given him any real reason to be this furious with you, have you? I mean, apart from buy a whole load of dodgy luxury goods?'

'Oh ha-ha. Of course I haven't done anything! Apart from try to get myself a better job. Why is that so terrible and threatening to him?'

'Why would a perfectly sensible and tasteful architect be planning a surprise tenth wedding anniversary party with a ceremony. Men are strange. The older they get, the more peculiar they go.'

'Oh great! We have just so much to look forward to then.'

The very first pair of glossy magenta and gold Timi Woos on Annie's eBay store looked like they were going to close down at £111 for the first pair . . . then there was a little last-minute flurry . . . £122, 124, 128, 131 . . . going, going, gone for £131.

Blimey!

Not only that, but every one of the losers emailed her within the next ten minutes to ask if she had more and in different sizes and colours.

Yes, yes, yes, were her replies.

Just ninety-nine pairs to go.

And the Celestron Firstscope, she'd looked that up too. It was a telescope 'suitable for beginner astronomers', priced £120.99. Good present, she couldn't help thinking, a little resentfully.

Chapter Twenty-five

Operation Harrods started with a hiccup or two. The children slept in, so Annie had to chivvy them to the kitchen table and force cornflakes down their throats, even though she was too nervous to eat herself.

'I have a meeting at 10 a.m.!' she kept wailing at them, 'you have to be out of here, gone! We all have to be on our way. I have to get my head together.'

She raced around the house in a flurry, trying to decide which of the bags to take. Three . . . she'd decided three was a good number. Or four? Was four better? Five?

All the cab numbers she tried were busy, or promising a car in 'about forty minutes, maybe sooner'.

'Just go by tube,' Lana told her. 'It'll be much quicker.'

'Tube! I'm a business mogul.'

'Mum, you're a lady selling bags . . .' Lana contradicted her scornfully, 'a bag lady.'

On her most sober high heels, Annie trotted at speed to the tube station. It was a good fifteen-minute walk down a steep hill, hot enough for the little grey jacket over her painstakingly chosen cream and black dress to have to come off.

Inside the carriage, the teeming throng of the rush hour Northern Line was upon her. Two cheeky-looking black twin schoolgirls were giggling together on the seats Annie would have killed for.

They looked about ten or eleven. Hair tamed in careful rows of braids, white school polo shirts setting off their bright smiles as they drank from little juice cartons and did more mischievous giggling.

Annie looked away from them and into the sea of humanity crammed at wonky angles into the belly of the tube train.

'Excuse me,' one of the twins suddenly seemed to be saying to her, 'we're getting off here, d'you want a seat?'

'Oh! That's very kind!'

What a sweet little face this girl had, with dimples in her cheeks when she smiled.

Annie swung round so that her legs were pressed against the seat they had vacated, guarding it from any other weary passenger. She watched the two girls approach the door, then just as she sat down, she saw them hop merrily out of the train. It took a moment or two for the Ribena on the carefully sabotaged chair to soak through Annie's dress. She looked frantically out of the window after the girls and saw their grins spread. As they saw her glaring at them, they began to laugh.

Annie stood up immediately, but it was already too late. She couldn't see, but she could feel the large blackcurrant stain. Drat. Damn. Bollocks. Crap. What was she supposed to do now? She looked at her watch. There was no way she could phone and tell them she'd been delayed. That would just be so unprofessional. It would take ages to go home and change.

No, she'd just have to brazen it out . . . keep her back to the wall, always walk behind them . . . and if worst came to worst, tell them she'd sat on a Ribena stain on the tube. Hey, it could have happened to anyone.

Even the Harrods accessories purchaser must occasionally sit on a dodgy chair, rub against a bit of chewing gum, spill a coffee, miss a step. They were only human, after all.

Coming up to the surface in Knightsbridge, Annie felt much better. The sun was out, the sky was blue, the shoppers were gorgeous, their expensive bags and jewellery glinting in the sunshine. Manes of below-the-shoulder hair swishing and every single one – man, woman, even delicious OshKosh B'Gosh baby in Bugaboo Frog – wearing sunglasses.

Annie took hers (Chanel, but via eBay . . . possibly very, very good fakes, hard to tell) out of her bag and strode forward, head high, knowing that this was the way you walked in Knightsbridge.

303

She was buzzed through the Harrods office intercom and shown into a pleasant waiting room.

'Tom Dickinson has been called away . . . very last minute . . . accessories purchasing manager . . . her office, waiting to meet you . . . show you straight through,' were the words Annie, suddenly overcome with nerves, was able to pick up from the receptionist.

Annie clutched her three, no four, handbags.

'No, after you,' she insisted when the receptionist held open the door. 'No, no really. I insist.'

'No, after you.'

'After you.'

Finally the woman gave in.

'And what's her name?' Annie asked as they approached a smart wooden door. There was a nameplate on it, but the receptionist pushed open the door before Annie could read it and then she was standing at the threshold of the office, looking directly into the face of the one woman she'd hoped never to see again.

Oh no. No, no, no! Not here. It just couldn't be!

Annie almost dropped every one of her bags straight onto the floor.

There, standing in front of her, was Donna Nicholson, her former floor manager at The Store. The woman who'd once made a part of every day miserable. The woman who'd had Annie dismissed on completely spurious and unfair grounds, the woman she'd danced a little victory dance about when she'd heard of her resignation. Annie had only returned to The Store when 'ding dong, Donna the wicked witch was dead'.

'Ms Valentine to see you,' the receptionist announced.

Donna didn't look quite as surprised to see Annie as Annie was to see her. Tom Dickinson must have mentioned her name, of course.

'Thank you, Celia,' Donna said, raising an eyebrow at Annie and saying with totally mock politeness, 'Come in, Ms Valentine and take a seat.'

'Shall I bring in some tea or coffee?'

'I think we'll be fine, thanks,' Donna answered and Annie was sure she could see the woman's eyes glitter.

As soon as the door closed on Celia, Annie knew Donna's gloves would come off and the nastiness would begin. How could she have been so naïve? Why didn't she check with Tom Dickinson? Why hadn't she asked who else she was going to meet? It wasn't so unlikely, was it? Donna had held a high-powered position at The Store, where else in London would she go? Harrods, Selfridges or Harvey Nichols had to be the top choices. The chances of Annie opening the door to find Donna in the Harrods accessories buyer's chair had in fact been: *too high!!*

'So, Annie Valentine . . . still moonlighting from The Store, are we? Or have you told your new boss about this?' Donna couldn't help snarling as she stalked across her little room, ultra-stylish light grey trouser suit swishing about her as she went. 'Maybe I should give her a call? I used to work with Raquel.'

Annie didn't even want to show Donna the bags. She just wanted to get out from under her poisonous glare as soon as she possibly could.

Putting on a horrible baby voice, Donna asked, 'Shall I have a look at Annie's special little handbaggies?'

'I don't suppose there's any hope of you being

professional, just for once?' Annie asked as calmly as she could when she'd found her voice again.

'No!' Donna snapped, 'I don't think so. Not when I've got you here at such a pathetic disadvantage.'

Annie could suddenly remember, in far too much detail, her final conversation with this woman on the day Donna had sacked her. Annie had definitely called her a bitch and it had been very ugly. Donna certainly wasn't going to be rushing to sign up a deal with Annie and Mr B's handbags, Annie could swear to that.

'I think I should just go,' Annie told her.

'No, no, I want to take a look. It's only fair, after you've brought them all the way here.'

Donna's hand went out for the bags, which Annie still had clasped to her side. For a moment, there was almost a slight tug-of-war, until Annie decided to let go.

Let Donna see them, she reasoned, let her see what fantastic stuff Annie was proud to be representing.

She handed the bags over, pulled back her shoulders and lifted her chin. She had no reason to quail under Donna's vicious gaze.

'Nice,' Donna said, running her hands over the leather and holding them up one by one to admire the shape and the colours, 'very nice.'

For a moment Annie felt a whiff of triumph. Even her one and only enemy had to admit that the bags were good.

Donna had the burnt orange one in her hands now and she was opening it, popping the satisfyingly large magnetic metal button.

'Nice lining,' she said, stroking over the pink quilted satin.

'Yeah,' Annie tried to sound just the faintest bit enthusiastic. She might as well play along, she thought.

'And the price?'

'Negotiable – but extremely reasonable for the quality.'

'Shame no zip, though,' Donna added with the happy glint back in her eye and the very beginning of a smile on her face. 'I mean selling handbags in central London, you can't sell them without zips. No one would buy them. Thieves everywhere, pickpockets. A handbag without a zip is a bit of a liability.'

'No zip?' Annie repeated. 'Yes, there's a zip!' She stood up to look closely at the top of the bag.

Where the bloody hell was the zip? There had been a zip in the factory bags, she had checked. She had double-checked, because what Donna had just said about pickpockets was totally true.

'No zip,' Donna assured her with a wicked smile and a look of pure evil.

Annie, the bag clutched between her hands, searched frantically for the zip. But there was no sign of one.

'There must be some mistake,' she said.

'Yes,' said Donna, 'there certainly is. The mistake is *you* coming in *here* trying to persuade me that you know something about handbags when in fact you don't.'

Annie could not believe that, once again, she was going to be shot down in flames by Donna. This could not be happening. Please, please no. The fate of Mr B's handbags at Harrods surely could not rest in the hands of this most horrible of harpies.

'I know about handbags,' Annie's voice was low but clear, 'believe me Donna, I know about handbags. The first women to start carrying handbags were the ancient Egyptians. In medieval Europe, the quality of a bag's embroidery and leather revealed your social status – so not much has changed there, then. The handbag proper began life in eighteenth-century France where it was called a reticule.'

'How very entertaining,' Donna sneered. 'Bye-bye, Annie Valentine.'

But Annie didn't move. 'Louis Vuitton opened his first shop in Paris in 1854. In 1856, Thomas Burberry set up shop in Basingstoke. Together they are responsible for the most copied luxury goods in the world.

'Coach of Manhattan: established in 1941. Hermès of Paris began to produce the handbag now known as the Kelly back in the 1930s, a good twenty years before Princess Grace ever carried it. Jackie O preferred the Hermès Constance, and in 1981 the iconic Birkin was designed for actress Jane Birkin, who blames its weight for her tendonitis.

'In the 1970s in Somerset, Roger Saul started his Mulberry workshop. When he sold out over twenty years later, deciding to run a hemp-seed oil farm instead, the brand went global, with prices tripling. But purists will still tell you that a Saul bag, with its tartan lining and oiled brass zips, is better than the modern Mulberry.'

'Good bye Annie, take your bags off to Primark, where they belong,' Donna said with a dismissive wave.

'Mrs Thatcher's handbags were Ferragamo,' Annie went on, determined to finish. 'Princess Diana preferred Dior, who returned the compliment by creating the Lady Dior in her honour. The average thirty-year-old British woman owns twenty-one handbags and will buy a new one every three to four months, owning about 160 in her lifetime. My Italian bags are vegetable-tanned using a process perfected in Italy over five hundred years ago.'

Annie paused for breath. 'So, don't tell me I know nothing about bags.' With that, she picked up her samples and, head held high, tried to leave the office with her dignity at least intact.

But, just as she'd turned to make for the door, Donna's voice rang out with glee. 'Oh Annie, I think you've sat in something.'

'It's Ribena,' were Annie's parting words. She gave the door as hard a slam as she could manage and stomped down the corridor straight past the reception desk.

'Nice boss,' Annie managed, heading straight for the stairs.

Sunglasses back on, shoulder bag lowered awkwardly over the Ribena stain, out on the pavement, Annie struggled to regain her composure. 'You are not going to cry about Harrods,' she told herself, 'you are not going to cry about Harrods.'

And anyway, if the Harrods accessories department was run by Donna, then it was bound to be awful. And she wanted nothing to do with it.

Sod the expense, she was going to treat herself to a taxi home. She stepped off the pavement and stuck out her arm at the next passing cab with its light on.

In the back of the taxi, face firmly towards the window, Annie watched the street scene in front of her eyes become blurry. Then she brushed the tears away from her cheek.

'All right, love?' the taxi driver asked her.

'Yeah . . . just one of those days,' she told him, trying to snap a smile back into place, 'I'll survive.' She smiled even harder, fishing in her handbag for emergency lipgloss and the other thing she found helped crying outbursts more than anything else. She popped two slivers of extra strong chewing gum in to her mouth and bit down.

Blinking hard, she cleared the blur from her eyes and told herself there were plenty of other shops. All over London. Just look out of the window! There were shops on every corner selling women the four handbags they bought every year.

The taxi was cutting through the side streets, short-cutting the clogged main arteries of London and winding them up towards Camden now, heading north to Annie's home in Highgate.

Yes, she was supposed to be going back to work, but she'd decided to go home, drop off her handbags, drink coffee, change out of the Ribena dress and recover before braving the shop floor again.

The taxi came to a halt in a side street. A big, silver four-by-four had stopped right in the middle of the road, put its hazard lights on and now the passenger's door was opening.

'Act like they own the blooming place,' the taxi driver complained.

Out stepped the passenger and Annie recognized her at once by the soft and sexy short bob and the glamor-ously foxy outfit. It was Svetlana's hairdresserphobe friend, Kelly-Anne.

The passenger door shut and the driver fired up his engine again. From her cab window, Annie watched as

Kelly-Anne ran her fingers through her hair and walked happily down the pavement, her touchy-feely pale grey knitted coat, belted at the waist, hugging her cosily. She looked great and that made Annie feel a lot better. She would miss styling women when she was a shoe and handbag mogul.

The taxi pulled out and into the top of Camden High Street where, under umbrellas opened to offer shade against the bright autumnal sunshine, café-goers were sipping their drinks.

And there was Ed. What!? Her head snapped round so she could take a second look. His coffee cup was in mid-air and he was laughing over the top of it . . . and right beside him, laughing back, was a very attractive woman.

Who the hell was that? And what was he doing having coffee in Camden High Street anyway? Shouldn't he be at school?

Annie, passing briskly in the cab, had not had the chance to have a proper look at his companion. The only details she'd taken in were that the woman was pretty, with dark hair and a delighted-looking laugh. Annie certainly didn't recognize her.

'Maybe she was Italian?' she wondered, panicking. Maybe it was Giovanna? Maybe this was why Ed was back at his sister's and not making any attempt to contact her. He'd lured Giovanna back from Italy . . . and now he wanted to move her back into his life.

No. She was being ridiculous. She was being irrational. Ed was allowed to have coffee breaks. He was allowed to meet women that she didn't know. There was probably a completely innocent explanation. That woman was probably a supply teacher who'd been assigned to the music department . . . and Ed was buying her a coffee to be friendly. But in Camden? So far from the school?

There had been no word from Ed since he'd stormed out of the house on Wednesday night. Since then she'd tried very hard to shut him out of her thoughts because the situation was making her very tense. Hadn't he realized yet that nothing was solved by silence? Did he seriously think she was just going to phone him up one day and say, 'Come back, I totally agree with you, I'm going to do everything you want'? If he thought that, he was deluded. She was too far along the road now. The Timi Woos were flying off the eBay site. She'd already made nearly £400 in profit and she was about to place a new order with Mr Woo.

As the taxi wound uphill into Hampstead her phone began to ring and she delved into one of her bags. *Ed?* she wondered nervously. Mr B, wanting to know about Harrods? That was going to be an awkward conversation. But where were the zips? What had he done with the zips? She snatched up the phone and looked at the screen. To her relief, she saw that the number was Connor's.

'Hello you!' she greeted him, trying to sound as bright as she could.

'Hello gorgeous girl, did I just see you whiz past me in a taxicab? You looked bloody miserable. And how come you're whizzing past in taxis while I have to walk everywhere?'

'Yes I am in a cab,' Annie told him, 'I thought you were so famous now that you had a car and a driver to take you everywhere.'

'As if . . . are you all right then?'

'Oh I'm fine . . . Ed seems to have another woman. But I couldn't be better.'

She was both surprised and hurt when Connor replied, 'You know what, my agent is on the other line, I'm going to have to call you right back. Sit tight.'

Chapter Twenty-six

Ralph Frampton-Dwight does lunch:

Light grey suit (vintage Gieves & Hawkes)
Pink shirt (same)
Pink silk tie (same)
Pink silk socks (holiday in Sorento)
Brown leather slip-ons (same)
Total est. cost: long forgotten

'Where the bloody hell are you?'

Connor was on his way home. He'd been partying at a friend's house, which had involved staying up drinking and gossiping until 5 a.m., kipping on the sofa for several hours and then leaving before noon. He'd still managed to dash out before the host emerged and roped him into clearing up.

Hell, he'd been rude. Never mind, he'd take the guy an extra-nice bottle of something the next time he went round. Hector had been at the party, just briefly for half an hour or so; in fact as soon as Hector had realized Connor was there, he'd left.

Once Hector had gone, Connor had felt, for the first time in a very long while, lonely in a crowd and without giving it too much thought, he'd turned to the wine bottle in front of him for comfort.

Now his T-shirt was sticking to him underneath his jumper as he walked. He was sticky, sweaty, unshaven, his hair was grubby and messy and he needed to get home and shower from top to toe. He needed to get last night out of his head, his mind and definitely out of his hair. He needed to get his act together for the Big Lunch with Sam Knight tomorrow.

The bridge of his nose hurt. He gave it a rub and realized that he must have knocked the scab off at some point. It felt a little crusty, as if some dried blood was sticking round there. God, he needed a wash. He could at least have washed his face before leaving. What if he bumped into someone important? He was walking up Belsize Park Road for God's sake.

That was when he saw Annie speeding past in the back of a cab. Or thought he saw Annie.

After giving her a quick ring to find out, he cut her off to answer the call from his insufferable, pompous arse of an agent Ralph (*Rafe*) Frampton-Dwight, known to his clients as Frightful-Twit. Still, the man got him lots of great work and other actors queued round the block to get onto his books, so he could hardly complain.

'*Rafie* darling, lovely to hear from you,' Connor gushed as charmingly as he could through the increasing pain of his hangover.

'Where the bloody hell are you?' came Ralph's angry response.

This took Connor by surprise. Where the bloody hell was he? Where the bloody hell was he supposed to be? OK, yes, yes, over the years, there was the odd little meeting or appointment . . . hell, even audition he'd been a tad late for . . . or, only very occasionally, missed. But he was sure there was absolutely nothing scheduled for today . . . Thursday?

'Where am I?' Connor asked *Rafe*. 'I'm walking up Belsize Park Road in search of a bloody bacon butty. Wrong place to look, really. Where are you?'

'Connor McCabe!!' Ralph Frightful-Twit erupted but in a low voice, as if he didn't want to be overheard, 'I am sitting in the sodding Chelsea Dining Room waiting for Sam Knight to turn up for a meeting arranged five weeks ago because he's thinking of casting you in his next sodding film. That's where I am, you imbecile. Get. Over. Here. NOW.'

'Oh fuck,' was Connor's pithy response, 'I thought that was on Friday.'

'This *is* Friday you hopeless wanker.' Clearly the gloves were off now.

'Have I got time to go home and change?' Connor wondered.

'No you bloody well do not. In fact – *fuck's sake*,' Ralph muttered under his breath, 'that's him now. Just get here!'

In the back of the taxi, Connor attempted to smooth down his hair. Then he flapped his sweater and T-shirt to try and let some fresh air circulate. Better keep the sweater on, he reasoned; less chance for the stale sweaty smell to escape.

Bloody shit damn expletive buggering bloody hell.

He'd been preparing for this meeting for weeks . . . months! He'd been to AA! Detoxing! Wheat-free! Pumped up! Annie herself had approved the perfect outfit for today: subtle designer jeans, just the right side of broken in, a very flattering blue cashmere T-shirt, shoes the perfect groovy crossover between shoe and trainer, and a Ralph Lauren blazer.

Now, here he was speeding towards Mr Knight in a stinky T-shirt, a jumper with holes and a pair of chinos which, on closer inspection, appeared to have a wine stain on the knee. He didn't even want to think about the stinky, ragged baseball boots on his feet. Shit!

And Mr Knight was one of those Californian health nuts. Only ate raw vegetables and seeds, swam a mile before breakfast, all that kind of crap.

Connor fell into something of a gloom as his taxi sped towards the Dining Room. Would they even let him in? he wondered.

Just as the cab pulled up outside the restaurant and Connor was digging about in his deep pockets for the fare, his mobile went off.

Handing over a jumble of pound coins and 50 pence pieces to the irritated driver, Connor could see that Hector was calling him. He cheered up immediately.

'Heck!' he said affectionately into the phone. 'Hello! Nice to hear from you.'

'Is it?' Hector asked moodily. 'I thought you were avoiding me last night.'

'No, you avoided me!'

'You definitely avoided me.'

'No,' Connor insisted, aware that the cab had pulled

off, that two men seated right at the window, in the restaurant's best table, were looking at him with . . . well . . . looks that ranged from angry to kind of surprised.

'You're not going to believe this . . .' Connor began, 'but I'm going to have to call you back because I'm just about to meet—'

'No!' Hector interrupted, 'you're not allowed to hang up on me, Connor. I don't care if you're about to go and meet Steven bloody Spielberg himself. You have to talk to me right now!'

'I can't,' Connor pleaded, 'I will phone you as soon as I've finished . . .'

The line went dead.

Connor cast his eyes back to the men at the window. Even at this distance, he could see how scarlet Rafe was turning. With a casual ruffle of his messed-up hair, he jogged towards the restaurant's reception.

A waiter ushered him to the table where he made fulsome and apologetic greetings: 'I am so, so sorry . . . grovelling . . . honestly, Mr Knight, if you'd let me lick your shoe leather, please.'

'No, no,' Sam Knight, tanned, shiny with health and wealth, just exactly as you'd want a Hollywood film director to look, insisted, sounding a little bewildered.

'Sam, allow me to introduce Connor McCabe,' Frightful-Twit began.

'I couldn't get a taxi, then the taxi got stuck in traffic . . .' Connor wondered whether he should explain his outfit and general state of unwashedness. Frightful-Twit seemed to be staring at his nose with an expression set in utterly alarmed disbelief.

Connor made a mental note to leave at the same time

as Knight. He didn't really want to hear what Frightful-Twit might have to say to him as soon as Knight was out of earshot.

Jesus, look at Knight. He had a totally smooth neck and chubby cheeks. Did people from Hollywood really think it was normal to go around looking like a chipmunk's bum?

'Been in London long?' Connor ventured as he headed towards his chair.

'I'm just here for three days. Back-to-back meetings, no chance for sightseeing,' Sam replied briskly. Clearly this was going to be a quick lunch.

'So Ralph here—'

'*Rafe,*' F-D chipped in smarmily.

'He tells me you're a big TV star over here. Sunday night ratings of over eight million.'

Connor suspected he was supposed to give 'power meeting' now. He was supposed to sit down and wow Sam Knight with his energy and brilliance and dedication and commitment and determination and drive . . . blah, blah, blah. Just how had an acting interview managed to get so like an accounting interview?

'Oh . . . well, yes,' Connor began . . . and all of sudden he just truly couldn't be bothered. He leaned back, tipping his chair dangerously. 'Well, there are a few old ladies who like to tune in to *The Manor* every now and again.'

Frightful-Twit's face was returning to a dangerous shade of red.

'A few old ladies, huh?' Sam Knight repeated.

'Connor's being modest . . .' Frightful-Twit began to intervene.

'No, no. Old ladies love me,' Connor broke in: 'obviously they're in denial about the fact that I . . .' his voice dropped low and he had Knight's full attention now, *'sleep with other men.'*

'Right,' Knight said.

'Because, let's not beat about the bush. I'm good-looking, I can act the socks off anyone you'd like to name, but I'm a great, big, raving poof' – Connor had decided to give it to him straight, so to speak – 'and you're not going to have me walking the red carpet with a fake girlfriend or keeping coy in interviews about my "other half" and "very good friend" and all that bollocks.'

'Right,' Knight repeated.

'So here I am. This is me. Take it or leave it,' Connor added, 'I'm not giving you any of that marketing wank about myself.'

Connor suspected he'd blown it. No, make that, he *knew* he'd blown it just as soon as he'd pulled up in the taxi outside the restaurant . . . so he decided, on the spot, that since he'd so blown it, he might as well go down in style.

'And I'm not going to go on about how much I love your work either,' he continued. 'Your first two films were cracking, but that thing you brought out last year: *The Geologist's Nightmare?'*

'The Biologist's Daydream,' Knight corrected him.

Frampton-Dwight's mouth hung open slightly, his face frozen in an expression of horror.

'That was a steaming pile of horse manure,' Connor announced bluntly, 'and you're good, so you must know it.' He sat up straight now. 'Yeah, right, well, I'd absolutely love to come and work with you, but not on a stinker like that.'

Connor heard his mobile phone beep, and making another sudden decision, he stood up, muttered an apology or two and left to finish off this call. It really couldn't wait.

He hurried over to the restaurant's lobby. Phoning Hector back now seemed far, far more important than chatting up some big US director dick. And then there was Annie: *what* had Annie just said about Ed? He was going to have to call her too.

Back at the table, Sam Knight began to laugh.

'The Brits!' he exclaimed to Ralph Frampton-Dwight. 'That guy!'

Frampton-Dwight was struggling to read the expression on the movie man's face. He was just about to tell him that Connor McCabe was no longer on his books and would he be interested in meeting Steve Crookston, who could be here within fifteen minutes, when Knight asked, 'D'you think he was in a fight last night? Did you see his nose? He looked like he hasn't slept or washed in a week. No one, no one in the States would dare to meet me looking like that!'

'I know. Deplorable,' Frampton-Dwight agreed, 'absolutely deplorable. So unprofessional—'

'It's great!' Sam Knight said picking up the menu and looking seriously as if he intended to stay for lunch after all, 'He's gonna be perfect for the part. I wanted a sort of retro *Withnail and I* feel to the thing anyway. And you know what? I think I'll make his character gay. Let's have a gay lead. And yeah . . . he's right about *The Biologist's Daydream*. That's what happens when you listen to too much . . .' he paused and then tried out the phrase uncertainly, 'marketing wank?'

As Frampton-Dwight tried not to choke to death on the large swig of wine he'd just taken, Knight sipped at his still mineral water and added calmly, 'Yesterday I met one of your actresses. Big name . . .' he gestured vaguely, 'Kate?'

'Blanchett? Winslet?' Frampton-Dwight offered eagerly.

'Yeah . . . something like that,' Sam said. 'And you know what? She brought her baby! To the meeting!'

'Oh God,' Frampton-Dwight offered with a grimace.

'No, no, listen up. It was a big baby. It could walk and everything . . . and she said she had to bring it, because it's still breastfeeding! And then, she starts feeding it, during the meeting! I mean *that* is different. I'm not going to forget a meeting like that.'

'No . . .' F-D had to agree, 'and I suppose that way you know she won't have a problem with a nude scene.'

'Oh, you are so wrong!' Sam exclaimed. 'She's sitting there with a toddler hanging off her nipples. Great tits, by the way. And she's telling me on no account will she do nude. Not even a partial buttock, not even upper thigh.'

'Really?' F-D felt a little at sea. Was he supposed to be admiring or disapproving? He seemed to have lost his bearings here. Was McCabe hired or fired? He should have stuck with the mineral water too.

'That is what I love about the Brits,' Sam continued. 'They don't care. In LA everyone is sucking A so hard their faces are distorted.'

Sucking A? What did he mean? The man spoke a

different bloody language. 'So you've cast this Kate?' he ventured in confusion.

'Sure! And her baby too if she wants and you know what? I think your guy will be great with them. Just great. I'm hoping he gets off the phone soon so he can tell us what he did last night. What do you think we should order for him? Another round of beers?'

Chapter Twenty-seven

Tilly B-P's Blitz spirit:

Red skirt suit (Valentino)
Wide black patent belt (The Store's
accessories department)
Red pillbox hat with veil (same)
Black seamed stockings (same)
Black patent shoes (Chanel)
Total est. cost: £1,200

'This looks like a bloody bit of satellite.'

'Are you still at home?' Connor's voice was fever-pitch with excitement.

'No, I'm at work now. I'll be here till eight,' Annie informed him.

'I've got something to tell you!' Connor exclaimed. 'It's huge, it's immense! Enormous! It can't wait.'

'What?' Annie asked him. 'Babes, I really have to go.'

'Wait! I'm going to be one of the stars in Sam Knight's

next film. Annie, I'm going to be famous! Really, internationally, *movie star* famous!'

'That is fantastic!' Annie told him, 'I am so, so pleased for you. But I have to go.' She glanced over at Tilly B-P, one of her favourite clients, who had an enormous Prussian blue hat, trimmed with metal, balanced on her head and was drawing a line with her finger across her throat. This didn't mean 'Get off the phone or else.' Annie knew it was Tilly's shorthand for 'If you want me to wear this, you'll have to kill me first.'

'I'm coming round later,' Connor informed her, 'to check on you.'

'No, you don't have to,' Annie told him. 'Dinah's feeding the children and once I get home, I'm going to bed early. Anyway, you should go out with your glamorous friends and celebrate.'

'But you are my glamorous friends,' Connor said and all of a sudden Annie had to swallow hard. 'See ya later?' Connor asked.

'OK doll.'

'Annie! What are you thinking? Are you feeling a bit off-colour today? PMT?' Tilly was asking her, now that she'd put her phone away. 'This looks like a bloody bit of satellite fell out of the sky and landed on my head. I didn't live through cancer only to get hit by a sputnik! '

Much as Annie wanted to laugh, she astonished Mrs Brosnan-Pilditch, who was in the suite to choose an outfit for her 70th birthday lunch, by welling up with tears.

'Oh dear! I'm sorry!' Mrs B-P soothed. 'It's not your day today, is it?'

'It's not the best,' Annie agreed, pressing hard at her eyes and gulping tears back. Streaked mascara all over the place wasn't the best personal shopper look.

'And you, being you, will definitely not want to talk about it, will you?' Mrs B-P said next, 'you'll just want to fix it.'

'Well, it's not very professional to be gushing all over my clients. But I've not been very professional,' Annie blurted out, thinking of the conversation she'd had with Mr B about his zipless bags half an hour ago in her office with the door tightly shut.

She'd given it to him straight: 'Harrods won't take the bags because they have no zips.'

'No zips!' she'd heard him declare. 'But why they need ugly metal zip? We have beautiful brass button with magnetic closure, much, much more elegant and easy.'

'But this is London,' she'd insisted. 'We have thieves. And anyway, the bags you showed me had zips. The bags I ordered had zips!'

'No, no, no! No zips,' he'd countered.

'Yes they did, I checked . . .' she'd said, realizing how naïve and amateurish she'd been. She'd taken no photos of the original bags she'd ordered, she hadn't written up any sort of detailed specification. No contract. She'd certainly not thought of making Mr B sign anything. Oh, she could just about scream at herself for being so green!

'Annie, I have to phone you back,' he'd told her and abruptly, the line went dead.

*   *   *

'You're always 100 per cent professional to me my dear,' Mrs B-P told her, 'that's why I can't buy anything by myself any more. I'm totally dependent. An Annie addict. Now come on, cheer up. Unless it's fatal, I don't think you should cry about it. That's my new motto. And even if it is fatal, at least you're not dead yet!'

Annie put her hand on Mrs B-P's skinny, narrow shoulder. 'Are you going to be OK?' she asked her. 'Are you properly in remission now?'

'Darling, we are all in remission,' Mrs B-P smiled at her serenely. 'It's going to come and get us all one day. Worth remembering that.'

'Is that the spirit of the Blitz?' Annie asked with a smile.

'I'm not that old!' Mrs B-P reminded her, 'but damn right! Now take this bloody thing away.' Mrs B-P passed her the sputnik hat and picked up the deep red pillbox trimmed with a huge silk rose and a spunky little red net veil, 'I think this is much more like it.'

'Everyone's fine, everyone's great. Owen's already in his pyjamas, Lana's doing her homework and I have to run,' were Dinah's words of greeting when Annie arrived back at her home that evening.

Annie gave her sister a big hug of gratitude and asked, 'No phone calls or anything?'

'No, Ed has not phoned,' Dinah told her, 'but Annie, you need to do something. You're the grown-up! You're the one who's been married. You know how these things work. You'll have to step in and sort him out. Or he's going to wreck this.'

Annie didn't even have her feet properly inside the

door, didn't even have her coat off and she was already being bombarded with Ed advice.

'Dinah, not right now, babes. Not right now . . . are we all organized for tomorrow then? And by the way, your face! Your face looks lovely. The rash went right away!' Annie enthused.

'You owe me eighty-five pounds, Annie,' Dinah said huffily. 'That's how much it cost to see Connor's dermatologist.'

'It was worth it,' Annie told her. 'Shall I give you a bag instead?'

'No, I would not like a blinking bag! I have to go. Bryan's got squash.'

'So tomorrow,' Annie began. 'Lana, Owen and Billie are going to Mum's first thing, I'll come and get Billie and the car seat. We are then left to spend the entire day at the spa, then we get dressed up at my house and meet Bryan at the hotel for the surprise "dinner" he thinks you think he's arranged.'

'Oh God,' Dinah looked properly nervous all of a sudden, 'you do think it will be OK, don't you?'

'It is far, far too late to worry about that now, you might as well just enjoy,' Annie told her, adding, 'I've booked you in for the full top to toe at the spa, by the way.'

'What does that mean?'

'Look, you're in there, you might as well go for the works: facial, mani, pedicure, all the waxing. The more you have done, the cheaper it gets. This is not the time to economize,' Annie pointed out. 'The second-biggest party of your life is happening tomorrow night. There won't be many more jamborees in your honour before your funeral probably, so make the most of it. You might not be looking your best at the next one.'

'Oh please!' Dinah said, gathering up her things and heading out of the door. 'See you tomorrow.'

As Annie was coming down the attic stairs after chatting to the children, her mobile beeped with a text.

She fished it out of the bag she still had draped over her shoulder and eyed the number, registering the little hope that Ed might be getting in touch.

'*Speaking to* Marie-Claire, *what to wear???! Danni xxxx*'

Annie carried on down the stairs and then made straight for the spare room and her stack of cardboard boxes. She delved into them for the beautiful red pair of Timmi Woos in Dannii's size four. The ones with a light tan trim. They were high heeled, shiny crimson red with a low strap, and a nice little red and tan button to hold the foot in place. All in all they were the sexiest, classiest shoes Annie had ever seen.

Dannii should definitely wear these. What she would wear with them was just a detail. A detail which Annie would be able to sort out inside an hour at The Store on Wednesday, and she texted Dannii back to say as much.

Annie leaned back against the comfortable male arm under her neck and wriggled in a little closer to the warm body lying across the length of the sofa beside her. She picked up her nearly empty wineglass and pushed it up into the air: 'To you,' she said once again, 'what would I do without you?'

'Get a dog, maybe?' came the reply. 'You could snuggle up on the sofa with a dog. If it was a big one.'

Annie slapped Connor's thigh. 'You're not my dog,' she told him.

'Yeah, but you're my bitch, girl,' he said, making himself laugh.

She had heard every last detail of Connor's meeting with Sam Knight, including the catastrophic outfit, which she was sure had clinched him the part.

'A *retro "Withnail and I"* kind of feel,' Connor was repeating again. 'Annie, if I'd worn the Ralph Lauren blazer, I wouldn't have got the part. Even the scab on my nose helped!'

'I didn't like the blazer,' Annie reminded him, 'that was Dale from Menswear's idea, remember? I didn't think it said "creative". It was more "accountant on day off". You're right, what you wore screamed "creative". You were very clever,' she teased, digging him in the ribs, 'and he's going to make your character gay . . . you're a star!'

'Drink up' – he pointed at her glass – 'because you know I'm about to ask you about your boyfriend.'

'Oh no, not my boyfriend!' she grumbled.

'Are you two OK? Why is he not staying here at the moment? And what are you doing about it? And how do you feel?' were the questions Connor fired at her.

'How do I feel?' she repeated wearily. 'I feel as flat as a hedgehog on the M25 and I have no idea how we're going to work this out . . . but there is one thing I want to ask you . . .'

'Anything you like,' Connor assured her.

'Was Roddy ever unfaithful?'

There was a time not long after Roddy's death when Annie and Connor had had to talk about Roddy constantly. Roddy's wife and his best friend, who hadn't even been very close before, had felt obliged to discuss every memory, every little joke, conversation and nuance. They'd been determined to keep Roddy as alive as possible in their minds. They'd almost been frightened to stop talking about him, in case they forgot some detail when they were knocked sideways by grief and desperate to remember everything.

Now it was an occasional treat to talk about Roddy: not nearly so desperate or painful as it had once been. They could reminisce bittersweetly, just once in a while.

Annie listened for several moments to Connor breathe.

'You know,' she went on, 'you were away together filming when I was back at base with the babies. I've worked on film sets, I know how incestuous they get on a long shoot.'

Still Connor said nothing.

'You have to tell me, Connor, because if you don't say anything, I'm just going to suspect the worst.'

'Why do you have to suspect the worst?' Connor asked, breaking his silence.

'For some reason, I think if anything ever happened, it happened on that four months you were in Romania. Did it?' Annie prompted him.

'Annie,' Connor began, hauling himself up so he could look at her, 'why are you asking me this?'

'So he did, then,' she said in a small, flat voice.

'No, I'm not saying that. I'm not saying that at all. But why are you asking me about it?'

'It just seems important! I'm looking back at my marriage and thinking no one and nothing can ever match up to it. But maybe I'm totally wrong,' she tried to explain.

'OK. Well, here's what I'm going to tell you.' Connor swirled the remains of the wine around in his glass and drank it down: 'In Romania there was this girl. A Romanian girl, Irena. She was very pretty, very sparky and she was absolutely besotted with Roddy. She always arranged to sit beside him and talk to him and do his costumes and be with him. She did all the running, and he wasn't interested.'

'Oh really . . . not at all,' Annie's sarcasm was obvious.

'OK, he was flattered,' Connor had to admit, 'he was flattered . . . and we were over there for four months . . . and I think,' Connor hesitated, then decided to say as gently as he could, 'I think there might have been a very, very little . . . *thing* . . . but as far as I could see it was over before it had even begun and he was not interested. He felt really, really guilty . . .'

'Oh well, that's all right then,' Annie snapped. She looked dangerously as if she was going to cry. Connor decided to plough on.

'And Roddy was horrified when this girl started phoning him once he was back in London. He didn't want you to find out anything about it. Because,' and now Connor's arm went round Annie and held her tight, 'he didn't want to spoil anything with you and with the children. He didn't want to do a single thing to hurt his family.

'Annie don't you dare cry about this, because it's nothing. You and the children were the most, most important thing to him in the world. Annie' – Connor was looking exasperated now – 'Don't tell me you've forgotten that? That would just be an insult!'

And because Connor looked quite genuinely upset as he said this, Annie had to agree with him. Really, she knew it was true anyway. And she knew, really, that of course this wasn't important, not in the scheme of things.

'I don't know why you're asking me about this. Just forget it, please.' Connor was now overcome with remorse that he'd mentioned a word about the girl.

'Irena?' Annie was asking now. 'You know, I think I've met her. Jesus, Connor, I think she came into The Store and had a session with me.'

Connor looked completely taken aback.

'Before we went to Italy! A Romanian girl called Irena came in for a consultation and she asked all sorts of personal questions, about the children . . .'

'She knew who you were?' Connor sounded incredulous. 'And where you worked?'

'Roddy must have told her. She must have known he'd died, someone must have told her that.'

'I told her,' Connor admitted straight away.

'Oh Jesus. Well . . .' Annie stumbled, 'that was nice of you.'

'Annie,' Connor began, 'she phoned me up soon after it happened, saying she was coming to London, she hadn't heard from Roddy in ages and she wanted to contact him. And I told her . . . and she was quite upset.'

'Obviously – what with them being such close friends.'

'Annie, he's the one who told Irena all about you, all about the children. That wasn't me.'

Annie sank back against his arm, realizing that she could find a lot of comfort in that.

'And no,' Connor added, kissing her on the forehead, 'your marriage was great, but it wasn't perfect. No one's is. We have to make do with the best we've got. So get off your bum and go and phone Ed. Do whatever it is he needs you to do, or you're going to be a very sad and lonely lady all over again, and we can't have that – not when I can't look after you because I'm away *filming*,' he shot her a grin. 'Meanwhile, I'm going to go and investigate the contents of your fridge.'

'Good luck,' she called after him. 'There's a soya yoghurt, a quorn sausage and a diet quiche. They're all mine, I have a party dress to get into. Owen ate everything else.'

'It's a nightmare in here, you need Ed back!' Connor shouted from the kitchen.

'What about you?' she shouted back. 'If no one's perfect and we've got to make the best of what we have, why don't you get off your bum and go and see Hector?'

'I'm going to do that,' Connor said, speaking through a mouthful of diet quiche as he came back into the room, 'right now. He's not home till 11 p.m. God, this is disgusting!'

'Better get used to it, Hollywood boy!' And suddenly Lana was standing at the sitting room door in her pyjamas.

'Hey babes,' Annie greeted her, 'I thought you'd gone to bed.'

'I did, but I forgot to tell you . . . I spoke to Ed today and he said he's at a concert tonight, that he can't get out of . . . and he'll see you tomorrow.'

'But I'm spending the day with Dinah tomorrow,' Annie replied.

'Maybe he means at the party then.'

Chapter Twenty-eight

The fifty-something woman on the swing:

Long below-the-shoulder gunmetal grey hair (herself)
Extensive waxing (The Spa)
Sparkly pink nail varnish on all twenty nails (MAC)
Total est. cost: £95

'Even being naked is expensive.'

Dinah walked into the sauna with one thick white towel wrapped around her head and another round her body. She was brandishing a long, chilly glass of champagne and as soon as she spied Annie, she announced, 'I cannot believe how much that hurt! I am never, ever doing that again.'

Annie tried hard not to burst out laughing at Dinah's shocked face. 'Babes, it will be so worth it. Think of the surprise Bryan will get tonight. His baby's had a Brazilian.'

'I don't know how good it looks, though,' Dinah confided, 'I'm not exactly twenty any more. I've given birth, there are baggy bits, purplish bits . . .'

'Enough!' Annie screeched. 'Once the swelling goes down, you'll be fine.' Annie patted the space on the bench beside her, although there was no one else in the tiny Swedish pine cabin right now, 'So . . . ten years!'

'Yeah.'

'You should know that the next three years are really, really tough, according to all my clients. Best to be prepared. Apparently it's when you pass through the: *shall I really stick with this man and all his many faults and flaws for the rest of my life? Or shall I get out while I still have some looks left and a slight hope of attracting someone else?'*

'Thanks, Annie.' Dinah nudged her. 'That's so cheering.'

'Do you know in which year a divorce is statistically most likely to happen?'

'No, but you're about to tell me, aren't you?' Dinah swigged her champagne.

'Year eleven.'

'No! You are lying!'

'I'm not. That is the truth, I promise you. And I bet it's because the wives didn't get good enough anniversary presents. Seriously! They're thinking: *I put up with you for TEN YEARS and you give me a rubbish little AMBER PENDANT which cost about thirty pounds.* I think if you want to guarantee another ten years of bliss, you have to fork out big on your tenth. Spend even more than the engagement ring.'

'You would say that because you're so materialistic,' Dinah said, with a quick smile at her sister.

'And you would say that because you're so . . . so . . .

337

untainted!' Annie countered. 'It's not materialistic, it's about wanting to be properly appreciated.'

'Bryan appreciates me,' Dinah said, 'and I don't need some bit of rock dug out of the ground by some poor, exploited, Third World miner to prove that. He's having this party for me, isn't he?'

'Yes,' Annie agreed quickly, 'I think it's great! I think it's fantastic you've been married for so long. You always seem really happy.'

'We are happy,' Dinah said thoughtfully, 'we are definitely happy enough. We've fallen in and out of love so many times. That's the difference between people who stay married and people who split up: we just hang on in there, convinced it's going to get better. And it does. No one tells you that . . . that you can fall in love with someone all over again, and even be desperate to be with them all over again. It's the work of a lifetime to learn how to live very happily with someone else.'

'You're right,' Annie agreed and raised her glass. 'Here's to your very happy marriage.'

'What the hell are the vows going to be like, though?' Dinah worried. 'How can there be renewing of vows when I've not even seen them? What's he going to make me promise and how cheesy will it be?

'As long as there's nothing about being your ickle little sexy kittie for the next fifty years and not a word, not one whisper about till death do us part. That's like the marriage small print,' she added, 'we all skim over it without a thought. When you're in your wedding dress, you never, ever once think about standing at a grave-side . . .'

'But weddings are like childbirth. You're so focused

on the day, when really you should be preparing for the lifetime that's going to come afterwards,' Dinah cut in.

'You can't knock a little bit of healthy denial, though . . .'

'I do occasionally think about Bryan being dead,' Dinah confessed, 'but only in a fashion shoot kind of way: look at me in my veiled black pillbox . . .' Dinah added. Then, as lightly as she could, she reminded Annie, 'you were devastatingly gorgeous at Roddy's funeral. No one could take their eyes off you.'

'Yeah, well I spent a lot of time and a huge amount of money on that outfit. Because I had no idea what had just hit me,' Annie recalled: 'the emotional equivalent of a two ton lorry. I was still unconscious at the funeral.'

'Here's to all the devastatingly gorgeous widows out there,' Dinah raised her glass.

They chinked glasses and after taking a swig for bravery, Annie felt compelled to ask, since they were obviously having an emotional detox in the sauna today, 'Have you ever cheated on Bryan?'

Dinah swallowed down her mouthful of champagne and to Annie's utter astonishment replied, 'Yes.'

What was going on? Was everyone apart from her cheating? And there was Ed thinking that she was cheating when she wasn't.

'No!' Annie spluttered in reply. 'You cheated on Bryan? Why don't I know about this?'

'I didn't want you to know . . . I didn't want anyone to know. Not when it was happening and not afterwards because it was just so embarrassing.'

In the dim light of the sauna, Annie tried to read Dinah's expression. Was she guilty? Glad? Was she proud of herself now, or ashamed? She looked very, very thoughtful. But then Dinah tended to. She always had to think about everything, analyse it and figure it out.

'We were going through a rough patch. Billie was a toddler—'

'Oh my God!' Champagne just about flew out of Annie's nose at this. 'You managed to have an affair when Billie was a toddler, how did you do that?'

'I met a dad at toddler group and he used to come back to my flat, and when the children had a nap . . .'

'Oh. My. God.'

'It only went on for a week or two . . . three weeks. Then we were both overcome with guilt and he started going to a different group.' Dinah couldn't suppress a giggle at the recollection.

'Yeah, adultery can really impact your kids,' Annie couldn't resist saying. 'They can lose all their little toddler friends. Oh. My. God . . .' She was still scandalized, 'You were a little distant that winter when Billie was eighteen months and not sleeping and I thought you were just shattered and didn't want to hear any more of my sleep training advice.'

'No . . . no. Billie was getting plenty of sleep training. The blinds were all drawn at naptime. And the sex was . . . I'm sorry, I know people are always supposed to say the sex wasn't that great when they had an affair because they were so guilty and they were so used to one person and blah, blah . . . but the sex was . . .' she lowered her voice, 'absolutely thrilling.'

Annie tried to laugh, but it stuck in her throat as she thought of Roddy and Irena. Maybe that had been absolutely thrilling too.

'It wasn't about me and Will – that's what his name was, by the way. I didn't even like him much, he was a jerk, just a good-looking jerk.' Dinah went on. 'It was about me and Bryan. I'd been at home with a baby for a year and a half. I was bored and totally boring. Instead of taking him away on holiday, instead of doing something new and interesting with him or with myself, I channelled all this energy into fantasies about Will. The fantasies went on for weeks, *months* before we actually did anything,' she confided.

'And when you did?' Annie prompted.

In a confessional whisper, Dinah admitted: 'Because we were so guilty about the sex, we used to have foreplay for just about the full two hours the children were asleep . . . and then a tiny two minutes of sex at the end.'

'Sounds about right,' came Annie's comment.

'It was! I used to just kiss him for the first half an hour until my knickers were in meltdown,' Dinah whispered.

Something about Dinah with a towel on her head and a raw new Brazilian saying this was suddenly so funny that Annie began to laugh and then Dinah joined in and they both roared uncontrollably for several minutes.

'This must be why you're not allowed to drink in the sauna. It gets you high,' Annie managed to say finally. And then, without even meaning to, she found herself telling Dinah all about Irena, dehydrating herself with tears in the process. When the story was all out and Dinah had said as many consoling words as she could think of, she had to suggest to her big sister, 'You know, it is maybe just a little bit possible that you idealize slightly how it was when you were with Roddy. You had plenty of ups and downs too.' Annie had a suspicion about what was coming next.

'So are you going to tell me what's happening with Ed?' Dinah asked. 'He's not still at his sister's, is he?'

'Yes he is at his sister's. But he's said he'll see me tonight.'

'Tonight?' Dinah sounded surprised. 'Tonight's not going to be a great time to talk.'

'You know that, babes, and I know that . . . but Ed seems to be a complete and utter beginner as far as serious adult relationships are concerned.'

'Blame his Italian girlfriend,' Dinah said.

'What? Has he said anything about her?'

'No, I was just being . . . I dunno, flippant.'

Annie just gave a shrug. 'You know what, I think I'm finally ready to go on the swing!'

'The swing over the pool?' Dinah asked.

'Is there another one?'

'The naked swing? The one we watched the naked old ladies swing on?'

'Oh yes!'

Annie screamed as she launched, tits flying, off the swing and into the freezing cold pool. When her head surfaced, she urged Dinah on with the words, 'You've got to do it . . . free yourself!'

Dinah dropped her towel.

Chapter Twenty-nine

Dinah's party outfit:

Sleeveless silver dress with crystals and
sequins (Monsoon)
Silver and blue sensational shoes (Timi Woo)
Leggings and underwear (still under discussion)
Total est. cost: £90 . . . well the shoes were a gift.

'You have to give me my present!'

'No, Dinah!' Annie just about snatched the offending item out of her hands, 'You can't wear leggings!'

'Why not?' Dinah demanded.

They were in Annie's bedroom – well, obviously Annie and Ed's bedroom, but clearly currently Annie's – getting ready for the Big Surprise. In another twenty minutes or so the taxi would be here. The hair was done, the make-up was on, now it was time to get dressed. Quickly.

'Because leggings are not sexy,' Annie said slowly, as if speaking to a child. 'No man will ever, ever fancy you in leggings. Men our age are confused by leggings. They think: tights with no feet, they wonder why you didn't put your trousers on . . . they see gym teachers and Jane Fonda and all sorts of disastrous dates they'd rather not remember from the eighties.

'Dinah, on your tenth wedding anniversary, you wear stockings! I mean it's like your wedding night, right? Tonight is *guaranteed* sex. There is guaranteed lovemaking at the end of the night for you and Bryan. You're all smooth and delicious down there,' she quirked an eyebrow, 'so you wear stockings to frame the painting. Don't worry, I have some,' she added. 'I've not had much use for them lately.'

'Annie, I think we're past stockings,' Dinah protested. 'I mean we still do it if I'm wearing a thermal vest and tartan pyjama bottoms. And suspenders are so uncomfortable.'

'Yeah, but tonight is special! Hold-ups then?' Annie offered. 'Please! You should make the extra effort. I know I would.'

'Annie you're wearing tummy-tuck tights!' Dinah pointed out.

'Yeah, but I'm as good as single,' came Annie's reply, 'it doesn't matter how I look under my clothes, only how I look in them. Anyway, I'm trying to squeeze into my Valentino from three years ago. There's no way I can pull that off without the tummy-tuckers. Make that, there's no chance of pulling it on without the tummy-tuckers.'

'The Valentino?' Dinah sounded impressed. 'That is a very, very nice dress, but Annie . . .' her voice was almost quite stern now, 'in no way are you single. You shouldn't say it and you shouldn't even think it. You'll have to try and find some time with Ed tonight or more

344

likely tomorrow to iron things out and make up. You two have to get over this, or else I'm going to lock you both in a room together until you've worked out that you're the most stubborn pair of idiots I have ever known!'

Rattled by this outburst from her sister, Annie could only think to say, 'Right then, I'm not going to give you your present!'

'Yes!' Dinah pleaded, 'you have to give me my present. You always give the best presents. Do you really have a present for me? For today? That's very, very nice of you. Please, Annie! C'mon we have to hurry up, Mum will have just about driven our children insane by now.'

'Especially if she's been making comments about Lana's hair or Lana's outfit or anything to do with Lana at all. I warned them both,' Annie told her, inching herself slowly into the red Valentino and breathing in deeply as she edged up the zip.

'Present!' Dinah reminded her and Annie went out of the bedroom, instructing Dinah to wait there.

When she returned a few minutes later, she was holding a pair of Timi Woos in each hand.

The silver ones with navy blue trim she handed to Dinah saying, 'You like? They will be fantastic with your dress.'

For a moment, Dinah was about to say: *With this dress? Tonight? No, no, I have a pair of pink kitten heels which I was going to wear . . . along with my leggings.* But then she thought better of it.

'Thank you! They are gorgeous. Oh thank you!' she said instead and gave Annie a hug.

'Are those for you?' Dinah pointed to the gold and red pair in Annie's other hand.

'Oh yeah,' Annie confirmed, sliding them onto her feet then doing up the strap. The simple, draped but very shaped, strapless red evening dress, set off with the tummy-tuckers, a pair of silicone chicken fillets tucked into her bra, the Timi Woos, Chanel pillar box red lipstick and her tightest blondest ponytail, was – even if she had to say so herself – a knockout look.

'Check it out!' she said more to herself than to Dinah as she gave herself a final once-over in the mirror.

Plus, if she wore the shoes very gently and gave them a thorough polish up afterwards she could sell them on again as nearly new. Used Timi Woos were already popping up on eBay, slightly worn, within weeks of her first sales.

She did genuinely have the feeling that she was on to something here. They were going to be huge! It was high time she had a proper conversation with Mr Woo and signed up some exclusive rights for her 'esteemed corporation'.

To Dinah she said, 'If Nic had been able to drag her fragile pregnant self along to the party tonight, I'd have given her a pair too. Then we could have all matched . . .'

'And done a dance routine,' Dinah joked.

'Oh God, do you remember when the three of us sang "By the Rivers of Babylon" at Mike's wedding?'

'NO!' Dinah screamed. 'Never, ever remind me of that. EVER!'

'Maybe Bryan's got a karaoke machine for tonight?'

Chapter Thirty

Party Ed:

White shirt, severely ironed (M&S)
Dinner suit, freshly cleaned (second-hand)
Tie-up bow-tie, properly tied (second-hand)
Black shoes, polished to a shine (cupboard)
Silver cufflinks (his mum)
New haircut (Toni & Guy)
Aftershave (Italian BTW)
Guitar and violin (own)
Total est. cost: in denial

'Have you any idea how much they charge?'

'OK, my girl, here we go,' Annie said as their taxi drew up at the front of the Parkes Hotel. 'Good luck!' she added, 'Break a leg and all that. And just remember to look really, really surprised. Or Bryan's going to like me even less than he already does.'

'Bryan does like you!' Dinah hissed.

'And stop looking so nervous!' Annie insisted.

* * *

As she'd been instructed, Annie told the woman on reception that they were here for a family dinner, and gave Bryan's name.

'Oh yes, it's straight up the stairs and into the function room on the left hand side. I hope you enjoy your evening.'

Dinah wobbled ever so slightly in the Timi Woos. They were an inch or so higher than her normal heel but she was getting the hang of them and anyway, Annie couldn't help thinking, taking a long sideways look at her, it was worth it. She looked delicious.

'You're looking hot, baby,' Annie told her, to make her smile. 'You know what Connor's going to whisper in your ear as soon as he sees you?'

'Something typically filthy.'

'Yeah, he's going to say . . .' Annie's voice dropped low as she prepared to give her best Connor impression, 'Baby, Bryan just came in his pants.'

'Annie!' Dinah turned to look at her with a mock-scandalized expression, which meant her eye was off the door just as Annie threw it open. So she really did look quite genuinely shocked as sixty people shouted out at her, 'SURPRISE!'

The first twenty minutes of party flurry passed quickly for both sisters. They whirled from guest to guest, kissing everyone hello, hugging, chatting, laughing, joking.

Annie spotted Hector and Connor in matching kilt outfits, manning clipboards and party planner walkie-talkies, which made her crease up with laughter.

'Connor said it,' Dinah told her, when their paths crossed for a second in the whirl.

'I know him too well,' Annie told her, 'Oh, Billie is beautiful!' she added, spotting Billie in a purple velvet dress, accessorized with purple ballet shoes and another Billie touch of genius, fluffy purple deely boppers.

Annie was of course blindingly proud of her own children. Owen in a white shirt, black trousers and – at his own insistence – a black bow-tie. His fringe had been slicked oddly to the side, which he thought was incredibly cool. To Annie he looked alarmingly like a baby Donny Osmond, but she'd already decided to say nothing.

Lana was in frivolous, vivacious and terrifyingly flammable fuchsia pink and avoiding her slightly. She was on the arm of Andrei and both were terrified that Annie might have something incredibly tactless to say to him along the lines of: 'Cheat on my daughter?! Never darken my doorstep again.'

'Annie! Hello, lovely to see you and thanks for all your help with tonight.' Ah! She and Bryan were going to have to do their awkward kiss greeting, pretending they were delighted to see each other again.

'Oh, you're very welcome,' she said, bumping her left cheek against his. And then the right. They looked at each other and struggled for something else to say. Bryan was thin, balding and, Annie thought (not for the first time), just incredibly bland looking. He was in a white dinner jacket, which made him look like the head waiter and his tiny, frameless glasses made his entire eye socket looked glazed. Annie had decided long ago that he must have many, many hidden qualities which only Dinah fully appreciated.

'Well . . . time to kick off, I think,' Bryan said, looking at his watch and shooting her a parting smile. As he turned and walked away from her, Annie's heart gave a little leap of surprise, because there, standing hesitantly at the doorway, was Ed.

The longer she looked, the more trouble she could see Ed had gone to. He'd ironed his shirt, he'd acquired a dark and very dapper suit from somewhere. He'd tied on a bow-tie, his shoes were gleaming. He'd even brushed, no, definitely *cut* his hair. It was a long time since she'd seen him look so well groomed . . . or just groomed in any way at all, to be honest. And he looked great.

Before Annie had even caught his eye, Owen, violin in hand, was beside him. Ah! Of course, they were going to perform their music together.

Bryan called the crowd to attention and urged everyone to top up their drinks and move over to the semicircle of chairs.

'You don't think this is going to be too New Age, do you?' Fern slipped her arm into Annie's as they headed over. 'I'm just getting to that age where too much mushy sincerity is going to make me snort my G&T out of my nose.'

'You're a grumpy old git, you mean?' Annie asked.

'Well . . . maybe. They're happy enough though, aren't they? Dinah and—'

'Baldy? I think so. Don't think you need to worry about them. Pale pink really suits you, Mum,' Annie added. 'Matches your hair. What is going on with your colourist?'

'Don't be so cheeky!' Fern hissed at her as everyone settled into their seats and Owen and Ed struck up their melody.

'What's the song?' Fern whispered into Annie's ear.

'I don't know. I suggested "We've Lost That Loving Feeling" but they refused.'

When the music ended, everybody clapped loudly and Owen broke into a big beaming smile. Ed balanced his guitar on his knee and clapped Owen as well.

And then Bryan and Dinah, looking sweetly nervous, launched into their ceremony.

Annie glanced briefly over to where handsome Hector was sitting in the front row watching tensely with his earpiece still in place. Just one slip on the part of the happy couple now and all his weeks of party planning would be ruined. Poor guy. Annie made a mental note to go over later and tell him how utterly amazing this party was.

Bryan recited a poem (mercifully not home-made) for Dinah, who, bless her, had to wipe the tears from her eyes by the end of it. Then they said some truly sweet things to each other and to Billie, while Billie twanged at her deely boppers, setting off a ripple of suppressed laughter in the crowd.

It was all very touching and lovely and Annie might have enjoyed it all much more if she hadn't been working herself up into such a frenzy about Ed. Why did he not even glance in her direction? Why was he not even making eye contact for long enough to give her a smile?

This was just so unbelievably rude. She lived with this guy. She owned a property with him. He had made a commitment to help her bring up her children. Now he was perched on a stool, looking just about everywhere else in this entire room but at her. How long was this going to go on for? How long did an Ed Leon sulk last? Maybe she should phone his sister and ask. Why were Hannah and her partner not here tonight anyway? She knew they'd been invited.

If Dinah hadn't been tenderly promising Bryan that she would always be his best friend, Annie would quite like to have stood up now and shouted at Ed, 'Oi you, over here! Remember me?'

Then, with a flurry of applause, the ceremony was over. Dinah broke into smiles of visible relief and Owen and Ed started up again with a new melody.

'Hello Annie, lovely to see you – and in Valentino. How appropriate!'

She gave Hector a double cheek kiss. 'I know, I might change my name: Annie Valentino. Sounds good, huh?' She waved an arm at the room – 'it's fabulous, darling,' she told him. 'You look fabulous too.'

'Excellent. Now, there's dancing,' he continued briskly, 'and I want you with someone very handsome on the dance floor first so the video can capture you and B and D can look back on this and remember it as a glamorous event.'

Hector had her firmly by the shoulders and before Annie could have any say in the matter, she was being pushed against Andrei and together they were ushered onto a dance floor empty save for the happy couple.

'And dance!' Hector cried, as if he were directing a movie. Then he disappeared.

'Well, hi, Andrei,' Annie managed, shuffling stiffly and sensing that Andrei's hand was only hovering in the general vicinity of her back.

'I'm glad to see Lana so happy again,' she went on, shooting a fake smile of happiness at Dinah as she spun past. 'She was very upset about what happened.'

Andrei had the decency to blush and look down at his shoes. Well, hopefully it was his shoes and not her magnificent, fillet-enhanced cleavage.

'I'm very sorry about what happened, Ms Valentine,' he said.

'You're both young and I'm sure, in time, you'll both move on,' Annie told him, 'but be nice! Next time, you have the decency to break up just as nicely as you possibly can. Or else I'll . . .' Now what was she doing? Was she going to threaten to send the boys round? 'I'll be very angry,' she ended.

'Yes, Ms Valentine,' he said and looked so sheepish that she felt quite sorry for him.

As soon as the waltz was over, she and Andrei all but jumped apart and finally Annie was able to go off and do the one thing she really wanted to do: find Ed. She began to walk purposefully round the room, trying to avoid eye contact and unwanted chit-chat with anyone else.

But there was no sign of him. Or of Owen, it occurred to her. Not over in the quiet bar area. Not anywhere near the semicircle of seats, or dance floor. There wasn't even – strangely – any sign of them loitering near the tables being set up for the buffet.

'Where's Owen?' Annie asked as she walked into Lana.

'Maybe he went to the toilet,' was Lana's suggestion.

Annie made for the double doors leading out of the function room. Out there in the corridor, a little dancing party was going on. Ed and Owen were fiddling some manic jig while two elderly couples tried to dance to it and another handful of people were laughing and clapping them on.

Look at Owen go!

Annie spent a moment watching his crazed elbow bob up and down as he whizzed his bow over the strings. His foot was tapping and even his head was nodding up and down to the tune.

Right, never mind that for now.

She marched straight past the dancers and took hold of an astonished Ed's arm. He'd been too busy jigging to see her coming.

'Right, you!' she told him, 'I want a word with you.'

Ed, still playing to the end of the verse, let himself be led by the elbow through the double doors and towards the bar where Annie turned to him, the red dress spinning slightly with the speed of her movement and told him quietly but definitely, unmistakably furiously, 'That's it. Game over! You have to talk to me. You have to Deal With Me,' and with every one of these last three words, she jabbed angrily at his chest.

'Now let's get a few things straight,' she stormed on. 'Number one: there is not a single thing going on between me and Sandro Berlusponti-Milliau. Here,' she opened the teensy golden clutch bag she was carrying, took out her phone and handed it to Ed, 'you can phone him. You can ask.'

When Ed shook his head at this suggestion, Annie blustered straight on: 'Furthermore, I have decided to sell the shoes from Hong Kong and a few of Sandro's bags, On. My. Website.' These words were delivered with heavy emphasis.

'I've had a website on eBay for as long as you've known me, Ed. Yes, I may be expanding it a little, but right now I'm not doing anything different. Not yet.'

In a slightly contrite tone, she added: 'I'm sorry I didn't discuss my plans with you properly. And I made a big decision to borrow money without you. OK. I admit that. I shouldn't have done that. OK? In future, I will talk to you about the plans and I'm not going to do anything really different until they're . . . clearer.

'But *this* – you and me – this only works if we keep talking. Nothing works if you storm off in a great big sulk—' she broke off, almost out of breath with effort.

'I think we should sit down,' Ed said, 'or there's a danger we'll draw a crowd.'

Once they were sitting down at a table together, it didn't seem so hard any more. There was Ed, her Ed, looking slightly bewildered but still surprisingly good.

'You've had a haircut? And a proper one?' she said with some astonishment.

'Toni and Guy,' Ed replied. 'Have you any idea how much they charge? Hannah made me.'

'Oh!'

'Annie, that was not just a kiss on the cheeks. I saw it.' Ed was not going to let this go.

Annie gave a deep sigh and tried to think about what he could have seen: 'Were you standing behind me?'

she asked finally. Hadn't Mr B held on to the back of her head, stared into her eyes and pulled her closer? Trying to go for a full mouth-on-mouth?

'Look, you won't believe me,' she said, 'but I had something in my eye.'

Ed gave a bitter little laugh. 'Don't try and be funny.'

'After the cheek kiss, he tried to kiss me on the mouth,' Annie went on quickly, 'and I told him I had something in my eye, to get out of it, to get out of the kiss . . . but then he held my head and stared and stared into my eye for ages, right up close, right against my face . . . then he finally let me go. That's what you saw . . . you total tit,' she added for good measure.

Ed stared into the distance. She couldn't read much in his expression, she didn't have the slightest idea whether he believed her or not.

'Anyway what about you?' it was her turn to ask. 'I found Giovanna's phone number in the villa. What have you got to say about that?'

Ed looked at her in confusion now. 'Giovanna's phone number?'

'Isn't that your Italian girlfriend? Her name and number had been written down on the telephone pad.'

'My ex-girlfriend,' Ed said with emphasis on the *ex*, 'was called Janine.'

'Oh.'

Now Ed was the one struggling to think of an explanation.

'I spoke to someone about changing my flight and wrote down her name and contact number and took it with me on a piece of paper.'

'Oh.' Again that was all that Annie could manage.

'You must have seen the imprint of the writing.'

'Maybe . . .' She wasn't sure she wanted him to follow this line of enquiry too closely.

'Good grief – did you do that rubbing pencil over the letters and numbers thing that detectives do on the telly?'

'No! I could read it perfectly well,' Annie lied because the thought of being caught out here was just too pathetic.

'You pencilled it!' Ed insisted.

There was a warmth in Ed's voice now, as if he was starting to find this funny. Then came a pause. Ed looked over at her, Annie looked back at him. Neither of them was sure where to go from here.

'You told him you had something in your eye?' Ed asked finally.

'Yes,' Annie answered, wondering why something as small and stupid as this could have set Ed off on such a tantrum. Well . . . along with the thirty grand and the stack of expensive accessories accumulating in the spare room.

'In your eye?' he repeated, and the corners of his mouth were twitching but she couldn't tell if this was anger or if he was trying to suppress some sort of smile. 'Why didn't you just slap him in the face?'

'Ed! He'd just offered me a forty per cent discount,' Annie burst out.

'Oh! Well, that's OK then. You should have just snogged him straight back.'

'It crossed my mind. Believe me. If I'd thought it could have got me fifty per cent, I'd probably have done it. But I thought that was as low as he would go.'

'Have you sold his bags over here yet?'

'I've sold one on eBay – but the shoes are going a storm.'

'The shoes . . .' he leaned over the side of the table to take a look at Annie's dainty shoes.

'They are very nice shoes,' he had to agree, 'very, very nice shoes. And that's a very nice dress. Very nice.'

And that was the moment Annie knew she had to lean over and kiss him. Right on the mouth, hands clasped on his head, pulling him back to her again. Because of the way his hair bounced against his cheek and his voice was so warm and real and everything about him was better than she remembered it. And yes, the shiny shoes, the black suit and tie were probably a major attraction factor. She lifted herself slightly off her chair, so she could lean into him, fling her arms round him, kiss harder and more hungrily.

'Come home, please!' she said urgently, pushing herself against him.

Ed, who was already quite astonished at this reaction to his comment about her outfit, was even more surprised to feel the wobble of the back legs of the chair.

'Annie!' he warned. But it was already too late. In her enthusiasm to get to him, she'd pushed the chair back beyond the point of no return. If they'd been hoping to keep news of their reconciliation quiet, they were certainly disappointed when the chair went down with a crash, somehow taking along the tablecloth, two bottles of mineral water, glasses and a condiment set, as well as the embracing couple.

As Annie lay on top of Ed and the chair, listening to the loud hum of concern in the room as people hurried towards them, she was conscious of one thing and one thing only . . . a cool breeze. Ed had managed to pull up her dress.

'I think we've drawn that crowd,' Ed said.

A roomful of spectators was now being treated to a rear view of her orthopaedic beige tummy-tuck tights. She should have gone with the stockings. She so should have gone with the stockings.

Chapter Thirty-one

Party Lana:

Pink dress (Miss Selfridge)
Pink heels (Primark)
Blue fishnets (Topshop)
Blue eyeshadow (Superdrug)
Total est. cost: £85

'Is he staying the night?'

'So this is why Lana is suddenly getting As in French,' Ed teased gently. 'Lots of private tutoring.'

'Sir!' Andrei protested, pulling away from Lana's ear, which he had been nuzzling, as Lana blushed frantically and Annie and Owen burst into laughter.

'OK, break it up and please take your mug of the finest hot chocolate, complete with mini marshmallow toppings, that you are ever likely to taste outside of a campsite,' Ed continued, bringing the steaming drinks towards the table.

Although it was close to two in the morning, Ed had

promised everyone in the taxi home from the party that what they needed before bed was a taste of his 'world famous' hot chocolate.

'Obviously Owen knows all about this treat, being a veteran of the Ed Leon school of camping,' he added, making sure Owen was included in the first round of drinks.

Owen looked up and smiled a little shyly. He accepted his cup without a word and began to stir the marshmallows. His silence did not escape Annie. She was acutely sensitive to how her children were feeling about Ed being back in the house.

'So, sir,' Andrei began in Ed's direction, 'are you dressing up for the Halloween disco again this year?'

By way of reply, Ed threw his head back and gave his best horrible, hollow, ghost-train laugh. This set everyone around the table giggling again, including Owen, to Annie's relief.

'You'd make a very dapper Dracula,' Ed advised Andrei: 'you're tall, with dark hair, you just need a bit of talc on the face, some fake teeth – and Lana could be your victim! Put on a long dress, add a bite mark or two on your neck . . .' Ed was tempted, so tempted, to add, 'unless they're already there of course,' but he swallowed the comment back down.

As Andrei groaned at this suggestion, Ed turned to Annie, who was looking straight at him. She gave him a wink. He wondered if that meant she knew about the neck comment he hadn't made. He suspected that it did. Sometimes he felt as if his entire, complicated inner life and private thoughts were nothing but an open book to Annie.

And looking at her there, sitting bolt upright, her hair piled up on her head, mug of hot chocolate in her hand, winking at him with her eyebrow cocked, he thought . . . he thought that that was just fine. She could leaf through his open book any time. Any time at all.

Further chat about the Halloween disco established that the decorations last year were rubbish and desperately needed an overhaul, then Owen, under intense questioning, broke down and revealed that he was going to go as Beethoven. But finally the mugs were empty, Andrei's taxi honked at the front door for him and Ed showed him out.

'I'll lock up behind you,' he said. 'No, don't take that to mean I'm locking you out – but I am!' He winked at Lana.

Planting one final kiss on Lana's face, Andrei thanked them all for a lovely evening and disappeared out of the kitchen with Ed.

Which left Annie facing her sleepy but none the less curious children.

'Is he staying the night?' came Lana's whisper first.

'Is Ed moving back in?' Owen asked, before Annie had a chance to reply.

'We're just talking,' she told them, 'we're trying to sort out some of the things that were making us so upset with each other. OK? But . . . you do both want Ed to come back, don't you?' she added quickly.

'As long as that's what you want, Mum,' came Lana's reply.

'How about you, Owen?'

Owen gave a non-committal shrug. 'I'd like to go to bed.'

Ed's head appeared round the kitchen door and he said, a little uncertainly, 'I was thinking about going upstairs . . . to bed . . . if that's OK?' When the three serious faces turned in his direction, suddenly he wasn't sure if this was OK at all; he wondered if he should maybe be getting into a taxi just like Andrei.

'Yes . . . yes, that's fine,' Annie said, but now she felt slightly unsure too.

When Annie stepped into the bedroom, only the little flower lights were lit, casting their low pink glow. A fruity jazz saxophone was oozing from the stereo and Ed, still in the black suit, was sitting in the chair with a very thoughtful look on his face.

'Come here?' he asked gently, as she came into the room. As she got closer, he held out his hands to hers and stood up beside her. 'That is some dress,' he said, 'you look amazing.'

'Oh, it's the chicken fillets,' she said and he had no idea what she was talking about.

'Well, whatever they are . . . they're working,' he said.

He put his arm round her and with her right hand in his, he began to dance with her very slowly in a small circle round the room.

'Are you OK?' he asked and his hair brushed against her ear.

'I think so,' she said.

'I've missed you.' Ed's voice sounded a little ragged.

'You should have said . . . because I had no idea what you were thinking,' Annie told him.

'I'm sorry.' Ed leaned over to land a kiss on her shoulder. And then came another, which lasted until she felt a shiver, a shudder travelling up and down her neck. She leaned into him, closing her eyes and hearing only the melting notes of the saxophone solo.

But.

Why did she feel so frightened?

He was here, wasn't he?

He had his arms around her.

She thought of Owen's silence and Owen's non-committal shrug and now she understood it. Owen didn't know if he wanted Ed back because what if Ed went away again? Annie and her children had already lost far too much once before.

With a knot of fear in her stomach, she held onto Ed very tightly, because this was going to hurt. This was going to really hurt.

She let the saxophone play on to the end of the song and then she began to speak slowly and carefully. 'Ed . . . you can't be in my life. I'm sorry. I'm really sorry. I don't think you can know how sorry I am. But you can't be one of us.

'I have this little family . . .' she stumbled on, starting to cry now, 'me and Owen and Lana . . . and I just can't let you in.'

As Ed tried to pull back from her grip, to look her in the face, she clung to him more tightly and kept her chin firmly on his shoulder. She didn't want to look him in the eye as she said this, it was hard enough.

With a great hard knot in her throat she went on, 'I can't do it again. I can't go through it again. Because I've tried to be in love with you and I just can't go there. I can't lose it all again. I just want to look after my children, work hard and keep us all safe and happy. I can't have this unknown quantity in my life, someone who might choose to walk away when it suits him. I can't bear that. When you moved to your sister's, you didn't even think for a moment about how the children would feel.'

'Annie,' Ed began urgently, 'I'm sorry. I am really, really sorry. I misunderstood . . . everything. I will never let anything like this happen again. This is all so new to me. Annie, please?'

'But you should have talked to me. You should have come *to* me, not walked away from me.'

She was looking into his face now and could see the extreme anxiety there. But none of this mattered any more. All she could focus on clearly was that Ed didn't belong with them. She and Lana and Owen were inextricably linked. They were family. Ed was like a guest who had visited them for a year. He just couldn't be permanent. He couldn't replace Roddy. He couldn't be her husband or their father. She'd rather grow into an old lady alone, with her children and her grandchildren to love and care for and to love her back, than risk any love on someone who could let them down. She could not face losing someone she was in love with all over again.

Sitting down on the edge of the bed with Ed, she held him in her arms and told him this in every way she could, until he understood that she really, really meant it. She was telling him the truth.

The jazz CD had reached an end and there was nothing but a deep, painful silence hanging in the air between them.

After looking at her very closely and very carefully, Ed finally turned away, murmuring only 'I have to go now,' before leaving the house.

Chapter Thirty-two

The mysterious dark-haired lady:

Long red, black, olive and orange knit dress (House of
Fraser own brand)
Long black crotcheted cardigan (same)
Black maternity tights (Mothercare)
Low black boots (Russell & Bromley)
Total est. cost: £320

'Oh! You're Annie Valentine, aren't you?'

A decade of dressing women in The Store, in their
homes, even in random London changing rooms when
she just couldn't keep her advice to herself, had taught
Annie many, many valuable lessons.

But the number one, the Annie Valentine Golden Rule,
was that you never, ever Let Yourself Go.

Yes, it was tempting. When everything around you
was turning to rubbish, when you were going through
break-up hell, your house was about to be put up for sale
– even if it was for a fortune – and you were about to

begin the hassle of looking for somewhere new, packing up and moving.

It was tempting to reach for the beaten-up jeans, the drab old jumper, not wash your hair and put it in a scrunchie . . . get up too late to wash your face and put on your make-up. She knew just how tempting it was.

For six mornings in a row, she had woken up with a start, stared at the ceiling, let the full memory of what was happening come flooding back into her mind and she had wanted to roll over, pull the duvet back up over her head and stay there. Forget about it. Block it out.

But Annie knew that staying in bed was the beginning of the end. If she let the slightest thing slip now, where would it lead? Before she knew it, she'd be turning up at The Store in a fleece . . . *a fleece*! And maybe even clumpy shoes – and then she'd lose her job and no one would buy Timi Woos from her website either and she wouldn't be able to buy a new home of her own . . . far less afford the school fees and . . . . just the horror of these thoughts would get her out of bed on time. Force her to the bathroom, where the rigorous application of cleanser, toner, moisturizer and make-up would begin.

Annie had decided she had to go in the opposite direction. If other women let their appearance slide when things were going appallingly, she had to smarten up, over-groom . . . gleam and radiate. It was the only way to maintain morale.

She hadn't looked this good since the second year after the death of her husband, the worst and most grinding days of her life.

Her lipstick was now brighter, her eyeshadow more colourful: iridescent greens and purples had replaced the usual smoky brown. Hell, she even painted her nails; well she had time now, of an evening. Amazing how much more time there was, once you were properly single again.

There were strategies for maintaining morale against the odds. She didn't know how many times she'd sat frazzled women down in The Store and explained the strategies to them. Number one was to keep it simple. Develop a uniform which could be put on in the morning without too much thought. But not a jeans and sweatshirt uniform; a pressed trousers, pressed shirt and natty jacket uniform or a skirt and flattering blouse uniform, or in Annie's case, a great day dress with boots or shoes, with a jacket or matching coat, depending on the weather.

Number two was not to forget the details: necklace or earrings for sparkle, beautiful rings or watches for uplift. Hair had to be not just brushed, but curled with a hot air brush and no matter how bad the day ahead was looking, there was never, *never* any excuse not to wash face, apply tinted moisturizer, lipstick and even perfume, yes perfume. *Your* favourite. Not your ex-husband's, or your ex-boyfriend's or the one your aunty gave you for Christmas, but your very own favourite perfume. That had no associations. That you could carry about in a little bottle and revive yourself with during the day.

If it got too hard and too stressful to do this in the mornings, Annie recommended laying out clothes the night before, so that some effort and thought could be put into it ahead of the morning gloom. Anyway, it was another morale boost to wake up and see clothes carefully set out, necklace and earrings too. It was like having a ladies' maid, someone to take care of you while you slept.

That's really what this was about anyway, taking care of yourself through the rough times, when no one else was able to. When the natural tendency was to take it out on yourself, punish yourself and beat yourself up.

She would even tell clients with far too much stress and worry on their minds to care about the frivolities of wardrobe, to make a clothing chart.

'I know, I know,' she would insist, 'it sounds so dorky. But I promise you, you'll thank me. Write down four or five good outfits and stick the list on the back of the wardrobe door. Then, when you're standing there like a zombie, hands hovering over the comfy jeans and fleece, you will thank me, you will turn to the good outfit recipe and be able to come out looking like a woman who is surviving instead.'

Having followed her own advice, Annie was now in Operation Visit The School, striding on high patent, black shoes in a beautiful, not to mention brand new, black, white and orange dress, black raincoat and gorgeous, long, drapey burnt orange scarf (the exact colour of her nail varnish, by the way). Her hair was done, her lipstick was on and she was wafting something very spoiling by Diptyque towards her children's hoity-toity private school, St Vincent's.

For once, she was not late. She had arranged evening cover at The Store for the whole week, for ever. It meant she would miss out on hundreds of pounds of commission every month, it meant she could kiss goodbye to her almost guaranteed position of saleswoman with the highest monthly commission bonus. But never mind. She was back to single parenting, and her kids had to come first.

Maybe when she was living with Ed, she'd relied on him too much. She'd let her position slip, she'd delegated just a little bit more than she should have. But now she was making up for all of that.

There was an event on at school tonight, a big showy concert. Owen was playing, Lana was announcing two of the acts and it was a big deal for them both. So Annie was going to be there, beautifully turned out, calm and coping and, above all, their loving and supportive mum.

The chances of bumping into Ed at this thing were horrendously high. He was the head of the school's music department, after all. But she was going to cope with that just fine as well. She was a totally grown-up grown-up for God's sake. She was going to be perfectly civil.

Through the school's main entrance she went; its elaborate Victorian archway with massive wrought-iron gates. She still felt a rush of pride that her children went here, to one of the oldest and best schools in London. And if Timi Woos kept flying out of the boxes like they had been doing, long would her children continue to enjoy the gilded education with guaranteed stellar exam results which St Vincent's provided.

'Annie!' She heard her name being called over the cobbled courtyard. But it was OK, she'd already decided how she was going to answer the questions she could expect from parents she'd known since their children were little together.

'How are you? Looking wonderful, as always.' Suzie Wollstonecroft breezed over to her and kissed her on both cheeks.

'I'm really well, how are you?'

Suzie linked arms with her, filled her in on all the latest family Wollstonecroft news and then turned with the inevitable, 'And the lovely Mr Leon? How is he doing? I've not had the chance to speak to him since parents' night last term. I'm so glad you got him, by the way. He's great and he was definitely going to seed all on his own.'

'He's fine, very well,' Annie began, then as lightly as possible she added, 'but it's kind of run its course Suzie, no big deal. All very amicable . . . but you know how it goes sometimes.'

'Oh no!' Suzie gushed, pulling a face. Annie braced herself. 'No! That's terrible. He's a lovely man. I thought you two made a great couple. What happened?'

'Nothing dramatic,' Annie insisted. 'We've just decided to call it a day.'

Thankfully, they were approaching the entrance to the main hall where the headmaster was standing at the doorway to meet and greet, so Annie was spared from having to give any further details.

Suzie quickly peeled off from her side and Annie understood the move perfectly: she was rushing off to accost all the mothers she could find and relay this sensational new piece of parent/teacher gossip.

Annie settled in a seat beside two sets of parents she knew and although, once the lights were dimmed, she'd sneaked a look around to see if she could spot Ed, she was now going to concentrate very hard on watching Owen and Lana's performances.

After the nerve-racking, maternal pride-riddled minutes of Owen's tune and Lana's announcement, Annie finally felt she could enjoy the rest of the performance and the parent wine and cheese reception afterwards. Oh, why not? Everyone was going to be talking about her anyway, she might as well show up.

Annie tried to keep the conversations focused away from her. Instead, she asked lots of questions: 'How is Greta getting on?' 'What do you think of this year's form teacher?' 'Haven't you guys just moved house, how's that going?'

And to questions about how she was doing she just replied, 'Really well, thanks. I'm so proud of Owen and Lana, they did brilliantly tonight.'

When she was momentarily caught without anyone to talk to, and not knowing the people directly around her, she set off slowly through the crowd in search of a top-up for her wine glass and another familiar face. That was when she caught her first glimpse of Ed and turned abruptly, almost knocking straight into another woman.

'Oh I'm so sorry!' Annie exclaimed.

'No, no, totally my fault, I'm not used to my size yet,' the woman said gesturing to her stomach, the hard, swollen balloon of a pregnancy round about month six or seven. 'Oh! You're Annie Valentine, aren't you?' the woman said.

Annie nodded and smiled, trying to remember where she had seen her before. She was very pretty, with a dainty face and a sleek black bob. Nicely styled, high at the back and narrowing to two points level with her pointed chin. The bump was beautifully clothed in a long, subtly coloured knit dress with a flowing black crotcheted cardigan on top.

'I was going to contact you properly tomorrow but I hoped we might run into each other tonight. I'm Denise.' She stretched out her hand to shake Annie's, then head a little to the side, she asked, 'Ed's probably told you all about me?'

That's when Annie realized who this woman was. The one Ed had been sitting beside in the café in Camden. The one he'd been laughing and sipping coffee with, the one Annie had thought (ridiculously) must be his Italian girlfriend.

'My daughter's in the choir and we went on the school trip to Bavaria together and I got to know him really well,' Denise added with a happy smile.

'Right,' Annie smiled back.

'I'm one of the buyers for House of Fraser: shoes and leather accessories,' Denise went on. 'A few weeks ago Ed showed me a pair of the shoes you're importing. I've taken them into various meetings, you know how it is nowadays, no one person is ever allowed to make a decision. We have to get all the suits and creatives and one man and his dog to agree, but the bottom line is, we love the shoes and we'd like to talk to you about stocking them in some of our stores. That's why I was going to contact you tomorrow. I hoped we could meet up and discuss this further.'

If Annie was surprised, then Ed – now within earshot and seeing the two women together and guessing what they must be talking about – was very surprised and seriously flustered.

Annie, spying his approach from the corner of her eye could have rounded on him in total confusion. Could have demanded what the hell he was doing arranging meetings about her shoes? Sneaking around behind her back? Taking shoes from her boxes without asking? What on earth had he been thinking?

Instead, Annie remembered her promise to herself to be a totally civilized grown-up, even if it killed her. So before Ed could say anything, she quickly told Denise, 'What fantastic news! That's the best news I've had for weeks! Yes, well . . . when's a good time to come in and talk to you?'

As Denise got out her BlackBerry to make the necessary arrangements, Annie turned and offered Ed a very grown up and absolutely perfectly civilized smile.

As she left St Vincent's that evening with Owen and Lana in tow, Annie's mobile began to ring. She didn't recognize the number, but she knew it was Italian. Aha! Finally Mr B was phoning her back about the zipless bags. She'd only left about eight voicemail messages for him.

But to her surprise, the voice at the other end of the line informed her: 'Annah? It is Patrizia here.'

'Oh hello, Patrizia! How are you doing?'

'Very, very bad,' came the surprising reply, 'I have bad news.'

'Right.' Annie braced herself. Mr B was not going to cave on the zipless bags front. He wasn't going to give her the money back . . . Well, never mind, she would sell her stock, slowly but surely on the internet. It had been a lesson.

'Mr Berlusponti-Milliau is being investigated by the police,' Patrizia told her. 'The bags he sell you are copies. All the new bags, nearly everything he sell you, all copies of new bags coming out next year. It is very, very big trouble. Police. Fraud squad.'

'WHAT?!'

Chapter Thirty-three

Paula at The Store:

Silver lurex vest top (Zara)
Pink satin bra (La Senza)
Very tight pinstriped black trousers
(Joseph sale – staff discount)
High black wedges (Miu Miu sale –
staff discount)
Total est. cost: £180

'Your next client's waiting.'

The bag from Mr B had already sold on eBay for £145. But there was still time to contact the purchaser, say there had been a mistake and refund the payment. So technically, Annie had not sold a fake bag. So technically, Annie would not be drummed out of eBay and she was not wanted by the Italian fraud squad – both good things.

But she had a bad feeling about getting her money back on the great stockpile of bags she had already bought from Mr B and now had stacked incriminatingly in her spare room.

She needed a lawyer and she didn't think it should be the crusty old dear who had handled the conveyancing on the many properties she'd bought and sold over the years, and who had looked after Roddy's will.

In the cold light of a Monday morning in The Store with a cooling coffee on her desk as she waited for her next client to show, Annie knew there was one woman with excellent legal contacts she really had to call. Punching the number into her mobile, she waited for her to pick up.

'Svetlana?'

'Yes, this is she.'

'Hello babes, it's Annie Valentine here. How are you doing?'

'Vonderful! Ve have a date for my fourth vedding! Darling, I've done spring, autumn and winter, so this time I am going to be a summer bride!'

'That is fantastic, lovely!' Annie enthused, thinking of the shopping that this would entail. OK the dress would surely be couture, but everything else would come from The Store: the shoes, the underwear, the going away outfit, the honeymoon wardrobe. The outfits for most of the wedding party. This was excellent, excellent news.

'Babes, look, I need a good lawyer. Someone who can help me with a little business problem. Nothing serious,' she added quickly, she didn't want Svetlana to think she'd diddled her taxes or something. 'I need to get my money back from a supplier.'

'This is not a problem with the beautiful shoes, Annah?' Svetlana exclaimed.

'No, no problem with the shoes, the shoes are coming on just fine. I'm just wondering how I'm going to be able to buy as many shoes as people seem to want,' Annie added.

'Ha! You need an investor, someone with big bucks, ha?'

Annie had to laugh at this, 'Well, I might . . . House of Fraser is meeting with me at the end of the week. If they want to sell the shoes, then I have a problem, but a nice problem. More buyers than I have goods . . . but we'll see.'

'Annah . . .' Svetlana's voice was suddenly lower than usual, 'Harry tells me I need a little business. Not too much vork, you understand, but a little business on the side, tax deductible and I think I should vork with you on the shoes. The shoes are vonderful. And I meet so many people, go to so many parties. I vear the shoes, I talk about the shoes, I tell everyone . . . we get them onto television, we make big, big success. Then maybe I not need to keep marrying silly old rich men,' she broke off with a big throaty laugh.

'No Harry, he quite all right,' she added, 'I only joking with you. But you tell me, vhat you think of having former Miss Ukraine-Moneybags as your business partner? Ha, Annah? I think ve vork very vell together. No?'

For several moments, Annie was too surprised to speak. This was just too major. She just let all the possibilities, the amazing new opportunities this offered, fill her head, before finally making her reply.

'I think that is the best, best news ever!' Annie gushed. 'Babes I think *veee* are going to be *vonderful*!'

It was coming together – it was really going to happen. She already had a business mentor, someone who was going to tell her all about importing and exporting, Revenue & Customs and all that boring stuff. Chemical toilets whiz Bronwen had been delighted to get Annie's phone call and request for help.

'I'll obviously pay you for your time,' Annie had offered.

'No way!' Bronwen had assured her. 'Just keep dressing me. You've already dressed me all the way to my first pay rise.'

There was a tap at the door of her office and the scantily clad arm and shoulder of Paula appeared, followed by the delicate clatter of her long beaded braids.

'Your next client's waiting,' Paula whispered.

Annie nodded vigorously and held up a finger to indicate she would just be one minute.

'I've got to go,' she told Svetlana. 'I'll call you about my other plans as soon as I finish work tonight.'

'Perfect,' Svetlana told her before hanging up.

Now Annie just had to send a text. If she didn't, she would have put it off too long and too late. It was only polite to send it now.

'Shall we go with Foxtons est8 agents? I will if you will. U must come to Owen's b-party. Not same without u.'

Bleep. It was sent. To Ed, obviously.

Chapter Thirty-four

The mugger:

Grey hoodie (Gap)
Black tracksuit bottoms (Adidas)
Black and white trainers (Adidas – very brand loyal)
Black beanie (market stall)
Total est. cost: nil. All nicked.

'Aaaaaargh!'

A strange thing had happened to Annie. When she was in the house on her own at night, when Owen had fallen asleep and when Lana's light was finally off, Annie seemed to grow more and more awake.

She'd once enjoyed the wind-down hour before bed, taking off her face, showering, slathering herself in lotions and potions, snuggling down for the night . . . but now she couldn't settle.

Upstairs in her bedroom she was jumpy and seemed to wind herself up further and further. She found herself clickety-clicking on the internet into the small hours of the morning because all of a sudden, sleep just didn't want to come to her. She'd rather stay up now, because going to bed involved lying in the dark for far too long, worrying.

At night in the dark she had – and she hated to admit this to herself – become a bit of a scaredy cat. When she closed her eyes, the mugger – the man she hadn't thought about at all in the weeks after it had happened – came into her mind uninvited. She could see him striding towards her from a distance, then picking up speed, then at a brisk jog, holding out his arm and *wallop*! She would open her eyes in horror, feeling her heart thump hard in her chest.

Bad, bad habits were forming: she had begun to change into her pyjamas and bring her duvet to the sitting room, where she would have the TV on low and fall asleep on the sofa. When she woke at four or five in the morning, the birds were already singing and she would finally feel safe enough to go back to her own bed.

Not her bed . . . their bed. The sumptuous leather bed, glossy and luxurious, bought when they moved in together, when Annie's marital bed had finally been consigned to the spare room and her new life with a new man had begun properly.

Their bed. When she was lying in it, wide awake, wondering who would get it when the house was sold and they had to go their separate ways . . . jog, jog, jogging, into her mind would come the mugger again.

Tonight it had just turned 11 p.m. when Annie came down to the sitting room in her pyjamas with her duvet and a supposedly soothing cup of herbal tea. She was achingly tired.

She settled down on the sofa, tucked the covers around her and was quickly tuning out the gentle hum of chatter from the telly and dozing, finally falling into sleep . . . deeper and deeper until . . . the dull clunk of all the lights, appliances and the TV coming to an abrupt standstill woke her up with a start.

She sat up in the pitch darkness trying to understand what had happened. Then she heard a sound in the hallway outside.

With a lurch, sending her heart into overdrive, she realized she could hear footsteps in the hallway. Heavy ones, nothing like Owen's or Lana's. There was someone in the house.

Frozen in the dark silence of the sitting room, she heard the footsteps heading off in the direction of the kitchen. There was a burglar in the house! And he'd cut the electrics so that there was no chance of an alarm going off or of anyone waking up and pressing a panic button.

She'd read about burglaries like these. Burglars who waited until people were at home, robbers who woke people up and made them reveal the valuables. Burglars who pulled out knives and forced you to hand over your bank cards and PIN numbers. One went to the cash machine while the other stayed holding a knife to your children to make sure you weren't lying.

She could hear drawers and cupboards being opened in the kitchen. He was looking for a knife . . . The burglar was looking for a knife! The blood was drumming in her chest and in her ears. He was going to come out of the kitchen and start hunting round this room – what if he went upstairs? The children!

Annie wanted to stuff the duvet into her mouth to stop herself from moaning with fear. She wanted to scrunch down into the smallest possible space and hide from this. She wanted to faint to be out of it so that she couldn't even know this was happening.

What if it was her mugger? What if he had got her address from the bag or from her phone and he'd waited till tonight to come back to see what other choice items of YSL he could take? They had never got round to changing the locks!

Some instinct, not of self-preservation, but of the ferocious need to protect her children, kicked in and cleared the frozen panic from her mind.

Annie looked round the room, now slightly less dark as her eyes adjusted to the light, scanning frantically for something, anything with which she could defend them all from this intruder. The lamp looked far too big, the vases too flimsy. Picture frames weren't any use.

She could hear the kitchen door opening. It was now or never, there had to be something. On the coffee table were several heavy, solid hardback books. One of those would have to do. It was the only useful thing she could think of.

The burglar was already in the hall, she would have to be quick – very quick and totally silent. Without thinking any more about it, she slipped off the sofa, pulled the book from the table and carried it to the doorway. Then she hung back, waiting for the intruder to walk past. She'd surprise him from behind, it was her only chance.

Annie shook with fear as the footsteps came towards

her. She was going to have to go out, she couldn't wait, she couldn't bear to risk being caught without acting. With a scream of fright and fury, she stepped out right into the path of the burglar and whammed the book very hard at him.

She'd hoped to wallop him on the head: she'd hoped she would be able to hit him hard enough to knock him down. Maybe even knock him unconscious. But to her horror, the intruder shouted: 'Aaaaaaaargh!' in a voice which sounded even more frightened than hers.

The figure dropped something to the floor with a clatter before yelling, 'Jesus, Annie, what the bloody hell do you think you're doing?'

Then he added, 'For God's sake, my nose!'

The voice was unmistakably Ed's.

'Ed! You . . . you . . . you,' Annie shouted, terror instantly giving way to a wave of fury, 'what the hell are you doing? Creeping about here in the pitch black scaring me out of my mind!'

Cupping a hand over his nose, he explained in a muffled, but none the less, highly annoyed voice, 'I rang the bell. When you didn't answer I let myself in. I switched on the light in the hall and a bulb blew and tripped the whole house. So obviously I went to the kitchen to get a torch, so I could get to the fuse box . . . and the batteries in the torch are dead, so I was just going to look for some more when you shoot out of the sitting room giving me the fright of my life and whack me in the face with a bloody encyclopaedia or something.'

Annie looked at the book in her hand. 'Fantasy Footwear,' she informed Ed and bent down to pick up the torch, which had fallen down between them.

'I need some tissues,' Ed told her.

'Come and sit down,' she said, walking into the sitting room ahead of him and guiding him towards the sofa. 'Sit. I'll get some cold water and a facecloth.'

'And tissues,' he instructed.

'And I'll try and put the lights back on.'

'Yeah . . . OK.'

Several minutes later, the side-light and the TV jumped back on again and Annie appeared carrying a small bowl, a flannel and a tissue box.

'Let's see,' she said, approaching Ed, who was still sitting with both hands now cupped over his face. The nose didn't look too bad. The edge of the book had broken the skin at the bridge, so blood was trickling down from there as well as from the nostrils.

'It's a bit like Connor's Italian injury,' she told him, wiping gently at the cut with a wet corner of the cloth. 'He thinks it helped him get the part – you know, in the film.'

'Oh the film, yeah, he was telling me about that at . . .' but Ed's sentence tailed off as if he wasn't desperate to relive Bryan and Dinah's party, however briefly.

'Just pinch here,' Annie instructed, putting her fingers beneath the bridge of her nose to demonstrate.

'Yes I know,' Ed snapped. 'I *teach* First Aid at school.'

He looked huffy again.

She took a good look at him . . . pinching his nose with one hand, balled-up bloodstained hankies clamped against it with the other. He was dressed like a burglar in dark trousers and a dark hoodie. He also had a touch of stubble and unusually bluish rings under his eyes. Tired.

Just like her. No bloody wonder. It was close to midnight and they were still up.

'Why are you here?' she wondered out loud. 'I mean it's your house and everything . . . obviously you're allowed to come back . . . but I think you could have warned me.'

'I'm sorry, I didn't mean to give you a fright. Did you think I was the taxman?' he managed to joke.

'I've paid that bill, thank you very much,' Annie replied sourly.

'I'm sorry . . . it was just a . . .' Ed suddenly seemed at something of a loss, 'a spur of the moment . . . kind of thing . . .'

Annie wondered what this meant: spur of the moment drop in and pick something up? Spur of the moment chat about estate agents?

'I didn't think you'd be asleep, I didn't realize it was so late,' Ed added, rolling up a tissue and stuffing the tube into his bleeding nostril. 'That ought to do it,' he said.

There was a pause, during which Annie looked at him expectantly. Surely he was going to give her some sort of explanation for turning up after 11 p.m. and scaring her half to death.

Ed, feeling that he was required to say something, told her: 'I wanted to talk to you about Owen's birthday party.'

'Oh . . .'

She didn't add, 'Are you out of your mind? Couldn't we have done this at ten in the morning tomorrow like normal civilized people?'

'Why is your duvet down here?' he asked, as if he'd just noticed it on the sofa.

'I was just dozing, in front of the telly.'

'Can't sleep?' he asked, turning to her with his very familiar, gentle concern. Before she could deny this, so as not to seem too vulnerable and troubled, he added, 'Me neither. Far too much to think about. You still haven't signed the estate agent's agreement form.'

'Neither have you,' she reminded him quickly, not wanting to dwell on why she hadn't been able to bring herself to do this yet.

'No . . . it feels very sad.' He made a scratchy sort of throat clearing. 'Losing my mum . . . losing the house . . . and losing you.'

Now her throat felt very scratchy too. For a moment, all she could think about was how many hours she'd spent scraping the layers and layers of blackened varnish off the stair banister before polishing it up to perfection. And she'd done this willingly because she'd thought she'd be here to enjoy every corner of this lovely house for years and years to come.

'And it was about Connor, funnily enough,' Ed started up, almost out of nowhere. 'That was what I wanted to ask you about too.'

'Connor?' she said, sounding surprised, swallowing down the scratchy throat, 'has he been talking to you?' Not that this would have been so surprising. Connor, just like Dinah, still couldn't understand why she had finished with Ed.

'No. But I think Connor is the hole in your argument.'

Ed sounded quite detached, almost a little teacherish, as if some problem was going to be discussed, weighed up and counter-argued.

'Connor? What argument? What hole?' she asked as

if he'd gone mad. What was he talking about? Had she knocked him too hard with the shoe book?

'You *love* Connor, don't you?' Ed asked, 'and you didn't use to feel like that about him. Not before Roddy died. Do you see? Do you see what I mean?'

'No,' Annie told him, 'I'm not in love with Connor. That's not why I—'

'No!' Ed broke in, 'that's not what I meant. It's this . . .' He took a deep breath and, though muffled slightly by the hanky, began, 'Why is Connor allowed to be an honorary member of your family, when I'm not? Why do you let yourself love him? Why was he allowed in? Was there a cut-off point?

'Did I miss the date of entry and now the gates are closed and no one else will ever be allowed into your family again? I've been thinking and thinking about what you said, and I understand it from your point of view, but what about me?' Ed's voice was straining with the effort of these words. 'Where's my family? When do I get to be part of a family again? My mum and dad are dead and my sister's got a family of her own. So what am I supposed to do?'

Annie could not take her eyes from his face as he put a hand gently on her shoulder and told her once again, just to make sure, because he had to make one more attempt at this, 'I love the three of you. I accept that I do not love you as much as if I'd lived with you for years, but I love you enough to want to start to love you that much.

'Can you understand what I'm saying?' he asked, knowing that his heart was right out there on his sleeve. 'You're the only family I've got now and you've got to let me in. Because I promise, I just absolutely promise that I won't let you down.'

'But how do I know that?' was all Annie could say in reply.

'Because I really mean it,' Ed said and took hold of her hands.

There was a long, loaded silence before Annie, in a frightened whisper, managed to voice the question which was scaring the life out of her. 'But what if you die too, Ed?'

Ed's answer was to put his arm round her shoulders and pull her in tightly towards him. 'Oh Annie,' he said into her hair, 'Annie, Annie.'

For a moment they just held each other and Annie recognized how warm and how safe and how right it felt to be here.

'There can't be any new leaves without old leaves,' Ed said into her hair, 'but you've got to stop. How are you ever going to fall in love with me if you're busy picking out my coffin?'

When Annie was finally able to speak again, she leaned away from him, wiped hard at the tears on her face and told him, trying to make it sound jokey, but really meaning every word, 'If we're going to get back together, you've got to promise that you won't die first, Ed, that's the deal. You're not allowed to die first.'

Ed took her hand in his and told her solemnly, 'I will never cross the road without looking very carefully. I will never, ever overtake without being able to see a full mile ahead on the other side of the road and I will never, ever get on a plane if I know there's a terrorist on board. Is that OK?'

'I don't know!' she said, feeling yet another tear drip from the end of her nose, 'I don't know if that's enough.'

'We might get really, really old together,' Ed reminded her, trying to sound light-hearted too, 'and then you might kick me out because my bum's too wrinkly and there's a hot new waiter who thinks eighty-year-old women are funky. And it might all end very happily for you.'

'It never ends happily,' Annie told him darkly.

'Annie! Please! Put the coffin catalogue down!' Ed exclaimed. 'Baby, can't we just seize the day and all that? Enjoy today? Maybe you need to see someone professional.' He put a finger gently on her forehead: 'maybe you need to put your busy mind at rest. No amount of shopping is going to fix what's going on in there.'

Laying her head down on his comfortable chest, where she could hear his heart beat slowly and reassuringly, Annie told him gently, 'You're all right, Ed. I think I could quite get to love you, you know . . . once the tissue plug comes out of your nose.'

Chapter Thirty-five

Morning Ed:
Blue pyjama bottoms (vintage M&S)
Matching blue jewellery box (Tiffany)
Total est. cost: classified.

'Oh, Ed!'

On Sunday mornings, there was a new routine at number 8 Hawthorne Street. Ed and Annie slept in. Late. Ten o'clock late. Eleven o'clock late. Disgustingly, filthily late. Then finally, when Owen and Lana were completely restless and bored, they knocked on the bedroom door and brought in coffee.

This Sunday, there was something very special to go with the coffee: a gooey, homemade, Ed-baked, triumph of a chocolate cake. It was decorated with eleven candles. When Owen brought it into the bedroom, the candles were already alight and Owen was singing, 'Happy Birthday to me!' loudly.

'Happy birthday! Hello! Good morning!' Annie roused herself from the pillows and gave both her children a hug. Slowly, with a bit of poking and tickling, Ed came round as well, perking up remarkably at the prospect of chocolate cake for breakfast.

Once the candles were blown out, Ed began to cut slices and Owen fell on the pile of presents waiting for him in the corner of the bedroom. He was going to get to the big box first – that had to be the Celestron!

The white phone at the bedside table burst into life and Owen snatched it up. 'That'll be Grandma.'

But no, after he'd said hello and listened to the request on the other end of the line, he handed the receiver to Annie. 'For you, sounds like work,' he announced.

Probably Mr Woo, Annie thought, reaching over for the phone. The man never took a day off work and had not yet picked a good moment to phone. Still, the shoes were going to be trialling in four House of Fraser stores next month, so there were plenty of last-minute snaggles to attend to.

'Hello, Annie speaking,' she said.

And then someone began to talk to her and what he was saying was so extraordinary that she only seemed to be able to take in little bursts of it. 'Donnie Finnigan . . . TV producer . . . so sorry, Sunday . . . Kelly-Anne's husband . . . looking terrific, ten years younger, much happier . . . makeover show . . . auditions . . . Svetlana Wisneski . . . think you'd be perfect . . . you and Svetlana . . . prime-time TV. Need to come and meet us. Just say when and we'll send a car. What do you think?'

When Annie finally put the phone down she stared at her family in shock before screaming out, 'I've got an audition to go on TV! There's a new makeover show! Me and Svetlana! They think we'd be perfect!!'

*   *   *

Some time later, when every one of Owen's parcels had been torn open and greeted with rapturous enthusiasm (well, apart from the remedial-looking pyjamas from Aunty H), every cake plate had been scraped clean and Annie had relayed the conversation with the TV producer at least five or six times, Ed, in his pyjama bottoms, hopped out of bed and began to rummage around in his wardrobe.

'I've got a little, teeny, weeny present,' he announced. When he came back to the bed, he opened his hand to reveal a small, pale-blue box.

'Ooooh,' Lana, cuddled in beside Annie, was the first to comment, 'from Tiffany!'

'Oh, Ed!' Annie gasped, but she kept a rein on herself. They sold all sorts of things at Tiffany's. Yes they sold engagement rings with perfect round, white diamonds cut in the trademarked Tiffany way. But she didn't know if she and Ed were there yet. They were *somewhere*. They were somewhere very, very nice. They were settling into a new phase: one where Annie was learning to be truly open, was realizing that there was nothing she needed to hide from Ed any more. Nothing of herself she needed to protect or hold back from him.

Ed was beginning to understand much more about really talking and not storming off and sulking when he didn't know where the dialogue was going to go next.

But anyway, back to the little blue box which Annie was holding tightly in her hand . . .

She was reminding herself that at Tiffany they also sold Elsa Peretti pendants in sterling silver, chunky silver rings, decorative gold bracelets . . . but then the box was too small for a bracelet. Could it be earrings?

This might just be a *present*, which would be lovely. Very, very sweet. No doubt about it. This might not be the great, romantic gesture which . . . did she want? Did she not want?

'Mum!' Lana urged her with a nudge. 'Come on! Open it!'

'Yes!' Owen agreed

Annie stole a glance at Ed. His steady gaze was on her and there was a smile of expectant happiness on his face.

If this was a proposal ring . . . was it going to be a fabulous diamond or something much more modest? Looking from Ed to the box and from the box back to Ed, Annie suddenly realized that no matter how many times she'd told herself before that she was only going to settle Svetlana-style for the real deal, the mega engagement ring, she knew just looking at Ed that no matter what was inside, she was going to love it.

Because she loved him.

She really did. Maybe not as much as she'd once loved her husband. Not yet. But there was plenty of time for that. They had their whole grown-up lives ahead of them.

So she pulled off the ribbon and lifted open the lid.

'Oh! Oh babes,' she said, eyes shining and with a smile that lit up her face. 'Oh, Ed! That is absolutely perfect! Perfect!'

THE END

Acknowledgements

Yes, I know, it's that kissy, kissy, luvvie darling moment at the back of the book, but how else do I let everyone know how *wonderful* they are?

I am always so grateful for the kind advice and input of my wise agent, Darley Anderson, and for the support of the lovely people who work with him: Maddie, Zoe and Ella.

A very special thank you to my new editor Sarah Turner. It has been a pleasure to work on LNS with you. You've nipped and tucked my story with charming brilliance! As has copy guru Judith Welsh. Annie's latest adventures would not be as sparkling without you both.

I feel very lucky to have such a fantastic team behind *Late Night Shopping.* The covers, the website, the adverts, the sales pitch: all genius! Thank you so much for all your hard work on my behalf, I really do appreciate it hugely.

And finally, my home side: a ginormous thank you to Thomas, Sam and Claudie for putting up with all the stressy deadline weeks and to my Mum and Dad for their very hands-on help. Big hugs to my special scribbling amis, Shari Low and Lennox Morrison, and not forgetting the Wednesday night vino and kino club!

THE PERSONAL SHOPPER
by Carmen Reid

**Meet Annie Valentine: stylish, savvy,
multi-tasker extraordinaire.**

As a personal shopper in a swanky London fashion
emporium, Annie can re-style and re-invent her clients
from head to toe. In fact, this super-skilled dresser
can be relied on to solve everyone's problems
. . . except her own.

Although she's busy being a single mum to stroppy teen
Lana and painfully shy Owen, there's a gap in Annie's
wardrobe, sorry, life, for a new man. But finding the
perfect partner is turning out to be so much trickier
than finding the perfect pair of shoes.

Can she source a geniune classic? A lifelong
investment? Will she end up with someone from the
sale rail, who'll have to be returned? Or maybe, just
maybe, there'll be someone new in this season
who could be the one . . .

A fabulous read. A sexy read. A Carmen Reid.

**'If you love shopping as much as you love a
great read, try this. Wonderful!'
Katie Fforde**

9780552154819

A fabulous read. A sexy read. A Carmen Reid:

THREE IN A BED

Bella Browning is attractive, successful and **ambitious**. She works hard, plays hard but deep down she knows there's something missing . . . a baby.

When Bella falls pregnant, her husband Don is **terrified** by the prospect, but Bella's a top Management Consultant turning around multi-million pound corporations . . . she can handle this! **Can't she?**

'An entertaining and insightful tale of a 21st century working motherhood with a bittersweet edge'
Cosmopolitan

9780552155816

DID THE EARTH MOVE?

Meet Eve: 4 kids, 1 hectic job, 2 complicated exes and a lot on her mind.

Like, is sex with **the vet** better than no sex at all?

Is she too old to shop at **Topshop** or dye her hair pink?

Are **violets** the new geraniums?

What the hell is in the **fridge** for supper?

And, most important of all, has she let the **love of her life** get away too easily?

'Full of love, hope and a dash of sadness. A great summer read'
Sunday Mirror

9780552155809

A fabulous read. A sexy read. A Carmen Reid:
HOW WAS IT FOR YOU?

Five years of gruelling IVF still haven't brought **Pamela and Dave** the baby they long for. Their marriage is now so rocky, they need hiking boots just to negotiate dinner.

So they probably shouldn't be moving **out of London** to run an organic strawberry farm. Especially as out there in the countryside is **devastatingly handsome** farmer, Lachlan Murray.

Just how far is Pamela prepared to go for a baby?

'Carmen Reid's previous bestsellers were only a delicious taste of how brilliantly she can tell a story'
Daily Record

9780552155830

UP ALL NIGHT

There aren't enough **hours in the day** for Jo, overworked newspaper reporter, mother of two, and newly divorced after ten years of marriage.

She's close to cracking the **biggest scoop of her career** – if she knocks on the right doors and asks the right questions then a real exclusive could be hers . . .

But how will Jo meet her deadlines when her **distractions** include two needy daughters, a pompous ex-husband, his new 'girlfriend' and the romantic intentions of a scruffy but **delicious** young **super-chef**?

'Cleverer than the average and much more entertaining too'
Heat

9780552155823

And for teenage readers:

Secrets at St Jude's

New Girl

By Carmen Reid

Ohmigod! Gina's mum has finally flipped and
is sending her to Scotland to some crusty old
boarding school called St Jude's – just because
Gina spent all her money on clothes and
got a few bad grades! It's so *unfair!*

Now the Californian mall-rat has to swap her
sophisticated life of pool parties and well-
groomed boys for . . . hockey *in the rain,* school
dinners and stuffy housemistresses. And what's
with her three kooky dorm-buddies . . . could they
ever be her *friends?* And just how does a St Jude's
girl get out to meet the gorgeous guys invited to
the school's summer ball?

978 0 552 55706 1

www.rbooks.co.uk

Win a luxury holiday in Tuscany with

citalia.com
the leading italian specialist

Citalia are offering one lucky winner and their partner the ultimate indulgence - a four night spa and designer shopping stay at the 4 star Natural Spa Resort Bagni di Pisa.

The Natural Spa Resort is a magnificent and sumptuous building, once owned by the Grand Dukes of Tuscany, with beautifully restored palazzo style bedrooms. Bagni di Pisa is in an ideal location, close to great shopping in Pisa, Lucca, Florence and also close to The Mall - the fabulous designer outlet shopping centre in the Tuscan countryside where you can shop like Annie Valentine herself, and enjoy cut-price designer items available in the Gucci, Armani, Valentino and Stella McCartney stores!

The prize includes four nights for two people sharing a room on a half board basis, a complimentary massage, return flights from London to Pisa and car hire.

Simply enter online at
www.booksattransworld.co.uk/citalia
Closing date for entries is 30th September 2008
Terms and conditions apply - see website for details